The Outstanding Mysteries of Sherlock Holmes

Gerard Kelly

Paperback ISBN 9781908218674
Mobipocket/Kindle ISBN 9781908218681
ePub/iBook ISBN 9781908218698

Published in the UK by MX Publishing
335 Princess Park Manor, Royal Drive, London, N11 3GX
www.mxpublishing.com
Cover design by www.staunch.com

These stories are dedicated to the two women in my life. My wife Marlene, for her endless forbearance and countless cups of coffee, and my daughter, Antonia, for her encouragement, typing, proof-reading etc. My thanks are due also to friends and colleagues whose experiences have suggested ideas for some of the plots and for their assistance with my research. These friends now appear as characters within the stories themselves.

G. Kelly

3

Contents

A SLAYING IN SUBURBIA

There have been times, albeit few in number, when my friendship with Sherlock Holmes has been sorely tested, and just such an occasion took place in July of this year. For weeks he had been alternating between feverish activity and despondency bordering on melancholia.

If he was not frenetically searching his extensive files or experimenting with some evil-smelling chemicals, then as like as not he would be slouched in his chair, in dressing gown and slippers, staring vacantly into space.

Sometimes he would not speak a word all day, then other times he would berate me for having misplaced some letter or card, whether or not the blame was mine. Once I found him slumped unconscious on the floor of his bedroom, after going for three days and nights without sleep. Animated, I'm sure, by that accursed cocaine. Many were the times that I considered destroying his supply and syringe, but I knew that he would soon acquire more and, to be truthful, I blanched at the prospect of the rage such an act would precipitate.

I was certain that the underlying cause for his present state of mind lay in the singular lack of stimulating cases to challenge him.

Consequently it was with some relief and a fervent wish that I admitted Mr Mark Lowe to see Holmes one morning. He had made his appointment earlier in the week, and I prayed that his problem would engage and intrigue my morose companion.

Holmes was barely civil to our visitor and sat back in his chair staring at the ceiling. I invited Lowe to sit down and tell us his story.

He was a tall presentable young man with fair hair and a pale complexion. He sported a neatly trimmed goatee beard and was quietly spoken.

His navy blue pinstriped suit was well tailored, and he carried a brown leather attaché case.

When he was seated he said, 'My employer, Sir Lawrence Brinkley, recommended you to me, Mr Holmes. The name is familiar to you?'

Holmes nodded almost imperceptibly and replied, 'Faversham and Brinkley, solicitors, of Wardour Street.'

'That's right. I am a junior partner there and Sir Lawrence speaks very highly of you.'

Holmes nodded again and the young solicitor continued, 'I am tasked with defending a man accused of murder and, whilst I firmly believe him to be innocent, I am afraid that without assistance I am not going to be able to prove it.'

Holmes turned to look at Lowe and asked, 'This is your first murder trial?'

'Yes, Mr Holmes. You have probably not heard about it for it received scant coverage in the newspapers. On the face of it, it seems a parochial enough affair between disputatious neighbours, which escalated into murder, however; I remain unconvinced.'

Holmes responded, 'You are right, the case is not familiar to me. Pray fill in the details.'

Lowe recounted, 'On June 2nd my client, Mr Arthur Dunn, was arrested and charged with the murder of one Cedric Tomkins, a close neighbour. Mr Tomkins was shot through the head by a .22 calibre rifle, fired from the vicinity of Dunn's house.'

Holmes asked, 'What was the nature of the dispute?'

Lowe sighed and replied, 'Of all things it centred on a lurcher dog by the name of Bess.'

Holmes raised an eyebrow, and I rejoiced that the case seemed to be arousing some interest in him.

Lowe continued, 'It transpires that for some time Tomkins' dog Bess had been fouling in Mr Dunn's garden. The two properties back on to each other. There had been heated exchanges between the two men and when one night some of Mr Dunn's chickens were killed, he blamed Bess. Tomkins insisted that a fox was the culprit, but my client was not convinced and was heard threatening to shoot the dog.'

'Your client owns a .22 calibre rifle?'

Lowe nodded. 'Yes, Mr Holmes, he does.'

'Who is in charge of the case?'

'Inspector Gregson.'

Holmes sighed, 'Ah yes. The patient, plodding Tobias Gregson. As good as you will get at Scotland Yard, but still somewhat lacking. This is poor fare indeed, but as it is the only dish on the menu I suppose it will have to suffice.' Rising from his chair he continued, 'Perhaps we might see your client before consulting Inspector Gregson?'

Lowe jumped up immediately, saying, 'Splendid! I had hoped you would say as much.'

Holmes asked, 'We may use the carriage that awaits you?'

Lowe looked surprised. 'How did you know that I had retained a cab?'

Holmes replied, 'Not only am I aware that you have retained a cab, I even know *which* cab. The driver is Albert Gough and his dappled mare is called Petunia.'

'Ah! So you saw me arrive from the window?'

Holmes shook his head. 'As Dr Watson will verify, I have not moved from my chair for over an hour.'

I confirmed his statement and Lowe looked puzzled until Holmes explained, 'I know most of the cabmen who ply Baker Street and Albert Gough suffers from bronchitis. In my mental filing cabinet he is "Gough with the cough". Listen, you can hear him now. Also his mare, Petunia, is a restless creature that paws the ground impatiently. This also you will discern, if your ears are sharp.' Holmes was right, for we could faintly hear the repeated scrape of Petunia's hoof on the cobblestones.

Holmes and I donned our coats and hats and soon we were all seated behind Petunia heading towards Wormwood Scrubs Prison, where Dunn was being held on remand.

Presently we found ourselves sitting across from the accused, who was guarded by two warders. The introductions having been made, Holmes said, 'Mr Lowe here is convinced of your innocence and has enlisted my aid in proving it. Is he correct in his belief?'

Dunn, a fellow about my own age and build, looked haggard. His thin grey hair was dishevelled, he had unshaven stubble on his chin and there were dark circles under his eyes. In addition his hands trembled visibly.

He replied, in a quavering voice, 'Oh yes! Very definitely!' He looked pleadingly at my friend and continued, 'I am in Hell, Mr Holmes. I keep expecting to awaken from this nightmare, but it is all too real. As God is my witness I am innocent, but unless you can uncover the truth I'm afraid I'm done for.'

Holmes said, 'If I am to help you, then you must help me. Tell me everything that transpired.'

Dunn recounted the series of events that we had already heard from Mark Lowe. When he had finished Holmes asked, 'How long have you lived at your present address?'

'Almost ten years.'

'Tell me about your immediate neighbours on either side.'

'Well, on the left is Miss Sinton, an old lady with rheumatism. She is confined to a bathchair most of the time. Her niece looks after her.'

'And on your right?'

'A fellow by the name of Ambrose Fowler. A man in his late thirties, who works as a cooper in Lambeth, I believe.'

'How long has he been a neighbour to you?'

'Just a couple of months.'

'Is he a married man?'

'No, he lives alone.'

'How were your relations with this Ambrose Fowler?'

'Cordial enough. We passed the time of day, discussed the weather and suchlike. We also compared rifles, I recall.'

'Did you indeed?' Holmes was thoughtful for a moment before asking, 'Did you see Fowler on the day of the shooting?'

'Yes, in the morning. He was hoeing his vegetable patch.'

'And later?'

'He went indoors.'

'Did you threaten to shoot Tomkins' dog, Bess?'

Dunn wrung his hands together and cried, 'Yes, but I would never really have shot the beast. Let alone its owner. I just wanted to pressure him into controlling the animal.'

'If you did not kill Tomkins, then who do you think did?'

'I can only believe it was Ambrose Fowler. Though if you were to ask me for a reason, I could not furnish one.'

Holmes stood up and said, 'I will do what I can for you, Mr Dunn, but I make no promises.'

'Thank you, Mr Holmes, thank you. I will count the minutes until I hear from you.'

Soon we were en route to Scotland Yard and an interview with Inspector Gregson. We had to wait some considerable time before we were finally ushered into his inner sanctum. The flaxen-haired inspector greeted us cordially enough and invited us to be seated. Introductions were unnecessary as each was known to the other. Mark Lowe explained, 'I have enlisted the aid of Mr Sherlock Holmes in an attempt to prove my client's innocence, Inspector. Perhaps you would not mind answering a few of his questions?'

Gregson turned and said, 'As you wish, Mr Holmes.' Glancing at his timepiece he continued, 'However, I would appreciate it if you could be as brief as possible, for I have pressing engagements within the hour.'

'Thank you, Inspector. This won't take long. Cedric Tomkins was killed by a .22 rifle bullet in the head, was he not?'

'That's correct.'

'No doubt the Yard's ballistics experts have determined the trajectory of the bullet?'

'Indeed they have, it was from above and behind. From the position of the body we have determined that the shot was fired from an upstairs window of either number twelve or number fourteen Rydal Avenue. The accused lives at number twelve.'

'Then Ambrose Fowler resides at number fourteen?'

The inspector nodded. 'That's right.'

'So there are really only two possible suspects, our client or Ambrose Fowler. Both of whom own .22 calibre rifles, I believe.'

'So they do, Mr Holmes, but whereas your client's is a powerful firearm, Ambrose Fowler has only an air rifle, which is incapable of inflicting death at such a range.'

There was a sharp intake of breath from Holmes, and he glanced at Mark Lowe as if to say, *Why was I not told this?*

Turning back to Gregson, he asked, 'Your experts have verified this statement as fact?'

'Of course. They tested both weapons extensively. Also, the neighbours reported hearing a loud bang at the time of the shooting. They thought it was a backfire from one of the new motor cars in the area.'

Holmes was thoughtful for a few moments before asking, 'Did you retrieve the bullet?'

'Yes. It was lodged behind the victim's forehead. The impacts against the bones of the skull have left it a misshapen lump of lead.'

Holmes nodded and murmured, 'I'm not surprised.' He regarded Gregson for a moment before asking, 'Was there any animosity between the victim and Ambrose Fowler?'

'None that we can establish.'

'From what you have told me, Inspector, it does not bode well for Mr Dunn.'

Gregson leaned forward conspiratorially and said, 'I have suggested to Mr Lowe here that his client might profitably plead manslaughter, in that he was trying to shoot the dog and mistakenly killed its master, but he will have none of it.'

Mark Lowe protested, 'Why should he confess to manslaughter when he is totally innocent? Indeed it is his refusal to plead the lesser charge which convinces me of his veracity.'

Holmes asked, 'May we inspect the scene of the crime?'

Gregson shrugged, 'Why not?'

'And perchance question Ambrose Fowler?'

'We have already questioned him at length *and* extensively and painstakingly searched his property.'

'And your conclusion?'

'He is not a suspect, Mr Holmes. We have our man.'

'Nevertheless I would still like to speak to him.'

'Then you had better contact his solicitor, Mr Major, for Ambrose Fowler has had his fill of being questioned.'

Holmes glanced at Mark Lowe, who nodded and said, 'I have the address.'

Holmes stood up and said, 'Well thank you, Inspector, for your time and trouble. Until we meet again.'

'Goodbye, Mr Holmes.' Soon we were in a cab heading towards Pimlico and the offices of Fowler's solicitor, Mr Major.

Holmes asked of Lowe, 'Did you not know that Fowler's gun was only an air rifle?'

'Well yes, but I'm no expert on weapons, Mr Holmes, I assumed it to be powerful enough to kill a man, and the loud bang *could* have been a backfire.'

Holmes responded, 'I have seen air guns of such power. One was built by the blind German, Von Herder. Another by the master gunsmith Straubenzee, but both were very specialised weapons. From what Gregson told us, Fowler's gun was run of the mill.'

I suggested, 'Perhaps Fowler had more than one rifle.'

Holmes shook his head, arguing, 'According to the inspector, the police searched Fowler's premises thoroughly, but found only the air rifle.'

Lowe sighed, 'Things go from bad to worse for my client.'

Holmes countered, 'It is always darkest before the dawn. Ah! It looks as though we have arrived, gentlemen.' The cab had drawn up outside a respectable sandstone building on Chatham Street, and the sign over the door proclaimed, Mr N. Major. Solicitor and Commissioner for Oaths. We rang the bell and waited. An elderly lady with grey hair and watery eyes opened the door. She peered at us and asked, 'Can I help you?'

Holmes replied, 'May we speak to Mr Major?'

'Do you have an appointment?'

Holmes shook his head. 'I'm afraid not, but if you will convey to him that this is an extremely urgent matter involving murder, I'm sure he will see us.'

'Wait here please,' she said and shuffled off down the hall. Eventually she returned to say, 'Mr Major has asked me to tell you that he is a very busy man and that if you insist on seeing him, then you will have to wait.' She indicated some chairs and we sat down. In the event we had to wait almost fifteen minutes before Major granted us an audience. Finally we were summoned and followed the old woman along the corridor to the lawyer's office. It was bright and spacious and was not typical of other law offices I had been in. Those had been book-ridden and cluttered to the rafters, but this was neat and tidy. What books there were were racked on shelves and his oak desk was uncluttered.

Barely rising from his chair, Mr Major indicated some seats and said, 'Sit down if you must, though I pray you not to make yourselves too comfortable,' and he glanced pointedly at his fob watch. He was tall and lean. One might almost describe him as scrawny. His dark hair was thinning and brushed straight back, though what he lacked on his head was amply compensated for on his face. He sported the most rampant beard and eyebrows I had seen. His eyes appeared grey behind thick spectacles, and he peered at us inquisitively.

Holmes made the introductions and continued, 'Thank you for seeing us without a prior appointment. We will take only enough of your time to request permission to speak with your client, Ambrose Fowler.'

'To what end?'

'We feel sure he can shed some light on the murder of Cedric Tomkins.'

Major said, 'Scotland Yard already hold Tomkins' murderer in chains.'

'Nevertheless we would still like an interview with Mr Fowler.'

The lawyer laughed a high falsetto giggle and responded, 'So that you and this young upstart can divert suspicion away from your client and direct it towards mine? You must take me for a fool.' He turned towards Mark Lowe and continued, 'Yes, I know who you are and whom you represent.'

Holmes rejoined, 'We seek only the truth.'

'Then you must trawl your net in other waters, for I will sanction no such interview.'

Holmes argued, 'Should not the final decision rest with your client?'

Major replied; 'If you leave your card I will see that he gets it, but you live in vain hope.'

Holmes stood up, scribbled something on the back of one of his cards and left it on the desk. 'Good day to you, sir,' he threw over his shoulder as he strode from the room. We followed him outside, where he shook his head in disbelief. 'What an odious fellow, Watson. He has all the charm of a boa constrictor!'

As Holmes hailed a cab, I asked, 'What did you write on the back of your card?'

He smiled archly and replied, 'It's a long shot for sure, but I wrote, *I KNOW YOUR SECRET!* It has been my experience, Watson, that everyone, except perhaps the saints in heaven, has some guilty secret. A skeleton they would rather keep locked in the proverbial cupboard. You can be sure that friend Fowler has some such secret, and I hope to lure him out with this bluff.'

The cabby opened the door for us and Holmes ushered Mark Lowe and me aboard saying, 'I am going to take the fellow at his word and trawl other waters. I shall see you later at Baker Street, Watson. Rest assured, Mr Lowe, that I will contact you as soon as I have something to report.'

As the hansom pulled away, we saw Holmes hurrying across the street to hail a cab travelling in the opposite direction. We journeyed to Wardour Street and I dropped Lowe off at his office before heading back to Baker Street.

I hardly saw Holmes for the next three days. He would rise before me and return usually after I had retired for the night. Finally one morning I met him at breakfast.

'Well there you are, Holmes. How goes the investigation?'

He replied, 'I've no doubt, Watson, that your readers have no notion of the mundane nature of much of my detective work. You, quite rightly, concentrate on the pertinent aspects of the cases, but the whole is much less glamorous. I have just endured three days of drudgery, looking through parish records of births, deaths and marriages. I have searched electoral registers and military archives. I've even waded through extensive files at the Home Office, and the result is amazing.'

'How do you mean, Holmes?'

'The murder victim, Cedric Tomkins, does not exist!'

'What?'

'I decided to approach this case from the other end and find out what I could about the *victim*. I'm afraid that the sum total of my efforts does not amount to very much. He has lived at 21 Clarendon Street, in the garden of which he died, for only three years. The neighbours describe him as quiet and taciturn, almost reclusive. He lived alone, apart from a housekeeper, and had few visitors. He spent long spells away from the house, fuelling rumours that his employment involved overseas travel. He would walk his dog, Bess, of an evening and tend his garden, but did not fraternise with his neighbours. He was aged about forty-five and spoke with a Cockney accent.'

'Then what did you mean when you said, "he did not exist"?'

'I can find no trace of him *officially*. There *was* a Cedric Tomkins born in Chelsea who would now be about the right age, but the lad died from diphtheria whilst still an infant.'

'So what does this mean, Holmes?'

'It means the deceased was living under an assumed name. There may be many different reasons why a man might do such a thing. He could be a criminal trying to avoid arrest; he could be the victim of a personal tragedy, trying to re-build his life; or he could conceivably be a government agent living a double life.'

'Ah! I see what you mean. Then how can you find out the truth?'

'Well, I have already discounted the first option. With Scotland Yard's assistance and photographs of the deceased we have virtually ruled out the "criminal" possibility.'

There was a knock at the door, and presently our landlady delivered an envelope for Holmes.

'Thank you, Mrs Hudson,' he said as he tore it open. 'Well, well, well!' he continued. 'Perhaps my little bluff worked after all. It's from Mr Major and we are granted an interview with Ambrose Fowler at three o'clock this afternoon.'

Three o'clock saw us knocking at the door of Fowler's house on Rydal Avenue. We were admitted by Mr Major himself who said, 'I have advised against this interview and insisted that I be present throughout to protect my client's interests.'

Holmes shrugged and said, 'As you wish.' We followed the lawyer through to the garden where Ambrose Fowler, wearing thick leather gloves, was pruning his roses. He was not at all as I had imagined him, being below average height with close-cropped ginger hair and moustache. His green eyes were heavily lidded, but had a quickness about them which suggested that he missed very little.

Holmes said, 'Just a few questions, Mr Fowler, if you don't mind.' The man nodded, but made no reply.

'How long have you lived here?'

'Two months.'

'Do you own the house or rent it?'

'I rent it.'

'You are a single man?'

'Yes.'

'Did you know of the feud between your neighbours?'

18

'I would have to be blind and deaf not to.'
'Do you own a .22 calibre rifle?'
'Yes, but it is only an air rifle.'
'May I see it?'

The man looked at his lawyer, who nodded in agreement. Fowler beckoned us to follow him and led us to a lean-to wooden tool shed. He unlocked a large chest and took out an unremarkable air rifle. Its wooden stock lacked polish and there were traces of rust on its barrel. Holmes sighted down its length and asked, 'Is it for pest control or target shooting?'

Fowler replied, 'Both. It keeps the crows off my vegetables, but you need to practice to hold your accuracy.'

Holmes nodded as he glanced around the shed. 'I see you make your own pellets,' he commented, pointing to a small crucible with lead in it, sitting on a gas burner. There were pellet moulds, tongs, files and such like on the workbench, which was splashed with the solidified remains of molten lead. Ranged on shelves, amongst tins of paint and boxes, were an oil can, some small bottles labelled machine oil, lubricating oil and diesel oil, and alongside these were several paper targets with concentric rings.

Fowler said, 'It's cheaper to make your own.'

Major asked peevishly, 'Is any of this in any way relevant?'

Holmes ignored him and reached for one of the targets. As he did so his sleeve brushed against a thin glass pipette, which almost rolled off the bench. Fowler prevented it from doing so, but could not pick it up because of the gloves he wore. Tutting irritably, he removed a glove, retrieved the

19

tube and put it on the shelf. The incident was so trivial that I would have missed it completely if it were not for the change it initiated in my companion.

He hesitated briefly, glanced at me, then said, 'Well, gentlemen, I need take up no more of your time. Thank you for being so accommodating.'

Fowler asked, 'What was all that nonsense about you knowing my secret? I don't have any secrets.'

Holmes smiled, 'I'm sure. That was just a little ruse to secure this interview. Good day, gentlemen.'

When we were seated in a cab, bound for Baker Street, I asked, 'What did you see, Holmes?'

He replied, 'Did you not notice the tattoo that was revealed when he removed his glove, Watson?'

'No, what was it?'

'On his wrist was a small black scorpion, which is familiar to me. Somewhere in my files there is a reference to a man with such a mark, and his name is not Ambrose Fowler!'

'The brew thickens, Holmes.'

'Indeed it does, Watson, indeed it does.'

As soon as we reached Baker Street, Holmes threw himself into searching his extensive reference books and files until presently he exclaimed triumphantly, 'Aha! Here we have it,' and he held a card aloft. He continued, 'So Ambrose Fowler *did* have a secret after all. His real name is Thomas Pritchard and he has hovered on the fringe of the law for some time. So far he has managed to avoid arrest, but he was a suspect in the McNaughton art robbery. However, he has changed his appearance dramatically, and but for the tattoo I would not have placed him.'

'Perhaps he is now on the straight and narrow path, Holmes,' I ventured.

He smiled and replied, 'I'm afraid, Watson, that I lack your optimistic nature. To my mind once a criminal, always a criminal.'

'But how could it profit him, the death of a neighbour?'

'That is what I must find out, old fellow. At the very least I am now convinced that this is no longer a prosaic affair.' He picked up his hat and cane and said, 'I'm off to see my brother Mycroft, Watson, for he holds keys that open many doors.' He did not invite me along, and I would not presume.

'Very well, Holmes,' I said, 'I shall see you later.'

It was indeed very much later when Holmes returned in thoughtful mood. He flopped down on the sofa and stared at the ceiling.

I asked, 'Did Mycroft's keys open the right door?'

'What?' He looked questioningly at me, then said, 'Oh yes, Watson, yes they did. Mycroft has sworn me to secrecy, but of course I can trust your integrity.' He rose, lit his pipe and stood with his back to the fireplace. 'As you know, Mycroft acts as adviser to their Lordships at the Admiralty and has the ears of Cabinet Ministers and Generals. He intimated that the occupant of 21 Clarendon Street was indeed an agent of the Crown whose periodic absences from that property coincided with missions abroad on behalf of Her Majesty's Government.'

I exclaimed, 'Good lord, Holmes! This means that what we have here is an *assassination*, no less!'

He nodded seriously, 'I'm afraid so, Watson.'

'And you suspect Fowler, I mean Pritchard, not his neighbour, Dunn?'

'I do.'

'But how could he accomplish it when all he has is an air rifle? Don't forget that neighbours reported hearing the crack of a firearm being discharged. An air rifle is virtually silent.'

'I have not forgotten the point, Watson. Indeed I am acutely aware that it is central to the whole problem.' He puffed on his pipe, deep in thought for several minutes, then suddenly his eyes lit up.

'Wait a minute, though. Could it be?' He laid his pipe in the ashtray and began pacing up and down, up and down. Abruptly he stopped and turned to me with a gleam in his eyes.

'Watson, I am a "Wise man of Gotham". A fool of the first order!' He was tense with suppressed excitement. 'I can scarcely believe it,' he continued, 'the clues were lining up to present themselves to me and I *missed* them!'

'What on earth are you talking about, Holmes?'

He replied, 'Here's presumption for you, Watson, but I believe I know how a simple air rifle was transformed into a deadly firearm!'

'You do? How?'

'You recall the small bottles of oil in the garden shed?'

'Yes, machine oil, lubricating oil and...'

'Diesel oil! What would he want with diesel oil?'

I shook my head in puzzlement. 'I don't understand, old chap.'

Holmes said, 'Herr Diesel's great discovery was that if the compression generated by the flywheel was high enough, the induced air would become hot enough to *ignite* the injected diesel oil. The resulting explosion would then drive the piston. His new engine does not need a *spark* to ignite its fuel, it explodes due to *pressure!*'

'I'm still not sure what you are implying.'

He explained patiently, 'If Pritchard were to add a drop of diesel oil into the hollow of a lead pellet and fire it from his air rifle, the compression from the spring would heat the air, ignite the oil and *Presto!* The air rifle becomes a firearm!'

''Pon my soul, Holmes! What an incredible idea!'

'And,' he continued, 'that would explain the thin glass pipette that almost rolled off the bench. Pritchard could have used *it* to apply the oil.'

I held up a warning hand. 'Hold hard a moment, though. I am an old soldier myself and know a little about guns. The flaw in your reasoning is that the breech of an air rifle is not designed to withstand the pressure of an internal explosion. Anyone firing such a weapon would risk death from a breech-piece exploding in his face.'

'A very good point, Watson, and one that I have already considered.' He picked up his pipe and re-lit it before continuing, 'If you think about it you will see that my hypothesis is still intact, for there is a built-in safety feature with such a weapon.'

'How so?'

'The spring, old fellow, *the spring*! When the weapon is fired, the major portion of the charge propels the pellet down the barrel, but a significant part of that charge, enough to prevent the breech from exploding, is expended in *RE-COMPRESSING* the spring! Simplicity itself: the spring becomes a self-damping safety device.'

'By Jove! I believe you have it, Holmes,' I exclaimed.

'Naturally some test firing would be required before such a weapon was used in anger, but there are many secluded places where such tests could have been carried out.'

I said, 'Pritchard has gone up in my estimation. To have devised such a plan displays an intelligence I would not have attributed to him.'

Holmes nodded in agreement. 'You have just voiced my own thoughts exactly, Watson. I seem to sense a familiar malevolent intellect behind all this.' He paced the floor puffing on his pipe before continuing, 'For some time now I have been monitoring the emergence of another master criminal in the mould of my old adversary Professor Moriarty. I suppose it was inevitable that someone would move in to fill the power vacuum left when Moriarty's chief of staff, Sebastian Moran, was imprisoned.'

'Who is he?'

'I believe it is a man who has access to the accumulated wealth of the Professor's evil empire and who was himself a devotee of the Napoleon of Crime. His name is Jonas T. Rimmer and it is said that he is very nearly the intellectual equal of the Professor. He controls the American end of the criminal network set up by Moriarty and has been investigated by Pinkertons for some time. They have been singularly unsuccessful, and he scorns their attempts to call him to task.'

I asked, 'You think he has moved here to London, then?'

Holmes sat down facing me and leaned forward. 'Consider the facts. One: a Crown agent, no less, is cruelly murdered. Foreign governments hostile to this country would pay hugely for such a coup. Two: the assassination is carried out in such a way that an innocent man is charged with the crime, thereby deflecting suspicion away from the real culprit. And three: the conversion of the murder weapon, which was brilliant in its conception. Jonas Rimmer possesses a first-class mind and is quite capable of devising such a scheme. Also it is particularly characteristic of the man to take the inspired work of a great inventor like Rudolph Diesel and twist it into a tool for evil. This fellow is a worthy successor to Moriarty and he is just as ruthless. The fact that a totally innocent man stands to die on the gallows because of him weighs not a pennyweight with the callous fiend.'

I asked, 'So what will be your next move? How can you draw him out into the open?'

Holmes began pacing again. 'That, Watson, may well prove to be very difficult. I've an idea of what the fellow looks like, for I have seen an early Pinkerton photograph of him, but he is elusive. He rarely puts his head above the parapet and invariably directs underlings to carry out his schemes. He has learned his trade well from the master.' He was thoughtful for a moment before continuing, 'Even though Rimmer could name his price for the assassination of Cedric Tomkins, I do not believe he is motivated by wealth. By my reckoning he must now be an extremely rich man, after a lifetime of lucrative crime. And you can be sure that it is *his* money that is paying Mr Major's fees. Jonas Rimmer is, I'm convinced, stimulated solely by the crime itself. The planning, organisation and successful execution of the most outrageous acts against society are what he revels in. His contempt for Pinkertons and the Sûreté is well known to both those organisations, and now he challenges Scotland Yard itself.'

Holmes finished his pipe and knocked out the ash into the grate, then turning to me he continued, 'We are rather in the position of shutting the stable door after the horse has bolted, old fellow, for the deed is done and Tomkins is dead.'

'So there is nothing to stop Rimmer from slinking away into obscurity again?'

'Unless I can tweak his tail feathers by exposing the conspiracy, revealing the true murderer and exonerating Dunn. Rimmer's vanity is perhaps the only chink in his armour, and I may yet be able to taunt him into an indiscretion.'

'Are you going to notify Inspector Gregson about your deductions?'

'Not yet, Watson. I intend to confront the odious Mr Major and his client with my conclusions about the air rifle and the fact that we know the bogus Fowler's real identity. That should definitely stir things up somewhat.'

I grinned. 'I can hardly wait, old fellow.'

Holmes arranged for us to meet Pritchard and his lawyer two days later at Rydal Avenue, and when we arrived Mr Major demanded, 'So just what is this startling development you spoke of, Mr Holmes? Mr Fowler and I grow weary of your presence.'

Holmes replied, 'Surely you mean, Mr *Pritchard*! For that is his real name!'

A quick glance passed between lawyer and client before Major blustered, 'I'm sure I don't know what you are talking about, Mr Holmes.'

Holmes responded, 'You may not, but your client most certainly does.' Turning to Pritchard he continued, 'The scorpion tattoo on your wrist betrayed you, Thomas. You should have kept your glove on.'

Pritchard glanced down at his wrist then glared at Holmes, but maintained his silence.

Major sneered, 'And *this* is your startling development, that my client used an alias?'

Holmes shook his head. 'That is only part of it. You see I know *how* Pritchard contrived to kill Tomkins with his air rifle.'

Major giggled and said, 'You really are a wag, sir. These flights of fancy are *so* entertaining.'

Holmes responded, 'Inspector Gregson may not find it quite so amusing when I tell him.'

The smile faded from Major's face. 'So just how was my client supposed to have achieved this minor miracle?'

Holmes outlined his theory in detail, alluding to the diesel oil and the glass pipette.

Mr Major responded, 'I've never heard anything so preposterous in all my life. You really must be desperate, Mr Holmes, to have concocted such a hare-brained notion. I'm not altogether sure that you are not suffering from brain fever!'

Holmes countered, 'You ridicule my hypothesis, but I believe you talk a better battle than you fight. I'll wager neither you nor your client would have the nerve to stand in the line of fire of such a modified weapon.'

The lawyer bristled and replied, 'Allow me a word with my client and we may just accept your challenge.'

The two men withdrew out of earshot and conversed in whispers for a few moments. Presently they returned and Major said, 'Very well, Mr Holmes, you shall have your little demonstration. My client shall be the target and *I* shall pull the trigger.'

I interjected, 'I really *must* protest. This has gone far enough; someone is going to get killed.'

Holmes responded, 'Don't worry, Watson, they won't go through with it.'

We all trooped out into the garden shed, where Pritchard produced the air rifle and passed it to Holmes without a word.

My friend propped the gun against the bench, then taking a pellet he carefully filled its hollow with diesel oil from the glass pipette. He picked up the rifle and loaded it, then cocked the spring ready to fire.

We went out into the garden and Holmes passed the weapon to Mr Major. Pritchard walked to the very far end of the garden and turned to face us.

I made one last attempt, crying, 'For God's sake, gentlemen,' but my plea fell on deaf ears. The whole scene took on an air of unreality. Here we were in a sunlit garden, with birds singing overhead, and one man was lining his rifle-sight on the heart of another. The lawyer took careful aim, held his breath and pulled the trigger. There was a sharp crack, a burst of blue smoke from the muzzle and a strangled cry from Pritchard. He clutched his chest, staggered backward a few paces and fell to the ground amongst his roses.

I cried, *'There, you see! Why wouldn't you listen to me?'*

I caught a glimpse of shocked horror on Major's face before I found myself sprinting to aid the stricken man. I am familiar with gunshot wounds and have saved the life of many a soldier in the field, but I could do nothing for Pritchard. He was dead before I reached him. I turned back toward the others. Holmes looked stunned and Major had sunk to his knees babbling and weeping. I have never seen such a change in a man. From being arrogant and cocksure, he was reduced to a gibbering wreck.

He tugged at Holmes' sleeve, imploring him, 'You must intercede for me with Inspector Gregson, Mr Holmes. It was an accident. An accident I tell you. I shall be ruined...'

Holmes shrugged him off and came over to me, asking, 'Is he dead, Doctor?'

I nodded. 'I'm afraid so. There was nothing I could do for him.' We both looked at the spreading crimson stain on Pritchard's shirtfront.

Holmes ran his hands through his hair, saying, 'I have stirred things up a shade too much, Watson.'

I responded, 'You have vindicated your theory, but at a terrible price.'

We turned around and the garden was empty. The rifle lay on the ground where he had dropped it, but of Major there was no sign. Holmes ran into the house calling his name, but the fellow had disappeared.

We reported the incident at Scotland Yard and gave Inspector Gregson a detailed account of all that had transpired.

The police officer was scathing to Holmes, saying, 'I should lock you up for instigating a murder, Mr Holmes. There were other ways for you to prove your hypothesis.'

When we finally left Scotland Yard, Holmes was as subdued and crestfallen as I have seen him. We took a cab to Wardour Street and the offices of Faversham and Brinkley, and before long Holmes was relating the sequence of events to Mark Lowe. The young solicitor was ecstatic.

'You have saved my client's life and launched my own career, Mr Holmes,' he enthused. When he saw my friend's lukewarm response, however, he urged, 'Pray do not be so hard upon yourself. Pritchard was soon to die anyway, at the end of a rope, and Mr Major will only be charged with manslaughter, I'm sure.'

Later, back at Baker Street, I asked, 'Do you think that Major will try to flee the country, Holmes?'

'He may try, Watson, but I doubt he will get very far. Gregson knows where his office is on Chatham Street and will doubtless soon apprehend the fellow.' There was a ringing of the doorbell and presently Mrs Hudson entered with a calling card for Holmes.

'It's a Mr Major to see you sir.'

Holmes leapt to his feet crying, '*Is it, by Jove?*' He took the card and glanced at it. His face hardened and he said to Mrs Hudson, 'Tell him I am a very busy man and that if he insists on seeing me he will have to wait.' To me he said, 'He kept *us* waiting, Watson, so now I return the compliment.'

He sat down again and looked at the calling card. After a moment he smiled a grim smile and said musingly, 'So the fellow would beard me in my own den, would he? Still, it is no less than I would have expected.' Passing me the card he asked, 'Does anything unusual strike you about this, Watson?'

I looked at the card and read; MISTER N. MAJOR SOLICITOR AND COMMISSIONER FOR OATHS CHATHAM ST. PIMLICO LONDON. I handed it back saying, 'I see nothing special, Holmes.'

He responded, 'Ah, Watson, still you look without really seeing.' The minutes ticked by until eventually, glancing at his pocket watch, he said, 'Mayhap we have kept the fellow waiting long enough.' Striding to the door, he called down, 'You may admit our visitor now, Mrs Hudson.'

Next moment a very subdued and servile Mr Major sidled in. He carried his hat in his hands and smiled obsequiously at Holmes. 'I believe you have been interviewed by Inspector Gregson, Mr Holmes. I do hope you told him that the unfortunate incident was a complete accident?'

Holmes replied, 'I gave him the facts, leaving it for him to decide. Now, however, I must report to him that it was cold blooded, premeditated murder, Jonas T. Rimmer!'

I leapt to my feet crying, 'What's that you say?'

The lawyer smiled and bowed slightly. 'Congratulations, Mr Holmes. You did not disappoint me.' All the obsequiousness had vanished and the self-confident arrogance had returned full fold.

Holmes said, 'You will note a singular lack of hospitality on my part, but murdering villains are not welcome here.'

Rimmer strolled around our room as if he were a prospective buyer assessing the property. 'So this is the famous 221b Baker Street. I simply had to see it for myself.'

I cried, 'You *knew* that rifle shot would be fatal to Pritchard, didn't you?'

Turning to me, he replied, 'Of course, Doctor. Who more so than me, since it was *I* who devised the modification to the weapon?'

'But why would you kill your own henchman?'

Holmes answered for him, 'Elementary, Watson. He could not risk Pritchard talking out of turn to the police. Once my theory about the weapon was validated, Pritchard's incarceration became inevitable.'

Rimmer said, 'Quite right, Mr Holmes. I had to tidy up the loose ends, and your challenge gave me the perfect opportunity.'

I asked, 'But how on earth did you get Pritchard to agree to the demonstration?'

The American replied, 'Simple. I told him I would aim to miss and he held an unused rifle pellet in his hand. He was to produce this as if it had bounced harmlessly off his chest.

30

The fellow always was gullible to a fault, and I can be very persuasive.'

Holmes asked, 'How many pieces of silver did they pay you for the assassination of Cedric Tomkins?'

Rimmer replied, 'I never discuss my business arrangements.'

Holmes responded, 'Nor would I if my business was murder.'

'Shall we just say that a certain European country wanted the activities of a particular agent, known to you as Cedric Tomkins, curtailed. I know no better way of curtailing a man's activities than assassination, do you?'

'So you installed Pritchard at Rydal Avenue to spy on him and report back to you?'

'Of course. As any good general will tell you, surveillance before a campaign is essential. From my man's detailed reports I learned that Dunn owned a .22 calibre rifle and that he was at loggerheads with Tomkins. The rest was easy.'

Holmes said, 'You have made your first big mistake in coming here. I intend to hold you here until you can be taken into custody and charged with murder.'

'Tut tut, for shame, sir. Threatening violence no less.' With a movement that was a blur the American produced a small chrome-plated revolver from his pocket and pointed it at Holmes. He continued, 'I think not, sir. At this range I can choose in which ventricle of your heart to put the bullet.'

I snatched up the poker and urged, 'We can rush him, Holmes. He can only shoot one of us before we are upon him.'

Turning the gun on me, Rimmer sneered, 'How brave the old soldier is, but before you try it, let me point out, Doctor, that it is *you* I will shoot first and you would be dead before you reached me. Pray do not make the mistake of underestimating either this little gun or my ability to use it.

At such close quarters you won't stand a chance.' As we hesitated he went on, 'John Watson, the servile lap dog ever faithful to his master. Waiting for the command to attack. The difference between Mr Holmes and myself is that *I* have the fortitude to dispatch my first lieutenant, whereas *he* does not. You will not give that order, will you Mr Holmes?'

I looked at my friend, willing him to say the word, but he shook his head. *'No, Watson! I forbid it,'* he commanded.

Turning back to Holmes, the American smiled a supercilious smile. 'Just as I thought. The Professor told me all about you, Mr Predictable.'

Holmes was white-faced with impotent rage, and he rejoined, 'You are an abomination masquerading as a man. You have killed two men, without the least compunction, and would have sent another innocent man to the gallows. You perceive decent human values as weaknesses. The good Doctor here would have laid down his life for me, yet you mock him for it. You have a God-given intellect most men would envy, yet you prostitute it on the altar of crime. If it is my last act on earth I shall end your malignant existence and rid the world of your cankerous presence.'

The words were spat out with such venom that the smile was wiped from Rimmer's face and he actually took a backward step. He raised the gun and pointed it at Holmes' face, but the detective stared him down without flinching. I swear that the hand that held the gun trembled a little.

The American said, 'You have cost me a great deal, Mr Holmes. The façade of a successful lawyer and the premises in Pimlico are now lost to me, as is a very able lieutenant. Perhaps I should kill you now, before you can carry out your threat.'

I raised the poker and hissed, 'Then *I* will most certainly kill *you!*' He looked into my eyes and saw that I meant every word. For long moments it hung in the balance, but in the end he opted for self-preservation.

As he backed slowly towards the door he warned, 'Don't try to follow me or Mrs Hudson becomes my next target. *Au revoir,* gentlemen. Perhaps we shall meet again.'

Holmes said icily, 'You can count on it.' Next moment he was away and gone. I ran to the sideboard, snatched my revolver from the drawer and rushed to open the window, only to see him leap into a waiting carriage and speed off into the night.

I urged, 'Come on, Holmes, we can be after him!"

But he shook his head. 'It's no use, old fellow. He knows all of the Professor's dozen or so safe houses and a hundred boltholes. You'd as like search for a needle in a haystack.'

I slumped as I realised that Holmes was right. *'Damn the man's eyes!'* I exclaimed in frustration.

Holmes gently took the revolver from me and placed it back in the drawer, saying, 'His time will come, Watson, you can be sure of that. Though when I finally settle the score with him, I too shall be the loser, for he tasks me as no other man has since Moriarty himself.'

I nodded, knowing exactly what Holmes meant.

Eventually I said, 'His English accent was faultless. How on earth did you know that, under all the facial hair and glasses, he was really Jonas Rimmer?'

'Why, he told me so himself, Watson.'

I argued, 'I recall no such thing, Holmes.'

He smiled as he explained, 'He was testing me, and fortunately I was not found wanting. Remember when I showed you his calling card and asked if you noticed anything unusual?'

'Yes.'

'Well it struck me as strange that his title was written as MISTER. Usually the title is abbreviated to Mr. I immediately realised then that *Mister N. Major* was an anagram for Jonas T. Rimmer!'

I smiled and shook my head. 'I *never* would have noticed that, Holmes.'

Arthur Dunn was acquitted, a warrant was issued for the arrest of Jonas Rimmer, and the young solicitor, Mark Lowe, settled his account with Holmes very generously indeed.

THE MYSTERY AT THE GOLDEN COCKEREL

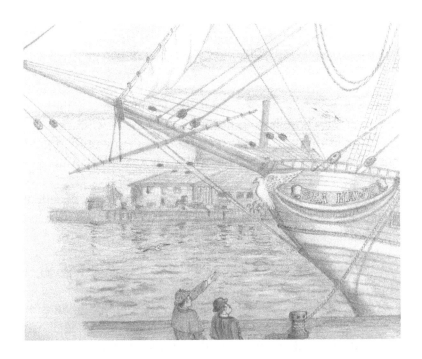

'**I**t is indeed that season of mists and mellow fruitfulness, Watson,' Sherlock Holmes observed as he peered from the window of 221b Baker street. 'Though I fear,' he continued, 'that the mists will soon give way to those damnable pea-soup fogs for which London is infamous.'

I glanced up from the morning paper to see him creating a veritable fog of his own, as he puffed busily on his favourite Meerschaum pipe. 'Unusually lyrical for you, old fellow...' I began when Holmes suddenly interjected,

'Helloa! What's this? Unless I'm very much mistaken we have our first client of the day.'

I joined him at the window in time to see a slightly built man with a baldpate nimbly dodging the hansom cabs and the droppings of their horses, as he hurried across the Baker Street cobbles towards our door.

Holmes tapped the windowpane with the stem of his pipe and said, 'Our fellow is a local for he comes on foot and he has just discovered something of great import for he has rushed out without donning either hat or coat.'

That much was apparent even to my untrained eye. However he went on, 'I further deduce that he is a Parisian restaurateur whose house speciality is Duck a L'Orange.'

I turned to my friend in amazement. 'How on earth...' I began, but he held up a hand and with a twinkle in his eye replied,

'Elementary my dear fellow. I have dined in his excellent restaurant more than once with my brother Mycroft who, incidentally, rates his cuisine one of the finest in London.'

I laughed, 'You caught me that time, Holmes.'

He chuckled along with me. 'Forgive me, Watson, I could not resist the opportunity.'

It was good to see my old friend in such high humour, for of late he had been in some dark moods indeed and had resorted more than once to that infernal cocaine. Next moment we heard a pounding on the front door and the murmur of voices as Mrs Hudson admitted our visitor. He took the stairs two at a time and burst into our room with barely a knock.

'Monsieur 'Olmes,' he blurted out in a strong French accent. 'A catastrophe 'as 'appened. I will be ruined.'

Holmes raised his hands. 'Pray calm yourself Monsieur, please.' He took the fellow by the arm and led him to the chair I had just vacated. 'Watson, a measure of brandy for Monsieur Fontaine I think.'

I hurried to comply and presently our Gallic guest regained some of his composure. As he sipped his drink I took the opportunity to appraise him. He was below average height and slightly built. His eyes, and what remained of his hair, were dark, and a small neat moustache grew beneath his aquiline nose. Apart from his white shirt his ensemble of waistcoat, tie, trousers and shoes were black.

Holmes said, 'This is my friend and colleague Dr Watson who has assisted me in many of my investigations. You may speak freely in front of him.'

Monsieur Fontaine looked up at me and said, *Mon Dieu!* A physician. That is providential for I 'ave work for the both of you.' He took another sip from his brandy glass before continuing, 'Gentlemen, I 'umbly apologise for my ill mannered entrance, but I 'ave just discovered a corpse in my restaurant.'

Holmes gave a start. 'The devil you say!'

'Oui c'est ca, though it is not the devil, it is Monsieur Brentwood. Jeremiah Brentwood.'

'Have you notified the police?' I enquired.

'Not yet, mon ami, but I suppose I will 'ave to and then the newspapers will find out and the scandal will ruin me. Who will want to dine in a...a...*mortuary!*'

He was becoming agitated again and all but wringing his hands. Holmes gripped the man's shoulder. 'Steady, old chap, he urged, 'you have done the right thing in coming straight here. We don't want the hob-nailed boots of the Metropolitan Constabulary trampling all over the evidence. Time enough later to involve Scotland Yard. Tell me, have you touched anything?'

'No nothing. As soon as I knew 'e was dead I came 'ere directly.'

'Excellent, excellent,' murmured Holmes. He drew up a chair so that he could face the Frenchman and said, 'Now tell us the whole story pray.'

Monsieur Fontaine drained his glass and began, 'As you know, Monsieur 'Olmes, I own a small restaurant called "Le Coq D'or" on Portland Place, not ten minutes from 'ere. On Tuesday morning, the fifteenth, I received an unusual request from this same Jeremiah Brentwood. He asked that I prepare a meal for 'im and a friend and leave everything set out on warming plates for 'imself to serve, no?'

Holmes leaned forward. 'What, no waiters?'

'Non. In fact 'e insisted no one was to be present, not even myself. 'E paid me one 'undred guineas for this privilege, over and above the cost of the meal. As you can imagine, such a sum is more than I can make in a week so I could 'ardly refuse. 'E said 'e would lock up the restaurant and drop the key through the letter box when 'e left.'

'And that was how you found it this morning?'

'Oui.'

'What time was this meal scheduled for?' Holmes asked.

'Midnight.'

'And how, pray tell, was it arranged? Did he meet you in person?'

'Non, I received a letter which was delivered by messenger.'

'Was it hand-written?'

'No it was type-written.'

'Was it signed?'

'No, just the name Jeremiah Brentwood, type-written.'

'Do you still have the letter?'

'Why no, I do not. I was instructed to append my response at the bottom of the note and return it to the messenger.'

'Damn!' muttered Holmes and he rose and began pacing the floor. 'No clues to be unearthed there. And of course no return address either.' He turned to face the Frenchman again and asked, 'How was the fee paid, after you agreed to this bizarre arrangement?'

Monsieur Fontaine gave a Gallic shrug, as only the French can, and replied, 'Later that same day I received a sealed envelope with banknotes to the full amount, once again delivered by courier.'

'Was any reason suggested for the lateness of the meal and the absence of staff?' Holmes enquired.

'Oui, the letter hinted strongly that this was a romantic assignation. A midnight-tryst with a respectable married lady, hence all the secrecy. All the world loves a lover, Monsieur 'Olmes, and we French cannot resist affairs of the 'eart.'

Holmes drew on his pipe again, seemingly unaware that it had gone out. I proffered him a box of Vestas, but he brushed them aside impatiently. 'Come, Watson,' he said as he grabbed his ulster and hat, 'It is high time we took a look at the mortal remains of Mr Jeremiah Brentwood.'

I grabbed my own coat and cane and Monsieur Fontaine and I followed Holmes down the stairs and out into the mist. We crossed Baker Street and headed down Marylebone Road towards Portland Place, with myself and Fontaine hurrying to keep up with my friend's long-legged stride.

I remarked, 'All this could be perfectly innocent, Holmes. The fellow could have died from natural causes.'

'You could be right, Watson, and of course I expect you to be able to ascertain exactly that when you examine the body. However my instincts tell me that there is a mystery here and my instincts are seldom wrong.'

I lapsed into silence knowing this to be true. I also deemed it prudent to save my breath because at this pace Monsieur Fontaine and myself were soon panting. Holmes on the other hand seemed totally unperturbed.

Presently we arrived at the Coq D'or and the Frenchman ushered us inside. Then with a quick glance around outside, he locked the door behind us. He led the way through to the dining area and stood aside motioning us to enter.

The salon was small, but exquisitely appointed in blue and gold. Heavy damask curtains framed the windows and two crystal chandeliers hung from the ornate plaster ceiling. There were seven unlaid tables and one, near the far wall, which was set for two, with crisp white linen and blue and gold crockery. A triple-branched, silver candelabrum bore the burnt down stumps of white candles and molten wax had dripped from them onto the tablecloth. Draped in the chair facing us was the body of Jeremiah Brentwood. His head was thrown backwards and rested on the back of his chair. His mouth was open and his sightless eyes stared at the chandeliers.

I have seen death many times, from the bloody brutal death on the battlefields of Afghanistan to the quiet peaceful death of the old woman who dies in her sleep, but I never get used to it. After all my years as a doctor I suppose I should be inured to the work of the grim reaper, but I confess I am not and this man's death was no exception. He seemed so young, at most five and twenty, and was clean-shaven. His brown hair was swept back from his face with very little pomade and he wore a black evening suit with a white shirt.

Forcing myself to be professionally detached, I busied myself with examining the corpse and was soon able to tell Holmes, 'It is my considered opinion that Brentwood died from heart failure.'

Holmes looked at me keenly. 'Are you absolutely sure, Doctor?'

I shrugged, 'As sure as I can be without a post mortem examination. All the classic symptoms are very evident. And from the degree of rigor mortis, I should say he has been dead for between six and eight hours.'

Holmes joined me beside the body and studied it carefully, even to the point of looking at the man's hands and peering into his mouth. Turning to me he said, 'Watson, do not for one moment imagine that I impugn your professional judgement, but is he not a trifle young to be the victim of a heart attack?'

Another doctor might have bristled at such a question, but I am used to Holmes' directness and answered, 'It is a common misconception that heart attacks strike only at the aged. Admittedly such a death in an apparently fit young man as we have here is rare, but not unheard of. He may have carried an hereditary defect or once suffered from rheumatic fever, which seriously weakens the heart.'

Holmes nodded, 'Thank you, Doctor. As ever I bow to your experience.'

He then turned his attention to the table, his keen eyes flitting over everything; the remnants of the various dishes, the cigar butt in the ash tray, the wine glasses and half empty wine bottles.

Turning to Monsieur Fontaine he said, 'This meal you prepared, was the menu selected by yourself or by your customer?'

'By Monsieur Brentwood. In fact 'e was most particular about each course.'

'And did he also choose the wines?'

'Non, In the matter of the wines 'e deferred to my judgement, saying only that they should be of the 'ighest quality.'

Holmes deftly fished a leather wallet from the dead man's jacket pocket and showed me the initials "J.B." which were chased in gold leaf on the front. 'Please list for me each course you prepared, Monsieur,' Holmes requested.

'As you wish. The first course was beef consommé without croutons, followed by pate de foi gras with untoasted bread. For the main course 'e requested omelettes supreme, a 'ouse speciality, and for dessert a fruit melange consisting of blackberries, strawberries, plums and cream.'

Holmes had been studying the contents of the dead man's wallet and he stopped and looked up at Monsieur Fontaine. 'You are sure that is all?' he questioned.

'Oui, that is what 'e requested and that is what I prepared.'

Holmes replaced the contents of the man's wallet and returned it to the jacket pocket. 'Watson, I discern an unpleasant odour like bad meat, you don't suppose...?' and he indicated the deceased.

I shook my head, 'Of course not, Holmes. He has not been dead for long enough and the weather is cool.'

'Do you not smell it?' he asked.

I sniffed and for sure there *was* a faint disagreeable odour, though with deference to Monsieur Fontaine, in whose dining room we were, I pretended not to notice. 'I am sure you are imagining it, old fellow,' I remarked, and gave a surreptitious shake of my head to Holmes.

He indicated that he understood by the slightest of nods and hurried on, 'Monsieur Fontaine, your testimony has been lucid and extremely enlightening. I have no doubt it will go a long way towards unravelling this mystery.'

I said, 'So there *is* a mystery here then Holmes?'

'Very much so, Watson. My instinct was, after all, correct and I had determined it within minutes of our arrival.'

'Pray keep us in suspense no longer then,' I urged, 'tell us what it is.'

He sat in the vacant chair opposite the corpse and steepled his fingers saying, 'The letter implied this was an illicit tête-à-tête between Jeremiah Brentwood and a respectable married lady.'

'Just so,' I said.

'*Not* so, Watson,' he replied. Then sweeping a hand towards the table he announced, 'Jeremiah Brentwood's dinner guest of last night is a *man*. Indeed I would go so far as to say that he is a toothless, middle-aged American who smokes Cuban cigars and is of a nervous disposition.' He turned towards the Frenchman and continued, 'Furthermore, it was *he* who arranged the meal and paid you in excess of one hundred guineas. Not Brentwood.'

Monsieur Fontaine's mouth fell open in amazement. I, who am used to Holmes' incredible feats of deduction, have long since managed to retain a firm lower mandible, but I was equally amazed.

Monsieur Fontaine spread his hands and asked, "Ow can you know all this?'

Holmes replied, 'All the evidence is right there on the table. What is it that you fail to see?'

Monsieur Fontaine asked, "Ow do you know it was a man?'

Holmes smiled, 'I can't imagine our dead friend here would have agreed to a midnight rendezvous with a toothless woman who smokes cigars.'

I said, 'Surely Brentwood could have smoked the cigar?'

Holmes shook his head. 'I very much doubt it. Look, old fellow, the butt sits in the ashtray pointing away from Brentwood. I've never seen a smoker reverse a cigar on an ashtray so that the lighted end is likely to burn him when next he picks it up. Furthermore there is not a trace of nicotine staining on the dead man's fingers.'

'Could he not have used a holder?'

Again Holmes shook his head. 'Do you perceive one? In any case, a holder leaves a ring impression on the end of a cigar. This one is pristine.'

'Ah!' I exclaimed, 'that is how you deduce that the smoker is toothless.'

'Very good, Watson, you show improvement. It is as you say, for Brentwood has excellent teeth. However you still miss the obvious. The major clue to the toothlessness of our mystery man is in the meal itself. Each course sets a pointer. No croutons in the soup, untoasted bread with the pate. Omelette as a main course, I ask you! Where is the meat or fowl, or even fish? And lastly for dessert, soft fruit. Rather convincing, wouldn't you say?'

'Of course,' I agreed, 'and from this you also deduced that *he*, not Brentwood, selected the menu?'

43

Holmes nodded. 'That was one of the clues, but there are others. For example you must be aware that even a typewritten letter is normally signed in person, yet the signature on this one was typed. Also the letter writer agreed to drop the key through the letterbox as Monsieur Fontaine found it. Brentwood could hardly have done so, could he?'

'You make it seem all so obvious, Holmes,' I remarked.

He shrugged, 'To me it *is* obvious, Watson.'

Monsieur Fontaine interjected, 'But 'ow do you know 'e is a middle-aged American?'

Holmes responded, 'How many young Americans can there be in London who have no teeth? Also it has been my experience that old men, with passions spent, rarely indulge in plots and conspiracies. As for him being an American, this is by way of being a likelihood more than an absolute fact. Our stateside cousins have a penchant for cutting up their food into bite-sized pieces then, rejecting the knife; they transfer their fork to the right hand to eat. You will observe our mystery man's main course knife is as clean and bright as a whistle and still resides on the table where Monsieur Fontaine placed it. His fork however is well used and rests here with the empty dishes. With such moderate courses he did not need to use the knife. An Englishman would use both knife and fork, even for eating an omelette, as Brentwood did.'

'Bravo Holmes!' I exclaimed, but Fontaine held up his hand.

'But 'ow do you know Brentwood is English?'

Holmes replied, 'Because I have just verified the fact from documents in his wallet.'

The Frenchman persisted, 'Ah! But what of your claim that the man is of a nervous disposition?'

Holmes replied, 'Take a look at his napkin and compare it to Brentwood's. The latter's is mildly crumpled whereas the former's shows severe stress. It is crushed and creased as though repeatedly twisted and is even stained with nicotine from the man's fingers, so heavily has it been wrung. These are hardly the actions of a calm man.'

Monsieur Fontaine and I were both nodding in agreement when suddenly Holmes leaned forward and seized the wineglass nearest to him. He peered at it intently, sniffed it and exclaimed, 'Pah! I am a fool, Watson. If you see me display signs of complacency again you have my full permission to use your boot on the seat of my pants.'

Without waiting for a reply from me he turned to Monsieur Fontaine and said, 'Tell me, my friend, which wines did you select to accompany each course of the meal?'

The Frenchman picked up one of the bottles and replied, 'As an aperitif I chose this *Alsace Pinot Blanc*, and to follow a Sauterne from *Sainte Croix Du Mont* a superb wine to complement the fois gras. For the main course I selected this Cabernet Sauvignon or, as you English say Claret, from the village of *Margeaux* in the *Haute Medoc* region of Bordeaux. Formidable!' and here he kissed the tips of his fingers in the Gallic fashion. 'And finally for dessert, what better than this sweet *Coteaux Du Layon. C'est magnifique!*'

Holmes listened attentively and when the Frenchman had finished, remarked, 'Though I am no connoisseur, even I can appreciate that you have graced this table with a superb selection of wines, Monsieur.'

The little Frenchman gave a slight bow as though to say, 'But of course.'

Holmes continued, 'Is it not odd then that the stranger drank none of it?'

Monsieur Fontaine exclaimed, *'Sacré bleu!* Is it true?'

Holmes nodded, 'I believe so. His glass is clean and dry and bears no trace or smell of wine.'

'So 'e is an abstainer or a Philistine, no?'

'So it would seem. It may or may not be significant, but I should have detected it earlier.' Holmes picked up one of the discarded dessert bowls and drew my attention to it. 'What do you make of these plum stones, Watson?' he asked.

I looked and could see several plum stones together with some blackberry seeds. 'What *can* I make of them Holmes?' I replied. 'They are just plum stones.'

'Do you not see that many of them appear misshapen compared to the others?'

'Well, now that you mention it, yes. But they are probably just a different variety.'

'I wonder...' he mused. Then taking one of the stones, he popped it into his pocket and turning to Monsieur Fontaine declared, 'You know, mon ami, that we *must* inform the police?'

The Frenchman sighed, 'Yes of course.'

'Can you arrange to get a message to them?'

'Oui d'accord I will see to it,' he said and reluctantly left to do so.

Holmes regarded me for a moment then said, 'Look, old fellow, I've little patience with Inspector Bradstreet and there are lines of enquiry I wish to pursue. You must stay and inform him of the cause of death, and so on. Please make my apologies to Monsieur Fontaine, and I will see you later at Baker Street, agreed?'

'Very well, Holmes,' I replied, and Sherlock quickly departed, leaving me alone with the body of Jeremiah Brentwood.

Eventually Bradstreet arrived and Monsieur Fontaine and I told our stories. The Inspector asked a few questions and after a cursory inspection of the wine bottles, seemed prepared to accept that this was indeed death from natural causes, brought on by an excess of imbibed alcohol.

Arrangements were made to transport the body, (through the back door, at Monsieur Fontaine's insistence) to the mortuary. I made Holmes' apology to the little Frenchman and assured him that we would contact him directly.

I confess I was relieved to put the place behind me and, as I had no patients to see until the afternoon, I took a stroll through Regents Park, which is close by. The early morning mists had lifted and dappled sunshine filtered through the leaves on the trees. Listening to the birds and watching the parade of nannies wheeling their young charges in perambulators soon lifted my spirits, and presently I headed back to Baker Street quite ready for lunch.

It was long after darkness had fallen before Holmes finally stumbled in and flopped down on the sofa, with a heavy sigh.

'Pray pull my boots off for me, Watson, for truly I am spent.' I did so, then poured him a glass of sherry.

'I don't suppose you have eaten all day either,' I ventured.

'No time old fellow, no time. She sails on the morning tide and there was much to do.'

'Who sails on the morning tide?' I asked.

He passed a hand wearily over his eyes and replied, 'The Sea Hawk. A full-rigged clipper bound for the Malay Archipelago. You should see her, Watson; she's a beauty. An ocean flyer, but then of course she *had* to be, for time was of the very essence.'

'I haven't a clue *what* you are talking about, Holmes,' I said.

He laughed, 'Sorry, Watson, but so much has happened since I left you this morning that my head is in a spin.'

'Look, I said, 'I've saved you some cold beef from supper. I'll make you a sandwich while you tell me your story.'

'Bless you, Watson. You are a friend indeed and of course you are right, I *am* famished.'

'Come along then,' I said, 'out with it.'

He stretched out his long legs towards the warm fire and began, 'When I left the Golden Cockerel this morning, I took a very pleasant ride in a hansom cab out beyond Chiswick, where I met a Doctor Geoffrey Croft. It is extremely gratifying to meet someone who is as expert in their own field as you or I in ours, Watson; perhaps even more so. Croft is the Head of Tropical Plants at Kew Gardens, and his knowledge of exotic fruit and flora is encyclopaedical. He has helped me to confirm that Jeremiah Brentwood was *indeed* murdered.'

I almost dropped the bread knife I was using. 'But Holmes...' I began.

He held up a hand, 'Hear me out, old friend, please.' I let him continue. Holmes took the plum stone from his pocket and held it between thumb and forefinger, as if it were a priceless gem. 'This, Watson, is the bullet, or at least the spent cartridge, of the murder weapon. It is the seed of a fruit called the Durian, or *Durio Zibethinus* of the family *Bombaceae,* and is the favourite food of the old man of the forest.'

'What old man,' I asked.

'"Man of the forest" is the English translation of the Malay "Orang Utan". You recall, Watson, those red arboreal apes from Asia? Well it seems they locate the ripe fruit by its very disagreeable smell, which is so strong it can be detected from miles away.'

'Ah!' I said, 'the unpleasant odour you noticed in the Coq D'or.'

'Exactly! Well paradoxically, although this fruit smells abominable, I am reliably informed it tastes delicious, sublime almost.'

'I'm amazed,' I said, passing Holmes a plate of sandwiches.

In between munching, he continued, 'An admirable arrangement don't you agree, Doctor. The tree broadcasts by the smell that its fruit is ripe, the ape finds and gathers the fruit, and disperses the seeds around the forest in its droppings.'

I nodded in agreement, 'As you say, Holmes, admirable, but apes and men are both primates and share a similar physiology, therefore this fruit can hardly be poisonous or all the apes would die.'

Holmes smiled, 'A good point, and one that bothered me also. We know that our toothless friend ate the fruit, as witnessed by the stones in his dessert bowl, yet he survived. Now, here's the rub, Watson, and this is what Croft was able to tell me. The Durian is deadly poisonous *if taken with alcohol!* It will induce a massive and fatal heart attack!'

I was speechless for a moment. 'Well, I'll be damned! So that was why Mister X drank none of that excellent wine?'

Holmes nodded in satisfaction, 'Precisely,' he said, 'and by the by, you need no longer refer to him by the euphemism of Mister X. His name is Mervin J Kingsley of New York City.'

'You *know* him then?' I exclaimed. 'Holmes you really are a marvel.'

He smiled with pleasure. 'Thank you, Watson. As ever you are my most consistent admirer.'

I poured us both a glass of sherry each, then asked, 'But how on earth did you track him down?'

Holmes finished the last of his sandwiches and replied, 'Well, once I knew where the Durian came from, I went along to Lloyds to check the shipping register for any craft arriving from Malaya on the thirteenth, fourteenth or fifteenth of the month. You will recall that Fontaine was contacted on the fifteenth. The records for those dates showed that two vessels had berthed at the Port of London, from Malaya, both on the fourteenth and none on the thirteenth or fifteenth. The first, the Adelphi, carried a cargo of tin and no passengers. The second was the Sea Hawk with a cargo of tea and rubber and three passengers.'

He took a sip from his sherry glass and continued, 'I declare, Watson, it is amazing what information can be purchased for the price of a gold sovereign. For that amount the First Mate of the Sea Hawk, a Mr Michael Hughes, showed me the manifest of cargo and passengers and even included a guided tour of the ship. So, armed with the passenger list it became immediately obvious to me who I was after. The first two passengers were a Miss Simpson, the daughter of an army colonel, and her chaperone. They had been despatched to England for the girl to be educated here at boarding school. That left Mervin J Kingsley, Finance Director of the Imperial Rubber Plantation near Kuala Lumpur.'

He drained his glass, set it upon the table and said, 'From there the trail ran cold. Kingsley disembarked from The Sea Hawk carrying a large valise and promptly disappeared. It was as though the metropolis had swallowed him. I employed the Baker Street Irregulars* to question every cabby in the dockland area to see if one could be found who remembered Kingsley as a fare. Nothing; absolutely nothing. I reasoned that perhaps he had not taken a cab and was therefore staying at an hotel near the docks. I spent hours checking them all, but to no avail. I confess, Watson, I was at a loss to know what to do next. You are familiar with my methods, so will not be surprised when I tell you that, as a last resort, I endeavoured to put myself in the other man's boots. I tried to anticipate what my next move would be, by imagining that *I* was the murderer and considering *my* next move. It occurred to me that very few people would know that I was here in England and the sooner I could leave again, having carried out the dirty deed, the better. With this thought in mind, I returned to The Sea Hawk and spoke again to Mr Hughes. I tell you, Watson, I must be fast approaching my dotage or I would surely have thought to check with him first, but the relief I felt at his news was immense.'

'Why?' I asked. 'What did he tell you?'

'Just that Mervin J Kingsley was the sole passenger booked on the vessel's return voyage to Malaya.'

'Ah!' I said, 'we have him then.'

'We should, if Bradstreet acts on my telegram to the Yard. I told him to meet us at the Royal Albert Dock at seven a.m. tomorrow, if he wishes to further his career with the arrest of Jeremiah Brentwood's murderer.'

'Do you think he will come? He seemed fully inclined to accept that the lad had died from natural causes.'

Holmes yawned and stretched. 'Bradstreet is, like most policemen, a little dim, but he is not a fool. I believe he will be there.' He rose and stretched again saying, 'Well, Watson, I think I'll retire, for we have an early start on the morrow. That is if you wish to accompany me?'

'I would not miss it for the world, Holmes,' I replied. 'There is just one thing however. You said that the ship had to be fast because speed was of the essence. What did you mean by that?'

'Simplicity itself, Watson. Kingsley had to reach England with all possible haste, before the Durian became over-ripe and inedible.'

I nodded in understanding. 'Of course. As you say, Holmes, elementary.'

'Good night, old fellow.'

'Good night, Holmes.'

I was awakened the following morning, at first light, by a fully dressed Holmes shaking me gently and saying, 'Come along, Watson. The game's afoot. There's a cup of coffee waiting for you on the table.'

'Righto, Holmes,' I mumbled as I rubbed the sleep from my eyes.

Very soon we were crossing Baker Street and hailing a hansom to take us to the dock. The morning air was chill and a heavy mist shrouded the cab as we clattered over the wet cobbles towards the river. I turned up my collar and huddled down in my seat, yawning at the early start. Holmes sat forward alertly, resting both his gloved hands on the silver head of his cane.

'I see you have brought your sword stick,' I remarked. 'Do you think he will make a fight of it?'

'You never can tell, Watson. Even a rat will turn and attack if he is cornered. Do you have your service revolver with you?'

I patted my pocket. 'Just in case,' I replied. Presently we reached the waterfront and stepped down from the cab. The mist was even thicker over the Royal Albert Dock and we could see nothing of the river beyond. Holmes paid the cabby and we watched as the cab rumbled away into the mist. There was the mournful hoot of a foghorn from down river and the slap and surge of water around the piles, but apart from that the quayside was very quiet.

'Come along, Watson. This way.' Holmes led me eastwards along the waterfront. We passed a few vessels moored to the capstans and then, emerging out of the mists, we saw the Sea Hawk. She was, as Holmes had said, a beauty. Her bow was long and thin to cleave the seas beneath her acres of sail, and her figurehead was a swooping bird of prey with talons outstretched.

Holmes took out his half hunter and glanced at it. 'Nearly seven,' he muttered. 'Bradstreet is late, if indeed he *is* coming.'

I was about to say something in reply when he held up his hand. 'Hark, a carriage approaches.'

At first I could hear nothing, then I too detected the rattle of wheels on cobbles and the clip clop of horses hooves. Soon a four wheeler hove into view and the driver barked at his horse to whoa! The animal clattered to a halt and snorted, its breath visible in the damp morning air. The carriage door opened and Inspector Bradstreet stepped down, closely followed by a uniformed police constable.

Holmes hurried forward to greet the man from the Yard and drew him to one side out of earshot from the constable and myself. He spoke earnestly to Bradstreet while the constable and I discussed the weather. I assumed that Holmes was appraising the Inspector of the situation. After a few moments the two of them joined us and Bradstreet drew a hip flask from his pocket and took a draught saying,

'I don't normally when on duty, but to keep out the chill, you understand.' He was about to offer the flask to Holmes, when we all heard the approach of another cab, which soon rattled into view. It stopped behind the first one and a portly fellow, carrying a large bag, stepped down. We heard him thanking the cabby in a distinct American accent before that cab also left.

The man turned in our direction and walked towards us. He was hardly dressed for the weather, wearing only a lightweight jacket and trousers and no hat. When he saw us waiting he hesitated and the Inspector stepped forward.

'Mr Kingsley?' he enquired.

The man shook his head. 'No, no my name is Brown. John Brown.'

Holmes stepped forward and said firmly, 'It's no use, Mervin. We know everything. We know about the Durian,' and he held up the little stone saying, 'you should have disposed of these.'

There came into the American's eyes a wild desperate look and he suddenly threw his case at Holmes and Bradstreet. Holmes ducked out of the way, but the Inspector was struck on the shoulder. Kingsley, with a speed that was surprising in so heavy a man, turned and ran.

'After him, Jones!' commanded Bradstreet, and the young constable pounded in pursuit, his hob-nailed boots clashing on the cobblestones and his cape billowing out behind him. The outcome was predictable. Jones easily overhauled the villain and by the time we caught up with them Kingsley was securely handcuffed.

'Well done, lad!' Bradstreet said as he patted Jones on the back. The constable smiled happily. 'Right, get his bag, Jones, and you sit up with the driver,' the Inspector ordered as he held open the cab door for the rest of us. He instructed the cabby to take us back to Scotland Yard and we all climbed aboard.

Kingsley slumped forward in dejection, his head in his hands.

Bradstreet said, 'I am Inspector Bradstreet of Scotland Yard and I am arresting you for the wilful murder of Jeremiah Brentwood on or around the fifteenth of this month. Anything you say may be used against you in a court of law.'

The American did not respond other than to let out a sob. Bradstreet said more softly, 'The judge will be notified of any assistance you may give us in this matter.'

Kingsley sat back with another sob and I could see tears in his eyes.

'I didn't want to kill Jerry,' he blurted out. 'I hardly knew the lad and God knows, he had done me no wrong.'

'Then why...?' I began, but Holmes held up a restraining hand as though to say, 'let him speak'.

Kingsley wiped his eyes with the back of his sleeve, as well as the derbies would allow, and continued, 'I am a weak man, Inspector. I suppose some would say dissolute. I have lived and worked in Malaya for seventeen years. The owner of the rubber plantation where I worked was Saunders Brentwood, Jerry's father. I had a good job and was well paid, but when is enough ever enough? My weakness is gambling and the Malays are great gamblers. I lost and lost. Soon I was stealing from the company. I did not think of it as stealing, for I fully intended to repay the money as soon as my luck changed. But it didn't change. Oh sure, I won sometimes, but seldom more than I lost. It went on for years, but I was able to hide it. Saunders trusted me implicitly with the company's finances. I might still have gotten away with it, if poor old Saunders hadn't trodden on that damn snake. It was a hooded cobra and it bit him behind the knee. We couldn't save him. I knew then that I was in big trouble. The company would pass to Saunders' only living relative, Jeremiah. The books would be audited, my larceny would be exposed and I would go to jail. As I have said, I am a weak man and I know what the jails are like in Malaya. The filth, the rats, the cockroaches and the lice. I couldn't face that. It was then that I decided on a desperate gamble, for that is what I am, a gambler.' He laughed a mirthless laugh, 'And it looks as though I've lost again.'

When he had composed himself he continued, 'I should tell you that a few years earlier I had managed to persuade Saunders, in what was for him an uncharacteristic moment of weakness, to add a codicil to his will saying that if anything happened to himself *and* Jeremiah, that the company be left to me, rather than let it revert to the Malay Government. I suppose he saw no reason not to, as there was every likelihood that Jerry would outlive both of us. That then was my gamble, if I could gain control of the plantation my crime would never be exposed. Instead I now face the gallows.'

Holmes said, not unsympathetically, 'At least you have confessed and confession is the first step towards redemption.'

There was silence in the cab except for the rattle of its wheels on the cobbles, until Holmes asked, 'Did Jeremiah know of his father's death?'

Kingsley shook his head, 'Hell, no! I insisted that no wire be sent to England and that I must go in person to break the sad news to Jeremiah myself. Naturally I made no mention of it to the lad, or he would never have agreed to join me for a meal. I told him I was here for a flying visit on company business, and the reason for the lateness of the meal being the extent of my business and the early departure back to Malaya. It didn't bother Jerry. He always was a nightbird and often stayed out until the early hours. His father had wanted him to take a more active interest in the plantation, but Jerry was a city boy. He couldn't stand the heat and humidity of the tropics. I entertained him with tales of the jungle and told him how well his father was doing and how prosperous the company had become. One of my few talents is as a raconteur, and I kept him amused until the Durian had done its work.'

There was another long silence, which no one seemed inclined to break. Presently Bradstreet drew the hip flask from his pocket again and, after taking a sip, he offered it to Holmes and myself. We both declined, but Kingsley asked, 'May I? The condemned man's last drink and all that.' Bradstreet only hesitated for a moment before handing it to the American. He took a long pull and sighed, 'Thank you, Inspector, I am eternally grateful,' and he even managed a weak smile. He regarded Bradstreet for a moment then said, 'My compliments, Inspector, on the way you tracked me down. I had no idea that the Metropolitan Police were either so astute or so efficient.'

Bradstreet squirmed, then with a loud cough conceded, 'Scotland Yard cannot take the credit, which is rightly due to the gentleman sitting beside you. He is Mr Sherlock Holmes, Consulting Detective of Baker Street, London, and this is his colleague, Doctor Watson. Mr Holmes has from time to time er...assisted us at the Yard.'

Kingsley inclined his head to me, then turned to look at Holmes with new interest and not a little admiration. 'You are to be congratulated, sir. You must possess a remarkably analytical and logical mind to have targeted me so quickly.'

Holmes gave a stiff little bow in response and replied, 'It was fortunate for me that you are not an habitual criminal, otherwise you would hardly have left so many obvious clues for me to follow.'

By now we were approaching the vicinity of Scotland Yard and presently the cab lurched to a halt and Jones jumped down from his perch to open the door for us. Holmes stepped out and Bradstreet took hold of Kingsley's arm to lead him from the cab, when suddenly the American jerked forward violently. I assumed he was making another attempt to escape and grabbed him around the waist, but it was soon evident that the man was in serious trouble. He was gasping for breath and his eyes were rolling as he made gurgling noises in his throat.

'My God,' I exclaimed, 'he's having a heart attack!'

We dragged him out of the cab and laid him on the ground. I did what I could for him, but it was no use. He died right there before our eyes.

Holmes alone amongst us seemed unsurprised and he turned to Bradstreet saying, 'Congratulations, Inspector, you have saved the taxpayers the cost of a trial and a hanging.'

Bradstreet looked startled, 'What the devil are you talking about, Holmes?' he blurted.

'The whiskey you gave him reacted with the Durian he had eaten and killed him!'

Bradstreet's mouth dropped open in dismay. 'But how was I to know?' he pleaded.

Holmes responded, 'Calm yourself, Inspector. You are quite right, you could not have known. As far as you are concerned it was an accident, but I'm afraid as far as Kingsley was concerned it was suicide!'

Later, when Holmes and I were alone in the cab returning to Baker Street, I remarked, 'What an incredible series of events, Holmes.'

He was thoughtful for a moment before replying, 'Just so, Watson, just so. I expect the late Mervin J Kingsley will be facing an even higher court than the Old Bailey, come judgement day.'

I nodded in agreement and commented, 'Who would have thought he would take his own life like that?'

Holmes smiled, 'I would for one, Watson. Pray never disclose this to Bradstreet, but I very nearly prevented him from passing his hip flask to Kingsley. Then I thought, 'if the fellow wants to take his own life perhaps it is better all round.'

'But the Durian he had eaten, during his meal with Brentwood, would surely have passed through his system by now,' I argued.

'I should tell you, Watson, that the Durian, which by the way means "thorn" in Malay, is a large spiky gourd, filled with plum-like fruit. That was why Kingsley had to have such a large valise to carry it in. Doubtless there was still enough of it left over from the meal for him to have breakfasted on it this morning.'

'Are you surmising, Holmes? That's not like you.'

'Not at all, Watson. Don't forget that I sat next to him in the cab, and the simple fact is that I could smell it faintly on his breath!'

'Well, I'll be damned!' I muttered.

Holmes laughed, 'Elementary my dear fellow, or should I say *Alimentary!'* And we both chuckled.

Later that day Holmes went to see Monsieur Fontaine and assured him that, contrary to what he believed, the notoriety gained by his restaurant being the scene of a murder would probably swell, rather than diminish, his clientele.

On his return Sherlock announced, 'Tonight, Watson, we dine at the Golden Cockerel as the very special guests of Auguste Fontaine. We may eat and drink what we like, for as long as we like and, since I am to receive no other fee for this case, I propose that we take full advantage of the offer.'

I laughed, 'Splendid, Holmes, splendid. I'm with you all the way!'

- For the benefit of readers who have not before encountered any of my chronicles of Holmes' exploits, the Baker Street Irregulars are a gang of street urchins who will do Holmes' bidding for a few shillings.

THE MYSTERIOUS DEATH OF THE KENNINGTON VERGER

It was the worst winter I can remember during my years at Baker Street with Sherlock Holmes. Indeed it was so stubbornly reluctant to give way to spring that even long after the calendar proclaimed officially that the seasons had changed, London was still snowbound. The view from the window of 221b was enchanting and the trees in Regents Park, with the sunlight reflecting from their snow-covered branches, resembled a scene from a Christmas card.

Much of this was lost on me however, as I had an irksome duty to perform. It was imperative that I ask my friend Sherlock Holmes for a great favour, and I had procrastinated for long enough. He sat at the table totally engrossed in his paperwork, leafing through his reference books and making copious notes.

I said, 'Holmes, I hate to disturb you when you are busy, but there is something I must ask you.' He did not appear to have heard a word I had said and carried on writing.

I tried again. 'Holmes, could you please listen to me for a moment?'

He sighed heavily and said rather peevishly, 'What is it, Watson? You know how I hate to be interrupted when I am working.'

'I'm sorry, old chap, but it is essential that I speak to you.' He laid his pen down with great deliberation, folded his arms and leaned back in his chair. 'Come along then, out with it.'

'I am aware that you are weighed down with casework, but I have a personal favour to ask of you. I have been asked, nay beseeched, to intercede with you for help. My niece Anne, of whom I am extremely fond, is in desperate straits.'

He replied, 'I'm sorry, Watson, but it is out of the question,' and he picked up his pen to resume working.

I persisted, 'Holmes, our friendship has survived many years and even more deadly dangers. I believe I can truthfully claim to have saved your life, as you have saved mine, on more than one occasion. In the name of that friendship I beg you to at least consider it.'

He replied, 'I have the Carstairs legacy to unravel before the twelfth, the Pilkington jewel robbery to investigate and I am threatened with assassination by the brothers of the blackmailer Phelps. I simply cannot take on another case at the moment.'

I nodded in resignation. 'Of course, of course.' I paused for a moment then said, 'I have never told you this, Holmes, but I look upon my niece Anne as the daughter I never had and even though I knew you would be bound to refuse, I *had* to ask, you understand?'

'Of course, Watson. I really am sorry.'

'No matter, old fellow. Between you and me I believe her cause is already a lost one. As I said to her, Sherlock Holmes is only human. He cannot work miracles, and what you ask is almost certainly beyond even *his* powers.'

I confess that this ploy of mine was a little unworthy, but knowing Holmes as I do, better than any man living, I was sure that a slight pricking of his vanity was perhaps the only strategy that might prove successful.

He looked at me keenly for a moment then said, 'My curiosity is piqued despite myself, Watson. What on earth is the situation she finds herself in?'

I suppressed a sigh of relief as the bait was taken and replied, 'No doubt you read in Tuesday's Daily Telegraph the account of the murder of Mr Soames, the verger at St. Albans church in Kennington?'

'Certainly. An unremarkable case in which Inspector Hopkins has already arrested the likely culprit. What of it?'

'The young man charged with the murder is my niece's fiancée.'

'Ah! Now we have it,' he said. 'She wants me to prove his innocence by finding the real murderer,

'Exactly, Holmes.'

'Look, old fellow, the chances are that all I would achieve would be to prove categorically that the lad *did* commit the murder. Inspector Hopkins may be still a little inexperienced, but he has studied and applies my methods and as a result is now a capable officer of the law. If he has already charged the fellow then he must be fairly certain that he has his man.'

'That is what I told Anne. Apparently there is a wealth of evidence stacked against the youth and he seems to have no alibi.'

'Well then?'

'For all that, Holmes, if you could at least speak to the boy I would be forever in your debt. I promised Anne I would do my best to persuade you.' At that moment there was a ringing of the doorbell and presently a timid knock on our door. I opened it and Anne herself stood on the threshold.

'Please don't be cross, Uncle John,' she pleaded. 'I know you asked me not to come, but I simply *had* to know Mr Holmes's decision.' She was as pretty and demure as ever, even though her red-rimmed eyes betrayed her recent tears. She clutched her bag tightly and looked imploringly at Holmes. They had met once before so introductions were unnecessary.

Holmes said, 'Anne, if you knew a fraction of what I am involved in…'

She said, ' *Please*, Mr Holmes, Simon is innocent. I *know* he is, and you are the only man in the world who can prove it.'

Holmes finally relented and throwing his hands in the air he said, 'Very well, I will take a look. However, I give it just one day, no more. And, young lady, you must be prepared to accept as the truth whatever I find, however unpalatable it is. Agreed?'

'Oh! Yes, Mr Holmes. I agree. Thank you from the bottom of my heart.' She clasped his hand in her two and more tears welled in her eyes. Holmes can be surprisingly gentle with the fairer sex, and offering her his handkerchief, he consoled her with soothing words, before finally asking,

'Where is Simon now, at Scotland Yard?'

Anne nodded, 'Yes, Inspector Hopkins has him in custody, but he is being transferred to Pentonville tomorrow to await trial.'

'Then I should get over there without delay. Coming, Watson?'

'Yes of course, Holmes. Can we drop you off on the way, Anne?'

She shook her head. 'I have to go into Town, but thank you anyway. And thank you for interceding with Mr Holmes, Uncle John.' She kissed me on the cheek and whispered, 'Give my love to Simon.'

In the cab on the way to Scotland Yard Holmes asked, 'So what is the connection between young Simon and Mr Soames, Watson?'

I shook my head. 'I was not aware of any connection between them, Holmes,' I replied. 'I know nothing of this Soames fellow and precious little about the lad, other than what Anne has told me. By her account he is a gentle giant with a heart of gold.'

Holmes looked thoughtful for a moment then responded, 'I pray she is not deluding herself, Watson. Not for nothing is winged Cupid painted blind.'

I nodded in silent agreement. Presently we arrived at Scotland Yard, where Holmes's reputation and standing soon secured us an interview with Inspector Hopkins.

'My dear Mr Holmes,' he said when we came to his office, 'and Dr Watson, an unexpected pleasure. Come in and take a seat.' We sat down and Hopkins asked, 'Would you like a cup of tea, gentlemen?'

Holmes shook his head. 'Thank you no, Inspector. I know how busy you must be and we would not want to take up too much of your time.'

'Then how can I help you, gentlemen?'

Holmes gave a little embarrassed cough and said, 'I am persuaded to enquire about a prisoner of yours, a lad called Simon who is charged with murder.'

The welcoming smile left the face of Inspector Hopkins and he looked hard at Holmes. 'At whose direction do you enquire?'

Holmes replied, 'It is a family matter concerning Dr Watson. His niece is engaged to the fellow.'

'Ah!' Hopkins said as he turned to me. 'I am deeply sorry, Dr Watson, but it looks very black for the lad.'

I asked, 'Could you give us an outline of the case, Inspector?'

Hopkins sat back in his chair and replied, 'Such that it is, Doctor.' Then turning to Holmes he continued, 'It is a very straightforward affair and involves nothing of the mysterious that I know you enjoy, Mr Holmes. Indeed I would go so far as to say that it is probably the simplest challenge I have had to date and is in the nature of an open book.' He put his hands behind his head as he continued, 'On the evening of Monday the eighth, Constable Butler, one of my best men, was passing the front of St. Albans in the high street, on his regular beat when he noticed a bundle lying on the path near the front doors of the church. He opened the gate and went up the path to investigate. It turned out to be the body of Mr

Arnold Soames the Verger and he had been stabbed in the back. Butler checked for a pulse but could find none. What he did notice however, and this is crucial, was that the body was still warm.'

Holmes asked, 'What time was this?'

The inspector replied, 'A little after six-thirty PM.'

Holmes nodded and the inspector continued, 'As I have said, Butler is one of my best men, and will probably make Sergeant this year. He summoned help on his police whistle, but had the sense to avoid the only other footprints in the snow, apart from his own. He stationed the constable, who answered his alarm, at the gate with strict instructions to admit nobody into the churchyard, then hurried to alert me.'

He leaned forward and smiled at Holmes as he continued, 'I think you will appreciate my immediate decision, Mr Holmes. I ordered the official police photographer to accompany Butler and myself back to St. Albans and had him photograph the boot tracks in the snow, before any thaw could set in.'

Holmes was nodding in approval, 'Very good, Inspector. I commend both your decision and your reasoning.' Then after a pause he asked, 'Would it be possible for me to see those photographs later?'

Hopkins nodded, 'Yes I don't see why not. I will arrange for it.'

'Thank you, Inspector. Tell me, should there not have been at least three sets of footprints on the path? Butler's, Soames' and the murderer's?'

'No, Mr Holmes. It transpires that Soames was in the church for over an hour and during that time there had been a further light snow shower.'

'Ah! I see,' said Holmes nodding. 'Then presumably Soames had just left the church when the murderer struck?'

'That's how I see it, Mr Holmes. The verger's few footprints can be seen leading from the door of the church then stopping next to the other tracks. There is disturbed snow in a small area indicating a scuffle of some sort, then the tracks of the murderer heading back the way he had come through the gate. Fortuitously the returning tracks did not completely obliterate the incoming impressions and the texture of the snow was perfect for recording the imprints in very fine detail.'

'And presumably those imprints led you to young Simon?'

'They did literally, Mr Holmes. Again fortune favoured us, for at that time of the evening, in such cold weather there were few people abroad and it occurred to me that we should try to follow the tracks. The imprints were very distinctive. Apart from their huge size, there was a split in the sole of the left boot and a cleat missing from the heel of the right one.' Inspector Hopkins permitted himself a wry little smile as he continued, 'We followed the tracks back across the river, over Vauxhall bridge and there we lost them. I told Butler and Williams, the police photographer, to fan out and try to pick up the trail again. Carriage wheels and horses hooves play the merry devil with footprints, as you well know, Mr Holmes. Finally I picked up the tracks again on Lupus Road and they led me straight to the Red Lion hotel. I went into the bar and it was immediately obvious to me who my man was. Simon Jurgens is a giant of a fellow with feet to match. It was hardly even necessary to examine his boots, but we did so anyway and they mirrored the footprints exactly. I arrested him then and there and he came without a struggle, though he denied the charge vehemently and continuously.'

Holmes asked, 'Did you find the murder weapon?'

Hopkins shook his head. 'I'm afraid not, but we know it must have been a long circular knife or bayonet. Or it could have been a poker.'

I asked, 'Would it be too much of an imposition to take a look at the body, Inspector?'

Hopkins only hesitated for a moment before replying, 'Not at all, Doctor. We have it in the police mortuary. Come along, I'll show you.'

We followed him downstairs to the mortuary and he removed the sheet covering the mortal remains of Arnold Soames. He was a man in his late forties or early fifties, with greying hair. He was of average height and weighed about twelve stones. We turned him over so I could examine the wound and I was soon able to tell Holmes, 'The poker, or whatever, was plunged into his back with tremendous force, for it has shattered the seventh thoracic vertebra and severed the spinal cord. I should say he would have died almost instantly.'

Holmes asked, 'At what angle to the body is the wound?'

I replied, 'About thirty degrees to the vertical, if the man was standing.'

Hopkins said, 'Thirty-two degrees, to be exact. Our pathologist has already measured it, and he says it would have to have been made by someone well above average height and with great strength.'

I nodded in agreement saying, 'I have to concur with his findings.'

As we left the mortuary Holmes asked, 'Was there any indication of robbery, Inspector?'

'None, Mr Holmes. The verger's purse, with one pound seventeen shillings and sixpence inside, was still in his pocket, and his watch and chain were intact.'

Holmes was thoughtful for a moment before asking, 'Would it be possible to speak to Simon?'

The inspector looked at his watch and replied, 'I can allow you a half hour and of course you must be accompanied.'

'Naturally, Inspector. I appreciate your co-operation and a half hour should be sufficient.'

Hopkins led us along a cream coloured corridor to cell number seventeen and the duty jailer unlocked the door for us.

Simon Jurgens had been sitting on the edge of his bed with his head in his hands, but now he stood and faced us. He was indeed a huge man. He must have been at least six foot five and he was broad at the shoulders and narrow at the waist. His open necked shirt was stretched over his biceps and across his pectoral muscles and torso. He had striking blue eyes, a square jaw and an unruly mop of blond hair. He looked at us warily and Hopkins said, 'These gentlemen would like to speak to you. Perhaps you will tell them more than you have told me. This is Mr Sherlock Holmes and his colleague Dr Watson.'

The lad's face lit up and he stepped forward with hand outstretched. 'Mr Holmes, Dr Watson. Anne said she would do her best to persuade you to look at my case. I can't tell you how happy I am to see you.' He shook hands with both of us and although my hand was lost in his giant fist, he was surprisingly gentle. I remember thinking; here is a fellow who *does* know his own strength.

Holmes said, 'We do not have much time, Simon, so I suggest you tell us your story, and if I am to help you I only want to hear the truth.'

The smile faded from the lad's face and he replied, 'The truth will probably hang me, Mr Holmes, even though I did *not* kill Soames.' He sat down again on the edge of his bed and continued, 'That is the reason I have said so little to Inspector Hopkins. For the truth is that I *was* at the church and I *did* threaten the verger.'

Holmes asked, 'What was your relationship with Soames?'

Jurgens hesitated for a moment then admitted, 'He was my stepfather.'

I said, 'Anne never told me that.'

69

He replied, 'Anne did not know. I hated him and denied his existence. I never admitted the relationship to anyone.'

Holmes said, 'Perhaps you should start at the beginning.'

Simon nodded and with a sigh he said, 'My real father was a Norwegian seaman called Arne Jurgens. He was a big man also. My mother called him her Viking Warrior and she loved him deeply. He was lost at sea when his ship, the Miramar, sank with all hands off the Azores. I was nine years old at the time. We had never been rich even when my father was alive, but after he died we came to know what *real* poverty was like. My mother is not a very strong woman and though she took in washing and did cleaning work for the big houses, we were always poor. Arnold Soames desired my mother, for she was still a handsome woman, and he courted her. I'm sure my mother never loved him. To her no one could take the place of my father. Eventually Soames wore down her resistance and they married. Though she has never admitted it, I believe she married him more for my sake than for any other reason. We were certainly not so poor afterwards. At first life was good and he treated us well, but gradually his true colours began to emerge. He had a violent temper and the slightest thing could throw him into a furious rage. I was always the focus of those storms. He beat me regularly with his leather belt, even when I had done no wrong. He seemed to take pleasure in it. He usually waited until my mother was out and threatened further beatings if I told her. I left home as soon as I was old enough and now I earn a living as a builder. No man in the trade can carry as many bricks as I can,' he said proudly.

Holmes smiled, 'I can believe that.'

'And I have ambitions, Mr Holmes. I won't always carry the hod. Mr Henderson, my old school master, tutors me in the evenings and Anne helps me with my figures.'

Holmes nodded, 'Very commendable, Simon, but I need to know what took place on Monday evening at St Albans.'

Simon sighed, 'I had just called on my mother. I visit her each Monday when I know Soames is at the church. I found her weeping and she tried to hide the ugly bruise on the side of her face. At first she would have me believe she had walked into a door, but finally she admitted that Soames was behind it. I remembered other occasions in the past when she was marked, but she always had an innocent account of it. I had thought the fiend only enjoyed beating me because I was not his real son and because he could not make me cry, but when I knew that he had also been beating my mother, who is the most gentle, loving soul in London, I went berserk. I wanted to kill him - yes I freely admit it - but she implored me not to and I could never deny her anything she asked of me.'

He swallowed hard and unclenched his huge hands, which had formed fists of rage, as he recounted his torment. He took a deep breath and continued, 'I finally agreed to let him live, but I told her that I intended to warn him that if he ever laid a finger on her again I *would* kill him. I went directly to the church and as I approached the front doors, he emerged. I grabbed him by the throat and lifted him off his feet, shaking him as a terrier would a rat. I hissed my warning into his face and he whined and pleaded like the coward he is. I left him there by the church, trembling and weeping and that was the last I saw of him.'

'Then what did you do?'

'I just walked, trying to calm down. I did not even notice where I was until finally I came to an inn where I stopped for a tankard of ale. That was where I was arrested.'

Holmes said, 'And you did not kill Arnold Soames?'

'No, sir. As God is my witness, I did not.'

'Then who did, would you say? Your footprints were the only ones found there.'

The lad shook his head in perplexity. 'That is the question that goes round and round in my head, Mr Holmes, and the only answer I have is that God himself must have struck down the beast. Arnold Soames wore two faces. His public face was pious and God fearing, but his private face was the face of a devil. God is not mocked, Mr Holmes. He saw the real Arnold Soames and I believe He was not pleased by the sight.'

Holmes responded, 'Such a defence plea would carry very little weight at the Old Bailey, Simon.'

The lad nodded forlornly in agreement. 'I told you that the truth would probably hang me,' he repeated.

Inspector Hopkins looked at his watch and Holmes said, 'Simon, you are in a desperately serious situation and although I will do what I can for you, I want you to harbour no vain hopes.' Putting on his hat he said, 'We may yet meet again.'

'Thank you, Mr Holmes, and you too Dr Watson.' I passed on Anne's message to him and we left.

Back in Hopkins's office Holmes said, 'Tell me, Inspector, do you still have a constable guarding the churchyard?'

Hopkins nodded, 'Yes, but I was going to call him off this morning. We have all we need.'

'Pray humour me, Inspector, and leave it so for another few hours. I would take a look at the scene of the crime, if I may?'

'Certainly, Mr Holmes. You had but to ask. Now if you will excuse me, gentlemen, I have much to do.'

'Of course, Inspector, but the photographs?'

'Ah yes. I will have a set of prints sent round to you at Baker Street. Will that suffice?'

'Excellent, Inspector. Your generosity and co-operation exceed all expectations.'

Hopkins rose and said, 'If you are planning to visit the scene of the crime directly, we could share a cab, for I am just on my way to Vauxhall Bridge.'

Holmes nodded. 'Of course. To check on the progress of your men, who even now drag the riverbed below the bridge.'

Hopkins looked at him sharply and asked, 'How did you know?'

Holmes shrugged, 'I didn't, but it was a simple deduction. You said that the murder weapon had not been found and that Simon had crossed the river by Vauxhall Bridge. What better place to dispose of the evidence than the river Thames?'

Hopkins smiled. 'You are absolutely right as usual, Mr Holmes.'

Presently we were trotting along in a carriage towards Kennington in quieter fashion than usual, for the snow muffled the sound of the horse's hooves and the carriage wheels. Half way across the bridge Hopkins ordered the driver to stop and we clambered out.

The inspector shouted down from the guard rail to his men in a boat below, 'Found anything yet, Butler?'

'Nothing yet, sir,' came the faint reply.

Holmes and I joined Hopkins at the rail and looked down. Three constables were dragging on chains whilst a fourth controlled the boat with his oars. Holmes said, 'I take it they are using grappling hooks on their chains?'

Hopkins nodded. 'Of course. What else?'

'Have them try strong magnets. Grappling hooks are unlikely to snare a long thin blade.'

Hopkins smiled, 'Good idea, Mr Holmes. Never let it be said that I was too proud to take advice. I shall try it.'

Holmes said, 'Watson and I shall walk to the church from here. Once again my thanks to you, Inspector.'

Vauxhall Bridge before being enlarged in 1896

We all shook hands then Holmes and I set off on foot for St. Albans. As we walked away Hopkins called after us, 'My man at the church is constable Jennings. Tell him I grant you leave to pass.'

'Very well, Inspector.'

When we were out of earshot Holmes said, 'I proposed this walk, Watson, because I wanted the opportunity to discuss this case with you. What do you make of young Simon? Is he, as he seems, a naive, ingenuous lad or the biggest fool in Christendom?'

'What do you mean, Holmes?'

'Well, old fellow, in my experience even the dimmest petty thief, or wharf rat who plunders cargo at the docks, would have been able to tell a better story than Simon's. Every sentence he uttered tightened the noose more securely around his own neck.'

I nodded in agreement and replied, 'I must say, Holmes, that for that very reason I am inclined to believe the fellow. Though as you well know, I am not the worlds best judge of human character.'

Holmes smiled, 'Truly spoken, Watson. You are one of the most honourable and trustworthy people I know and unfortunately you ascribe those same qualities to others, very few of whom deserve it.' To spare my blushes he hurried on, 'Could the lad have carried out the deed and not remember having done so?'

I nodded. 'Though it is not my field, I have read some of what has been written recently in the journals about disorders of the mind by men such as Charcot in Paris and Josef Breuer in Vienna. There are conditions, so it is postulated, where the trauma of an incident can be so painful that the mind deludes itself into believing that the incident never actually happened. I repeat I am no expert, but I have to say that Simon seems to me to be vigorously healthy in both mind and body.'

Holmes was thoughtful for a moment then said, 'As I see it, Watson, there are two things in Simon's favour. Firstly his story, which is so damaging it almost *has* to be true, and secondly the weapon. Hopkins said a poker or something similar, but the fact is that Simon Jurgens would not *need* a weapon to kill a man. He could have snapped Soames' neck like a rotten branch if he had wanted to. The verger was not exactly a small man himself, yet Simon was strong enough, in his fury, to pick him up and shake him. Such a man would, I feel, disdain a poker as a weapon.'

We walked on in silence for a while until Holmes said musingly, 'There are ways, Watson, to inflict a stab wound without actually being in the immediate vicinity of the victim.'

I said, 'You mean like throwing a spear or lance?'

'Exactly, or with a bow and arrow, or a cross bow and quarrel.'

'You might have something there, Holmes,' I enthused. 'We could examine the perimeter of the churchyard for other footprints. And,' I continued with excitement, 'if the arrow or shaft had a string attached, then it could have been retrieved without running the risk of leaving footprints in the snow.'

Holmes did not seem too enthusiastic about my supposition. 'There are drawbacks to such a scenario, old fellow.'

'Like what?'

'Well, the main one is the angle of entry of the wound. Thirty-two degrees to the vertical means that the spear or arrow would have to have been projected in a looping arc to strike the verger at a downward angle. That would have been some shot, and why would anyone even loose a projectile in such a fashion?' I was crestfallen as I realised the truth of Holmes's words. He continued, 'As for retrieving the arrow or whatever with string, it would need a formidable pull to dislodge a missile which is embedded into the bone of a vertebra.'

I nodded in forlorn agreement. 'Of course you are right as usual, old fellow.'

Holmes said, 'Well well, here we are already and the bored looking guardian of the law ahead must be Hopkins' man.' As we approached Holmes enquired, 'P.C. Jennings?'

'Yes, sir,' the man responded with a salute.

'Inspector Hopkins sends his compliments and instructs you to allow us entry. My name is Sherlock Holmes and this is my colleague Dr Watson.'

'Very good, sir. I know you by reputation of course. Did the inspector give a hint as to when I'll be relieved?'

'As far as I am concerned, Jennings, you can leave when we do. However, I've no doubt Hopkins will send for you presently.'

As I followed Holmes through the gate I noticed a hoarding by the wall exhorting the public to donate generously towards the roof restoration fund. As I glanced up at the roof I could see why, for some of the guttering was hanging down and a large section was missing completely. As I followed Holmes up the steep path I could hear Jennings muttering and stamping his feet against the cold.

Holmes soon discerned Simon Jurgens' footprints and carefully avoided them. He peered all around and indicated to me the red stain in the snow where Arnold Soames' lifeblood had spilled. 'See, Watson, it is as Simon told us. Soames was facing towards the gate before he was struck down, for you can plainly see his outline in the snow. Hopkins also read the signs aright. There *was* a brief struggle between the two men.'

I watched as Holmes quested hither and thither like a bloodhound seeking the scent. Presently he returned from examining the perimeters of the graveyard and exclaimed, 'No luck, Watson. I can find nothing to indicate that a third person was involved. If there had been another assailant he would have had to fire an arrow over the church roof to strike Soames in the back, because standing as he was, the verger had the body of the church directly behind him.'

I added despondently, 'And we would still have to account for how the arrow was retrieved.'

'Just so, Watson. I am afraid it really *does* look black for the lad.'

I said, 'Poor Anne! I just don't know how I am going to tell her.'

Holmes put a comforting arm around my shoulders and offered, 'I will convey the news, if you prefer, old fellow.'

'Thank you, Holmes, but no. I feel it my duty to tell her myself.'

We thanked P.C. Jennings and left, hailing the first available cab back to Baker Street.

As we arrived we were met by a messenger boy who had an envelope for Holmes. 'Compliments of Scotland Yard,' announced the courier.

'Ah yes. These will be the photographs that Hopkins promised. He was exceedingly efficient in dispatching them.'

Holmes tipped the lad and carried the package up to our room. As I poured each of us a glass of sherry, Holmes glanced casually through the photographs. When he had finished he tossed them onto the table and picked up his drink. Suddenly I saw him stop, his glass half raised to his lips. With slow deliberation he put down his glass and picked up the photographs again. His whole demeanour changed in an instant and I could sense that he was struggling to control his emotions.

'What is it, Holmes?' I asked, 'What have you seen?'

'The chains, Watson, *the chains!*' he breathed. 'I remember thinking, as we watched Hopkins' men dragging the river bed with their chains, it is rarely appreciated that even the strongest chain, with no weak links, will break under its own weight, *if it is long enough!'*

I said, 'Well yes, I suppose that is correct, but what-'

He interrupted, 'How's your Latin, old fellow? Do you know the expression; *Mole ruit sua?'*

I smiled, 'I would be a poor physician indeed, Holmes, with no knowledge of Latin. It means, "falls by its own weight".'

'Exactly! Watson.' He bounded to the sideboard and snatched his magnifying glass from the drawer. Returning to the photographs he began studying one of them in particular. I stood beside him and peered at the image over his shoulder. It was a view of St. Albans taken from the gate showing the front façade with its double oak doors, square clock tower and crennelated buttresses. At the four corners of the tower, just below the castellations, were gargoyle-headed waterspouts. The clock showed Seven Fifteen and by the darkness of the picture it was plain that dusk was falling. On the path was the shapeless form of Arnold Soames' body.

I repeated, 'What is it that you see, Holmes?'

He put down his magnifying glass and I noticed that his hand trembled slightly. When he spoke there was a tremor in his voice. 'Could it be so? *Could* it be so...?' Turning to me he said, 'Watson, you must be weary of hearing me say that when all other possibilities have been excluded, whatever remains, however improbable *must* be the truth.'

I said, 'Well I don't deny-'

He interrupted me again saying, 'I would despise myself if I raised false hopes in your breast, old fellow, only to have them dashed later. So perhaps it is best that I say no more at present, but I have to return to St. Albans.'

'Then I'm coming with you,' I announced and grabbed my coat and hat.

Soon we were galloping back towards Kennington as fast as the snow would allow. I tried to draw him out further, but all he would say was, 'You have on occasions remarked, old fellow, that you believed my powers to be a divine gift, and I, on each occasion, have refuted the notion. Well, if I am right *this* time I may begin to believe that there is perhaps a grain of truth in your assertion.' He was introspective for a moment before continuing, 'I sometimes feel, Watson, that the Gods on Mount Olympus make sport of us mortals for their own amusement. They ensnare us with their guile, but allow a clue to the riddle to be seen dimly, as through a glass darkly, by a select few with the sight, or insight, to pierce the gloom.'

I was not sure that I knew what Holmes was talking about, but I replied, 'If it is so, Holmes, then you are surely the best of that select few.'

As the cab approached St. Albans, we saw P.C. Jennings and another constable walking towards us, obviously heading back to the Yard. Holmes ordered the cab to pull up and he leapt out crying, 'Cabby, take these officers to Scotland Yard as quickly as possible,' and he thrust some coins into the driver's hand. Turning to Jennings he said, 'Summon Inspector Hopkins to meet me at the church as fast as he can. Tell him Sherlock Holmes suspects an innocent man has been charged with murder!'

Jennings saluted and said, 'Very well, Mr Holmes, it shall be as you say. Come along, Smith!' and the two of them scrambled into the hansom.

Holmes and I hurried on to the church, and when we reached the gate he stood and stared at the tower. 'It fits!' he said, almost in a whisper. 'It all fits!' Turning to me he said, 'If the good people of this parish had been a little more generous with their donations, Watson, young Simon would not now be languishing in a prison cell.'

'I'm sorry, Holmes, but I am completely in the dark. I don't know *what* you are talking about.'

He smiled fondly at me and said, 'Poor Watson. I forgot to include, among your many attributes, your unending patience. If you will bear with me for a moment more I hope to be able to answer all your questions.' He walked slowly up the path casting his eyes from side to side. Suddenly he let out a cry of, *'Eureka!'* and he stooped to pick up a snow-covered object from the side of the path. 'Behold, Watson,' he cried, 'Exhibit A, the murder weapon!' As he brushed the snow from it he revealed a huge icicle.

'That is what killed Soames?' I asked incredulously.

'Without a doubt, Watson.' He pointed up at the tower and said, 'Look at the gargoyles and tell me what you see.'

I looked then said, 'By Jove, Holmes, there is a great long icicle hanging from each of them, except this nearest one.'

'Exactly, Watson, for I hold it in my hand. Remember when I said that even a chain would break under its own weight, if it were long enough? Well, I don't pretend to know the tensile strength of ice, but this big fellow grew beyond that limit and down it came. There, you can see its track in the snow on the roof. After it fell from the tower it slid down the roof, which I'll wager is exactly thirty-two degrees to the vertical, and buried itself in the verger's back.'

He hefted the icicle in his hands and said, 'I estimate this thing must weigh more than three pounds. There is a correlation between mass and velocity called force, Watson, and the force this must have generated, as it whipped off the roof, is evident in that it knocked Soames flat and shattered his spine.'

I was overcome with admiration for my friend. 'Holmes, I'm left speechless. Except to perhaps repeat that your powers of deduction really *are* a divine gift.'

He smiled with pleasure and said, 'Now you will have only good news to impart to your niece Anne.'

I shook his hand warmly and said simply, 'Thank you, Holmes.'

He nodded in satisfaction, 'You are very welcome, old fellow.'

After a few moments I said, 'There are just a few things I don't understand, Holmes.'

'Fire away, Watson. We have time to kill while we wait for Inspector Hopkins.'

'What have the roof-fund donations got to do with it?'

He laughed, 'Because if the guttering had been replaced in this area, it would have trapped the icicle in its slide and protected anyone standing below.'

'Of course! How obtuse of me.'

'And number two?'

'Well, how come the inspector or Butler did not find the icicle?'

'Because they were looking for a metal implement. I only found it because I knew what I was looking for.'

'But it is some distance from where the body lay. I would have expected it to be beside the body.'

Holmes shook his head. 'Try to picture the scene, Watson. The icicle falls, strikes the roof and the tip almost certainly breaks off. The rest of it plummets down the roof and embeds itself into the verger. He falls to the ground and dies. Now the icicle is leaning forward at an angle of nearly sixty degrees to the vertical. The warmth of Soames' body melts the ice locally and the major part of the icicle falls forward and rolls down the sloping path, away from the body, picking up a dusting of snow as it does so. Because it is tapered, it rolls in an arc to the edge of the path where I found it.'

'Brilliant, Holmes, simply brilliant!'

Holmes shook his head and said, 'Not so brilliant, Watson. I missed it when we were here earlier. I was so busy looking for footprints, I never thought to look up, and as a consequence an innocent man could have hung.'

Presently a cab drew up outside the church and Inspector Hopkins stepped down. 'What's this then, Mr Holmes?' he called as he walked up the path. 'Jennings tells me you have another suspect besides Jurgens.'

Holmes smiled, 'You could put it that way, Inspector. In which case Simon was closer than any of us when he said that God had struck down the beast.'

'What on earth do you mean?'

Holmes proffered the icicle, which he still held in his gloved hands, to the inspector saying, 'Behold the murder weapon. And since nothing moves without the Prime Mover, you now know who killed Arnold Soames.'

'You're not serious, Mr Holmes?'

'I was never more serious in my life, Inspector.' Holmes went on to explain to the incredulous officer the train of events leading to the death of St Albans' verger, concluding, '...and if final proof be needed, Inspector, take a look at the end of the icicle. It is still stained red with Soames' blood!'

Hopkins tipped his bowler hat and said, 'I compliment you, Mr Holmes. Your case is conclusive and, though it makes me look a fool, I will enjoy freeing young Simon, for

I have taken a shine to the lad.' Hopkins took off his muffler, then packing the icicle around with snow, he wrapped it all in his scarf saying, 'This is going back to the Yard as evidence. My thanks to you, Mr Holmes, for preventing a serious miscarriage of justice. Perhaps you would like to return with me and break the good news to Simon yourselves?'

I said, 'What a splendid idea, eh, Holmes?'

'Absolutely,' he agreed. Soon we were retracing our steps along the cream corridor to cell number seventeen. When we entered Simon stood up and looked at us apprehensively.

Holmes said simply, 'You are a free man, Simon. I have proven to the Inspector that you did not kill Arnold Soames.'

The lad swayed on his feet and for a second I thought he was going to faint. He began to laugh and cry at the same time and he pumped Sherlock's hand vigorously for long moments. Finally when he had regained his composure he said seriously, in a voice husky with emotion, 'For as long as you live, Mr Holmes, if you ever need a strong back and a willing heart, I am yours to command.'

Holmes smiled and said, 'Make Anne a happy and contented woman and the debt will be paid,'

Simon nodded vigorously. 'That I will, sir. That I will.'

The three of us took a cab to Anne's home and as we alighted she espied us from the window. The smile on Simon's face told her all she wanted to know and the next moment the front door burst open and she flew down the path with arms outstretched. She did not, however, leap into her lover's embrace as I had expected, but instead threw her arms around Holmes's neck and covered his face with kisses.

For the first time in my life I saw the great misogynist, Sherlock Holmes, blushing like an awkward schoolboy!

THE RIDDLE OF THE CARSTAIRS LEGACY

As Sherlock Holmes and I stepped from the hansom cab outside 221b Baker Street, he said, 'Watson, I am delighted that your transparent ruse to inveigle me into investigating the death of the Kennington Verger had such a satisfactory outcome. No doubt it is destined to become one of your inimitable chronicles?'

I stopped short and said in dismay, 'You knew all along then, Holmes?'

'Of course, old fellow. However, since you had gone to so much trouble to try to enlist my aid, I realised that it meant a great deal to you.'

I smiled and said, 'I should have known better than to try to outwit the master.'

As we climbed the stairs, he said, 'I just hope that the loss of a day will not seriously jeopardise the outcome of the Carstairs investigation.'

'I'm sure you would agree, Holmes, that Simon's case, being literally a matter of life and death, *should* have had priority?'

'Absolutely, Watson, I could not agree more. It just means I must burn the midnight oil tonight if I am to conclude my investigation of the Pilkington blood sample before we leave for Cambridge in the morning.'

'If there is anything I can do, Holmes, you have but to ask.'

He was thoughtful for a moment, then replied, 'If you can sort out the travel arrangements, secure us tickets on the morning express and pack our bags that would be a great help, Watson.'

I smiled, 'Consider it done, old fellow.'

I checked in my Bradshaws for the train times, hurried down to Liverpool Street station to purchase the tickets, then returned to begin packing my own and Holmes' travel bags. As I did so, I reflected on the contrast between this evening's activity and the tranquillity of the previous Sunday. It had been one of those crystal clear frosty evenings when the snow sparkled like jewels under the light from the gas lamps and a breath hung long in the air. I was enjoying a pipeful of tobacco by the fireside and Holmes was writing, when the doorbell rang and presently Mrs Hudson introduced an agitated young man to us.

His name was Andrew Newton, and his opening question was, 'Mr Holmes, how would you like to earn a small fortune for a few days legitimate work?'

Holmes replied, 'I play the game for the game's sake and am not motivated by wealth. However, if you will outline your problem, perhaps it contains enough to intrigue me.'

Andrew Newton smiled with relief and said, 'You have just spoken the appropriate word, Mr Holmes, *intrigue!* My problem abounds with it.'

Holmes, inviting Newton to sit down, said, 'Pray tell us your tale of intrigue then.'

Newton was tall and slim with dark hair, a friendly demeanour and a pleasant smile. His manners and speech implied that he had some education, though his threadbare appearance indicated that he had yet to make his financial way in the world.

He began, 'I earn a barely adequate wage as a chandler's clerk at the docks, and am striving to better myself. Last week a Mr Barker, a senior partner in the law firm of Faversham and Brinkley, contacted me. His telegram urged me to call in to their offices in Wardour Street if I wished to learn something to my advantage. As you can imagine I rushed round there straight away and was shown into Mr Barker's office. What he told me was simply amazing. I stand to inherit Northcliffe Grange, a Tudor manor house, and two hundred acres of land just outside Cambridge.'

Homes raised his eyebrows and said, 'My congratulations to you.'

Newton shook his head and replied, 'Your felicitations may be premature, for there is a catch.'

Homes nodded, 'I rather thought there might be. Tell me, who is, or was, your benefactor?'

Andrew Newton Esquire

Newton replied, 'That is the strangest thing of all. It transpires that he was the late James Fitzroy Carstairs, errant son of Lord Edward and Lady Elizabeth Carstairs, and last male heir to the Carstairs fortune. I am told that the paintings in the Grand banqueting hall alone are worth a King's ransom.'

Holmes asked, 'Why is it so strange. Have you no connection with the Carstairs family?'

'None whatever, Mr Holmes. At least none that I know of. Until last week I had never even heard of them.'

Holmes said, 'Tell me a little of your own background.'

Newton paused for a moment, then said, 'I was born here in London in '67, the same year that my father died. He was a soldier and was killed in the Fenian uprising of that year. My mother was a gifted musician who taught music and piano to the families of the wealthy. She made enough money to give me a reasonable education before she died a few years ago. She never mentioned the name of Carstairs.'

Holmes said, 'The solicitor, Mr Barker. Is he not able to shed any light on the matter?'

'Apparently he is forbidden under the terms of the will. However, if I can answer the riddles, all will be revealed.'

'The riddles?'

'Yes, Mr Holmes. The catch I told you about involves solving several riddles and clues and finding a hidden message.'

Holmes' eyes lit up at the prospect. 'Aha! The intrigue you spoke of. Pray tell me more. This I find infinitely more stimulating than money.'

Newton continued, 'Barker informed me that James Fitzroy Carstairs was a headstrong rebel who refused to be constrained by the strictures of his aristocratic family and its traditions. He was an adventurer who wanted to live life to the full. After a scandal of unknown circumstances, he sailed to Argentina to make his own way in the world. Reports of his life out there are sketchy and include tales of prospecting for silver and diamonds. He must have been successful at one or the other because he bought a huge ranch by the Rio Negro, raised cattle and married a local beauty. He only returned to England, after the death of his parents, to secure Northcliffe Grange in the hands of a warden, with an annual stipend for maintenance and repairs. I am told that all the contents of the house have been placed under dust sheets and mothballs.'

Holmes said, 'And Carstairs then returned to Argentina?'

'Yes, Mr Holmes, where he remained until his death last month. Carstairs' widow, Rosa Maria, inherits the ranch and the villa, Casa Grande, in Argentina. However, I will inherit the Grange if I can present the hidden message at the offices of Faversham and Brinkley before noon on the 28th day after his death. If I fail, Rosa Maria inherits everything.'

Holmes asked, 'On which day of last month did he die?'

Newton replied, 'The 12th'

Holmes leapt to his feet and exclaimed, '*The 12th!* Good Lord! That only leaves us four days. Why did you not contact me sooner?'

Newton replied, 'I only found out myself last week. It has taken the solicitors almost three weeks to trace me.'

Holmes began pacing the room and said, 'These riddles, have you solved any of them yet?'

Newton nodded, 'Just a couple of the simpler ones. The others, however, have me baffled.'

Holmes stopped pacing and asked, 'Will the legacy be compromised if you enlist outside aid?'

The young man shook his head, saying, 'I asked Mr Barker that self same question as soon as I realised that I would need assistance. He said he did not believe so, since it was not expressly forbidden in the terms of the will.'

Holmes nodded in satisfaction, saying, 'Then I think you should show us your riddles now.'

Andrew Newton held up a hand saying, 'Even though you have said money means little to you, Mr Holmes, I insist on paying you 10 per cent of the estate's value, if you are successful. After all, I would rather receive 90 per cent of something than 100 per cent of nothing! The only stipulation being that if you fail then I can't pay you a penny. Agreed?'

Holmes nodded impatiently saying, 'Yes yes, I agree. Now the riddles, pray.'

Newton took a large manila envelope from his pocket and handed it to Holmes. Written on the front in black ink, in a beautiful copperplate script, was the name, Andrew Newton esquire. On the reverse was the embossed family crest of the Carstairs of Cambridge, and this was repeated in the red wax seal at the flap. Holmes reached for his magnifying glass and peered at the coat of arms. He began listing its heraldic features:

'A shield with per cross lines of partition; Lion rampant regardent in the Dexter chief; Inverted horseshoe in the Sinister base and Honey bees in the Sinister chief and Dexter base.'

None of this meant anything to me and from the look of puzzlement on Newton's face, not much to him either.

Holmes asked, 'Can you decipher the Latin text, Watson?'

I looked and translated it as, 'Strength and fortune through endeavour.'

Holmes nodded and said, 'Predictable. The lion for strength, the horseshoe for fortune and the honeybees for industry.' Finally he reached into the envelope and extracted a folded piece of parchment. As he unfolded it and spread it out on the table I stood at his elbow the better to see. It carried the family crest at its head and the writing was the same copperplate script as on the envelope. It read;

You Fillius Nullius will be (1) of any (2) if you turn up a shoe not of leather made by four kings together. Find the (3) inside its secrets to hide. Page (4) line (5), if you've read this aright, then this is your fate. If these things you have done welcome home now (6).

Below this cryptic paragraph were four riddles entitled, *THE FOUR KINGS*

The King of Hearts forever tries, when fed lives, when watered dies.

The King of Clubs is HIJKLMNO that is all you need to know.

The King of Diamonds, when he's done, is Old Sol's third son.

The King of Spades is simply that, what's over 'ead but under 'at.

Next were listed the following six riddles.

(1) God has never seen it, royalty seldom do, yet I always see it when I look at you.

(2) This animal walks on four legs, in the morning sun. At noon it's down to two legs, but heavens see it run. By evening it's stranger its legs they number three. This is a curious animal, whatever can it be?

(3) My first is a letter, an insect, a word, that means to exist, it moves like a bird.

My next is a letter, a small part of man, 'tis found in all climes, search where you can.

My third is something seen in all brawls, my next you will find in elegant halls.

My last is the first of the last part of day, is ever in earnest, but never in play.

(4) Six books stand straight upon their shelf, 100 pages to each itself, how many pages are there held fast, twixt first of first and last of last?

(5) Young monkey at bottom of forty foot well, each day he climbs three feet, slides two feet to hell. In the well there's no water, nary a drop, which day will young monkey reach up to the top?

(6) Brothers and sisters have I none, yet this man's father is my father's son.

Newton said, 'The ones I have deciphered are...' but Holmes held up a hand saying,

'Pray let us try them ourselves first. What say you, Watson?'

I shook my head and replied, 'I was never very good with riddles, Holmes, even when I was a child. Once I had heard the answer they seemed ridiculously easy, but before...'

Holmes responded, 'Looking at the four kings, diamonds and spades seem simple, but the other two are far from it.'

I said, 'Old Sol's third son? Who the devil is old Sol?'

Holmes laughed, 'That one must be the simplest of all, Watson. Sol is the sun, and his third son would be the planet in the third orbit, which is the earth!'

Newton was nodding, 'That's right, Mr Holmes, that was my conclusion also.'

I smiled, 'As I said, simple once you know.'

Holmes urged, 'Come along, Watson. The King of Spades. What is it that is over your head, but under your hat?'

'By Jove!' I exclaimed, 'it can only be your *hair*!'

'Well done, old fellow,' Holmes said encouragingly, 'you have it!'

I smiled with satisfaction and said, 'Right, that's two out of four. What's the next one?'

Holmes was puzzling over the King of Clubs. 'HIJKLMNO', he mused. 'Eight letters, but not quite the middle third of the alphabet. What on earth can they mean?' His concentration was intense for long moments, then suddenly he banged the table so hard that both Newton and I jumped with fright. *'Of course!'* he exclaimed, 'the man was *brilliant*! Don't you see, Watson? HIJKLMNO. H to O.'

I shook my head. 'See *what*, Holmes?'

'H to O,' he repeated. 'H2O. *Water!*'

'Of course, Holmes. Well done! I *never* would have seen it.'

Newton applauded, 'Bravo! Mr Holmes. I have obviously come to the right man for this task.'

Holmes said, 'Having found the King of Clubs I now know what the King of Hearts *must* be.' He turned to Newton and asked, 'When are they expecting us at Northcliffe Grange?'

Newton looked surprised and replied, 'Anytime from today onwards, but how did you know that they were expecting us at the Grange?'

Holmes answered, 'Well, it is obvious that the secret message will be there, and if we are to find it then we will have to be there also.'

Newton smiled, 'Of course. How obtuse of me. Mr Barker has wired Finch, the caretaker, to have rooms prepared for us, so we can travel up there whenever you are ready.'

Holmes took out his half-hunter and glanced at it. 'The hour draws late. Pray call round tomorrow morning, Mr Newton, and we can travel up to Cambridge by the most convenient train. I take it you have no objection to Dr Watson accompanying us?'

'Not at all, Mr Holmes.' Turning to me he said, 'You are most welcome, Doctor. After all, three heads are better than two.'

As I packed the last few items into our valises, I fretted that the 24-hour delay I had caused, over the verger's death, would come back to haunt me. Now there were only two days to go to the deadline and I confess I did not sleep too well that night.

The following morning found Holmes, Newton and myself hurrying to board the eight o'clock train for Cambridge. As we settled ourselves in a first-class compartment, Holmes took the parchment from its envelope and spread it out on the table, saying, 'We must make full use of the journey time to unravel the remaining riddles, otherwise I fear we will miss the deadline.'

We all huddled around and peered at the parchment again. I said, 'You implied, Holmes, that you already knew what the King of Hearts was.'

'That's right, Watson. You don't even need to decipher the riddles to know that it *must* be Fire.'

I said, 'I fail to see the connection between the earth, water, hair, and fire.'

Holmes laughed, 'It's not hair, Watson, but *air*. Remember it was what's over '*ead* but under '*at*. Now you can see the four primitive elements; earth, air, fire and water.'

'Of course! For if you feed a fire it lives, but if you water it, it dies.'

'Exactly,' he said, 'Now plainly we must insert the answers to the six riddles into the spaces in the text to make sense of the opening paragraph.' We both nodded in agreement as Holmes read aloud the first of the six riddles. *'God has never seen it, royalty seldom do, yet I always see it when I look at you.'*

Newton shook his head saying, 'This is not one that I mastered.'

I pointed out, 'This riddle is a *real* puzzler, Holmes, because after all God is omnipotent and is supposed to see *everything.'*

Holmes was quiet for a few moments, then he snapped his fingers, saying, 'Watson you are inspired! That was precisely the clue I needed. Don't you see? There *is* only one God; therefore the answer has to be *an equal*! Royalty seldom see their equal, but I see it when I look at you.'

I shook my head, 'Hardly, Holmes. Few men indeed could claim to be *your* equal. You are right again.'

He smiled, saying; 'I'm beginning to enjoy this.'

Newton read out the second riddle. *'This animal walks on four legs in the morning Sun. At noon it's down to two legs, but heavens see it run. By evening it's stranger, its legs they number three. This is a curious animal, whatever can it be?'* He continued, 'This one I know because I have seen it before.'

Holmes said, 'Then for expediency's sake tell us the solution, pray.'

Newton smiled and replied, 'The animal is man. When he is a baby, in the morning of his life, he walks on all fours.

In other words he crawls. When he is grown he walks erect on two legs, and when he is old, i.e. in the evening of his life, he walks with a stick. Three legs!'

'Well done, Andrew,' Holmes enthused. 'I believe you are absolutely right. That makes two down and four to go. Now then, number three...' and he read out the longest of the riddles. He repeated some of the first lines. *'A letter, an insect, that means to exist, and moves like a bird.'* After a few moments he said, 'I suppose it could only be a B. To be is to exist, and a bee flies like a bird.'

I nodded in agreement, 'I'm sure that's it, Holmes.'

Newton said, 'I think I see the second letter. *My next is a letter, a small part of man, found in all climes, search where you can.* A small part of man is M, which is also found in CLIMES.'

Holmes shook his head saying, 'I doubt it, Andrew. If it were so, we would have a word which began with the letters BM. I don't believe there is a word in the English language which starts like that. I'm sure that the letter *has* to be a vowel.'

Newton looked a little sheepish and acquiesced.

Holmes said, 'I believe that it must be an 'I' since there are only two vowels in climes and 'I' can be a man, whereas 'E' cannot be.'

'Right,' I said, 'so that means we have a five-letter word beginning BI...'

Newton suddenly exclaimed, '*I see it*! It's the *Bible*! The second B is in brawls, the L is in elegant halls and E is the first part of evening. You see it reads; *"my last is the first of the last part of day, ever in earnest, but never in play."'*

'Bravo! Andrew,' Holmes and I sang in unison.

'Excellent,' said Holmes, 'which gives us: *an equal*, *man*, and the *Bible*. What do you make of the first paragraph, Watson? Your Latin is better than mine, so what does *fillius nullius* mean?'

I replied, 'It means "Son of nobody" and is a polite way of saying "The bastard son of."'

'Ah!' Holmes exclaimed, 'So now we have, *"You, my bastard son, will be an equal of any man if you can turn up a shoe not of leather made by four Kings together."* So what is a shoe made by earth, air, fire and water?'

Newton asked, 'Could it be a wooden clog? The tree grows in the earth, and needs air and water.'

Holmes responded, 'But it doesn't need fire.'

Suddenly I exclaimed, 'By Jove! I believe I have it, Holmes,' and I was so excited I could hardly speak. 'It has to be a *horseshoe!* The iron comes from the *earth*, you need *fire* to forge it, *air* for the bellows and *water* to quench it!'

Newton smiled broadly and Holmes patted me on the back, saying, 'Well done indeed, Watson. This time you have excelled yourself. I thought you said you had no eye for riddles?'

I grinned like the Cheshire Cat. 'I seem to be getting the hang of it now, old fellow.'

Holmes observed, 'A horseshoe appears in the Carstairs' family crest, but what is meant by "turn up" a horseshoe?'

Newton replied, 'I believe it means, *to find.* When something turns up it usually implies that it has been lost or misplaced.'

Holmes nodded, 'I think you may be right. So now we have, 'Finds the *Bible* inside its secrets to hide. Plainly riddle four tells us which page in the Bible and riddle five tells us which line, so come along, gentlemen, we must decode riddle four next.'

I read out, *'Six books stand straight upon their shelf, 100 pages to each itself. How many pages are there held fast, twixt first of first and last of last?'*

Holmes said, 'This one seems almost too easy. One hundred pages per book equals six hundred pages. The ones between first and last, therefore, must be five hundred and ninety-eight.'

Newton and I nodded in agreement. 'I would go along with that, Holmes,' I said.

He did not appear to be totally convinced, but pressed on, saying, 'Number five is the monkey in the well. Each day he climbs three feet and slides back two. Which day will he reach the top?'

I said, 'Considering there is no water in the well, he will *never* reach the top because he will die of thirst before then.'

Holmes said, 'Try not to think like a doctor, Watson. These riddles are not meant to be taken literally.'

Newton said, 'Surely since he effectively only climbs one foot every day he would reach the top after forty days?'

Holmes shook his head saying, 'That would be too easy. We are missing something.' After a few moments his eyes lit up and he exclaimed, 'Ah! I have it. He would reach the top after thirty-eight days, since on that day he would be at the top briefly before sliding back two feet!'

'Of course,' I agreed, and Newton nodded, saying,

'Spot on, Mr Holmes. And I believe I know the answer to the last riddle, *Brothers and sisters have I none, yet this man's father is my father's son.* This has to be *my son.* Holmes agreed but I had to think about it for a minute or two before the penny dropped.

Sherlock smiled at each of us and said, 'Well done, gentlemen. Between us I believe we have solved all the riddles, so it just remains for us to find the horseshoe, discover the hidden Bible and look at line 38 on page 598, agreed?'

We both nodded in agreement. Holmes looked at his watch and, after a glance out of the window, declared, 'We have made good time. I believe we will be in Cambridge in less than half an hour.' It was as Holmes predicted, and soon we were rattling along in a dogcart, heading due West out of the city.

*   *   *

After a ride of perhaps twenty minutes, we turned into an imposing gateway and along a driveway between stately beech trees. Fallow deer pawed away the snow to browse among the trees, and rooks cawed overhead. Presently we came to the Grange itself and Newton's eyes grew wide with wonder. It was more than a house and only just less than a Palace.   Hexagonal columns flanked the great oak doors, with similar towers at the four corners of the building. The roofline was castellated, and tall latticed windows looked out over sweeping snow-covered lawns and formal flowerbeds. Carved in stone over the portal was the Carstairs coat of arms, and two rows of statues, lions and gryphons, lined the approach to the house. Through the trees to our right could be glimpsed a large lake with the sunlight reflecting from its frozen surface.

Newton was beside himself. 'I can hardly believe that all of this could be mine,' he whispered.

Holmes laid a cautionary hand on his shoulder, saying, 'Pray do not get carried away, Andrew.   There is still some way to go.'

The big doors opened and Finch the caretaker came down the steps to greet us.

'Good day, gentlemen, I have been expecting you.   Here, let me take your bags.'   He was a red-faced jovial fellow, with mutton-chop whiskers and a sizeable paunch.   He led us inside, saying, 'Mrs Finch has laid on a cold buffet as we did not know just when you would arrive.'

We passed through the impressive entrance hall, with its paintings of Carstairs ancestors and its suits of armour, and came to a morning room.   A welcoming log fire burned in the grate of a large stone fireplace, and stags' heads and antlers adorned the walls. In the centre of the room a long dining table held platters of cold meats, cheeses and the like and there were decanters of red and white wine and crystal goblets.

'Please help yourselves, gentlemen. I imagine you must be hungry after your journey up from London.' We thanked him and he withdrew.

When we were alone again I turned to Newton and said, 'This is an incredible inheritance.'

He shook his head in disbelief and replied, 'It is beyond my wildest dreams.'

Holmes was already seated and began helping himself to the food as he urged, 'Come along, gentlemen. The sooner we eat, the sooner we can begin searching for the horseshoe.' We joined him at the table and for the next hour enjoyed a delicious repast. Later, as we sipped an excellent claret, Holmes said, 'So to recap what we know, I think it is now fairly obvious that the scandal of unknown circumstances, that precipitated your benefactor off to Argentina, must surely have been a love affair with his music teacher, i.e. your mother, Andrew. I believe that you are the progeny of that liaison and, even though *fillius nullius*, you are the last of the Carstairs.'

Newton nodded slowly, saying, 'I was coming to the same conclusion myself, Mr Holmes. When I think back, I can recall being surprised that mother never had any letters or mementoes of my soldier father.'

Holmes lit his pipe with an ember from the fire and said, 'We can now complete the opening paragraph, which should read something like; *You fillius nullius will be an equal of any man if you turn up a shoe not of leather, made by four kings together. Find the Bible, inside its secrets to hide. Page 598, line 38, if you read it aright then this is your fate. If these things you have done, welcome home now my son.*'

'That's it, Holmes,' I said, and Newton nodded in agreement.

'Now, where do we start looking for a lost horseshoe?' I asked.

Holmes was thoughtful for a few moments, then said, 'The more I think about it, the more uneasy I feel about this horseshoe being lost. Carstairs gives us no clues at all about where to begin searching for it. All he says is to "turn up" a horseshoe. What if he meant that literally?'

I replied, 'By Jove, Holmes, I believe you may have something there. I remember thinking, when you described the Carstairs crest as having a horseshoe in its design, that it is considered unlucky to invert a horseshoe. Tradition has it that if you do, all of the good luck it contained will run out. If Andrew can turn it the right way up, he might restore enough good fortune to inherit Northcliffe Grange!'

Holmes smiled, 'Succinctly put, Watson.'

Newton asked, 'So we must look for an inverted horseshoe which we can turn upright to discover a secret hiding place?'

'That's how I see it,' Holmes confirmed, and he tugged on the velvet bell rope by the fireplace.

When Finch appeared, Holmes said, 'If it is not too much of an imposition, Mr Finch, we would very much like you to show us around the rest of the house.'

'Of course, sir. No imposition at all. This way gentlemen,' and he led us from the room. The adjoining room was the library and it was very impressive. Glass-fronted oak bookcases containing hundreds of volumes lined the walls from floor to ceiling. Tall windows presented panoramic views over snow-covered lawns and above the fireplace was a large gilt-framed painting depicting the nine Muses of Greek legend. All the tables and chairs were shrouded with dust covers. The next room was the long gallery, richly decorated in crimson and gold leaf. Large paintings and tapestries lined the walls and fine Persian rugs almost completely covered the polished floor. We visited the music room, the billiards room, the gun room, dining rooms and so on, each seemingly more opulent than the last, but we saw no horseshoes.

Finally on the ground floor we entered the grand banqueting hall. It was majestic with a high vaulted ceiling of carved oaken beams. In addition to the paintings, the walls were adorned with the stuffed heads of wild boar and red deer and over the huge stone fireplace, above a bronze Carstairs crest, was an elaborate array of pikestaffs, halberds and breastplates. The centrepiece of the display comprised a ring of fine sabres, ranged around a circular bronze shield. Down the centre of the hall ran the longest table I have ever seen, with chairs to seat upwards of fifty people.

Holmes strode over to the bronze crest and peered at it. 'I wonder...' he muttered. Taking one of the chairs from under its dustsheet, he stood upon it to reach up to the horseshoe emblem. He pushed it to the right, but nothing happened. He then pushed it to the left, and as it pivoted on its central nail a section of the shield, carrying a carved bumblebee, swung open to reveal a dark recess. Newton and I held our collective breath as Holmes reached his hand inside. With a cry of Eureka! he withdrew an old dust-covered Bible. It was bound in red leather and printed in gold leaf. It had a thick gold hasp and staple and it carried the Carstairs escutcheon on its front cover.

'Well done, Holmes!' we cried as he blew the dust from it and stepped down. He laid it on the table and opened it to page 598.

Counting down to the thirty-eighth line he shook his head, saying, 'Something is amiss. Line 38 has just one word and that is "Gentiles". One word can hardly constitute a message.' We were crestfallen as we realised that Holmes was right. We counted the lines again, but with the same result. Outside it began to snow heavily and it suddenly felt very cold in the great hall. I suggested we repair to the dining room, with its warm fire, and consider the situation.

Finch said, 'I'll away and light the fires in your rooms, gentlemen. I take it that you *will* be spending the night here?'

I looked at my watch and said, 'We would be hard pressed to catch the last train back to London today, and we have still not found the hidden message. However, there is a train leaving at nine in the morning, which will get us into town before the deadline.'

Holmes said, 'So be it. We shall sleep here tonight. Thank you, Mr Finch.' Later, as we sat by the fire sipping a sherry, Holmes stared into the flames deep in thought. Eventually he said, 'I'm convinced we successfully decoded all the riddles with the possible exception of number four. If you recall, Watson, I said at the time it seemed too easy.'

I nodded. 'You did indeed, Holmes. Shall I read it out to you again?'

'If you would, old fellow.'

I took the parchment and read, '*Six books stand straight upon their shelf, one hundred pages to each itself. How many pages are there held fast, twixt first of first and last of last?*' He steepled his fingers and closed his eyes. I could see his lips moving as he repeated the phrases over and over to himself. Finally he began to laugh. He laughed long and heartily, and we found ourselves laughing along with him even though we knew not what we were laughing at.

Holmes said, with tears in his eyes, 'It is so simple that it's beautiful. The answer is not five hundred and ninety-eight but *four hundred*.'

'Why so?' I asked.

He replied, 'You have to imagine the six books sitting on their shelf with their spines visible and their titles readable, yes?'

'Naturally.'

'Well then,' he said, 'the *first* page of the *first* book is 100 pages in from the left-hand side of the shelf, and the *last* page of the *last* book is 100 pages in from the right-hand side. Therefore the number of pages in between *has* to be four hundred!'

'Of course! That's it!' Newton and I exclaimed.

Holmes opened the Bible again, at page four hundred, and counted down. 'That's more like it,' he said, and nodded his head with satisfaction.

'What does it say?' I asked.

'It is from Samech in the Book of Psalms and says, *'Thou art my hiding place and my shield.'*

'That's it!' we both chorused. 'Bravo! Holmes.'

Newton topped up our sherry glasses and said, 'I propose a toast to the remarkable Mr Sherlock Holmes.'

It was a much-relieved trio that went to their beds that night. I stood at the window of my room and looked out at the snowy scene, lit by the light from the Grange's many windows. The snow was still falling and it was calm and peaceful. I was not sure whether I envied Newton or not. This really was a fabulous inheritance, but with it came great responsibilities, for which the lad was ill prepared. Obligations that were once too much for his father, the late James Fitzroy Carstairs. With a sigh I climbed into the large four-poster bed and was soon fast asleep.

The following morning I was awakened early by Mr Finch, who warned, 'The snow is still falling, and unless you make a prompt start, I'm afraid you might miss your train.'

I thanked him and hurried through my ablutions. Downstairs I met a worried Holmes and Newton. As we ate our breakfast, Holmes said, 'Finch has summoned a cab for us, but with this heavy snow it is sure to be late.' After we had eaten and re-packed our bags, all we could do was wait with growing impatience for the carriage's arrival. Eventually we saw it making slow progress up the long drive. We thanked Mr Finch for his hospitality, and kicking the snow from our boots climbed aboard.

Holmes said to the cabman, 'There is an extra gold sovereign for you if you get us to the station in time for the nine a.m. train to London.'

The man nodded and said, 'I'll do my best, sir,' and he whipped up his horse for the journey. The snow had finally stopped and the clouds were beginning to break up, but the going was treacherous. Deep drifts lined the sides of the road and the horse slipped and slithered alarmingly. I looked at my watch and was horrified to find that it was already three minutes past nine. At last we pulled up outside the railway station and Holmes thrust the money into the cabby's hand. Grabbing our bags, we ran, as fast as the snow would allow, into the station. I was mightily relieved to see that the train had indeed been delayed, but as we rushed up, the guard slammed shut the last of the open carriage doors and blew a long blast on his whistle.

Holmes sprinted forward, wrenched open the nearest door and, as the train moved off in a cloud of steam, we threw ourselves into the compartment. We sat there gasping and panting and smiled at each other. 'That was a shade too close for comfort,' Newton said with feeling. I was too winded to reply and just nodded my head.

Holmes said, 'I hope the snow will not delay the train too much.' In the event, that is exactly what *did* happen, and we arrived at Liverpool Street station with barely 15 minutes to get to Wardour Street. We bundled into the first available cab and Holmes gave the same challenge to this cabby also. In London the snow was not so thick, and though it had been churned to slush by the traffic, we made good progress.

I glanced again at my watch and said, 'We should make it now.' At my age I should have known better. Fate does not like to be anticipated, for no sooner had I spoken the words, than the horse lurched and whinnied before stopping completely. The driver jumped down and bent to see what the problem was.

Holmes leaned out and asked, 'What is it, cabby?'

The man shouted back, 'I'm sorry, gents, she's thrown a shoe and lamed herself. You'll have to get another cab.'

'Damn!' Holmes muttered as he grabbed his bag. ' Come on chaps, no time to lose!' We followed him from the cab and cast around for another, but the only ones we saw were all occupied.

Holmes said, 'There's only one thing for it, gentlemen, we must make it on foot. It is but a few blocks from here.'

I said, 'You two go on, I would only slow you down.' When they hesitated I shouted, 'GO ON! Don't wait for me. I'll see you there.' They left at a run and I hurried behind them as fast as I could. Despite the cold I was perspiring freely by the time I entered the offices of Faversham and Brinkley on Wardour Street. I was directed to Mr Barker's office, and when I got there I found my two friends slumped dejectedly in their chairs.

Mr Barker was saying, apologetically, 'I'm very sorry, my hands are tied. The terms of the will are quite specific.' He looked at his timepiece and continued, 'This watch keeps excellent time and it was seven minutes past twelve when you presented yourselves.'

I looked at Newton and he was almost in tears. He just sat there shaking his head.

Holmes said, 'There is a bitter irony here in that because of one horseshoe, young Newton had gained a fabulous inheritance. Then, because of another horseshoe, he has had that inheritance snatched from him.'

I nodded in silent agreement. I could think of no words of comfort for the lad. We trudged from the building and out into the bustle of London at midday.

Holmes put his hand on Newton's shoulder and said, 'I'm most dreadfully sorry old fellow.'

Newton forced a smile and responded, 'You did everything humanly possible, Mr Holmes. It just seems it was not meant to be.'

I asked, 'What will you do now?'

He shrugged and replied, 'Go back to being a chandler's clerk, I expect. A far cry from Lord of the Manor, eh what?' He turned to Holmes and said, 'I just wish that I could repay you for all the effort you have put in.'

My friend shook his head and smiled, saying, 'I agreed to the terms.' Then glancing at his watch, he suggested, 'What say we have lunch at Simpson's?' When young Newton hesitated, Holmes continued, 'Don't worry, I'll pay.'

We set off up the street in leisurely fashion each wrapped in our own thoughts. Presently we found ourselves in the cosy restaurant, sitting down to lamb cutlets and roast potatoes. Half way through the meal Big Ben struck the hour of one o'clock and Holmes automatically checked the accuracy of his half hunter. Suddenly I saw him stiffen, and for a moment he was introspective, before resuming his meal with gusto. He was in buoyant mood and entertained us with amusing anecdotes and tales of bizarre events from his illustrious career. Gradually Newton began to shake off his air of despondency and even managed a smile or two.

When we had finished, Holmes said, 'Dear me! I do believe I have left my gloves in Mr Barker's office. Would you mind, gentlemen, if we retrace our steps?'

We both shook our heads. 'Of course not, Holmes,' I said.

Ten minutes later we were back in Mr Barker's office and Holmes said to the solicitor, 'Just as a matter of interest, to recap on the will, it specified that Newton here must present the secret message to you before noon on the 28th day after Carstairs died. That is correct, is it not?'

Barker nodded, 'Yes, Mr. Holmes, that is correct.'

Holmes continued, 'And you have already agreed that the message he gave you *was* the right one?'

'Absolutely!'

Holmes looked at his watch and said, 'Then I believe, Mr Barker, that since there is still some time to go before the deadline, Andrew Newton *should* receive his legacy!'

Barker asked, 'Whatever do you mean, Mr Holmes? Plainly the deadline is long past.'

Holmes shook his head and replied, 'Argentina is nine hours behind Greenwich Mean Time. It won't be noon, where Carstairs died, for another seven hours!'

As the realisation dawned on Barker's face he exclaimed, 'By Jove! I believe you may be right, Mr Holmes. Wait here while I consult Mr Brinkley,' and he rushed from the room.

Newton's face was a picture as expectancy and doubt fought for supremacy across his features. Moments later Barker returned with a distinguished-looking grey-haired lawer in frock coat and pinstriped trousers. He was introduced to us as Sir Lawrence Brinkley, son of the founder, and he looked at Holmes with an interested smile on his face.

'Tell me, Mr Holmes, did you ever consider becoming a lawyer before you embarked on your career as a consulting detective?'

Holmes shook his head. 'I am afraid I would have found it a trifle dull, Sir Lawrence.'

Brinkley nodded, 'It can be, but events like this add spice. I can find no flaw in your reasoning, Mr Holmes, and I will be happy to settle the legacy on Mr Newton.'

Andrew let out a whoop of delight and went around shaking everybody's hand vigorously.

Brinkley said, as Newton shook his hand, 'I sincerely hope that this company can continue to provide your legal requirements into the future, Mr Newton, or should I say, Lord Carstairs?'

Andrew smiled and replied: 'You can rely on that, Sir Lawrence. And your first duty shall be to draw up a cheque, to the value of ten percent of my estate, made payable to my very good friend here, the incomparable Mr Sherlock Holmes.'

THE MYSTERY OF THE LOCKED STUDY

Sherlock Holmes reached for the Persian slipper from the mantelpiece and began filling his pipe with the dark shag tobacco it contained.

'Let us hope, Watson, that the beginning of the Twentieth Century brings more in the way of interesting cases than the latter part of the Nineteenth did. I declare, I can hardly recall a time to match it for its dearth of challenges.'

I knocked out my pipe in the fireplace, then sat back on the sofa. 'I'll second that, Holmes,' I agreed, 'and though you have been far from idle, it is the mundane nature of much of your recent casework which has precluded it from my chronicles.'

He sighed heavily. 'Just so, Watson, my point exactly. Oh for the emergence of another master criminal in the mould of my old adversary, Professor Moriarty.'

I held up a hand in protest. 'Beware, old fellow, lest what you wish for comes true.'

'I mean it, Watson. If I am not soon stimulated mentally, then I am convinced that my cognitive powers will seize up completely, like a carriage wheel deprived of grease.'

I laughed, 'That will be the day, Holmes. It will also probably be the day that they measure you for your coffin!'

Just then there was a loud rat-tat on the front door and presently we heard the murmur of voices, followed by a heavy tread on the stairs.

Holmes put down his unlit pipe and said, 'I wonder what brings Mycroft on a fraternal visit.'

I looked at Holmes in surprise. 'How do you know it's your brother Mycroft?' I asked.

Holmes smiled, 'I'd recognise that laboured step anywhere. Also his knock is distinctive. The letter M, for Mycroft, in Morse code. Just one of his more recent foibles.'

Sure enough, moments later the bulky frame of Mycroft Holmes almost filled our little domain.

'Sherlock, why the blazes do you insist on staying in these cramped upstairs quarters, when you can surely afford more spacious ground floor premises?' he gasped breathlessly.

Holmes smiled at him and replied, 'Stop fretting, the exercise will do you good.'

Mycroft flopped down in the armchair and mopped his brow with a silk handkerchief. 'I think the modern pre-occupation with regular exercise is downright unhealthy, don't you agree, Doctor?'

'Well...' I began, but he interrupted me saying,

'I'm as fit as I need to be to do the things I need to do, and climbing those damned stairs is not something I need to do.'

I enquired, 'Would you like a brandy?'

'Is it Napoleon?'

'I'm afraid not.'

'Then thank you no, Doctor. I see this cheese-paring brother of mine still resists spending on the essentials of gracious living.'

'It's a perfectly good Cognac,' I protested, but Sherlock interjected, 'Pay him no heed, Watson. He is always irritable when his equanimity is disturbed by unaccustomed endeavours. Speaking of which, it must be something quite extraordinary to drag you all the way up here, Mycroft. More, I suspect, than Brotherly love.'

Mycroft fastidiously folded his silk handkerchief and put it in his pocket.

'Something has occurred which displays interesting possibilities, and if I were not a martyr to ennui and lassitude I should investigate it fully myself. I have just come from the house of an acquaintance of mine by the name of Cavendish who is, or was, a fellow member of the Diogenes Club. We usually strolled to the club and played a little chess, each Wednesday. Well I'm afraid his chess-playing days are over. The poor fellow is dead.' Holmes was about to speak when Mycroft held up a hand. 'No questions please, Sherlock. If you have nothing more pressing to engage your time, then I suggest you return with me now and take a look. I'm sure you will find it interesting, though hardly rewarding, for there will be no fee involved.'

Sherlock rubbed his hands together and said, 'At last! Something to get my teeth into. And don't worry about the fee, Mycroft, it is *I* who should be paying *you* for delivering me from the apathy of stifling boredom.' He picked up his hat and cane and cried, 'Come, Watson. The game is afoot!'

I grabbed my medical bag and hat and soon the three of us were seated in Mycroft's cab heading towards Pall Mall.

'Have the police been informed?' I enquired.

'Not yet,' Mycroft replied, 'However, I suggest we call in at Scotland Yard on the way and report it.'

This plan was put into operation, and before long we were speeding along towards Cavendish's house with Inspector Lestrade seated beside me in the cab.

'Well, Mr. Holmes,' he said, 'tell me more about the circumstances leading up to the discovery of the body.'

Mycroft shrugged, 'It is soon told, Inspector. I called on Cavendish at about seven-thirty p.m. on my way to the club as usual. I was met by a very distraught housekeeper, Mrs. Allot, and a frantic maid. They both babbled on about Cavendish being locked in his room and there being a strong smell of gas. Well as you can imagine I hurried up the stairs, his study is on the first floor, and pounded on the door. It was as they had said, firmly locked and there was indeed a very strong smell of gas. Mrs. Allot said that Cavendish had the only key with him, so I was forced to break open the door.' Mycroft rubbed his shoulder at the memory and said to me, 'You might take a look later, Doctor. I'm not entirely convinced that I have not seriously damaged myself in the process.'

I nodded, 'Of course.'

Lestrade said, 'And what did you do after you burst into the room?'

'Well, my first action was to switch off all four taps to the gas mantles before rushing to the window and throwing it wide open.'

Sherlock asked, 'Was the window locked?'

Mycroft shook his head, 'Closed, but not locked.'

I asked, 'And Cavendish?'

'He was dead, of course. Slumped in his chair in dressing gown and slippers, for all the world fast asleep.'

At that moment the cab drew up outside a large Georgian town house in the middle of a terrace. Mycroft paid the cabby before leading us up the steps to the front door. Mrs Allot, a tall thin lady who dabbed her red-rimmed eyes with a handkerchief, admitted us.

'Oh! Bless you, sir,' she cried, 'I'm so glad you're back. I didn't know what to do.'

Lestrade stepped forward officiously and said, 'Don't fret yourself, Mrs. Allot. Scotland Yard is here now. I am Inspector Lestrade and I will take charge of everything.'

'Thank you sir, thank you,' she repeated. 'This way gentlemen.' She led us up to the first floor landing, but would go no further. Mycroft stepped forward and into the first room on the right. He held the door open and we followed him in. Even now, so long after the study had been ventilated, one could still smell the gas that had filled the room. It seemed to pervade everything and clung to the soft furnishings and curtains. I went over to the body and examined it. The symptoms of gas poisoning, the bluish lips etc. were very evident and I said as much to Lestrade. By the degree of rigor mortis I was able to determine that Cavendish had been dead for about three hours.

The Inspector jotted down notes in his book and muttered something about 'An obvious suicide.' Holmes was examining the door and remarked,

'You said that the door was locked, Mycroft, but you omitted to say that it was bolted as well. Little wonder that you now have a damaged shoulder.' Mycroft nodded and ruefully rubbed his injury.

Holmes glanced around the room, then turning to his brother remarked, 'You were right, there *are* interesting features here. The room is exactly as you found it?'

Mycroft nodded, 'Exactly.'

'Then I think I see why you suspect it was not suicide.'

Lestrade turned around and asked, 'What else could it be? A locked room. The door not just locked, but bolted on the inside. The only key right there on the bureau. What makes you think it was anything *but* suicide?'

Holmes replied, 'The absence of a suicide note.' Mycroft was nodding in agreement.

The inspector snorted, 'Good lord! Is that all? I've seen many a suicide with nary a note. Doesn't prove a thing.'

Holmes responded, 'We'll see. No doubt all will be revealed in the fullness of time.'

Mycroft said, 'Well come along, Sherlock. Tell us what you have deduced about the late Cavendish.'

Holmes looked around the study and responded, 'Just a few obvious conclusions. He was a retired Captain in the Royal Navy who had travelled in the Far East. He hunted big game and contracted blackwater fever or malaria there. He was a non-smoker though a heavy drinker and somewhat vain. He was still mourning the recent death of his wife and apart from his weekly visit to the Diogenes Club was practically housebound. He was dextrous of hand and keen of eye, albeit with the aid of spectacles, and he has a son who by now should be in his early twenties.'

Mycroft said, 'Very good! And what about his rheumatism?'

Holmes replied, 'I had concluded that his bunions were the cause of his incapacity.'

Mycroft smiled, 'Not good enough, old chap. You don't need walking-sticks for bunions. I should know, I've got one on my right foot.'

Lestrade asked, 'What the devil are you two talking about?'

Mycroft replied, 'Pay us no heed, Inspector. Sherlock and I like to play this little game of observation and deduction. It stimulates the old grey matter,' and he tapped his forehead with a finger.

'You mean to say that what Mr Holmes has said is all true?'

'But of course,' Mycroft responded.

Lestrade looked around the room with new interest. 'Aha!' he exclaimed, 'the large sea chest under the window with A. Cavendish inscribed on it.'

'The most obvious clue,' Mycroft conceded.

'The tiger-skin rug and trophies of big game on the walls,' Lestrade continued.

'The second most obvious clue,' responded Mycroft.

Lestrade strode around peering at everything. He picked a framed photograph from the mantelpiece, which showed Cavendish in captain's uniform with his wife and small son.

'There's the evidence for the boy and Cavendish's rank of Captain,' he announced proudly.

'Obviously,' sighed Mycroft.

Lestrade walked over to a drinks cabinet in the shape of a globe of the world. Lifting the top to display a good stock of spirits, he proclaimed, 'The evidence of a heavy drinker.' He was warming to the game now and had a smile on his face as he searched for the next clue.

Sherlock remarked, 'I did not need to see the contents of the cabinet to draw my conclusion, Lestrade. Take a look at his nose. Even the pallor of death cannot disguise the characteristic disfigurement of an habitual spirit drinker.' I looked and could see that Holmes was absolutely right.

'As you say, Mr Holmes,' Lestrade agreed. 'Now, how did you deduce that he had malaria?'

'Ah! I see it,' I cried, 'the half empty bottle of quinine medicine on the bureau.'

Holmes smiled, 'Well done, Watson. I suppose you of all people would know that blackwater fever or malaria commonly affect Europeans who have returned from the tropics and can recur intermittently for many years afterwards.'

Lestrade mused, 'I suppose the absence of ashtrays might suggest a non-smoker.'

Holmes shrugged. 'Perhaps not on its own, but together with the absence of pipes, pipe-racks, tobacco pouches, cigar-holders or vesta-boxes it seems to me to be fairly conclusive.'

Mycroft said, 'All of those were elementary. Now what about the more obscure deductions like the man's vanity, or the fact that he suffered from bunions, or his being a recent widower?'

I could see nothing to indicate any of these things. His dressing gown was of good quality, but it was hardly flamboyant. His feet were encased in a large pair of carpet slippers and, apart from the fact that his wife was not here, I could see nothing else to indicate that she had died recently.

Lestrade scratched his head in puzzlement. 'I'm afraid I have come to the end of the road, gentlemen,' he said.

Holmes strode over to the corpse and lifted a wig from the man's head. 'An excellent quality wig, Lestrade, but a wig nevertheless. So much for vanity.'

'Well, I'll be blowed!' exclaimed the Inspector.

I bent to remove the man's slippers and discovered he had a huge bunion on each foot.

'I don't know how you knew, old fellow,' I said.

In answer, Holmes walked round to the other side of the fireplace and picked up a pair of brown brogues from the hearth.

'Look at how the leather has been stretched so that it bulges out on the side of each shoe. The classic signs of a bunion sufferer.'

I nodded, 'Of course. So simple when pointed out.'

Lestrade asked, 'But what about the evidence of his wife's death?'

Mycroft took down a man's coat that hung on the back of the door. On the left sleeve was pinned a black armband. 'Elementary,' he said.

'But he could be mourning almost anyone,' Lestrade argued.

Holmes responded, 'Quite so, Inspector. However, he is a reclusive man with presumably few close friends; even Mycroft here described him merely as an acquaintance.

That, together with the fact that his wife has not yet put in an appearance, even though Mrs Allot has had over two hours to inform her of her husband's death, prompts me to suggest that the black armband is for Mrs Cavendish.'

Mycroft was nodding again, 'I can confirm that his wife died almost two months ago.'

I said, 'Well done, Holmes. There is just one thing though. Twice you have implied that Cavendish was reclusive. Where is your evidence for that?'

Holmes replied, 'Do you not consider it unusual for a man to have his study on the first floor? I asked myself why and the obvious conclusion is that it is adjacent to the bedrooms and bathroom. The two walking-sticks by the fireplace reinforce the notion that he was loath to use the stairs more than was absolutely necessary. And if more proof be needed, look at the model ships he has built. I count five including this one,' and he indicated an incomplete model of a three-masted schooner on a table by the window. Together with the model were woodworking tools, sandpaper, glue etc. and the surface of the table was scattered with sawdust, as were the polished floorboards nearby. Holmes continued, 'An absorbing hobby to while away the hours.'

I nodded, 'Of course, and there also is your evidence for him having dextrous hands and a keen eye. However, I fail to see any spectacles.'

Holmes went over to the dead man and deftly withdrew a pair of pince-nez from the pocket of Cavendish's dressing gown.

I pointed out, 'They were not visible. How did you know they were there?'

Holmes explained, 'The spring pressure of pince-nez leaves slight indentations on each side of the nose, especially when worn consistently, and these are plainly visible on Cavendish.'

Lestrade became the officious Scotland Yard man again, saying, 'This is all very well, but it gets us no nearer to what took place here.'

Holmes went to the open window and looked out. Glancing back over his shoulder, he said, 'Apart from a small overflow pipe below the window, there is absolutely no hand or foothold on the entire wall. No drainpipe, no ivy, no tree within fifty feet.'

Mycroft joined him at the window and asked, 'What about a ladder?'

Sherlock shook his head, 'I very much doubt it. The flowerbed below is undisturbed, as is the dust on the windowsill.'

I asked, 'Could it have been an accident? Perhaps a freak gust of wind blew out the lamps and slammed shut the window.'

Holmes turned to me and smiled, 'I'm afraid not, old fellow. As you can see, it is only now approaching dusk. Earlier on Cavendish would not have needed the lamps lit.' I felt rather foolish for having made the suggestion and decided to say nothing more.

Lestrade said, 'I've still not seen or heard anything to make me change my original conclusion of suicide, and if you gentlemen don't mind I'm going down to question the housekeeper.'

Holmes said, 'Good idea! I'll join you if you have no objections.'

We trooped downstairs and through to the kitchen where Mrs Allot was being comforted by the maid.

'Just a few questions, Mrs Allot, if you feel up to it,' said Lestrade.

'Yes, of course,' she replied.

'How long have you worked for the Cavendish family?'

'Fourteen years come October, sir.'

'And you live in?'

'Yes sir. My room and Mary's here, are on the third floor.'

'After the death of Mrs Cavendish were you three the only residents here?'

'Oh no, sir. Master Giles lives here too. His room is on the second floor.'

'Master Giles is the Captain's son?'

'That's right, sir.'

'And where is he now? Does he know of his father's death?'

'Not yet sir. He went up to St John's Wood this morning to visit friends and has not been back since.'

'Do you know who his friends are and where they live?'

'No sir.'

Holmes said, 'Tell us about Master Giles and his relationship with his father.'

Mrs Allot squirmed uncomfortably and replied, 'Well, sir, I'm not one for gossip, but if you are sure this will remain confidential like...'

Lestrade assured her, 'You can count on that, Mrs Allot.'

'Well, Master Giles is nearly twenty-one and has been a great disappointment to his father. He lacked for nothing and attended the best schools, but somehow the lad went astray. His father calls, I mean called, him a wastrel. He always needed money for something or other and could not settle to any career. His father wanted him to carry on the family naval tradition, but Giles failed to graduate. His parents tried to interest him in the law, but without success. Father and son had blazing rows about Giles' drinking and womanising until in the end Captain Cavendish warned him that he would be disinherited if he did not mend his ways before he came of age.'

'Holmes said, 'You stated that Giles had gone to St John's Wood this morning. What time was that?'

Mrs Allot replied, 'I don't rightly know, sir. I had slipped out to see my sister, who is not very well, and when I got back Master Giles had gone. He left me a note saying that if his father asked, he had gone to visit friends in St John's Wood and did not know when he would be back.'

Holmes asked, 'What time did you return from your sister's?'

'About midday, sir.'

Holmes turned to the maid and asked, 'Did you see Giles leave, Mary?'

'No, sir. I was in the scullery doing the washing and ironing.'

Lestrade said, 'Would you say, Mrs Allot, that Captain Cavendish was still depressed over the death of his wife to the point that he could take his own life?'

Mrs Allot looked thoughtful. 'I suppose that's possible sir. Naturally he was devastated and I don't think he ever really got over it, but he seemed to be beginning to come to terms with it, if you know what I mean.'

Lestrade scribbled in his notebook. 'When did you last see the Captain alive,' he asked.

'When I collected his lunch tray about two o'clock.'

'How was he?'

'He was fine, sir. I poured him a whiskey and soda and left. He usually had a few stiff drinks and would then sleep well into the evening.'

'When did you last check on him?'

'About seven p.m. I knocked, but got no answer so I left him.'

'Did you try the door?'

'No, sir.'

'So it could have been locked then?'

'I suppose so, sir. I thought he must be still sleeping, but later, when we smelled the gas...' Here she broke down and began weeping again.

'There there, Mrs Allot, I don't believe I have any more questions. I think I have everything I need for the time being.' Turning to me, he asked, 'Can you write out the death certificate, Dr Watson, so that the undertakers can be called?'

I nodded. 'Certainly, Inspector.' After doing so I turned to leave with the others when Holmes said, 'Mrs Allot, if I could impose once more, I would very much like to take a look at Master Giles' bedroom.'

'Of course, sir,' she agreed, 'This way.' Lestrade raised his eyes to heaven, but said nothing. The four of us followed Mrs Allot up to the second floor and into Giles' room. As bedrooms go it was unremarkable. There was a bed, a wardrobe, a chest of drawers and so on. The bay window area held a chair and a bureau on which reposed writing equipment and a few books. Two shelves by the fireplace held more books. Holmes looked in the wardrobe, then walked over to the bureau.

As he picked up each book in turn, he read out its title aloud. *'Scaramouche,* by Raphael Sabatini; *The Count of Monte Cristo,* by Alexandre Dumas; Homer's *Odyssey.'* Suddenly he stiffened, then said, *'The Odyssey...*Helen Of Troy...*THE WOODEN HORSE!'* With that he sprinted from the room and ran down the stairs. We followed as fast as we could and saw him rush into Cavendish's study. When I got there he was raising the lid of the iron-bound sea chest. His shoulders drooped and I hurried to see what was inside. It was almost empty, save for a sextant, a leather-bound telescope, some books and a tartan blanket.

Mycroft stood in the doorway and said, 'You really *are* slipping, Sherlock. The chest is not airtight. Anyone hiding in there would have been gassed along with Cavendish!'

Holmes turned around sheepishly and replied, 'To err is human, Mycroft. At least for us mere mortals.'

Mycroft yawned. 'Look, old chap, it seems as though I may well have led you up a blind ally. Perhaps it *was* suicide after all.'

Lestrade said, 'That's what's going in my report. A man stricken with recurring bouts of fever, practically crippled with rheumatism, cursed with a ne'er do well son and devastated by the death of his wife. Reasons a-plenty to take his own life.' He put on his hat and turned to leave.

Mycroft said, 'I'm off too. Are you coming, gentlemen?'

Holmes shook his head. 'Thank you, no. There are just a few more questions I would like to ask Mrs Allot.'

After Lestrade and Mycroft had left, Holmes turned to me and said, 'Watson, I do believe my brother is right. I *am slipping*. Oh, I don't mean this embarrassing little episode. I've *missed* something. A clue has presented itself to me and I have failed to spot it. Something in what we have seen or heard this evening is vitally important to this affair, but it has only partly registered in my brain. I shall not sleep tonight until I recall what it is.' He led the way downstairs again to where Mrs Allot was waiting in the hall.

'Just one or two final questions, Mrs Allot, if you don't mind.'

'Yes, sir... I mean no, sir.'

'I maintain that the Captain was highly reclusive, is that true?'

'I'm afraid I don't know what that means, sir.'

'That he did not go out much.'

'Oh, yes, that's true, sir. Apart from his weekly visits to the club, he barely set foot outside the door.' She hesitated before continuing, 'Except for his annual reunions of course.'

'Naval reunions?'

'That's right, sir. He would never miss the chance to see his fellow officers down at Portsmouth.'

'When was the last one?'

'Why just last week, sir.'

'How long did he stay?'

'Two days.'

'So you had only Giles to care for?'

'Not even him, sir. Master Giles gave Mary and me two days leave. He said he wanted a little peace and quiet. Mary went to her mother's and I visited my sister.'

'He gave you leave, did he? And what did you make of that?'

'Well, sir, at the time I thought he planned to throw a wild party for his friends, but when I got back the house was in good order. Between you and me, sir, I think he was womanising again.'

'Well thank you, Mrs Allot,' Holmes said, 'you have been most helpful. Dr Watson here will arrange for the undertakers. I would be obliged if you would present my card to Master Giles, when he finally puts in an appearance, and tell him I shall see him presently.'

'Very good, sir,' she replied, taking the card.

Later back at Baker Street, after the formalities with the undertakers, Holmes said, 'I can't wait to meet this Giles Cavendish, Watson, for if there *is* skulduggery here then that young man has had both motive *and* opportunity. Motive: to prevent his father from disinheriting him, and opportunity: by living under the same roof. What we don't have yet is method.'

I remarked, 'It is looking more and more like suicide to me, old fellow.'

Holmes said musingly, 'The three books that the lad had been reading, Watson. Do you know their common theme?'

'I can't say that I do, Holmes.'

'Revenge, old fellow. *Revenge!* Scaramouche became a master swordsman to avenge his friend's murder; Edmund Dantes, the Count of Monte Cristo, exacts the ultimate revenge on all his persecutors; and in *The Odyssey*, Odysseus kills Antinous and the other suitors of his wife Penelope.'

'So what is your point, Holmes?'

'Perhaps young Giles had vengeance in mind against a father who threatened to disinherit him.'

'If that were true, Holmes, then how the devil did he accomplish it? Don't forget the room was locked from the inside and the only key was on the bureau. Furthermore, since it was also bolted on the inside, even if a duplicate key is in existence, or had been copied from the master key, somebody still had to slide those bolts on the inside. You yourself have excluded the possibility of anyone having gained entrance through the window, which means that, dismissing anything fanciful like secret passages, Cavendish *has* to have taken his own life.'

Holmes was nodding. 'Everything you say is perfectly true, Watson, yet still I wonder.'

He built up the fire with more coal and arranged the cushions on the floor. Then he placed an ounce of tobacco, his favourite pipe and some vestas within easy reach. I was well used to this ritual and knew its portent. Holmes would sit up, all night if necessary, to ponder the problem.

'Well, old fellow,' I said, 'I shall say goodnight and leave you to your deliberations.'

'Goodnight, Watson.'

In the early hours of the morning I was awakened by a cry of *Eureka* from the living room and I smiled to myself as I realised that Holmes had pinpointed his elusive clue. I turned over and went back to sleep.

Sitting across from Holmes at the breakfast table there was no evidence that he had lost several hours sleep the night before. Indeed he seemed brighter and chirpier than I had seen him for months.

'Well, old chap,' I said, 'I gather that your deliberations of last night were fruitful.'

'Very much so, Watson. In fact I recalled *two* clues, not one.'

'And I don't suppose you are going to tell me what they are?'

'Not just yet, old fellow. However, I have arranged a little *denouement* for ten o clock this morning, which I venture to suggest you will find rather interesting.'

'Where?' I asked.

'In Cavendish's study of course.'

'You must have been up early then, Holmes,' I suggested.

'No, Watson, I never went to bed.'

'Good Lord!' I exclaimed.

Holmes smiled, 'I was far too agitated to sleep anyway, and fortunately Mrs Allot is an early riser. I have arranged to meet Master Giles, who, by the way, has now returned home. I have also left messages for Lestrade and Mycroft to meet us there.'

He glanced at his half hunter and continued, 'We have time for a pipeful of tobacco before the cab I ordered arrives to take us.'

Just before ten we pulled up at the Cavendish household, almost at the same time as Mycroft and Lestrade.

The inspector said rather harshly, 'This had better be good, Mr Holmes, for I'm a very busy man and have no time for chasing wild geese.'

Holmes responded, 'This should not take long, Lestrade. You will be on your way back to the Yard in no time.'

Mrs Allot admitted us and soon we were back in the Captain's study. The room was as before except that Cavendish's body had been removed.

Presently Master Giles sauntered in and introduced himself. He was a slim wiry individual whose otherwise good looks were marred by a rather weak chin. His dark hair was swept back and glistened with pomade, and his clothes were elegant, if not foppish. He sat on the edge of his father's bureau and said, 'Well, gentlemen, I've no doubt you have a thousand questions to ask me, so let us get on with it.

I would appreciate it if you could be as brief as possible, for I have a busy schedule.'

Holmes remarked, 'You appear to be taking the death of your father with great equanimity.'

The young man bristled and replied, 'Please allow me to grieve in my own fashion, Mr Holmes. We are not all weepers and wailers.'

Holmes made a stiff little bow and said, 'As you wish. I will endeavour to be as brief as possible.' He sat down on the oak sea chest and asked, 'Can you confirm Mrs Allot's account that you spent most of yesterday with friends in St John's Wood?'

'I can.'

'And if the inspector here requested the names and addresses of those friends, I've no doubt you could furnish them?'

'Of course.'

'Is it true that your father threatened to disinherit you, if you did not mend your ways?'

The young man looked keenly at Holmes and replied, 'Someone has been talking out of turn. Anyway, it was just another of my father's idle threats, and I know he did not mean it literally.'

Holmes looked around and said, 'You are a very fortunate young man to have inherited all of this. Did your father indicate, in his idle threat, who he *would* leave his estate to if not to you?'

Giles made a dismissive gesture and replied, 'He intimated that the staff would be provided for and that the bulk of his estate would go to the Seamen's Charity, but as I say, he was not really serious.'

Holmes nodded and patted the top of the sea chest, saying, 'So instead of going to charity this beautiful sea chest belongs to you now?'

'Naturally, since I am the only heir. Look, is any of this really relevant?'

Holmes stood up and replied, 'Please allow me to conduct this enquiry in my own fashion, Master Cavendish. We are not all procrastinators.'

I muttered under my breath, '*Touche, Holmes!*' The lad looked sullen, but said nothing.

Holmes turned and leaned on the chest. 'This is so well made,' he observed, 'and doubtless extremely heavy. So heavy in fact, that I doubt a man could lift it single-handedly.'

'That's right,' Giles agreed, 'it has not been moved in years.'

Holmes suddenly pushed the chest, which slid sideways a few feet on the polished floorboards.

'Though evidently not too heavy to slide,' Holmes continued. Then he said, with a note of surprise in his voice, 'Helloa! What have we here then?'

Beneath the sea chest a section of floorboarding had been removed, revealing a space between the timber joists. We crowded round and looked in. Nailed between the deep beams of the old house were canvas webbing straps, and a folded blanket lined the gap. Protruding into the space was a length of lead pipe, which disappeared through the external wall.

Holmes said, 'It looks to me like a cosy rat's nest.' Spinning round, he shouted, 'WATCH HIM, LESTRADE!' The young man had risen and was making for the door.

The inspector leaped forward and grabbed him by the arm. 'Where do you think you are going then?' he barked.

Giles glared at Holmes with a look of sheer malice, but maintained his silence.

Mycroft said, 'So my original suspicions that this was not suicide were correct after all?'

Holmes nodded, 'As you say, Mycroft, though I think perhaps it is *you* who are slipping. You saw the same two clues as myself and yet you missed them completely.'

Mycroft smiled at his brother and replied, ' Go on then, rub in the salt. What were they?'

Holmes replied, 'Remember when I pointed out there was an overflow pipe protruding from the wall below the window? Well it finally dawned on me that there should *not* have been one there. The bathroom is at the end of the corridor, three rooms away. *That* is where I would have expected to find a water overflow pipe.'

Mycroft was nodding with approval. 'Very good, Sherlock, and the other clue?'

'The sawdust! There was a liberal sprinkling on the table and more on the floor. The former, however, was fine and powdery and came from the model ship making, whilst the latter was courser and came from the sawn floorboards.'

I said, 'Bravo! Holmes, well done.'

Mycroft echoed my words. 'Well done indeed! Your notion of the Wooden Horse of Troy was, after all, not so far from the mark. And I'll warrant that the story *was* the inspiration for this little scheme.'

Holmes turned to Giles and said, 'I promised to be brief, and in my summary of events as I see them I will try to do just that.' He sat down again on the sea chest and continued, 'Counter to your claim that your father did not really intend to disinherit you, I believe he had every intention of doing just that. The prospect of having to abandon your spendthrift ways and earn your own coin alarmed you. As your maturation approached you became desperate and devised this diabolically clever scheme to murder your father, thus eliminating the threat and making you a rich man. Your father's absence when he went to Portsmouth gave you the perfect opportunity. Dismissing the staff, you were free to cut away the floorboards, chisel a hole through the mortar and insert the lead pipe. You covered the opening with the sea chest and waited. Soon your opportunity arose. Mrs Allot went to her sister's and Mary was in the scullery. You wrote a note saying you had gone to St John's Wood then secreted yourself somewhere in the house, probably in your own room. Finally, when you knew your father was in a deep alcohol-induced sleep, you went into his study, locked and bolted the door behind you and turned on all the gas taps. You then slid back the chest, slipped into your hiding place and pulled the chest back into position. I imagine the metal bindings on it provided enough grip. Then you lay in comfort in your improvised hammock, breathing fresh air through the tube, whilst your father expired above you. After Mycroft had forced the door then left to summon aid, you vacated your hiding place, re-positioned the sea chest and slipped out of the house by the back door. Finally you returned late last night making sure that Mrs Allot knew you were back.'

Holmes stood up and looked hard at the young man. 'The crime of parricide is particularly heinous, but it becomes doubly so when the only motivation is greed.' He pointed an accusing finger at the lad and declared, 'The hangman's noose awaits you, Giles Cavendish.'

The young man had listened to Holmes' account with increasing agitation, and with those damning words ringing in his ears he went deathly pale and collapsed on the floor in a faint.

I revived him with a small phial of sal volatile from my medicine bag, but not before Lestrade had locked the handcuffs on him.

The inspector went up to Holmes and shook his hand saying, 'It pains me to say it, Mr Holmes, but you are the best in the business.'

Holmes bowed slightly and responded, 'Thank you, Lestrade, praise indeed from a fellow professional.'

The inspector turned, and taking the subdued Giles by the arm, he led him from the room. We could hear Lestrade saying, 'Giles Cavendish, I am arresting you for the wilful murder of...'

Mycroft picked up his hat and cane and remarked, 'I particularly liked the way you elicited from Giles his father's true wishes regarding his legacy, before you exposed him. It is good to know that Mrs A and young Mary will be provided for. If you need my testimony for the executors you know where to find me. Once again, well done, Sherlock.'

'Thank you, Mycroft. And thank you for finding me such a stimulating challenge. It has done me a power of good.'

Later, on the way back to Baker Street in a cab, I said to Holmes, 'You took a frightful risk of further ridicule if there had been no bolthole under the sea chest, old fellow.'

He smiled at me and replied, 'I am not that big a fool, Watson. I had already tested out my hypothesis this morning when I visited Mrs Allot to make the arrangements. Master Giles was still asleep and Mrs Allot was sworn to secrecy.'

I nodded in understanding, 'Of course. As you say Holmes, elementary. At the risk of repeating myself, I still believe that the day you lose your powers will be the day they measure you for your coffin.'

THE ADVENTURE OF THE BLACK ARROW

CID Headquarters, Great Scotland Yard

My friend Sherlock Holmes is a man blessed with many unique talents, but I am sorry to say that 'musician' is not one of them. Indeed I would go so far as to say that if, instead of being a Consulting Detective, he aspired to earn his living as a concert violinist then he would surely starve to death.

He had been scraping away with his bow at the infernal instrument for the last hour or more and even my prodigious equanimity was beginning to buckle. I wandered over to the window of 221b Baker Street and glanced out, hoping that the rain had eased. I had planned an excursion for an ounce of tobacco to give my ears a rest, but the drizzle was as persistent as ever. Dusk was falling and the lamplighters of

London were already out in force, though it was not yet six of the clock.

The ringing of the doorbell sounded like music to my ears as the caterwauling finally ceased and Holmes laid aside his violin to cock an ear. There was a murmur of voices followed by footsteps on the stairs and Mrs Hudson knocked on our door.

'Come!' Holmes called. Our landlady introduced the visitor as Sir Charles Crichton from Richmond. He was as tall as Holmes himself and in his middle fifties, with grey hair and moustache. His face showed character and intelligence and would once have been handsome, but which now looked drawn and haggard. By the redness of his eyes I inferred that he had recently given way to tears.

He wore a black overcoat with a velvet collar and carried a black Homburg.

Holmes rose and greeted him, 'Do come in please and allow me to take your coat and hat.'

Sir Charles divested himself of them and said, 'Thank you for seeing me without a prior appointment, Mr Holmes. Your landlady implied that you were not overly busy at the moment'.

Holmes indicated a chair and replied, 'Nothing of momentous import. This is my friend and colleague Dr Watson who is discretion personified. You may speak freely before him.'

Sir Charles nodded in my direction then sat down with a sigh and passed a hand over his eyes. I noticed that the hand trembled alarmingly.

I asked, 'Are you all right? Would you like a brandy?'

'Thank you no, Doctor. I shall be fine in a moment.' He took a deep breath and began, 'You mentioned discretion just now, Mr Holmes, and I am assured that is just one of the many qualities which you possess. A friend who spoke very highly of your abilities gave me your card. His name is Auguste Fontaine.'

Holmes nodded, 'Ah yes! The owner of The Coq D'Or.'

I remarked, 'Most of Mr Holmes' clients are personally recommended, for my friend disdains advertising his services.'

Holmes sat back on the sofa, steepled his fingers and said, 'Pray tell us your story, Sir Charles, and try to include even minor details for they sometimes bear importantly on a case.'

'Very well. I am, or was until my recent retirement, a parliamentary private secretary to one of our cabinet ministers. I am sure you will understand if I decline to say which one.'

Holmes nodded.

'I am a moderately wealthy man in my own right as the Crichton family is well established, so the government post was perhaps icing on the cake. I live at Mauldeth Hall in Richmond and until this year was a happy and contented man. Now my world has crumbled and I am on the verge of insanity.'

He was unable to speak for a moment and I could see he was struggling for control.

'Would you like a cup of tea?' I enquired.

He nodded. 'Yes please, Doctor, that would be most welcome.'

I rang down for Mrs Hudson and asked if she would be so kind as to send up a tray of tea and biscuits. When Sir Charles had regained his composure somewhat Holmes invited him to go on with his story.

'This year has seen the two greatest tragedies of my life. In August my beloved wife, Margaret, died after a short illness and now my only child, my daughter Sophie, has been abducted.'

133

Holmes, who had been listening with eyes closed, gave a start. 'The devil you say!' He looked keenly at Sir Charles and asked, 'You came here in a hansom cab, did you not?'

'Yes, that is correct.'

'How else to travel from Richmond on such a miserable night?' Holmes mused. Then he said, 'I had wondered why you alighted from your cab at Oxford Street and walked the rest of the way here. *Now* of course the reason is obvious.'

Sir Charles looked at Sherlock Holmes in amazement. 'Are you a clairvoyant, sir? For how else could you know those were my exact movements?'

Holmes laughed, 'Would that I *were* a clairvoyant, Sir Charles, for my tasks as a criminologist would be infinitely eased with the gift of second sight.' He made a dismissive gesture and continued, 'A couple of trifling deductions. Firstly, if your cab had drawn up outside I would surely have heard it, even above the sound of my violin. Secondly, by the degree of dampness of your coat, which I have just hung up, I estimated that in this steady drizzle you could not have walked further than from Oxford Street which is on your route from Richmond.'

Sir Charles was nodding his head, 'Remarkable!' he enthused.

I asked, 'Why is his reason for leaving his cab obvious, Holmes? It is certainly not obvious to me.'

Holmes turned to me and explained, 'In almost every case of kidnapping I have ever experienced, especially concerning the children of wealthy parents, there is a ransom demand. Am I right Sir Charles?'

Crichton nodded his head. 'Absolutely,' he affirmed.

Holmes continued, 'What is also predictable about such ransom notes is that they invariably warn the recipients not to contact the police or other agencies. Am I still on track, Sir Charles?'

'Dead centre, Mr Holmes,' he confirmed.

'And lastly, they usually imply that the recipient is being watched in case he should disregard this warning. How now, Sir Charles?'

'Bulls eye, Mr Holmes!'

Sherlock said, '*Quad erat demonstrandum*, Watson. Sir Charles left his cab early to make sure he was not being followed.'

I clapped my hands together and said, 'Bravo, Holmes! Well done.'

Sir Charles stated, 'Auguste Fontaine did not exaggerate when he enthused about your powers of deductive reasoning.'

Holmes waved a dismissive hand and asked, 'Do you have the ransom note with you?'

'Yes of course, here it is.'

Holmes spread the note on the table and said, 'Watson, my glass if you please.'

I handed him his large magnifying glass then positioned myself at his shoulder so I could read what was written. It was a sheet of white foolscap paper to which were affixed, with paste, words cut from a newspaper or periodical. The message ran:

WE HAVE YOUR DAUGHTER AND IF YOU WANT TO SEE HER ALIVE AGAIN IT WILL COST YOU £1,000. DO NOT CONTACT POLICE. WAIT FOR FURTHER INSTRUCTIONS. YOU ARE BEING WATCHED. DICK AND JOHN.

Crudely sketched in pencil below this were the head and shoulders of a woman with an arrow, drawn in black ink, through her neck. Though childlike, the drawing was chilling in its portrayal.

Holmes peered at the note through his glass and murmured, 'Interesting...very interesting. Helvetica sans serif. Unusual, I wonder...' He turned to Sir Charles and said, 'One thousand pounds is a great deal of money, can you raise such a sum?'

Sir Charles nodded. 'It will take some time. I am already in the process of selling some family heirlooms and so on, but I should be able to amass that amount. Between you and me, Mr Holmes, I would sell Mauldeth Hall itself if it meant Sophie would be returned to me unharmed.'

Holmes replied, 'Quite so.' Then after a pause he continued, 'I would be failing in my duty, sir, if I did not warn you that the odds of a successful conclusion to this affair are not high. Many kidnap victims are killed, even after the ransom money is paid, so they can never identify their kidnappers.'

Sir Charles slumped visibly. 'Oh no!' he whispered, 'I couldn't stand that.'

At that moment there was a knock on the door and the maid entered with a tray of tea and biscuits. She passed a cup each to Holmes, Sir Charles and myself.

When she had departed, Crichton asked, 'Are you a family man, Mr Holmes? Do you have a child?'

Holmes shook his head, 'Alas no. I am not married.'

Sir Charles stirred his tea absently and said, 'Sophie is my *raison d'être*. I love her more than anything in the world and if you can save her life I will gladly pay double or triple your normal fee.'

Holmes made a dismissive gesture and replied, 'We can discuss my fee later, the important thing now is to plan our campaign.'

Sir Charles continued, 'I realise this is a heavy responsibility, but I place my own and my daughter's life in your hands. I will do anything and everything you ask of me, for I trust your judgement implicitly.'

Holmes squirmed a little under the weight of such a pronouncement then said, 'We will do our very best, of that you can be assured. Now tell me about your daughter and the circumstances leading up to her disappearance.'

Sir Charles replied, 'Sophie is twenty-four years old and a little headstrong. She is beautiful, though I am somewhat biased in that respect. I must confess that I may have over-indulged her somewhat, especially since her mother died, but she has rarely gone against my wishes. She is a student at St Anne's, Oxford and hopes to graduate this year. She disappeared on Saturday the tenth after a shopping trip to the West End.'

Holmes asked, 'Does she have any romantic attachment?'

'She had, until recently, been seeing a fellow student who was in the same drama group and there was talk of engagement, but I tried to dissuade her, at least until she had her degree.' He sipped his tea and continued, 'I suppose that if the truth be told I hated the thought of her leaving me entirely alone.'

Holmes nodded, 'A natural enough reaction. So Sophie failed to return from her trip to the West End?'

'That's right. By eight o'clock that evening I was becoming frantic. I contacted all her friends, but none of them had seen her. I even took a cab tour of the district in the hope of seeing her, but she had disappeared completely. There was still no sign of her on the Sunday so I went to the police. They have registered her as a missing person and said they would do what they could to find her. Then on the Monday that note arrived in the morning post.'

Holmes asked, 'Do you have the envelope it came in?'

'Why yes, here it is,' said Sir Charles, as he handed it over.

Holmes examined it and noted, 'It was posted in Islington. That could be to our advantage for it is not that far away.' Then turning to Sir Charles he continued, 'This is what I propose. We can do nothing until the next communiqué arrives, but in the meantime I think Dr Watson and myself should accompany you back to Mauldeth Hall and await developments there.'

Sir Charles replied, 'I think that is an excellent idea. Lord knows, with you gentlemen for company the Hall may not seem so oppressively empty.'

I informed Mrs Hudson that we would be away for a day or two and Holmes and I packed our valises. Soon we were seated in a carriage heading for Richmond.

Mauldeth Hall proved to be a double fronted Georgian manor house set in about ten acres of landscaped parkland. As we drew up outside, a butler hurried down the steps to open our carriage door.

'Ah, Jefferson,' Sir Charles said, 'these gentlemen are friends of mine who will be staying with us for the next few days. Please take their bags and prepare two of the guestrooms for them, will you?'

'Of course, Sir Charles,' responded Jefferson. 'This way, gentlemen.'

Soon we were sitting before a cheerful log fire in the billiards room sipping an excellent sherry. Conversation became a little stilted as Crichton was, not surprisingly, preoccupied, and Holmes and myself played a couple of games of billiards while Sir Charles gazed introspectively into the fire. He was still there when Holmes and I retired.

The following morning I was awakened by Holmes shouting up the stairs, 'Shake a leg, Watson, the next communiqué has just arrived.'

Soon I was shaved and dressed and had joined Holmes and Sir Charles at the breakfast table where they were studying the note. Again it was a single sheet of foolscap with cutout words affixed. It said: *PUT THE MONEY IN A BAG AND PLACE IT IN NUMBER FIFTEEN LEFT LUGGAGE LOCKER AT EUSTON STATION. THE KEY IS ENCLOSED. INDICATE YOUR AGREEMENT IN THE*

TIMES PERSONAL COLUMN. FAIL AND THE BLACK ARROW WILL STRIKE! DICK AND JOHN.
Holmes said, 'Excellent! This is just what I had hoped for. They have given us a way of contacting them. Now this is what I propose.' He stood and began pacing the room. 'Take this down Watson.' I produced a pen and note pad and as Holmes dictated, I wrote: *DICK AND JOHN. AGREE YOUR TERMS ON CONDITION MY EMISSARY CONFIRMS GOODS UNDAMAGED. RENDEZVOUS AT CORNER OF PORTLAND STREET AND REGENT STREET 6.30 p.m. ON THURSDAY 15TH. C.C.*

Sir Charles said, 'You are going to place yourself in their hands? Do you think that is wise?'

Holmes shrugged, 'It is the only way we have a chance of saving your daughters life, Sir Charles.'

I announced, 'I'm coming with you, Holmes.'

Sherlock smiled at me and replied, 'Thank you, Watson, I would appreciate that. Though it may well be dangerous.'

'Pish! When you have braved the cannon shells of Afghanistan's battlefields, then talk of danger.'

Holmes clapped his hands together and said, 'Well, that's settled then. Now I fancy I can do justice to those kidneys on the table.'

After breakfast one of the servants was despatched to place the advertisement in the Times and Holmes and I repacked our bags.

'Are you sure you won't stay a while longer, gentlemen?' asked Sir Charles.

'I think not,' Holmes replied, 'At Baker Street we are closer to the rendezvous point. We will contact you as soon as we have any news.'

Sir Charles shook hands with both of us and said, 'May God go with you, gentlemen.'

Six thirty p.m. on the fifteenth saw Holmes and myself waiting in the circle of light cast by the gas lamp under which we stood, at the designated corner. In my pocket was the comforting weight of my old service revolver and Holmes carried his silver handled swordstick. There was a light mist in the air and the evening was chill and damp.

We did not have long to wait before a horse drawn cab rattled to a halt alongside. The door was thrown open and a gruff voice from inside said, 'One only.'

Holmes stepped forward and announced, 'This gentleman is a doctor. He will ascertain if the goods are undamaged. He is also insurance against myself becoming your hostage.'

There was a pause and some whispered conversation inside the cab before the same gruff voice said, 'Right, get in.'

Holmes and I scrambled inside and the door was slammed shut. All the blinds were drawn and it was very dark inside the cab.

As we rattled over the cobblestones my eyes gradually grew accustomed to the gloom and I could make out more of the two men sitting opposite us.

The first one was broad shouldered and wore a long ulster, which was ripped and torn. On his head he wore an old cloth cap pulled well down over his eyes. A large muffler hid two thirds of his face and on his feet were scuffed hob-nailed boots. The other fellow was smaller and looked older because of his round-shouldered stoop. He wore a battered old bowler hat and a long astrakhan coat that had seen better days. He too wore a muffler, which hid most of his face, but I could see that he had thick bushy eyebrows above dark eyes.

I asked, 'Which of you is Dick and which is John?'

The man in the bowler hat replied in a hoarse gruff voice, 'What difference does it make?'

'Just trying to make conversation,' I said.

'Well don't bother,' he commanded.

I had heard voices like his before amongst patients of mine who had worked all their lives in the mills. Breathing the dust and having to shout above the noise of the machinery was what did the damage. I resolved to pass this clue on to Holmes at the earliest opportunity.

I glanced round at my friend and was amazed to see that he appeared to have dozed off. He sat slumped in the corner of the carriage with his hand over his eyes, seemingly asleep.

The cab rattled on down one street after another until at last, after perhaps half an hour, it pulled up and the bigger man, who I shall call Dick, jumped up.

John pulled a pistol from his pocket and said, 'Right guvnors, time to blindfold yer now.' Dick produced strips of black cloth and bound them tightly round my own and Holmes' eyes. We were led from the cab and along a gravel path, up three steps and into a house. The place smelled of mildew and dampness and we were ushered into a room where Dick removed the blindfolds. I glanced around and determined that we were indeed in an empty house with bare floorboards and peeling wallpaper. Great damp patches on the walls and ceiling were visible in the light of a single candle burning on the mantelpiece of an old iron fireplace.

Dick said to John, 'Go and check on the girl, then you'd best get her somink to eat. I want to talk to these two. Gimme the gun.'

John handed over the gun and left without a word.

Dick said belligerently, 'If you two are finking of being 'eroes and rescuing the girl forget it. This gun is loaded and the first target will be miss 'igh and mighty Crichton 'erself. Try explaining that to 'is lordship. 'As 'e got the money?'

Holmes answered, 'He is getting it together now. It takes time to amass such a large amount, even for a man like Sir Charles.'

Dick said, 'Well 'e better be quick about it 'cos I'm not a patient man.' He waved the pistol threateningly then said,

'Right, out the door and turn left.' We did as we were bidden with Holmes leading the way.

'Up the stairs,' commanded Dick. We climbed the creaking staircase then along a landing until Dick commanded, 'Right, stop there.' He pushed past us and fumbled with the lock on one of the bedroom doors. Next moment the door opened and he entered saying, 'In 'ere, gents.'

We stepped into the room and saw Miss Sophie lying on the filthy mattress of an old iron bedstead. Her left wrist was manacled by a chain to the bed head and she looked pale and anxious. She was fully dressed except for her shoes.

I stepped forward saying, 'My dear child, have courage. Your father, Sir Charles, sent us to determine that you are alive and well. I am a doctor. Tell me, have they molested you in any way?' I took her free hand in mine and it was cold and trembling.

'No not yet, Doctor, though they have threatened all manner of evils if father refuses to pay up.'

I took her pulse, which was strong and regular, though very rapid which was not surprising under the circumstances.

She said, 'How is Papa? He must be worried to death.'

Holmes joined me and bent low over Miss Sophie to say, 'Your father is beside himself with grief and anxiety, but he will be relieved when we tell him that you have not been mistreated. They have fed you adequately?'

'Yes, it's not like the Savoy, but it is edible,' she replied.

'And what about blankets?' Holmes asked.

She nodded, 'They bring me blankets at night.'

'You have been kept here since Saturday, then?' Holmes enquired.

'Yes, I've not been outside this room since then.'

Dick said, 'Right, that's enough! What d'yer want, 'er flamin' life story?' He prodded Holmes in the ribs and said,

'Come on, the visit's over. Move it!' He bundled us out, shutting the door behind us.

I shouted. '*Nil desperandum*, Miss Sophie, all will be well!'

Back in the ground floor room again, Dick produced the blindfolds once more. 'Right, Doctor. You do the honours this time,' and he indicated that I should blindfold Holmes.

After I had done so, Dick blindfolded me. I wondered whether I should have pulled my gun and tried to gain the upper hand, but with John loose in the house and Miss Sophie still at risk I decided the time was not opportune. We were led back to the cab, which still waited outside, and bundled aboard.

Once we were under way again Dick said, 'Right, you can remove your blindfolds now, but don't try raisin' the blinds or this gun might go off, accidental like.'

I said, 'You won't get away with this devilry, you know.'

He laughed a coarse laugh and said, 'Don't bet good money on it, gents.'

Dick continuously checked our location by peeking from behind his drawn blind and eventually he rapped on the ceiling of the cab to tell the driver to stop.

The cabby called, "Whoa!" and his horse clattered to a halt, snorting loudly.

Dick opened the door and said, 'G'night, gents, and don't try following me or else,' and he patted the gun in his hand.

Holmes and I stepped from the cab and it rattled away into the mist. I glanced around and realised we were back at the rendezvous point.

I turned to Holmes and said, 'I say, old fellow, I think that John, the little one, almost certainly worked in a mill for I've heard such hoarseness in patients of mine who were mill workers.'

Holmes gave a wry little laugh and responded, 'I doubt if John has ever even *seen* the inside of a mill, Watson.' Then hailing a passing hansom, he said, 'We must hurry to Mauldeth Hall for there is much to be done.'

Soon we were rattling along at a fair gallop towards Richmond. Holmes would not be drawn further and seemed preoccupied all the way. Finally we pulled up outside the Hall and Jefferson came down to meet us.

'Sir Charles awaits you in the library, gentlemen. This way please.'

In the library Sir Charles waited with bated breath. 'Holmes, Watson, thank God you are both safe! What news?'

'Good news!' I answered. 'Miss Sophie is well and undefiled.'

'Thank God!' whispered Sir Charles with real feeling.

Holmes however said, 'It is not all good news I'm afraid. It is going to cost you a great deal and you may *still* not get your daughter back, Sir Charles.'

Crichton nodded. 'I realise that we are not yet out of the woods, Mr Holmes, but the first part of this exercise has been a huge success. What now?'

Holmes was thoughtful for a minute, then said, 'I propose that we all go right now to Islington and see our friends Dick and John again.'

Both Sir Charles and I looked at Holmes in amazement. 'What's that you say?' I asked. 'How on earth can we find them?'

Sherlock smiled and replied, 'Watson, you know enough of my methods now to have realised that I was not sleeping in the cab ride to Islington. What I *was* doing was counting. By watching the strip of light below the bottom of the cab's blinds cast by each gas lamp that we passed, I was able to form a mental map of our route. East on Oxford Street for seven lights, north for four lights and so on. If my memory serves me, we should be able to retrace our route.'

'Bravo, Holmes!' I exclaimed. 'What a marvel you are.'

Sir Charles was equally impressed. 'You never cease to amaze me, Mr Holmes,' he said.

Holmes responded, 'Perhaps you should reserve judgement until we see how accurate I am.' He continued, 'Can you arrange a cab for us, Sir Charles?'

'Better than that,' he said, striding to the bell pull, 'I'll have my own teamed up.'

Crichton instructed Jefferson to have the groom harness up the brougham immediately, then turned to us and said, 'We must contact the police so these villains can be arrested once you have led them to the scene, Mr Holmes.'

Sherlock held up a restraining hand and said, 'Sir Charles, I recall you saying that you trusted my judgement implicitly. If that still holds true then I urge you not to contact the police just yet. I have my reasons.'

Crichton looked surprised, but agreed readily enough. 'Very well, Mr Holmes it shall be as you say.'

Soon we were sitting in Sir Charles' brougham making good speed towards the rendezvous point. When we got there Holmes sat in the same position as he had earlier in the cab and directed, 'East until I tell you to turn left.' The driver did as he was bidden, then Holmes said, 'Left here, but be ready to turn right soon.'

The brougham progressed in this manner for some time until Holmes said, 'This is far enough. Stop here driver.'

We were in a drab part of the city with old houses and run-down factories. Holmes said, 'If I am correct the house we seek is two lamp posts further down on the left.'

Sir Charles told the driver to wait for us and the three of us set out with Holmes in the lead. I gripped the butt of my pistol for reassurance. Presently Holmes held up a warning hand and indicated the gravel drive of a looming detached house with 'For Sale' signs in its small front garden. The place was in darkness, as were the properties on either side, and there was no sign of life anywhere. A dog barked

145

sporadically further down the street, but apart from that all was quiet.

Holmes drew close and whispered, 'I think we should reconnoitre the rear. Don't walk on the gravel. Follow me and watch your step.'

He moved ahead as silently as a shadow, with Sir Charles behind and myself bringing up the rear. It was so dark I had difficulty keeping in touch with the others and, in spite of Sherlock's warning, at one point I stumbled over something underfoot and all but pitched headlong. I smiled wryly to myself as I imagined Holmes' reaction if I *had* fallen and the gun had gone off. He would never have forgiven me.

Presently we found ourselves at the rear of the house and here we could see a little more clearly because a light burned in the kitchen. The window was partly boarded up and very grimy, but there was enough light to make out three stone steps and an iron banister up to the back door.

Holmes stealthily climbed the steps and peered in through the window. He seemed to slump and I'm sure he let out a sigh.

I whispered, 'What is it, old fellow? Have we come to the wrong house?'

Holmes shook his head and said quietly, 'I wish that were so.' He beckoned Sir Charles forward and said, 'Brace yourself, sir!'

Crichton crept up the steps and peered in and the look of amazement on his face was quickly replaced by one of bewilderment.

'I don't understand...' he whispered hoarsely.

I could contain my curiosity no longer and rather rudely pushed past the other two to look through the window. By the light of a hanging oil lamp I could see a broad-shouldered man sitting at a table on which were the remains of a meal. A fire burned in the grate of a black kitchen range and old clothes were draped over the backs of some chairs.

But what stunned me was the sight of Miss Sophie sitting opposite the young man, talking earnestly to him.

Holmes said, 'Meet Dick and John!' Instantly I understood, as did Sir Charles and the fury that filled his countenance was intense. Before either of us could make a move to stop him, he leapt forward and pounded on the back door shouting, 'SOPHIA, OPEN UP. THIS IS YOUR FATHER!' and he kicked the door with his boot. Next moment the door was thrown open and we all burst into the room.

Miss Sophie ran to her lover, who shielded her from her father's wrath and pleaded, 'Please, Sir Charles, this is all of my doing. I talked Sophie into it. Pray do not be too harsh on her.'

Holmes placed a restraining hand on Crichton's shoulder and urged, 'Please listen to me, Sir Charles, before you say or do something which you may regret for the rest of your life.'

Sir Charles was purple with rage and I feared he might have a seizure. I made him sit down and fetched him a glass of water.

Holmes said, 'Much of this is my fault. I could have warned you earlier, but I feared you would not believe me. I felt you had to see with your own eyes. We are apt to believe our offspring are incapable of evil.' He sighed heavily and carried on, 'Sometimes this profession of mine is not worth the candle, when I must expose the frailties of my fellow man.' He looked keenly at Sir Charles and said, 'I did try to warn you when I said it will cost you a great deal and you may still not get your daughter back. I did not mean monetary cost, nor did I mean that your daughter's life was at risk.'

Sir Charles slowly nodded in understanding. 'You did indeed, Mr Holmes, though your message was coded a shade too cryptically for me.'

I said, 'You have known all along then that these two were Dick and John, Holmes?'

Sherlock glanced at the young couple, still clinging to each other beyond the table.

'Almost from the first, Watson. The ransom notes were written in Helvetica sans serif, an unusual typeface and one I recall as being favoured by the Oxford University Press. I remembered it from my own student days. Sir Charles had said that Sophie and her paramour were students at Oxford. That on its own of course was insufficient evidence, but the other clue was in the grammar and syntax of the note. *We have your daughter*, for example. A semi-illiterate villain of the type they tried to portray would probably have written *We've got your daughter*, and there are numerous other examples.'

Holmes continued, 'They contrived their own downfall by calling themselves Dick and John. You recall the melodramatic sketch showing a black arrow through the woman's neck? Well, in Robert Louis Stevenson's latest novel, The Black Arrow, the two main characters are Dick Shelton and John Matcham. John, however, is in truth a young *woman* disguised!'

Holmes carried on showing how he had uncovered the conspiracy, and I realised that he was deliberately giving Sir Charles the time he needed to regain his composure.

He went on, 'You have on occasion, Watson, remarked that this nose of mine seems able to sniff out a clue from the unlikeliest of places. Well in this instance it was more a case of what it did *not* smell than what it smelled. When I bent low over Miss Sophie on the bed, she smelled fresh and fragrant. Hardly what I would have expected if indeed she had been a prisoner there for the last five days. I did not even see a chamber pot, yet she was supposed to have been manacled to the bed for nearly a week!'

He regarded the young couple and continued, 'Dressing yourselves in charity shop clothing, perhaps with an extra rip here and a tear there, is all very well, but genuine ragamuffins have an unwashed smell which you two lacked. I should know, for I have spent enough time amongst them in one disguise or another.'

Then turning to me he said, 'Poor Watson. Your vital clue about John's hoarseness being the result of having worked in a mill was simply Miss Sophie disguising her obviously female voice.'

I smiled a little shamefacedly and replied, 'As you say, Holmes, but you have to admit that their masquerade as ne'er do wells was very convincing.'

Holmes nodded, 'Indeed it was, until you recall that they were both members of an Oxford drama group. No doubt they played out their roles as if they were acting in a stage play.'

Sir Charles gave a huge sigh and said in a quavering voice, 'Sophie, how could you betray me so and put me through such torment?'

The girl was crying now and shaking her head,

'Oh, Papa,' she sobbed, 'I'm so sorry...it started out as a prank, then...'

The young man took up the tale. He said, 'I love your daughter, Sir Charles, almost as much as you do, and now that I see what a pass this has brought you to, I am heartily ashamed of myself. Sophie had sounded you out about our love and received no encouragement whatsoever. She felt you would never give your blessing and we had no money to strike out on our own. We joked about how we were sure you would gladly pay a four-figure sum as ransom for Sophie and one thing led to another. I can't expect you to believe me, but the truth is that we were just discussing how we could call the whole charade off, when you burst in tonight.'

Miss Sophie was nodding vigorously. 'It's true, Papa, every word.'

Sir Charles spread his arms in a pleading gesture and said, 'If you had only made your feelings known to me, Sophie, we could have worked something out, but this cruel subterfuge has very nearly destroyed me...'

The girl's sobbing increased and Holmes interjected, 'May I make a suggestion, Sir Charles. Pray take Miss Sophie and her young man back with you to Mauldeth Hall in your carriage and talk this through. Watson and I will make our own way back to Baker Street.'

Crichton stood and passed a hand wearily over his eyes. 'Mr Holmes, what can I say? Thank you seems so inadequate, and there is the question of your fee.'

Holmes responded, 'I will mail you my bill.' Then in what was little more than a whisper, he continued, 'A word of advice however, Sir Charles. Conciliation rather than confrontation, and you may yet get your daughter back.'

Crichton shook hands with us both and we left them there in the kitchen of the empty house.

Later in a hansom cab approaching Baker Street I asked, 'Do you think they will sort it out, Holmes?'

'I sincerely hope so, Watson. If only people would communicate more with each other, half these situations would never arise. But then of course, half my cases would never arise either.'

I nodded, 'Just so, Holmes, just so.'

It was almost a year later when Holmes received an envelope in the morning mail. After he had read the letter he smiled and passed it to me saying, 'A pleasant postscript to the Crichton case, Watson.'

I read; *'My dear Mr Holmes, I am writing to you to let you know the outcome of your inestimable advice, upon which I had the good sense to act.*

Mauldeth Hall is no longer a lonely place and now rings with laughter and joy.

My son-in-law, Rodney, is a boon companion and a formidable opponent at chess, whilst Sophie is more beautiful than ever, flushed as she is with the glow of motherhood.

We could think of no more suitable recognition of the debt of gratitude we all owe you than to tell you that we have named my grandson Sherlock, in your honour.
Your humble servant,
Charles Crichton.'

THE PADDINGTON PYROMANIAC

The long dry summer of 1889 is memorable to me for all the wrong reasons. Although it was the hottest and sunniest I could remember since moving into 221b Baker Street with Sherlock Holmes, that was not what makes it stand out in my memory. A series of raging conflagrations in London which caused tens of thousands of pounds worth of damage and the loss of many lives will, I am sure, be recalled by everyone who lived through that trying time.

It began in the middle of June with three huge fires in two weeks in close proximity around Paddington. The first was in a hostel for old soldiers where three veterans lost their lives. The second was a flax mill that burned for two days and nights, and the third was a brewery stable, which went up like tinder, because of all the bales of hay and straw. Five magnificent dray-horses died in that one.

I suppose that Holmes should have been alerted sooner, for as he was wont to say, 'Once is happenstance, twice is coincidence, but three times usually signals criminal intent.' However, in defence of my friend, he was at that time engaged in a particularly delicate case involving a high ranking-diplomat and an attempt at blackmail. I will not dwell on the details; suffice it to say that Holmes was somewhat preoccupied. The arrival of Inspector Lestrade at Baker Street followed close on the heels of the fourth fire. The top floor of a public house, called the Spinners Arms, was destroyed and the wife of the proprietor killed before the overworked London Fire Brigade could contain the blaze.

Lestrade displayed all the symptoms of extreme agitation as he mopped his brow and loosened his tie. It was obvious that it was not just the heat that was bothering him. 'Mr Holmes,' he said with a note of pleading in his voice, 'I need your help. I am enlisting the services of all and sundry in an attempt to prevent any further tragedy. I'm sure you must be aware that these fires are, in all likelihood, the work of an arsonist?'

Holmes nodded. 'I'm afraid I have reached the same conclusion, somewhat belatedly Inspector. Do you have any leads?

Lestrade shook his head. 'None at all, Mr Holmes.'

'What about known arsonists, like Adrian Phillips or Brendan Murphy?

Lestrade replied, 'Phillips is still behind bars in Pentonville and Murphy died last month.'

'What about the Berkshire Firebomber, Fielding?' Holmes' memory for the names of criminals and their particular crimes was prodigious. His mind was like a well ordered card index system with instant retrieval.

Again the inspector shook his head. 'He has been questioned closely and has solid alibis for all the dates.'

Holmes was thoughtful for a moment before asking; 'Do you know the whereabouts of Damien Applegate?'

Lestrade had to think for a moment before he could recall the name. 'Applegate? Of course, now I remember. Wasn't he the villain who set fire to all those business premises so their owners could claim the fire insurance?'

Holmes nodded, 'That's the fellow.'

'Your memory for detail is amazing, Mr Holmes,' enthused Lestrade. 'I will certainly check up on our friend, Mr Applegate.'

He jotted the name down in his notebook as Holmes asked, 'Does it look like any of these fires could have been initiated for insurance claims?'

The inspector shook his head. 'Hardly, Mr Holmes. The hostel was run by the Borough Council; the brewery are unlikely to have roasted their own animals, and the flax mill was not insured.'

Holmes leant on the mantelpiece and regarded Lestrade for a moment before saying, 'Then I am afraid it is the worst possible scenario, Inspector. We have a pyromaniac in our midst.'

I remarked, 'I thought anyone who deliberately started fires was a pyromaniac, Holmes.'

Sherlock shook his head, 'Not so, Watson. There are many criminal reasons for starting a fire. As we have just said, insurance claims for one. Also there is murder, political agitation, concealment of another crime, extortion. The list goes on. With all of these, however, there is some pattern, some underlying motivation, which once discovered may lead to a solution. But in the case of a pyromaniac the only motive is madness and the only pattern is randomness. The pyromaniac has an irrational compulsion to destroy by fire, and he almost invariably has a morbid fascination with fire itself. Often he will mingle with the crowd of onlookers that every fire attracts, to exult in his evil handiwork.' Turning to Lestrade, he asked, 'Have your men scanned the crowds at all these fires?'

The inspector nodded. 'Of course, Mr Holmes. We at Scotland Yard know all about these lunatics, who thankfully are a rare breed. All my men have been briefed to watch carefully, albeit discreetly, for anyone fitting the bill. Unfortunately nobody has yet been spotted.'

Holmes pointed out; 'They have been known to adopt disguises, so that they do not become noticed as they appear at each blaze.'

Lestrade nodded, 'Indeed, Mr Holmes, and again I reiterate that my men are aware of this and have looked for it diligently, but without success.'

Holmes went to the sideboard and withdrew his large-scale map of London. Spreading it out on the table, he said, 'Perhaps you can pinpoint the location of each fire for me Inspector?'

'Certainly,' said Lestrade. 'The hostel was here on Bishop's Bridge Road, the stables were on London Street, and what's left of the Spinners Arms is on Harrow Road. The flax mill was here on South Wharf Road.'

Lestrade pointed to each in turn, and Holmes responded, 'This is very unusual.'

'What is?' I asked.

'Why, the extreme closeness of each location to the other. They are, all four of them, little more than a stone's throw apart.'

Lestrade agreed, 'It *is* unusual, Mr Holmes, and as yet we cannot account for it.'

'I fail to see *why* it should be unusual,' I responded.

Holmes replied, 'Usually an arsonist, having set a blaze in one place and alerted the authorities and the general public in that area, selects a location some distance away for his second and third strikes. To have had four in a radius of a few hundred yards must be unique.'

Lestrade responded, 'We are, as you might imagine, concentrating our main effort in and around Paddington station. I have a dozen men in plain clothes, street-sweepers, lamp-lighters and so on, patrolling the area looking for anything suspicious, but so far there is nothing to report.'

Holmes mused, 'I suppose it could be someone who has a personal grudge against a resident or employer in the area of Paddington. Either real or imagined, for a pyromaniac is likely to suffer other manias, such as a persecution complex.

Lestrade responded, 'You could very well be right, Mr Holmes, but how on earth can I screen everyone in the area to determine if they hold such a grudge?'

Holmes smiled, saying, 'Of course you can't, Inspector, and that was not what I was implying. I was merely thinking aloud as a way to try to enter into the mind of the arsonist. Plainly you and your men are doing everything in your power to bring this fellow to justice.' He paced the room a few times before asking, 'Can you tell me the precise time each fire was reported?'

Lestrade took out his notebook again and replied, 'The hostel fire was reported at 1.15 p.m. on Monday the 15th. The flax mill fire at 2.05 p.m., three days later, and the stable blaze was a little before 2.30 p.m. on the twentieth. The Spinners Arms was at 1.35 p.m. on the 22nd.

Holmes abruptly stopped his pacing and turned to Lestrade saying, 'How very, very odd!'

'What is?'

'That every fire took place in broad daylight! In my experience most arsonists prefer night-time for the concealment of their comings and goings and for the dramatic spectacle of a conflagration against the night sky.' He was thoughtful for a few moments as he peered at the map. Eventually he observed, 'I'm sure you have already concluded, Inspector, that the most obvious target our man is likely to go for next has to be Paddington Station itself.'

Lestrade nodded forlornly. 'That is why I am so desperate for any help I can get. I dare not even contemplate the horror and loss of life that would ensue if he were successful in torching the railway station.'

Holmes nodded, 'Quite so, Inspector. Do you have men deployed at the station?'

'Of course, disguised as porters, guards, even passengers, but they have seen nothing.'

Holmes began to pencil in, on the map, a cross to represent the location of each fire and beside each cross he wrote the date and the time it was reported. Turning to the inspector he asked, 'Have you or your men found any indication as to how the fires were started?

Lestrade shook his head, ' I'm afraid not, Mr Holmes. Scotland Yard experts and the specialists of the Metropolitan Fire Brigade have been unable to determine *how* the fires were triggered. We have found no containers for fuel, no evidence of flammable material being piled up at the ignition point, *nothing*.'

Again Holmes was thoughtful. 'I recall,' he said after a while, 'that Damien Applegate used a simple timing device for some of his fires. It consisted of a cheap alarm clock rigged so that when the alarm went off, the hammer struck and smashed a small glass phial of phosphorus. If my memory serves me, the time of year was autumn and winter so naturally the phosphorus reacted with the moisture in the damp air and Whoosh!'

Lestrade was nodding in agreement, 'You are right again, Mr Holmes. In fact the alarm clocks, or what was left of them, led us finally to Applegate. But in these fires there has been nothing of the sort.'

'Has anybody involved reported seeing any strangers or suspicious characters in the vicinity of any of these blazes, prior to their starting?'

Lestrade paced the room and replied, 'Damn it no! Forgive me, Mr Holmes, but again I have to report in the negative. Nobody who could even remotely be considered as suspicious has been spotted. This case is getting on my nerves. I can't recall one like it for its complete lack of clues.'

Holmes placed a reassuring hand on the inspector's shoulder. 'Steady, old chap, I'm sure that between us we will bring the villain to justice. Pray leave it with me to cogitate on and of course if you have any news, however trivial, let me know immediately.'

Lestrade shook hands with Holmes and said, 'Thank you, Sir. I feel a deal more at ease having you on the case. Good day, gentlemen.'

After he had left I asked, 'Where on earth do you start, old fellow? It is like looking for the proverbial needle in a haystack!'

Holmes peered at the map as he answered, 'I'm afraid we still have insufficient data, Watson. I fear we must suffer further fires before we will be able to apprehend this lunatic. I just hope the next one isn't Paddington Station itself.'

In the event it was not, but it was bad enough. The fire broke out, two days later, in a haberdasher's shop on Praed Street, and before it could be contained, it took the life of the proprietor's bedridden mother. She had been in the bedroom above the shop and died, on her way to hospital, from smoke inhalation. We could see the pall of smoke, rising above the intervening buildings, from Baker Street.

Holmes said, when he read in the newspaper of the old lady's death, 'What kind of creature could do this, Watson? We must catch this madman and quickly.' He leaned back in his chair and continued, 'He is like no other pyromaniac I have ever encountered. He is a veritable phantom, seemingly able to come and go unseen, and when he has set his blaze he does not stand and gloat. He is able to start a fire on the first floor of a busy inn, like the Spinners Arms, and yet not be seen entering or leaving.'

I suggested, 'He could be triggering them remotely, somehow.'

Holmes nodded. 'I'm sure you are right, Watson, and I had already reached the same conclusion, but how? There has been no evidence of a timing device at any of the scenes.'

'Perhaps you should speak to your brother Mycroft. Maybe his keen mind can shed some light on the mystery.'

Holmes sat bolt upright and stared at me. 'Watson,' he declared, 'you are *inspired!* Once again you display that touch of serendipity that triggers my thought processes.' He began pacing the floor muttering to himself, 'Of course in this warm weather people will throw open their doors and windows. I'll wager that an upstairs window of the Spinners Arms was open.'

'More than likely, Holmes, and that will have aided the fire. The worst thing you can do, in a smoke-filled room, is to open a door or window, for the extra oxygen feeds the flames.'

Holmes nodded, 'As you say, Watson, but that is not what I was thinking. What has the weather been like these two days past?'

'Why, warm and dry with hazy sunshine.'

'Exactly! And I think you will find that on many of the other days when there was no fire, it was cloudy bright or overcast.' He strode to the table and peered again at the map. 'Yes it fits!' he declared. 'Watson, I am a dull-witted oaf for not seeing the possibility sooner. It needed your prompting to galvanize my mind, but I do believe we might just be on to something.'

I looked at him in puzzlement. 'All I said was, that you should speak to your brother, Mycroft.'

'Not quite, old fellow. You also said, *he might shed some light on the problem.* The operative word is *light!*' He beckoned me over to the table saying, 'Look here on the map. The first fire started there on Bishop's Bridge Street. The next on London Street, the third here at Harrow Road and the latest is on Praed Street. All of them have taken place in the middle of the day or early afternoon, and they each ring Paddington Station.'

I shook my head in bewilderment, 'I'm sorry, Holmes, but I fail to see what you are driving at.'

He smiled at my incomprehension and explained, 'If I wanted to set fires randomly from a safe distance, on a sunny day, all I would need is a large magnifying lens *to focus the sun's rays!'*

'By Jove! Holmes, I believe you have it!'

'And,' he continued,' since it would not be nearly as effective through glass, he chose open windows and doors.'

I nodded, 'Of course, but from where did he project his beam?'

'Isn't it obvious? Why from the roof of Paddington Station itself. *That* is why the building has not been a target and why he himself was not seen.' After a moment he continued, 'A guinea says that, since he is an aficionado of lenses, he watches the fires he has started through a telescope from his safe vantage point.'

I smiled, 'Well done indeed, Holmes, it all fits. So what will you do now?'

'We must lay a little trap for our fiendish firelighter. What is the weather forecast for tomorrow?'

I picked up the newspaper and read, 'Uninterrupted sunshine. Temperatures between seventy and eighty degrees.'

Holmes strode over to the window and looked up at the sky before saying, 'This is all still very much conjecture, Watson, and I don't have a scrap of evidence to substantiate it, so I propose not to involve Lestrade at the present time. I think perhaps that you and I should stalk this particular quarry.'

I smiled in anticipation. 'I can hardly wait, old fellow.'

He glanced at the clock on the mantelpiece and said, ' I propose we visit the Stationmaster at Paddington first thing tomorrow morning. If the villain decides to take advantage of tomorrow's sunshine, and is true to form, he will not put in an appearance until midday at the earliest.'

That very evening Holmes received a telegram, and when he had read it he passed it to me saying, 'Well, well, well! Who would have believed it?'

I read: *My dear Mr Holmes, Case closed. Under close questioning, Damian Applegate has confessed all. Appreciate your assistance.*
Best regards,
Lestrade.

I exclaimed, 'Great news, is it not?' and looked up to see Holmes donning his hat and reaching for his cane. 'But where are you going?' I enquired.

'I would very much like to speak to Damien Applegate myself, old fellow. Are you coming?'

'Absolutely,' I replied, snatching my own hat and following him through the door.

As our cab approached Scotland Yard, Holmes repeated, 'Pray make no mention of my speculation regarding the magnifying lens at this stage, Watson.'

'Of course not, Holmes.'

Presently we were ushered into Lestrade's office and Holmes asked, 'Did Applegate reveal how he initiated the fires, Inspector?'

'Not yet, but I am on my way to question him again. Perhaps you would like to accompany me, gentlemen?' Soon we were seated opposite the arsonist, who was a small, ferret-faced individual with lank greasy hair and a strabismus of his left eye. He watched us warily and licked his lips.

Holmes said, 'We meet once more, Damian, and you've been up to your old tricks again, haven't you?'

He smiled, displaying rotting teeth, and replied, 'No use trying to fool *you* Mister 'Olmes, but I never wanted no one to die, 'onest I didn't.'

Holmes asked, 'How did you set the blazes, Damian?'

A crafty look came into Applegate's eyes and he replied, 'If I co-operate what's in it for me?'

Lestrade replied, 'Nothing, you little rat. You'll hang for murder, I'll see to it personally!'

Holmes said, 'The inspector can do nothing for you, but *I* can. I could, for instance, see that your common law wife and children receive a little financial assistance. You're not going to be much use to them now, are you?'

He stared at Holmes for a few moments before asking, 'You're a gentleman, and must 'onour your word, right?'

Holmes nodded, 'Yes that's right.'

'OK, I'll tell you. I didn't use clock timers 'cause they leave traces. With this new method nothing's left behind. Give me your matches and I'll show you.' Holmes took a box of vestas from his pocket and handed them to Applegate. The arsonist opened the box, took out one match and said, 'If you trap a match like this…' and he propped the match upright with one end inserted amongst the live ends of the other matches. He then slid home the tray to grip the match tightly, 'all you've got to do is light the match and put the box amongst some paper or stuff that'll burn. It takes about a minute to burn down, which is enough time to get away, before the flame reaches the other matches. Then *WHOOSH!* Up she goes!'

Holmes was nodding. 'Ingenious and so simple. And you used this method for all the fires?'

'Sure, what else?'

'How did you secrete your matchbox in a first floor bedroom of the Spinners Arms? No one saw you enter or leave.'

Applegate smiled slyly. 'A geezer can't reveal *all* his trade secrets, can 'e, Mister 'Olmes?'

'He'd better if he wants his family provided for!'

Applegate's smile slipped, his eyes flitted from side to side and he bit his lip, 'See 'ere, Mister 'Olmes, back off a bit, can't you? I've told you what I can. Is it my fault that folks don't notice a little runt like me? I nipped in and back out again, that's it.'

Holmes stood up and said, 'You're a liar, Damian, and not a very good one at that. When you decide to tell the truth let me know. Come, Watson, we are wasting our time here.'

As we left we heard Applegate shouting, *'Keep your money in your purse! I'll be out of 'ere in weeks, just see if I ain't!'*

Lestrade followed us out and Holmes said to him, 'He's lying, but I don't know why. Previously he only ever set fires for financial gain and was invariably paid for his handiwork. You yourself pointed out that none of the fires could generate a profit. The only possible exception might be the haberdasher's shop, and the owner is hardly likely to have had his own mother murdered to prove his claim genuine.'

Lestrade responded, 'I did not expect you to be such a sore loser, Mr Holmes. You can't win them all. For once normal routine police procedure has apprehended the villain, and I would have thought that you would have the good grace to acknowledge the fact. No one in his right mind would knowingly put his neck in the hangman's noose for murders he did not commit.'

Holmes shrugged, 'Very well, Lestrade, we shall leave it at that, and let us hope you are right in your assertion. Good day to you.'

When we were in a cab on our way back to Baker Street I remarked, 'The inspector has a good point, Holmes. Why on earth would Applegate confess knowing the only outcome would see him kicking and struggling at the end of a rope?'

'I admit it seems bizarre, Watson, but the fellow never was a pyromaniac in the true sense of the word. His motive was always profit. I doubt he even watched the blazes he initiated, and no one ever died in one of Applegate's fires.'

'So we are still stalking our quarry?'

'Very much so, old soldier!'

Eight o'clock the next morning found Holmes and myself in the office of Mr Cunningham, the Stationmaster at Paddington. He was a small wiry man with sharp eyes and a quick mind. He immediately grasped the significance of what Holmes told him and he was anxious to help us.

Holmes asked, 'How can we gain access to the roof?'

Cunningham replied, 'Simplicity itself. Follow me and I'll show you.' He led us up a flight of stairs to the mezzanine floor, then through an access door on to the gantry. Up another flight of iron steps, we came to a platform and a steel door out onto the roof. The stationmaster produced a bunch of keys to unlock the door, but then let out an exclamation of surprise, 'This lock has been forced!'

Holmes bent forward and peered at it. 'It certainly has, Mr Cunningham. By a bifurcated jemmy, if I'm not mistaken. This suggests we might be, after all, on the right track.' He pushed open the door and stepped forward into the sunshine. We followed him out and looked around. The view from up there was impressive, and I picked out many famous landmarks. In the distance I could glimpse a bend of the River Thames as it glinted in the morning sunlight. Holmes was casting about hither and thither like a bloodhound after the scent. He went to the parapet and looked towards the scene of the last fire. Turning to us he said, 'Someone has been here for sure. There are footprints and even a handprint in the dust on the parapet wall.' He scanned the rooftop then began looking behind the brick built chimneys. Eventually he cried out, '*Eureka! Just as I suspected.*' Behind one of them he had discovered a leather bag and as we joined him he opened it to reveal a large convex lens, a small telescope and a steel jemmy.

'QED Watson!'

'Bravo! Holmes,' I cried, 'just as you predicted.' Holmes briefly explained the significance of his find to the Stationmaster.

Mr Cunningham nodded and remarked, 'The cunning devil. I wonder where he might have obtained such a lens?'

Holmes hefted the thing in his hands and replied, 'It has a long focal length so it is probably from an astronomical telescope.'

I asked, 'So what do we do now, old fellow?'

'We wait. That of course excludes you, Mr Cunningham, you must have much to do. Thank you for all your help, but Watson and I shall take it from here.'

The Stationmaster nodded, 'Very well, Mr Holmes, if you're sure you will be all right. Would you like me to contact the police?'

Holmes shook his head. 'I don't want anything out of the ordinary to happen which may warn our man off. He may even go to ground if he sees any increased police presence in the station. I think you and your staff should just carry on as normal and leave everything else to us.

'As you wish, Mr Holmes. Good luck!' and with that he left.

Holmes urged, 'We should conceal ourselves behind that large chimneystack over there, Watson, and await our friend. Do you have your revolver with you?'

I nodded, 'I certainly do, and I hope he gives me reason to use it, the murdering scoundrel.'

Holmes replaced the leather bag behind the chimney where he had found it, but he kept the lens with him. 'Come along then. We must make ourselves as comfortable as possible for we may have a long wait, if he comes at all.'

We positioned ourselves where we were hidden from view, but could peep out and watch the access door. Sitting down in the shade of the chimney, I prepared myself for a boring sojourn. The morning wore on and soon the sun moved around so that now we were in its glare and it became uncomfortably hot. The hard unyielding roof was making my posterior numb so I removed my coat, folded it and, unmindful of the dirt, put it down and sat upon it. I leaned back against the brickwork and wished that I had brought a bottle of water to drink. I glanced at Holmes, who sat cross-legged and immobile. He had the patience of Job in situations like this. He reminded me of those Asian mystics

166

and fakirs who could meditate for hours in the blazing sun and be seemingly unaffected. I must have dozed off, for the next thing I knew was feeling a hand clamped over my mouth and another gripping my upper arm. I began to struggle and opened my eyes to find Holmes' face not six inches from my own.

He whispered, *'Not a sound, Watson, the game's afoot!'* I nodded and he released me. I peered cautiously round the chimney to see the access door swinging open. Next moment a tall, slim individual, dressed in a railway porter's uniform, stepped onto the roof. He glanced quickly about, and both Holmes and I ducked back under cover before he could spot us. Presently we heard his soft footfalls receding and we peered out again. The fellow headed straight to where the bag was hidden and bent to open it.

Holmes stepped out from behind our chimney and I followed him. The man had his back to us and, as he scrabbled inside his bag, Holmes asked, 'Could this be what you are looking for?' The man jumped with fright and whipped around to face us. He glanced at the lens in Holmes' hand, then snarled at us like an animal at bay. What hair he had was brown, and he seemed to be aged in his mid twenties, but I winced at the hideous burn scars that covered half his face and neck. His left eye was dragged down by the crimson scar tissue that distorted his features, and no hair grew on that side of his head. His dark eyes stared at us, then flitted to his only escape route, the access door.

Before he could make a dash for it Holmes warned, 'Don't try it, we are armed!'

I muttered, *'Damn!'* My pistol was still in the pocket of my coat, which I had left behind the chimney. Holmes glanced at me and knew instantly that I was unarmed.

The fellow also realised the fact and, with a sneer, he drew a pistol of his own and aimed it at us.

With a warning cry of, *'Look out, Watson!'* Holmes suddenly raised the lens and shot a concentrated beam of sunlight into the man's eyes. The gun went off and I heard the bullet whistle past my ear then ricochet off the chimneystack beside us.

The man let out a piercing scream as he dropped the gun to cover his eyes with his hands. He staggered backward a few feet, and the next moment he had tumbled over the low parapet and disappeared from view. There was a long-drawn-out wail, then a sickening thud as his body struck the ground. Holmes and I rushed to the edge and peered over. He was sprawled on the pavement below with his limbs askew like a broken doll, and I knew immediately that he was dead.

I turned to my friend to say, *'Well done, old fellow!* My stupidity in leaving the revolver behind almost cost us dear.'

He shook his head, 'I am as much to blame as you are; I saw you take off your coat and did not react. No matter, the main thing is that we have successfully ended the murderous career of this maniac.'

* * *

Later we reported the events to Inspector Lestrade at Scotland Yard, who was grudgingly apologetic towards Holmes.

All three of us confronted Damian Applegate again and Holmes asked, 'So why did you confess to these fires when in reality you had nothing to do with them?'

Applegate said, 'So you've got 'im then, 'ave you?'

Lestrade answered, 'Yes, but he's dead. What in God's name is going on?'

Applegate replied, 'I 'ad to lie low for a while, or I'd be lying on a slab in the morgue as well. I don't suppose you know Ruben Darnley, the owner of The Spinner's Arms? 'E's a big devil and mean as 'ell. 'E earned the cash to buy the pub as a bare-knuckle street fighter around Bermondsey. They say 'e killed two men in those fights. 'E was sure that I 'ad torched 'is place and killed 'is missus. I 'ad to get away until the real firebug was caught. Ruben wouldn't 'ave done me in cleanly; 'e would 'ave made me suffer first. I figured the one safe place 'e couldn't get me was in 'ere, but I knew that if I'd asked for police protection they would have laughed in my face.'

Lestrade argued, 'But if Mr Holmes had not found the real culprit, you would have been *hanged!*'

Damian shook his head, 'Not a chance! I 'ad iron-tight alibis for two of the fires and I knew the geezer would strike again.'

Holmes leaned back smiling, 'So, finally we hear the truth.'

In the cab on our way back to Baker Street I remarked, 'A somewhat resourceful fellow, our Mr Applegate.'

Holmes nodded, 'As you say, Watson, definitely one of life's survivors!'

Postscript:

Holmes, being interested in all aspects of crime and criminals, not least their motivation, took it upon himself to delve into the background of the 'Paddington Pyromaniac', as he came to be recorded in the case files. It transpired that although he wore the uniform of a railway porter, he was not in their employ. He was presumed to have stolen it. His name was Cedric Waller, and as a farm boy in Sussex he had been badly burned and very nearly died. He was remembered as having a morbid fascination with fire and was suspected of crop burning. Indeed there were those who said that the fire he nearly died in was of his own making. As he grew older he could make no headway with the fairer sex, because of his disfigurement, and he became embittered.

He drifted as an itinerant labourer until he reached London, where he worked in a warehouse near Paddington.

It was never discovered from where he had acquired the telescopic lens, which now resides in Holmes' little museum at 221B Baker Street.

THE MYSTERIOUS DISAPPEARANCE
OF THE GOOD SHIP ALICIA

The Alicia

$\mathbf{A}$mongst the papers in my tin dispatch box, usually kept in the vaults of Cox and Co., are many of the unsolved cases of Sherlock Holmes. Just occasionally the great man is able to finally fill in some missing detail and solve one of the mysteries, after a lapse of some years. However, that was not the situation with this case; the Alicia file languished in the box for an altogether different reason. Although the Official Secrets Act was not in existence prior to the Great War, if it had been, Sherlock Holmes would most certainly have been required to sign it before undertaking the bizarre case of the Alicia. Indeed, as if in anticipation of the Act, the Admiralty imposed a strict prohibition of twenty years on Holmes not to reveal the details of the case to the general public. Those twenty years expired last month, so I now feel able to recount the incredible details of the case at long last.

* * *

The bare bones of the event may be summed up in one terse sentence. The Alicia sailed, one spring morning, into a patch of mist and was never seen again! The annals of mysterious happenings at sea are legion. The disappearance of every soul on board the drifting Mary Celeste. The loss of the barque, Sophie Anderson. The sinking of the SS Phoenix off the Cape Verde islands dragged under by a fearful sea monster, according to eyewitness accounts. The list goes on, but of all of them perhaps the most bizarre was the Alicia, for not only did she disappear from the surface of the sea, *she could not be found on the sea bed either!*

She was on the last leg of a voyage from South Africa to England. As she neared the coast of Portugal, she was seen to sail into a bank of sea mist by lookouts on board the SS Vagabond, bound for Tangiers. The two ships were so close that they were almost within hailing distance and the respective crews even waved to each other. But the Alicia did not reappear out of the mist. The lookouts aboard the Vagabond raised the alarm and their skipper, Captain Jacobs, took bearings from Cap St. Jorge, barely two miles distant, before putting about. The sea was calm and the strengthening sunshine soon burned off the sea mist, but there was no sign of the cutter. The Vagabond quartered the area searching for survivors, but there was nothing to indicate that a ship had even been there. They found not the smallest piece of flotsam. Captain Jacobs wrote up the incident in the Vagabond's log as possibly a 'phantom ship', i.e. the sea mirage of another ship miles away.

This was largely the account that appeared in the newspapers at the time, but recently Holmes has been able to acquaint me with much of the surprising background to the tale.

In 1877 the British Empire annexed the Transvaal and seized tons of gold bullion and uncut diamonds from the Limpopo mines in the Witwatersrand area of South Africa. In 1880 the Transvaal declared itself a republic, and after the British defeat at Majuba in 1881, steps were taken to ship this fabulous treasure to England.

The value of the hoard has been variously estimated to be between five and ten million pounds! In a top-secret naval operation, the treasure was loaded onto the cutter Alicia, which then set sail for England. Unfortunately, because the exercise *was* so secret, the cargo could not be insured. Indeed it is doubtful that Lloyds would have agreed to underwrite such a risk, even if they *had* been invited to.

Holmes himself became involved at the request of his brother Mycroft who, in his capacity as adviser to their Lordships of the Admiralty, recommended his sibling as *'The only man in England who might reasonably be expected to unravel such a complete mystery'*.

I believe I can do no better than to reproduce here Holmes' report to the Admiralty of his investigation, in its entirety.

To Admiral Sir Benjamin Bryant,
1ˢᵗ Sea Lord and Chief of the Naval Staff,
Admiralty House,
London

FOR YOUR EYES ONLY

Sir,

As requested, I respectfully submit the following report of my investigation into the disappearance of the Cutter Alicia on the 12th of May 1882.

Paragraph 1) is a re-iteration of the information presented to me by Naval Intelligence, upon which this report is based.

1) The Alicia disappeared with all hands at 8-30 a.m. on the date mentioned, two miles off Cap St. Jorge, Portugal in eight to ten fathoms of water. No trace of ship or crew has been seen since.

In view of the sensitive nature, not to say value, of the cargo every endeavour has been made by the Royal Navy, including the deployment of divers, to locate the ship. However, even in such shallow water, with calm seas and good visibility the divers reported the seabed to be completely empty.

2) Speculation as to the cause of the disappearance includes the possibility that the ship struck a submerged rock or reef. This has been discounted since there are no reefs shown on any sea charts for the area and the divers confirm that the seabed, at the known co-ordinates, is featureless flat sand and silt in every direction. Another speculation concerns the possibility that the Alicia was pirated for her treasure and her seacocks opened. This is patently impossible since there would not have been enough time to transfer the treasure to another vessel and sail away, out of sight of the Vagabond, before the mist lifted. Furthermore the wreck should still have been detectable on the sea floor. Further conjecture envisages the ship being rammed below her water line, by an enemy submarine, and towed away underwater. I believe we can safely discount the last scenario as being more in the realms of fantasy than fact.

3) My extensive enquiries, amongst seafarers that regularly sail these waters, have revealed that the area in question has a long history of strange phenomena. More than one told of St. Elmo's fire dancing among the rigging on dark nights off the Cape. Another talked of sea birds falling dead out of the sky to land in the sea or onto the decks. The region has gained such notoriety for its bizarre mysteries that it is variously called 'Poseidon's Pit' or the 'Devil's Cauldron'.

Part of my research into the area involved visits to the Maritime Museum, Lloyds and the British Museum. It now seems that the 'Devil's Cauldron' is an apt name because I have found that no fewer than 37 ships of all types, including a Roman galley, have sunk there over the centuries and only a few of these were caught in storms. In 1605 a full-rigged Spanish galleon, the Santo Domingo, was said to have been consumed by the 'Fires of Hell' as the sea itself burst into flames. In 1710 villagers, in the little fishing village of Cameno, watched from the shore as the night sky was turned crimson by the 'Incendio Del Mare' or 'Fire of the Sea'!

Seamen talk of seeing the surface of the sea heave and spew and of smelling the brimstone of the Devil's breath when all around was flat-calm and windless. We have all heard of such myths and legends. Indeed they are part of the folklore of the sea, but in my experience there is very often a grain of truth amongst the chaff of superstition.

4) I have long held to the axiom that when all other possibilities have been excluded, whatever remains, however improbable, must be the truth.

In short, Sir Benjamin, I believe that the solution to the mysterious disappearance of the Alicia can be summed up in one word: Gas!

It has been known for centuries that pockets of firedamp (or Methane, to give it its proper name) can be trapped under the earth. I know of a place in the Carpathian Hills where the steady release of such flammable gas fuels a fire that has burned among the rocks for decades. The place is well known among local shepherds and goatherds, who regularly warm themselves at the flames on cold winter days.

If gas can be trapped under terrestrial rocks, then why not under the seabed? One may then ask, how can gas sink a ship? Perhaps at this juncture you will permit me a little reprise on the basic principles of hydrodynamics.

As you well know, objects and substances float if their specific gravity is less than one. (The specific gravity of water.) A ship such as the Alicia, whilst built largely of wood, has however a specific gravity far greater than one and would sink if it were not for her displacement of seawater. (The well known Archimedean Principle.) If a stream of bubbles directly beneath the ship aerates the water supporting the vessel, the displacement principle is immediately and catastrophically destroyed and the ship will sink like a stone!

I have verified this phenomenon myself with model ships in the great water tank at the Oxford University physics laboratory. (The test results are appended for your inspection.)

When the bubbles rise up to the hull there is no warning, no gradual listing or capsizing. She goes under in seconds!

This is, I believe, what happened to the cutter.

Consider the evidence:

a) Sea birds falling dead from the sky? Rather like the canaries we use down our own coal mines to warn us of the same gas!

b) The Incendio Del Mare, or Fire of the Sea? With such huge eruptions of Methane all that is required is a flash of lightning or a lighted ship's lantern and Presto! The sea itself appears to blaze!

c) The Devil's breath making the surface of the sea heave and roil when there is no wind? Merely the eruption and bubbling of tons of escaping gas!

d) The smell of Brimstone on the Devil's breath? Methane smells sulphurous, as I'm sure you will know if you have ever smelled it!

So far so good, but now we come to what is perhaps the most perplexing aspect of the whole mystery. Why was there no sign of the sunken ship on the sea floor? For the answer to this enigma we must return again to our basic physics.

When a sinking ship settles onto the seabed, her mass will compress the sand and silt beneath her hull until it becomes compacted enough to bear her weight. She may sink several feet into the mud before this point is reached, but the bulk of the vessel should still be visible.

If, however, escaping gas is agitating the sand, the same principle as the displacement of water applies and the ship can not be supported. Sand and silt will be continuously distributed around and over the vessel, which will sink ever deeper into the mire to be eventually totally buried.

No one knows how deep these deposits are, but since they have been forming for millions of years they must be substantial. Enough, I maintain, to swallow a large number of vessels and leave no trace.

In conclusion then, Sir Benjamin, and in spite of the fact that, by the very nature of these events, I can offer no tangible proof of my assertions, I am totally convinced in my own mind that this is what happened to the good ship Alicia.

You can discount piracy, enemy action or the like in the almost certain knowledge that the cutter, with cruel luck, sailed into an intermittent submarine gas eruption and sank.

The other harsh twist of fate was that the bubbling and frothing of the surface of the sea was hidden from human eyes by a bank of sea mist!

By the time the mist had cleared, the eruption was over and the mystery complete.

Notwithstanding the loss of so great a treasure, the greater loss, to my mind, was the death by drowning of so many good men who never stood a chance.

Respectfully Yours,
Sherlock Holmes.
Consulting Detective.
221b Baker Street,
London

CATACAUSIS EBRIOSUS

It was in the third year of my eventful association with the remarkable Sherlock Holmes that this singular case transpired. To say that it was one of the most unusual events I have ever experienced would be a gross understatement. It was, for me, quite simply unique.

It began one afternoon in late autumn with the unannounced arrival of Inspector Lestrade at 221b Baker Street. After the usual greetings Holmes remarked, 'For once, Inspector, you do not seek my professional help. That much is evident from your relaxed manner and the twinkle in your eye.'

Lestrade smiled and replied, 'As usual you are quite right, Mr Holmes. I am here to invite you both to witness a scene you may never again in your lives behold. If you gentlemen have nothing more pressing I urge you to accompany me to Bethnal Green. My carriage awaits,' and he swept his arm towards the door. Immediately intrigued, Holmes and I quickly donned our outer garments and followed Lestrade downstairs. The inspector would not be drawn further on the journey other than to say, 'I myself have never before encountered this phenomenon and I would be amazed if either of you have. Ah, here we are now.'

The cab had pulled up outside a large terraced house of the kind that is often converted into several flats. A police constable, stationed at the front door, was holding back a small crowd of onlookers and two vociferous newspaper reporters. The constable saluted Lestrade as he led us past the cordon and up the stairs to the top floor. I noticed a pungent odour as we neared the second door on the right. Here, too, a uniformed officer stood guard. He saluted before opening the door wide.

Lestrade stepped to one side and motioned us to enter, saying, 'Brace yourselves, gentlemen!'

Holmes strode forward into the room and I heard him gasp. I was now consumed with a curiosity that was tinged with trepidation as I followed my friend inside. The first thing that struck me was the smell. It was a foetid oily stench that almost made me retch. The room was filled with a smoky haze, and the gloom was heightened by the dimness of the light that filtered through windows coated with a thin brownish layer of grease. All around the room, above a level of perhaps three or four feet, the walls were covered in a layer of oily soot. So, too, were the ceiling, gas lamps, mirror and clock.

'Fascinating!' Holmes muttered, as he crouched to study something on the floor by the fireplace. 'Simply fascinating.'

I peered over his shoulder and was horrified to see the charred remains of a female human body. All that was left were the extremities and the skull. There was still flesh on the arms and lower legs and the shoes were untouched. Everything else had been reduced to a pile of ash.

Holmes turned to me and said, 'My first-ever encounter with *Catacausis Ebriosus*, Watson!'

'Good Lord!' I exclaimed. *'Spontaneous human combustion?'*

Holmes nodded, 'Unless I'm very much mistaken.'

Lestrade concurred, saying, 'I knew you gentlemen would be interested to see it before the poor unfortunate lady's remains are disturbed. The Yard's photographers have recorded all the details.'

Holmes remarked, 'See how precise is the demarcation between burned and unburned,' and he pointed to a small pile of kindling in the hearth, which was untouched by the flames, and a pair of knitting needles in the woman's hand. The small woollen garment she had been knitting was not even scorched.

I said, 'I can scarcely believe that a fire intense enough to reduce the rib bones and spine to ash has not consumed the whole building.'

Lestrade nodded, 'As you say, Doctor, it's almost unbelievable.'

Holmes asked, 'How old would you say she was, Watson?'

I studied the teeth in the skull and touched her arm before replying, 'Judging by her teeth and the tone and condition of the flesh on her legs and arms, I would put her age at between 20 and 30 years.'

Lestrade confirmed my estimate, saying, 'Very good, Doctor, she was in fact 27 years old. Her name was Alice Murphy, a seamstress at Collins and Company. She lived here alone.'

Holmes was studying the skull, from which all the hair and flesh had been burned. 'What have we here then?' he murmured as he indicated a circular depressed fracture to the left-hand parietal bone.

Lestrade replied, 'Obviously she struck her head on the fender when she fell.' I nodded in agreement, for the black iron fender had brass corner knobs of just the right size, and her skull lay alongside one.

Holmes muttered, 'Not necessarily.'

Lestrade smiled and said, 'I think we can definitely rule out foul play this time. I'm aware of your inclination to look for mysteries even when there are none, Mr Holmes, but this bears all the classic signs of genuine spontaneous human combustion.'

To forestall any argument developing, I quickly interjected, 'I've read of the phenomenon, of course, but I still don't understand how the human body, which is perhaps 80 per cent water, *can* spontaneously ignite.'

Holmes stood up and asked, 'Who found her and at what time?'

The inspector consulted his notebook and replied, 'Her landlady, Mrs Bennett, found her at first light. The lady was alarmed at the smell of smoke and the lack of any response to her repeated knocking at the door. She let herself in, with her passkey, to find this horrendous scene. The poor woman has not yet fully recovered.'

I said, 'I'm not surprised.'

Holmes suggested, 'There is speculation that a lightning strike has enough energy to produce such results.'

I countered, 'I've examined the victim of one such strike and, whilst I agree that there *is* more than enough energy in a typical lightning bolt, the actual damage caused is different. The skin is burnt, the heart and nervous system usually shut down and I've seen bones broken by the massive muscle-spasms induced, but the body is never consumed like this. Indeed many victims survive the experience'

Lestrade observed, 'In any case there is no evidence that lightning has struck this room, and there was no storm last night.'

I asked, 'What about fireballs or ball lightning? That seems to occur about as infrequently as human combustion. Perhaps there is a connection between them?'

Holmes shook his head, saying, 'All the accounts I have read concerning fireballs seem to indicate that they are ethereal, will-o'-the-wisps that can pass through windows or walls, but do not burn people to ash.'

I pointed out, 'It does not seem likely that her clothing accidentally caught fire because such victims rush hither and thither beating at the flames. Yet here she lies with her knitting still in her hand.'

'An excellent observation, Watson,' Holmes enthused, 'I could not have bettered it myself.'

I felt a glow of satisfaction at this praise from the master of deduction himself.

Taking his handkerchief, Holmes wiped the soot from the face of the clock on the mantelpiece. The hands stood at 11-15 and this was one timepiece that would never tick again. He commented; 'The intense heat stopped the clock, so we know roughly when the fire approached its peak.' Turning to Lestrade he asked, 'Did Miss Murphy have any visitors last night?'

'I have not asked the question. The room was locked and no one had forced an entry. There was no commotion and no indication of a struggle. I repeat, I have no reason to suspect foul play.'

Holmes suggested, 'Perhaps we might ask Mrs Bennett. After all, it is as well to eliminate all other possibilities.'

Lestrade sighed with resignation. 'Very well, Mr Holmes, if you insist. This way,' and he led us downstairs to see Miss

Murphy's landlady. She was a grey-haired woman of matronly appearance in her fifties and was sitting on a sofa being comforted by a neighbour.

Lestrade said, 'I'm sorry to bother you again, Mrs Bennett, but this gentleman would like to ask you a few questions, if you don't mind. His name is Mr Sherlock Holmes.'

She dabbed her eyes with a handkerchief and replied, 'Yes of course. Would you gentlemen like a cup of tea?'

We all declined and Holmes said sympathetically, 'A terrible tragedy, Mrs Bennett. Tell me, how long was Miss Murphy a tenant of yours?'

'Two years.'

'Was she prompt with her rent?'

'Oh yes. Every Friday regular as clockwork.'

'Did she have many visitors?'

'No, apart from her man friend, Seamus.'

'You met him?'

'No, not really. I saw him coming or going from time to time, but he was always muffled up with a cloth cap over his eyes.'

'Was he indeed? Would you recognise him again?'

'I doubt it. He was as tall as you are sir, and spoke with an Irish accent. He always carried a walking stick.'

'Did he arrive on foot or by cab?'

'By cab.'

'Was he dressed as a gentleman?'

'No, more like a workman, but clean and neat.'

'Did he visit last night?'

'I didn't see him, but he might have. About nine o'-clock I went down to the Royal Oak for a nip of gin.'

'Did Miss Murphy drink gin to your knowledge?'

'Lord no! She was always against drink and drunkenness.'

'Indeed. Well thank you, Mrs Bennett, that's all I need to know. I hope you soon recover from this terrible shock.'

Lestrade walked us through to the hall, and Holmes asked him, 'Have the Metropolitan Police ever dealt with a similar case?'

The inspector nodded. 'Very few. The most recent was about sixteen years ago, before I joined the force. An elderly obese woman in Soho was discovered in similar circumstances. She was found sitting in an armchair, with an empty bottle of gin on the floor beside her. There was precious little left of the chair except the frame and springs, but her lower legs including her slippers were undamaged.'

Holmes nodded. 'I've read of several cases, documented in France, which were similar. Indeed, there are those who advocate that the empyreumatic oils, in the gin that fills the stomachs of these victims, is what fuels the fires.'

'As you say, Mr Holmes.'

'Would it be possible for me to see the records of this Soho incident?'

Lestrade nodded. 'Of course. If you call in at the Yard tomorrow morning I will arrange it.' As we stepped onto the pavement an impressive monogrammed carriage drew up behind Lestrade's cab and a stately figure stepped down. Lestrade immediately stood to attention and saluted smartly, as did the duty constable. Holmes whispered to me, 'Police Commissioner Sir James Marlowe; I wonder what he's doing here?' The fellow was tall and distinguished-looking in his frock coat and top hat. His beard was flecked with grey; he carried black leather gloves in one hand and a silver-headed ebony cane in the other. His grey cravat was held in place by a diamond pin and he strode forward imperiously.

'Ah, there you are, Lestrade. Dennison said you were investigating another of these mysterious blazes, and I was just passing by. A frightful business, eh what?'

'Decidedly so, sir. May I present Mr Sherlock Holmes and Dr Watson?'

We shook hands, and the Commissioner smiled and said, 'We meet at last, Mr Holmes. I'm well aware that you have assisted the Yard on several occasions.'

Holmes bowed slightly and responded, 'It has been my pleasure and my duty, sir.'

Turning to Lestrade, Sir James enquired a little querulously, 'You have asked for Mr Holmes' help here?'

'No, sir. The case is straightforward. Merely as a gesture of professional courtesy, I invited these gentlemen to witness a very rare event.'

The Commissioner relaxed, 'Capital. We don't want to turn this into some kind of fairground freak show. Let's wrap it up as quickly as possible, eh what?'

Lestrade asked, 'Do you wish to examine the scene, sir?'

Sir James looked a little squeamish and replied, 'No, that won't be necessary. Carry on Inspector.' He turned to the constable and instructed him to try to disperse the crowd. Then tipping his hat to us, he said, 'A very good day to you, gentlemen,' before boarding his carriage and being driven away.

We took our leave of the inspector, and Holmes said, 'Until tomorrow then, Lestrade.'

Soon we were heading back to Baker Street in a hansom, and I remarked, 'Another first then, Holmes?'

'Indeed. I remember reading about Old Krook, in Dickens' *Bleak House,* who dies in like manner, but I never really believed that one day I should encounter the phenomenon myself.' He was thoughtful for a while before continuing; 'I'm not entirely convinced about Lestrade's conclusions, Watson.'

'I rather gathered that. You suspect foul play?'

'I'm probably being overzealous, but there *are* aspects of this case that trouble me.'

'Such as?'

'Well, most of the incidents documented involve older, more sedentary people. Usually overweight, therefore with more fat to burn, and almost invariably they were heavy spirit drinkers. The greater part of all the French examples are linked to "spirituous liquors" i.e. brandy. Yet here we have a young slim woman, who does not drink, being struck down.'

'I suppose there are always exceptions to every rule,' I countered.

'I have some notions of my own concerning this paradox of water-rich human bodies becoming flaming torches.'

I nodded and said, 'I rather thought you might have, old chap.'

Holmes promptly stopped the cab and jumped out, saying, 'I've a few enquiries to make, Watson. I'll see you presently at Baker Street,' and with that he hurried away in the opposite direction. He was not gone for long and returned to announce, 'Watson, I've just spent the most macabre hour of my life, at the Borough crematorium, in the company of one Sidney Billings, the chief furnace operator. Apparently the sequence of events, when a body burns, is as follows. Firstly the hair ignites and burns with a blue flame, the head snaps back and the mouth opens. Then bizarrely the body actually tries to sit up as the tendons shrink. Bones start to explode when the temperature reaches 700 or 800 degrees Fahrenheit.'

'Dear God, Holmes! I wish you had not told me. I don't believe that I shall ever rid myself of the mental images you've engendered.'

'Sorry, old fellow, but you see my point? The difference between a cremation and what happened to Alice Murphy is that in the former the bones explode, they are *not* reduced to ash.'

I argued, 'They *must* be, Holmes, for are they not routinely scattered or kept in an urn?'

He shook his head. 'No, Doctor. The broken bones are ground to ash in a machine called a 'Cremulator', which is something else I was unaware of.'

'Well, I'll be damned!'

'So you see, a completely different process is at work here, and I intend to find out what.'

The following day he returned from Scotland Yard saying, 'That other incident in Soho many years ago makes me more determined than ever to discover just what is going on here, Watson, and I'm not at all surprised that Sir James was not inclined to inspect the scene.'

'Why is that then?'

'The young officer in charge of that investigation was none other than Inspector James Marlowe of K Division, on the lower rungs of the ladder towards Police Commissioner.'

I nodded. 'Of course, that would explain his reluctance. I don't believe that *I* would rush to see another such scene myself, if given the choice.'

I hardly saw Holmes for the next two days, then one afternoon he returned to Baker Street smudged with soot and carrying a lantern. He urged, 'Come, Watson, the game's afoot!' I followed him to an empty property, on nearby George Street, and he led me down to the cellar. My nostrils were again assailed by that oily odour.

I exclaimed in horror, 'Don't tell me that you are burning a *corpse*, Holmes?'

'Of course, Doctor. How else to test my theory? But fear not, it is only the body of a suckling pig, bought from our local butcher for this express purpose!' I sighed with relief and peered in through the doorway. The interior was so gloomy that all I could discern was a pile of glowing ash in the middle of the concrete floor.

Holmes stepped forward and held his lantern aloft. He explained, 'I chose a pig because its fat content is similar to a human's. Indeed the cannibals of the South Seas used to call their human victims *Long Pig*.'

After the smoke had cleared somewhat I could make out the remains of the animal, and the similarity to what had happened to the luckless Miss Murphy was striking. The bulk of the creature, including its ribs and spine, had been reduced to a calcined ash with just the legs and skull remaining. I was amazed and said as much.

'How did you achieve this, Holmes?'

He replied, 'From the very start I suspected that the clothes a person wears could act like the wick of a candle to support first the rendering and then the burning of subcutaneous fat. Therefore I wrapped the pig in a small blanket and set it alight. All this without the aid of gin, I might add. As you can see, the portion with the most fat burned up completely, but the bony lower legs and skull were spared.'

'How is it that the fire still burned even when virtually all the oxygen in the room was exhausted?'

'An excellent question, Doctor, and one that troubled me also. As I'm sure you recall the door and windows of the room in Bethnal Green were all closed, yet the fire continued to burn. It was this very question which demanded my little experiment. Look!' Here he pointed to several candles he had placed about the floor. 'I lit these candles at the same time as the blanket and watched developments through this crack in the door. These buckets of water here were to ensure things did not get out of hand.'

'So what happened?'

'At first the blanket burned brightly and the wick effect began to work. A thick black smoke rose to partly fill the room and began to deposit the soot you see on the ceiling and the walls. It was a slow process and very boring, but gradually, as the oxygen in the room became depleted, the flames died down and one by one the candles went out. However, this is the most incredible part, *the pig continued to burn!* It seemed to me that a form of anaerobic charring was taking place, which eventually reduced everything to ash. I do believe I shall write a paper on the subject one day.'

'This is truly incredible, Holmes.'

'Isn't it just?'

'So are you convinced that Miss Murphy died this way?'

'I'm convinced that this is what happened to her body at least. As to the actual cause of death I will need more information.'

I helped Holmes to clear the remains from the cellar and we used the buckets of water to sluice the floor. I confess that I was relieved to finally vacate the place, convinced all the time that a constable would discover us and charge us with trespassing.

Holmes was absent for most of the next day, but returned after teatime to say, 'Come, Watson, I must disguise us both.'

'Whatever for?'

'I have enlisted the help of a certain Miss Annie Cox, a friend of the late Miss Murphy, who also worked as a seamstress at Collins and Company. We are going to meet her this evening at the Royal Oak.' He then set about radically altering both our appearances.

As he worked, with false beards and make-up, he explained, 'I met and questioned Miss Cox, and she told me that Alice had confided in her that her friend, Seamus, is a married man. He had promised Alice that he would divorce his wife and settle down with her, but months wore on and nothing happened. When Alice tried to force the issue, Seamus became belligerent and threatened the girl. I asked how Alice communicated with Seamus, since he is married, and it seems that they corresponded via the personal column of the *Evening Standard*. That gave me an idea, and Miss Cox has agreed to assist me in carrying it out.' Holmes handed me that evening's copy of the newspaper, which was folded open at the personal column page. 'Look under Seamus,' he instructed.

I looked and read, *'Seamus, Alice told me everything. Meet me in the Royal Oak at nine p.m. I will be there tonight and tomorrow night only and will be wearing a red shawl. Annie.'*

I asked, 'Why do we need to be disguised? Seamus won't know us.'

Holmes smiled and replied, 'The Royal Oak is a workingman's pub with some rough and ready patrons. We would stand out like sore thumbs. I wish to observe without being observed and, since I am not exactly unknown in London, the disguises should ensure we attract no attention.'

Eight-thirty that evening saw Holmes and I seated at the bar of the Royal Oak. I looked at our reflections in the long mirror behind the bar and could hardly recognise either of us. We looked like a couple of bricklayers or millwrights in our rough working clothes and flat caps.

Behind us, sitting by the fireplace, I could see Annie in her red shawl, sipping her glass of beer and glancing nervously about. Nine o'-clock came and went and still we sat there. The noise level, in the busy inn, grew steadily and about ten o'-clock the first fight broke out. Amid the confusion a man approached Annie and bent down to speak to her. Holmes nudged my arm and we watched, poised for action. The fellow was obviously drunk, and seeing an unescorted woman alone was definitely interested. He sat down next to her and put his arm around her shoulder. She pushed him away, but he was not to be dissuaded so easily.

I heard him say, 'Come on, give us a little kiss, me beauty.'

Holmes strode over, dragged the fellow away and said roughly, 'Push off and leave my missus alone before I black both your eyes!'

Immediately the man was contrite. 'Sorry, guv, no offence. Didn't know she was wiv you.' Holmes winked at Annie and rejoined me at the bar. We waited another hour, but Seamus did not appear. We arranged to repeat the exercise the following night before seeing Annie safely home in a cab.

Once again we sat at the bar and watched Annie in the mirror. Holmes said quietly, 'If Seamus does not put in an appearance this time, then we must assume that he has nothing to hide and I shall be proven to have been overzealous in suspecting foul play in the first place.'

However, this time we did not have long to wait before a tall individual in a long black overcoat and cap approached Annie. He had his back to us and he bent forward and spoke quietly to her. She shook her head, but he gripped her arm and hauled her to her feet. I made to stand up, but Holmes placed a restraining hand on my arm.

'Not yet, Watson,' he whispered. The man led Annie out through the door and she threw a worried glance in our direction. '*Now, Watson!*' Holmes urged and leapt off his stool. We both ran after them and out into the street. He was dragging the struggling girl towards an alleyway a few yards away.

Holmes shouted, '*Leave her be, Seamus!* Or do you prefer the anglicised version- James?'

The fellow spun around to face us, and I was stunned to see none other than the police commissioner, Sir James Marlowe himself, glaring back at us. He held tightly on to Annie's wrist with his left hand and with his right he drew a revolver from his pocket and pointed it at us.

'Stay back!' he growled.

Holmes said, in a measured voice, 'Put away your gun, Sir James. How many more murders must you commit to cover up the first one? Will you shoot the good Doctor Watson here?' As he spoke he pulled off his fake beard, and I did the same.

The Commissioner's face registered total surprise. '*Holmes!*' he blurted.

My friend continued, 'Will you kill me and the innocent young woman beside you also?' Marlowe looked around wildly. It was evident the fellow was desperate and I had genuine fears for the safety of us all.

Holmes said, in those same calm tones, 'Don't compound the deed. You know in your heart of hearts that it's all over.' Still Marlowe would not concede. His eyes had a manic light in them, and I could sense he was ready to try something desperate. I had seen that same look in the eyes of soldiers in battle, and I fully expected the worst.

Holmes too could sense it, and he made one last plea, 'If not for our sake then for the memory of your unborn child, man!' Sir James suddenly crumpled before our eyes. He let go of Annie's wrist and lowered the gun. Tears rolled down his cheeks and he began to sob uncontrollably. Miss Cox ran to me and I threw a protective arm around her shoulders.

Sir James sank to his knees and bowed his head. 'What have I done?' he sobbed, 'What have I done?' He raised his tear-streaked face to Holmes and whispered, 'Thank you, Mr Holmes.' Then before any of us could react, he placed the muzzle of the pistol against his temple and pulled the trigger. I just had time to prevent Miss Cox from witnessing it by thrusting myself in front of her. Blood and brain matter were splattered against the wall, and he fell sideways, jerking convulsively. I told Miss Cox not to look, and Holmes and I bent to check on him. He was, of course, quite dead.

A woman behind us started to scream, and men piled out of the Royal Oak to see what all the commotion was about. Holmes took a police whistle from his pocket and gave several long blasts on it. Within minutes two constables were on the scene and taking charge. Holmes told them who we were and insisted that they should get Inspector Lestrade here at once.

The three of us repaired to the bar of the Royal Oak and Holmes ordered double whiskies for each of us. Never have I needed such a drink more. When Lestrade finally arrived, we all withdrew to the landlord's private room at the Inspector's insistence.

When the four of us were alone, Lestrade demanded, 'What in God's good name happened here?'

Holmes replied, 'The Commissioner killed Alice Murphy to prevent her telling the world that they were lovers. I expect Sir James could not stand the thought of losing everything he had achieved. His marriage, his family, his reputation and his career. It is not difficult to imagine his desperation.'

'How do you know all this?'

'I was concerned that the circular depressed fracture to the side of Miss Murphy's skull might not have been caused by her head striking the fender. I noticed that the silver knob on Sir James' ebony cane was exactly the same size as the brass knobs on the fender. Of course on its own that was merely speculation, but when the Commissioner seemed relieved that I was not to be involved in the investigation, I began to have my suspicions. Also, why would the Commissioner just happen to be passing the scene? I am always suspicious of coincidences. Finally, when I discovered that it was Sir James himself who had investigated the Soho blaze death, I was convinced that the possibility should be considered. The Commissioner was a very intelligent man and could easily have deduced, as I did, that the wick effect of a victim's clothes could account for spontaneous human combustion. By staging the scene we witnessed, he could eliminate the threats to his way of life and status by literally getting away with murder. I still did not know for sure that this was what had transpired. Therefore I had to fool the murderer into incriminating himself, so I contrived this little tableau with the aid of a very brave Miss Cox.'

I asked, 'But what was that you said to Sir James about his unborn child?'

Holmes sighed and replied, 'Alice Murphy was expecting the Commissioner's illegitimate child.'

Lestrade asked, 'How on earth could you know that?'

'I didn't know for sure and it *was* a bit of a gamble, but the little woollen garment that Alice had been knitting was for a newborn baby. Also I had noticed in the middle of the charred remains, away from ribs and backbone, a tiny amount of fine ash that could once have been a foetus.'

'My God!' I murmured. Then after a while I said, 'I suppose Marlowe had a key to the flat, since it was locked when Mrs Bennett tried the door.'

Holmes responded, 'I would be more surprised if the Commissioner did *not* have a key, Watson. After all, they had been lovers for some time, so it would be only natural that he should have a key of his own.'

Lestrade looked stunned. 'What on earth do I say to Mrs Marlowe? To learn that her husband has committed suicide is bad enough, but to compound it by telling her that he was also a murderer and an adulterer… ye gods!'

I pointed out, 'A *double* murderer. He also killed an unborn baby.'

Lestrade nodded forlornly. 'As you say, Doctor.'

Holmes was thoughtful for a few moments, then said, 'No good can come of it if the truth is told. The Commissioner's wife and family don't deserve to suffer for *his* sins.' Here he passed Sir James' pistol to Lestrade, saying, 'I slipped this into my pocket before the constables or any onlookers arrived. Only the four of us in this room know that he took his own life. He could have been on an important undercover operation, hence his rough clothing, and was shot by an unknown assailant.'

Lestrade looked at Holmes with something akin to awe. 'That is *brilliant,* Mr Holmes. I would be forever in your debt if we could explain it that way.' He turned to me questioningly.

I shrugged, 'Why not? As Holmes says, to what end should more innocents suffer?'

'Miss Cox?'

She nodded. 'Yes, I agree.'

Holmes said, 'As far as the world is concerned, Alice Murphy *was* just another victim of spontaneous human combustion.' Turning to me, he added, 'I won't be able to write that paper on the subject after all, Watson.'

I shook my head, 'Not for some time at least, Holmes.'

'Don't forget to search Marlowe's pockets for that key, Inspector,' Holmes instructed.

Lestrade looked like a man reprieved. It was as if a great weight had been lifted from his shoulders. He shook hands with each of us in turn saying, 'Thank you, thank you all very, very much!'

We escorted Miss Cox home safely and Holmes thanked her profusely for the part she had played. When we were in the cab heading back to Baker Street, I said, 'There is just one minor point, old fellow.'

'And that is?'

'Mrs Bennett said that Seamus spoke with an Irish accent, yet Sir James is, or rather was, quintessentially English.'

Holmes smiled and replied, 'An Irish accent is perhaps one of the easiest to mimic. In fact I can do a passable rendition of it myself,' and he proceeded to demonstrate. He was very good, and I could not but laugh when I heard him. It was the perfect balm for the depressing events we had both just experienced.

FOOTNOTE: Holmes wrote his paper on *Catacausis Ebriosus*, but he never did have it published and it languishes at the bottom of my tin dispatch box in the vaults of Cox and Co.

THE PRODIGAL QUEST

Readers of these chronicles, relating to the exploits of my good friend Sherlock Holmes, may not be entirely aware that I very often change the names of affected parties. The most obvious reason being, of course, to preserve client confidentiality. In this instance however, I could not follow my usual practice and the individuals involved in this account are truly named. Each of the survivors, for these events took place many years ago, has given written permission to be so named, and I record here my grateful thanks to those concerned.

The reasons for departing from the norm will, I'm sure, become evident as the facts of this intriguing case are laid bare. Though it happened back in the year 1881, I remember it as clearly as if it were yesterday. It was not long after I had moved into 221b Baker Street to lodge with Sherlock Holmes. On that particular evening I was deeply engrossed in *'The latest surgical techniques for limb amputation'* being cited in the current medical journal, and Holmes was diligently writing a monograph entitled *'On the dating of manuscripts'.* For once the bustle and hubbub normally associated with this part of London in general and Baker Street in particular was much reduced, due in part to the weather, for it was very cold, and the lateness of the hour for it was nigh on nine in the evening. You may imagine then our surprise and not a little annoyance at hearing the ringing of the doorbell and subsequent footsteps on the stairs.

Holmes muttered, 'I knew it was too good to last!' I sighed, nodded in agreement and put aside my journal. Next moment an apologetic Mrs Hudson was introducing our visitor to us as Mr Justin Clearwater. As we shook hands he also apologised profusely for the intrusion at such a late hour, but insisted his problem was a pressing one. As if in reproach of our intruder the clock on the mantelpiece chimed the hour and, in the distance, Big Ben echoed it.

Holmes remarked, 'You're a long way from home, Mr Clearwater.'

The young man looked at Holmes in surprise and replied, 'Please call me Justin, and yes, I am a long way from home. The other side of the world, in fact. How did you know?'

Holmes pointed out, 'Your antipodean accent, though slight, is unmistakable, and winter here means summer there, hence your healthy-looking tan.'

The lad nodded, 'Quite right, Mr Holmes. I'm from Brisbane and have worked my passage aboard ship to reach England.' Holmes raised an eyebrow but said nothing.

Clearwater was a robust individual with brown wavy hair, a strong chin and a hint of ruddiness beneath his tan. His clothes bore testimony to his words, for they were worn and patched and he carried a somewhat moth-eaten peaked cap in his hand. His eyes were green and he was clean-shaven. I estimated his age at around twenty-five or so. He continued, 'This is by way of being a 'return of the prodigal' or at least a second-generation version of it, for I have undertaken this journey because my father would never do so.'

Justin Clearwater

Holmes looked intrigued and, leading Justin to a chair, said, 'Pray tell us your story then, for it promises to be interesting.'

Once seated he began, 'I am searching for my roots, Mr Holmes, and I have precious little to go on. My father never wanted me to make this journey, and before he died he did everything in his power to dissuade me, but I am much like him and have inherited his own stubborn streak.'

Holmes pointed out, 'Clearwater is not such a common surname; it should be relatively straightforward to trace your immediate family.'

Justin shook his head. 'Would that it were so simple; unfortunately, Clearwater is *not* the family name.'

Holmes nodded, 'I anticipated as much. From what you have said I infer that there was animosity between your father and his family, so no doubt he disavowed the name when he sailed to Australia?'

'Exactly. While searching for a place to settle he found a small lush valley with a clear water spring where he set up a homestead. From then on he called himself Jack Clearwater and never again mentioned the family name.'

'What caused the family rift then?' Holmes enquired.

Justin sighed and replied, 'It's a story as old as the Genesis account of Cain and Abel. My father had an older brother, William, who was everything my father was not. He was tall, handsome, athletic and charming. He was also vain, arrogant, self-centred and cruel. What had been, in the early years, merely sibling rivalry, festered into hatred and loathing between them. William was the apple of his father's eye, who saw in him much of himself. Father and son rode to hounds, quaffed ale, shot deer and hawked with birds of prey. Jack was an outsider. His father considered him a mother's boy and a weakling because of his preference for the arts, music and nature. Jack would rather listen to the song of a bird than shoot the singer. He was more like his

201

mother. Sensitive, shy, artistic, intelligent and, of course, stubborn. The brothers clashed constantly, but the final rift came when William stole Jack's girl. Her name was Lucy, and Jack was besotted with her. William took her from his brother because he *could*. He did not love her as Jack did and proved it later by ending the relationship when he had tired of her. Jack never forgave him, and he actually cursed his brother and all the family, with the exception of his sister Victoria, before severing the ties. He stowed away on the SS 'Juliet' bound for Australia and only emerged out of hiding when he knew they were too far out to sea to turn back. The Captain, a gruff Scot by the name of McIvor, was furious and made Jack work like a slave to pay for his keep. As the ship neared the Cape of Good Hope she was overtaken by a violent storm that raged for three days and nights. She very nearly foundered, and at the height of the gale young Potter, the cabin boy, was swept overboard. Jack, who was about to go aloft to secure a torn sail, saw the lad get washed away and, lashing a rope around his waist, dived in after him. Though he was a powerful swimmer, both man and boy almost drowned. Eventually he managed to reach Potter, and willing hands soon hauled them back on board. As you can well imagine, Jack's standing with Captain McIvor and the rest of the crew soared, and from that moment on he enjoyed all the privileges of a full crew member. In fact McIvor offered to take him on permanently, but Jack declined. There were a few passengers on board, and amongst them was a young woman named Celia, a trained nurse bound for Australia to undertake missionary work with the aborigines. Jack and Celia fell in love, and when the Juliet finally docked they took off together. As I'm sure you have deduced, Mr Holmes, Jack and Celia became my parents.'

'Obviously. An intriguing tale, I'm sure, but nothing in it gives us any clues as to where to search for your roots, young sir.' Holmes pointed out.

Clearwater responded, 'As I've already indicated, my father was set against me making this trip, but when he realised I would not be dissuaded he gave me this letter.' Here he passed an envelope to Holmes, who opened it and read aloud,

My Dear Son, I suppose in my heart of hearts I always knew that the day would dawn when you would embark on a quest to find your roots. On reflection I now realise that my own reticence to discuss any and all aspects pertaining to my family virtually assured its inevitability. I have reluctantly agreed to assist you, but only indirectly. To find the family name and location you must decipher the attached cryptograms. I make no apologies for what must seem to be the placement of churlish and unnecessary obstacles in your path, but I have my reasons. Not least of which is a strong desire to protect you from contact with that damnable crew. Further, if you are to joust with them, (for believe me, they will not welcome you with open arms) then you will need wits, courage and tenacity. The latter two you already possess; deciphering the code will prove you also have the former. A word of warning, however: the family itself is bad enough, but its major-domo, Calvin Crowther, is much worse. He is ruthless, resolute and cunning. He runs the estate with an iron hand and will prove a formidable opponent. If you are successful (and if he still lives) you will certainly cross swords with him. Pursue your quest religiously and I know that Sanctified Frank and his friends Columbus, Shelley and King Harry will help you. Frank can be found at;
Catcalls, Rake-on-the-Mound, Aphrodite's Child, Anglia.
Good luck and God Speed!
Your loving father, Jack.

Below this were two cryptogram grids as shown;

S	D	Q	F	A	T	L	P
U	X	Z	E	J	K	E	J
D	B	Y	G	M	V	U	N
W	A	R	K	O	C	B	V
R	D	L	L	E	I	U	F
F	A	G	M	K	O	P	S
V	I	H	D	R	U	Y	T
X	C	B	S	G	L	H	X

V	C	T	W	E	R	H	Y
G	H	O	R	D	W	U	R
T	B	L	I	C	A	I	O
R	G	P	O	X	O	T	G
E	N	K	M	Z	P	S	D
W	K	G	Y	M	O	W	T
S	R	D	R	L	C	A	H
Z	M	S	E	Y	F	Z	K

Holmes' eyes lit up at the prospect of unravelling the clues.
'Here we are again, Watson, the game's afoot! I relish these
conundrums. It reminds me of the Carstairs case.'

'Indeed, Holmes; however, this looks somewhat trickier
to me.'

'I can't imagine Justin's father would make it *too* difficult
for him to decipher, and once we have the key it should be
simplicity itself.'

'And the key is?'

'Why, Frank and his friends, obviously. First we must
find where Frank lives, and *Anglia* is almost certainly
England, for that was its Roman name. However, if this *is* a
regular address then 'Aphrodite's Child' *should* represent a
county, but which one?'

Something stirred at the back of my mind, and then I remembered what it was. 'When I was a student at medical college I recall looking up something on Greek mythology in the encyclopaedia. I was researching a particular human condition called hermaphroditism, which is the union of the two sexes in one body, and I was interested in its derivation. It derives from *Hermaphrodito* who was the son of Hermes, the herald of the gods, and Aphrodite, the goddess of love. Hermaphrodito grew together with the nymph Salmacis into one person. I don't know if that helps.'

I should say it does, Watson! You are inspired! Don't you see? Aphrodite's Child represents an hermaphrodite who is neither one sex nor the other; therefore the county *has* to be Middlesex!'

'Of course! How very obvious. Well done, old fellow!' Holmes snatched his atlas from the shelf and opened it at the large-scale map of England. Almost immediately he began to chuckle, 'The next part of the address is *so* obvious.'

'Rake-on-the-Mound?' I asked, 'Wherever could that be?'

He was still smiling as he replied, 'To 'rake' is to 'harrow' as in the biblical Harrowing of Hell, Christ's delivery of the souls of the prophets. So obviously Rake-on-the-Mound must be *Harrow-on-the-Hill*, which is in Middlesex!'

Justin cried, 'Of course! Even I have heard of Harrow-on-the-Hill.'

I nodded, 'Now we are getting somewhere, but whatever could be meant by Catcalls?'

Holmes was thoughtful for a while before saying, 'I can think of only one instance where the call of a cat could also be a street or a road and that is Mews. Perhaps it is Feline Mews or some such and the best way for us to determine that would be to visit Harrow-on-the-Hill and look for ourselves.' Justin and I both nodded in agreement. As I had patients to see the following morning, we arranged to leave later and the afternoon saw the three of us heading off to Middlesex in a sturdy four-wheeler.

As we trundled along, Holmes opened the letter again and studied it closely. Presently he turned to Justin and said, 'Your father talks of pursuing your quest religiously; was he a religious man?'

'Not obsessively. He and my mother were good Christians, but living in such a remote place meant we could not attend church very often.'

Holmes nodded. 'This 'Sanctified Frank' he speaks of, do you recall him ever talking of a man called Frank here in England?'

Justin shook his head, 'No never.'

I said, 'These other people mentioned, Columbus, Shelley and King Harry, are they meant to be Christopher Columbus, the Lakeland poet and King Henry? And if they are, *which* Henry?'

Holmes shook his head, 'Hardly, Watson, they are all from different times and places in history, so could not have been contemporary friends of the mysterious Frank. It is more likely that they are just nicknames. Maybe Frank has a gang of cronies with these nicknames. It is commonplace among some of the London gangs to use such devices in an attempt to keep their real names off police records.'

Justin sighed and said, 'My father overestimated my intelligence when he set me this conundrum, because I haven't got a clue.'

Holmes smiled and responded, 'Don't worry, I'm sure we will be able to sort it out given enough time.' Presently we arrived in Harrow-on-the-Hill and Holmes instructed the cab driver to take us on a tour of the pleasant little town. Each of us scanned the street signs around us for the best part of half an hour, until suddenly Holmes cried out, *'Eureka!* Stop the cab!' He jumped out and we followed him. Facing us was a tree-lined road and the sign said 'Manx Mews'. Holmes asked, 'Isn't there a tail-less cat called a Manx?'

'There is indeed, old fellow,' I agreed. Holmes told the cab driver to wait for us, and the three of us set off to walk the length of Manx Mews. It was not a long road, and about half way down on the right we came to a small chapel.

Holmes said triumphantly, '*This* is what your father meant when he talked of pursuing your quest religiously. We have found Sanctified Frank!' The chapel was dedicated to St Francis of Assisi.

Justin beamed with delight, 'Well done indeed, Mr Holmes'. My friend led us inside the chapel, which was almost deserted. It was a simple, restful place with oak beams, plastered walls and a large stained-glass window, facing the altar, depicting St Francis surrounded by small animals and birds. He gazed out at us serenely with a dove of peace perched on his left shoulder and his right hand raised in the manner of bestowing a blessing. We all looked in vain for anything that might refer to Christopher Columbus, Shelley or King Henry.

Holmes glanced at his watch and said, 'It's getting late; perhaps we should find an hotel for the night and resume our search in the morning.' We both concurred. I for one was becoming distinctly peckish. We directed the cab back the way we had come to an inn we had seen earlier called the Blue Boar. Inside the low-beamed saloon, brasses gleamed and a welcoming log fire burned in the large open fireplace.

Mr Archer the landlord, a rotund, jovial fellow with mutton-chop whiskers, greeted us, 'Good evening gents, what will it be?'

Holmes replied, 'Three tankards of your best ale, a substantial meal and rooms for the night, in that order.'

The fellow smiled, 'No problem, sir, and welcome you are,' and he proceeded to comply with the first part of

Holmes' order. Soon we were seated by the fire quaffing excellent ale.

Holmes wiped the froth from his top lip and said to Justin, 'Well, so far so good. We have found the town and the chapel, and I am inclined to believe that your ancestral home is close by because your father displayed an intimate knowledge of this place in his clues.'

Justin nodded, 'As you say, Mr Holmes. I'm sure you are right.'

I suggested, 'We could ask the locals to name some of the established families in the area.'

Holmes shook his head saying, 'That could take quite some time to check them all out, and in any case I would prefer to try to crack the code first.' After we had dined well on roast beef followed by apple pie and cream, we retired to our cosy rooms for a good night's sleep.

The following morning, during a hearty breakfast, I pointed out to Holmes, 'You were a little wide of the mark when you suggested that Frank might have had cronies with the requisite nicknames, old fellow.'

Holmes smiled, 'Not necessarily, Watson. St Francis is always depicted as being friends with the animals. Perhaps Columbus and the others are nicknames of *animals*.'

Justin's eyes lit up. 'Good thinking, Mr Holmes. The stained-glass window shows the saint surrounded by little furry animals and birds.'

Holmes called the landlord over. 'Tell me, my good man, do you know of any naturalists who live locally?'

Mr Archer replied, 'To be sure, sir, Major Winstanley is your man. An animal expert he is. Collects butterflies and moths and stuffs and mounts his own birds. They say his collection is the envy of the Squire.' Here he glanced at the large grandfather clock in the corner and continued, 'He should be calling in any moment now for his morning constitutional. He always has a tot of whisky before his walk.'

Holmes nodded, 'Thank you, Mr Archer, we shall wait for him. Would you be good enough to introduce us when he arrives?'

'Certainly, sir, my pleasure.' We did not have long to wait before the door opened and a tall thin individual, with a beagle straining at his leash, bundled into the inn.

He propped his Penang lawyer against the bar; then turning to his dog he commanded, *'Sit Duke!'* He took off his hat and said to Mr Archer, 'Good morning, Sam. Damn cold today, better make it a double.'

'Morning, Major. This should keep out the cold,' and he handed him his double whiskey. As the fellow reached into his pocket to pay for the drink, Holmes stepped forward saying, 'Please, allow me,' and he asked the landlord to add it to our bill. Mr Archer made the introductions and the major joined us at our table.

He raised his glass and said, 'Thank you sir, your very good health.'

Holmes explained that young Justin was seeking his ancestral home and that the name was encoded in a cryptogram.

The major's eyebrows shot up, 'I say! How devilishly exciting!'

Holmes said, 'I'm led to believe that you are something of an expert on animals and insects; perhaps you might be able to help us?'

The major smiled and replied, 'Only too happy, if I can.'

'Would the names Columbus, Shelley and King Harry mean anything to you, other than historical figures?'

The major's brow furrowed, 'Well, I'm fairly certain that King Harry is an old English nickname for a goldfinch. Beautiful, colourful little bird. Eats thistle seeds, don't you know?'

Holmes nodded, 'Excellent, excellent. Then perhaps the other two are birds also.'

The major scratched his chin in concentration, before suggesting, 'I've a faint recollection that a Shelley is a chaffinch, but I've no idea what a Columbus is.'

I leaned forward and suggested, 'Perhaps *Columbus* is part of the bird's Latin classification?'

The major struck his thigh and said, 'Of course, how stupid of me! The doves and pigeons are classified under the order '*Columba*'; therefore a single specimen would be a *Columbus*! It *has* to be a dove.'

Holmes beamed, 'Splendid, splendid. I am indebted to you, sir. Landlord, another whisky for the major if you please.'

Winstanley smiled, 'Glad to be of assistance.'

Holmes asked, 'Could I impose one more time by asking you to accompany us to the chapel on Manx Mews to identify the birds for us? I'm afraid I would not know a chaffinch from a goldfinch myself.' The major agreed readily enough and downed his drink. In no time at all we were heading back towards the chapel with Duke leading the way. Major Winstanley secured his dog to a lamppost and we trooped back into the chapel. Once again we stood before the image of St Francis, and the major pointed with his walking-stick saying, 'Those three little birds by his feet are chaffinches and I count five goldfinches. Two in the tree and three on the wing, there.'

Justin exclaimed excitedly, 'And there's our friend Columbus, the dove on his shoulder!'

Holmes was nodding and smiling, 'As you say. Good work, gentlemen! Now we are well on our way.' He opened the letter and began studying the first cryptogram again. He mused, 'The birds are in the ratio of 1, 3, and 5, one dove, three chaffinches and five goldfinches. Perhaps that means a pattern of the first, third and fifth letter of each line in the grid?' However, he soon shook his head. 'That can't be right for it produces the letters, SZMWLKVB.'

I suggested, 'Perhaps it is the first, third and fifth letter from the *end* of each line?'

Again Holmes checked and again he shook his head, 'More gibberish, I'm afraid.'

We all scrutinised the grid for a while until Holmes suddenly exclaimed, 'Ah! I believe I have it! If you *skip* the first, third and fifth letters, that seems to produce something intelligible, see,' and he wrote out the following: D E V A L O I S.

I remarked, '*Devalois* doesn't look like a name I recognise, Holmes'

He smiled and replied, 'It's not Devalois, Watson, but *De Valois!* Which is French. It means, *Of Value* and it *is* a relatively common Gallic surname.'

Justin smiled and said, 'Well done, Mr Holmes. So my real name is *De Valois*. I like it, it has a certain quality.'

Major Winstanley exclaimed, 'The De Valois estate is not two miles west of here. It is an old established family, and the house is *Something* Manor, begins with 'C' I believe.'

Holmes asked, 'Could it be Cragmore?' He had quickly applied the key to the second cryptogram.

The major cried, '*That's it!* Cragmore Manor as I live and breathe! It's a large, sandstone pile somewhat the worse for wear. I suspect the family fortune has been in decline for some time, judging by the run-down condition of the estate.'

'Could you direct us?'

'Better than that, I'll take you. It will be part of my daily walk.' The four of us set off at a brisk pace with Duke foraging on ahead. It was a bracing morning with a keen freshness in the air, ideal for walking, and we soon covered the distance to Cragmore Manor.

Large wrought-iron gates barred the entrance to a long drive lined with laurels, and in the distance we glimpsed the ivy-clad manor house itself. It was, as the major had said, somewhat dilapidated, but not beyond restoration. Justin gazed through the latticework of the gates and said, 'So, at last I get to see where my father was born.'

Holmes nodded and said, 'Your quest is nearly over; however, I suggest we postpone the meeting with your relatives at least until tomorrow. There are one or two loose ends I wish to tidy up before then. Would you mind?'

'Of course not, Mr Holmes. Whatever you say.'

The major said, 'Well, gentlemen, Duke and I will take our leave of you now. It has been a pleasure making your acquaintance.' We all thanked him for his help and shook hands before he and Duke disappeared round a bend in the road.

We retraced our steps to the town and Holmes hailed a cab to take him back to London. He assured us he would return in the morning and was true to his word, arriving before 10 a.m. the next day. He seemed relaxed and at ease and after a glass of sherry said, 'Perhaps it is time for us to meet the De Valois family, and, though it is poor form to arrive unannounced, I believe in this instance a surprise visit should prove very revealing.' This time we took a cab, and as we approached Cragmore Manor, Holmes suggested, 'I think you should introduce Watson and myself as your legal representatives rather than investigators.'

Justin nodded and replied, 'As you wish, Mr Holmes.' The gates were now open as if the family expected company, and Holmes directed the driver to proceed on up to the house itself. As we alighted the big doors opened, and a tall, broad man in his late fifties, with grey-flecked hair and beard, came down the steps towards us. He held in check, on strong chains, two huge brindled hounds. They growled threateningly and bared their fangs in our direction.

Justin stepped forward confidently and said cheerily, 'Good morning!'

The man did not return the greeting, but asked, 'Are you seeking directions?'

Justin shook his head and replied, 'My name is Justin De Valois, son of Jonathan De Valois, and I am here to see my family.' The man looked shocked and swallowed hard. He seemed unsure of what to do. Eventually he asked, 'Are you expected?'

'No, I'm afraid not. I have only just managed to find this place. And you are?'

The fellow drew himself up to his full height, which was considerable, and replied, 'Calvin Crowther, the family's Major Domo.'

Justin said, 'This is Mr Holmes and Dr Watson, my legal representatives.'

The man's eyes narrowed then with a curt nod of his head he said, 'Please follow me,' and he led us up the steps and into the house. Holmes asked the cabby to wait for us before following us indoors.

The entrance hall was impressive with suits of armour, paintings and tapestries, but the carpets looked a little threadbare and the armour had not seen a polishing cloth for some time. Crowther ushered us into a reception room, untethered the dogs and told us to wait. He closed the door behind him and the two brutes sat before it and stared at us. It was disconcerting having those four black eyes watching our every move, and I began to wish that I had brought along my revolver. Presently the door opened and a distinguished looking young man in riding jacket, jodhpurs, boots and spurs strode into the room. He carried a riding whip in his hand, and there was no smile of greeting on his face. He had straight black hair, thin lips and piercing grey eyes, which looked hard at Justin. 'I am William Henry De Valois, head of the family and your first cousin, if you really are who you claim to be.'

Justin extended his hand saying, 'My father was Jonathan De Valois, your father's brother.'

William declined to shake his hand and said, 'My father is barely cold in his grave and already the vultures are gathering.'

Justin looked bemused, 'What are you talking about?'

Calvin Crowther, who had entered behind his young master, said, 'Surely you don't deny that you are here for this evening's reading of the will?'

Justin shook his head and replied, 'I didn't even know that my Uncle William had died. I've only just found out that my name *is* De Valois.'

Crowther countered, 'You come here dressed in rags, with two legal advisers in tow, and expect us to believe that you are not interested in the last will and testament of William De Valois?'

Justin's face hardened and he replied, 'I wasn't, but I am now. Perhaps I *shall* attend the reading. After all, I *am* family'

William replied, 'That remains to be seen. We have only your word for it.' At that moment the door opened again and a grey-haired lady entered the room. She was slim and elegant with fine features and blue eyes. I estimated her to be in her sixties, and she was dressed in a long, close-fitting black gown.

She smiled at Justin and asked, 'Is it true that you are Jonathan's son?'

He returned her smile and replied, 'Indeed Ma'am. My name is Justin.'

'I'm your Aunt Victoria,' she said, offering her hand.

Justin kissed it gallantly and said, 'My father spoke of his love for you.'

'How is he?'

'Unfortunately he died last year after a short illness.' Her smile crumpled and tears filled her eyes. 'I half expected it, as I have not heard from him for such a long time.'

'I'm so sorry, but I could not contact you. Until recently I did not even know my real name.'

She nodded in understanding, 'Jonathan left under a cloud, but I believe all that should be put behind us now. Don't you agree, William?'

Her nephew replied, 'We have no proof he is who he claims to be, and even if he *is* my cousin he is only here for a share of the spoils.'

Lady Victoria sighed and said to Justin, 'I feel compelled to apologise for the churlish way you have been received. It is high time this family displayed a little more hospitality,' and she rang a silver bell that stood on a side table. A butler appeared as if by magic, and she instructed him to bring us some refreshments. William and Crowther withdrew, and Victoria took Justin by the hand and led him to a sofa, saying, 'Tell me all about Australia. Was Jonathan happy there?'

Justin recounted to his aunt all about the country, its unique wildlife and its colourful flora. Holmes and I took a back seat, ate sandwiches and drank tea from china cups. Presently other family members began to arrive for the reading of the will, each and every one dressed in black. Finally the lawyers, Messrs Atkinson and Co., arrived and everyone gathered in the library.

Mr Atkinson, a slim wiry little man with silver hair and matching pince nez, addressed the assembly, 'We all know why we are here this evening, so without further ado I shall now read the last will and testament of William James De Valois.'

He read: *Being of sound mind and body I, William James De Valois of Cragmore Manor, in the county of Middlesex, made this 16th day of June in the year of Our Lord 1880, do hereby revoke all former dispositions made by me and declare this to be my last will and testament. I appoint my son William to be my executor and direct that all my just debts and funeral and testamentary expenses shall be paid as soon as conveniently may be, after my decease. I give and bequeath unto my only known surviving sibling, my sister Victoria, an annual stipend of one thousand pounds providing she continues to live at Cragmore Manor. To my faithful retainer and friend Calvin Crowther I bequeath five hundred pounds per annum and the continued use of Ivy Cottage in the manor grounds. To my various nephews and nieces upon each reaching maturation a single payment of one thousand pounds. To my late wife's grasping relatives I leave absolutely nothing. The residue of the estate including the house, grounds, horses, carriages etc I leave to my son William in the conviction that he will perpetuate my ideals, wishes and beliefs in the continuing administration of the estate. As witnessed this day, 16th of June 1880.*

Mr Atkinson folded the document and said, 'Ladies and gentlemen, that concludes the last will and testament of William James De Valois.' A murmur of conversation ensued as the assembly discussed the details until Calvin Crowther stood up and said,   'Mr Atkinson, I have a question. When you speak of nephews and nieces, I presume this applies only to legitimate claimants?'

'Naturally.'

Crowther continued, 'Not, therefore, the bastard son of William's brother Jonathan?'

Justin stood up and cried, *'How dare you, sir!'*

Crowther responded, 'Years ago I took the precaution of having your parents' background checked upon by a renowned Australian detective agency. They could find no record that your parents were ever legally married!'

Victoria demanded, 'How did you know where Jonathan was living?'

He turned to her and replied, 'You are altogether too trusting, my dear. I have had duplicate keys to your rooms for years. I took the liberty of monitoring all your mail, since you were the only one in correspondence with the runaway.'

She was beside herself with rage and stamped her foot in anger, exclaiming, *'You absolute cad! How DARE you invade my privacy so?'*

He replied, 'I was charged with looking after the interests of this family by your late father, and in my opinion the ends justify the means.' He turned to Justin and said, 'You and your representatives should leave now. There is nothing for you here!'

Holmes stood up and countered, 'On the contrary. My client has every right to stay, if he so wishes.' He took a piece of paper from his pocket and unfolded it saying, 'I have here the transcript of an entry in the log of the S S Juliet, written by Captain Duncan McIvor; it reads: *Today it was my very pleasant duty to perform the service of marriage for Mr Jonathan De Valois and Miss Celia Hobson, at midday on the fifth of May, 1855.* You perhaps forgot that ship's captains, as well as priests, are authorised to perform the ceremony.'

Crowther's face was like thunder, and William blustered, 'How do we know that this document is genuine?'

Justin said, 'Thank you, Mr Holmes.' Then turning to the others, he said, 'I have no intention of accepting any legacy, and I was telling the truth when I said that it was not my reason for being here. My father warned me about you all, with the exception of Aunt Victoria, but I had to find out for myself. He was right in every respect. That such mean-spirited, ungracious people are my own flesh and blood appals me. You judged me entirely on my appearance without knowing anything about me, which is exactly why I presented myself this way. The truth is that I could buy and sell the whole De Valois estate many times over and could easily afford to restore the house and grounds to their former glory. My father found a rich mother-lode of gold on his land and died a very wealthy man. You deny me a claim to what was rightfully mine, and so now I reciprocate by denying all of you, with the exception of Aunt Victoria, any claim to the considerable legacy of Jonathan De Valois!' He turned to his aunt and said, 'Why don't you come and spend some time with me in Brisbane and see Australia's beauty for yourself? It won't cost you a farthing.'

She smiled and replied, 'My dear boy, how absolutely marvellous! I believe I will.'

He said, 'My father was right when he said you had inherited all the grace and charm that had ever been allotted to our family!' He kissed her on the cheek and said, 'I will write to you when I have arranged your first-class passage. I look forward to showing you the charms of my homeland.' With a withering glance at Crowther he continued, 'Don't forget to have all the locks to your rooms changed!'

She shook her head, 'Don't worry, I shan't.'

With a disdainful look at the others, Justin strode from the room. Holmes and I also said our goodbyes to Lady Victoria and followed him outside. Our cab driver seemed relieved that we were ready to leave at last and held the door open for us.

Justin was thoughtful on the journey back to the Blue Boar, then he asked, 'So the 'loose ends' you spoke of, Mr Holmes, was to check the log of the Juliet?'

'As you say, Justin. I wanted to confirm that the name of the stowaway was indeed De Valois. The marriage information was an unexpected bonus.'

Justin smiled and said, 'It never occurred to me to ask *where* my parents were married.'

I remarked, 'I was very surprised to find that you are a man of substance, weren't you, Holmes?'

My friend shook his head. 'Not at all, Watson, I knew from the start.'

Justin looked surprised, 'How did you know?'

Holmes explained, 'You told us that you had worked your passage on board ship to reach England, yet when we shook hands I detected no calluses or roughness as I would have expected of someone who had been hauling on ropes and swabbing decks for weeks on end.'

Justin smiled, 'An excellent deduction, Mr Holmes. Anything else?'

Holmes nodded. 'Your clothes proclaimed you as a poor man yet you never once asked me about my fees. In my experience only the very richest of my clients display this tendency.'

Justin laughed and said, 'Well done, Mr Holmes, and now that my secret is out we can indulge ourselves of the very best food and drink that mine host of the Blue Boar has to offer us!'

A Chaffinch (or Shelly)

THE MAYFAIR STRANGLER

Sherlock Holmes and I were always determined that this particular account of his adventures would never see the light of day. At least, not in our lifetimes. Indeed, since we could still be arrested for our part in it, Holmes and I have resolved that it should not be published until after we have both shuffled off this mortal coil. The fact that you are reading this now should confirm that the publisher was true to his word and waited until after our demise before releasing it.

It all began in the year 1888 in what Holmes was apt to call 'The High Season of Crime', late autumn. When the nights were lengthening, adding their cloak of darkness to a multitude of nefarious activities, and yet before the bitter chill of winter kept even hardened criminals indoors. Holmes was slouched in the armchair with his feet resting on the mantelpiece, letting the glow from the fire warm the back of his long legs. As was his custom, in his indolent moods, he had asked me to read aloud any newsworthy items from the Times.

I read; 'ACTRESS MURDERED IN MAYFAIR! In the early hours of Saturday morning the 22nd, the brutal murder of promising actress Miss Harriet Perkins took place near Hyde Park. She had been defiled and strangled. Her partially clothed body was discovered on waste ground near Mount Street, by shift workers on their way to work. Miss Perkins is the third young woman to have died in like manner in the last five weeks and police are convinced that each has been the victim of the same murderer. In a statement issued by Scotland Yard, Inspector Lestrade asserted that investigations were progressing satisfactorily and he expected an imminent arrest. In the meantime he warned that women everywhere should be on their guard until this fiend has been apprehended. In his communiqué he urged ladies not to venture out at night unless accompanied by a man or a robust guard dog. As a direct consequence of these tragic events, it is reported that the sale of police whistles and long hat-pins has increased dramatically...'

Holmes gave a sardonic snort and said, 'Somehow I don't believe police whistles or long hat-pins will prove very effective against this fellow, Watson.'

I was about to reply when a ringing of the doorbell interrupted us. Presently Mrs Hudson introduced our visitor to us as Miss Molly Wright.

I have always found it extremely difficult to assess a woman's age, and since they are invariably coy about revealing it, I confess Miss Wright could have been anywhere between her middle twenties and her early thirties. She wore a brown coat with a fur collar, and her matching hat was held in place by just such a long hat-pin. Her hair was blond and her features fine. She was attractive enough, but she looked pale and anxious, her nervousness evident in the restless way she picked at the seam of her bag.

Holmes said, as he led her to a chair, 'Pray calm yourself, my dear. You are among friends. This is my colleague, Doctor Watson, from whom I have no secrets. Tell me, how may I help you?'

She regarded Holmes with a searching look, as though to assess the man before divulging her problem. Evidently satisfied with her appraisal, she said, 'We need your help, Mr Holmes, and if you are a man of honour, as I've been told, you will surely give it even if it means betraying one of your own class.'

Holmes said, 'Let me guess; you were a friend of Harriet Perkins?'

The young woman looked startled and asked, 'How on earth did you know that?'

Holmes shrugged and replied, 'A long shot, my dear. Since you are both actresses, I speculated that you might know each other.'

She countered, 'But you *could not know* that I am an actress.'

Holmes replied, 'There is still a slight trace of grease paint on the side of your neck and what looks like a stage script in your bag.'

She nodded and said, 'I'm impressed, Mr Holmes. You are right, of course; I have come directly from a dress rehearsal at the Oakwood Theatre, where I am in a new play.'

Holmes observed, 'Acting is a fickle occupation, notorious for its peaks and troughs. Pray do not be offended, but would I be far from the mark if I were to suggest that you might be forced to supplement your income from time to time?'

She flushed and replied, 'You are uncommonly blunt with your questions, Mr Holmes.'

'It *is* pertinent, I assure you.'

She looked him in the eye and answered, 'I'm not ashamed of it. My clients are gentlemen such as yourself, and your lives would be all the poorer without me and my kind.'

Holmes held up his hands in a gesture of placation and said, 'You misunderstand me, Miss Wright, I am never judgmental. I was merely trying to establish the connection between yourself and the unfortunate victims of the strangler. Since all three women were unaccompanied at night when they were killed, is it not reasonable to assume that they also supplemented their incomes?'

'The two that were known to me certainly did.'

'You knew them well?'

She nodded, but did not immediately reply. I could see she was close to tears. Finally she said, 'Hattie was my best friend, and that murdering demon has made an orphan of poor little Emily.'

I said, 'So Harriet Perkins had a daughter?'

She nodded again and the dam was breached as she dissolved into a flood of tears. Between her sobs she whispered, 'She is the sweetest little bundle you ever saw and was the joy of Hattie's life. I will love her and raise her as my very own, but I want the fiend who killed her mother to *hang*.' The last word was uttered with vitriolic hatred.

Holmes asked, 'Why do you come to me, when the newspapers assure us that Inspector Lestrade is about to make an imminent arrest?'

She gave a snort of derision and said, 'And the moon is made of green cheese!'

Holmes leaned forward in his chair and asked, 'What makes you think otherwise?'

She replied, 'When Kate Walters was killed the police seemed very concerned. Asking questions, taking statements, talking to the locals. But after the second murder took place, and poor Lizzy Banks was strangled, we hardly saw a policeman. We believe they think the strangler is doing them a favour by ridding London of women like us.'

Holmes frowned and shook his head; 'I can't believe that to be the case.'

Miss Wright said, 'If I thought Scotland Yard would help, I would not be here.' Reaching into her bag and taking out her purse, she continued, 'I have managed to raise five guineas. Will you find and bring to justice this devil's spawn for such a sum?'

Holmes shook his head and said, 'No, Miss Wright. I will do it for nothing. Keep your money in your purse.'

She started to protest, but Holmes said, 'Pray spend the money on baby Emily. I do not want it.'

She smiled and said, 'Thank you, Mr Holmes, I will do precisely that.'

224

Holmes said, 'You implied that the strangler is a gentleman of my class; how do you know this?'

'Because I've seen him.'

Holmes leapt to his feet. *'The devil you say!'*

'It's true all right. I've looked into his soulless eyes.'

'When was this?'

'Two weeks ago. I saw him murdering Lizzy Banks.'

Holmes began pacing the room and said, 'As I recall the newspaper report of that murder, Miss Banks was strangled in her own apartment off Marsden Street, and the murderer was disturbed in the act by the arrival of a third person. That was you?'

She nodded. 'It was.'

Holmes said, 'Perhaps you should tell me everything that transpired.'

Molly Wright sat back in her chair and recounted, 'It was about ten o'clock on a cold damp night and I decided to call on my friend Lizzy for a cup of tea. As I neared the top of the stairs I thought I heard a gurgling sound, but it was so faint I could not be sure. Her door was slightly ajar, and as I reached it I definitely heard another gurgle which was cut short. Then a man's harsh voice. I rushed in shouting, 'Lizzy! Are you all right?' He was kneeling over her on the bed, with his hands at her throat. As I entered he threw his left arm across his face, to prevent me seeing it, then leapt for the door. I opened my mouth to scream *murder,* but he struck me a savage blow that knocked me to the floor. Next moment he was gone.'

Holmes said, 'Describe him for me.'

She replied, 'He was as tall as you, Mr Holmes, but broader. His skin was olive, his hair black, and he had dark, evil eyes. He wore an evening suit, but no hat.'

Holmes asked, 'What about gloves?'

She nodded. 'Yes, he wore gloves ... and something else. He carried a lace or cord in his left hand.'

Holmes raised his eyebrows. 'Did he indeed?' He was thoughtful for a moment before asking, 'What was said in this harsh man's voice?'

She looked perplexed as she replied, 'It was very strange and made no sense, but what he said was, 'Ballet.' Then he spelled out the word socks. S.O.C.K.S.'

We both looked at her in surprise. I remarked, 'I've heard of ballet shoes, but never ballet socks.'

Holmes asked, 'Had your friend any connection with the ballet?

She nodded. 'Yes, she was a dancer, though not with one of the big companies.'

Holmes pondered this information for a moment before asking, 'Then what did you do, after he had knocked you to the floor?'

'I picked myself up and rushed to help Lizzy, but she was already dead. I could feel no pulse.' Here her weeping resumed as she continued, 'Poor Lizzy, she was such a lovely girl.'

Holmes prompted, 'Then what?'

'I was stunned. I sat on the edge of the bed and wept. I don't know for how long, but eventually I realised that I had to inform the police. I went to raise the alarm, and when I returned I noticed the medallion lying on the floor near the bed.'

'The medallion?'

'Yes. Lizzy must have torn it from his jacket as she struggled for her life.'

'Do you still have it?'

She shook her head. 'I handed it to the police.'

'Describe it to me in every detail.'

She said, 'It was a simple red cross with a circular centre and a crown at the top. Its ribbon was red and white stripes.'

'Horizontal or vertical stripes?'

'Vertical.'

'What colour was the circular centre?'

'Red and white.'

'Excellent, excellent! You are an observant woman, Miss Wright.' Picking up his pipe and tobacco from the mantelpiece, Holmes enquired, 'Do you mind if I smoke? I find it an aid to concentration.'

She shook her head. 'Of course not, Mr Holmes.'

He lit his pipe and drew on it thoughtfully for a few minutes. Presently he asked, 'Can you recall whether your friend Lizzy was lying face down or on her back?'

She replied, 'She was face down.'

Holmes nodded as though he half expected this answer. 'When you approached the house did you see anyone else?'

She shook her head. 'No, there was no one about.'

'There was no carriage waiting nearby?'

She was thoughtful for a moment, but again shook her head. 'No, none.'

Holmes pondered for a few moments more before saying, 'You have been extremely helpful, Miss Wright.' Handing her his card, he said, 'If you remember anything else, however trivial, contact me immediately. In the meantime you may rest assured that this case has my undivided attention.'

'Thank you, Mr Holmes, and God bless you. I shall pray for your success.'

When she had left, I remarked, 'There does not seem to be very much to go on, Holmes.'

He puffed on his pipe and responded, 'On the contrary, Watson, we have several clues which I shall now list.' Sitting down at the table with pen and paper, he wrote the following;

THE STRANGLER.

1) A gentleman, by reason of his clothes.

2) Has dark hair and olive skin.

3) Wore a distinctive red and white medallion.
4) Wore gloves and carried a lace or cord.
5) The strange utterance of 'ballet s.o.c.k.s.'

Holmes studied the list for a while, then said, 'I believe a visit to Inspector Lestrade at Scotland Yard is called for.' He jumped up and reached for his ulster and hat. 'Are you coming?'

'Of course, old fellow,' I said and grabbed my own coat and cane. Presently we were ensconced with Lestrade in his office at Scotland Yard, and for once the normally garrulous police officer was uncharacteristically taciturn.

'What can I do for you, Mr Holmes?' he enquired.

My friend replied, 'I was hoping to question you as to the progress you are making with respect to the Strangler.'

Lestrade regarded Holmes seriously for a moment before replying, 'You have read my statement to the press, have you not?'

'Of course, but I am talking specifics now, not generalities.'

'And what makes you think that you have any right to be privy to confidential police business, Mr Holmes?'

Holmes looked stunned. It was as though Lestrade had slapped him across the face. He stood up and said coldly, 'I was labouring under the delusion that I still had a special working relationship with Scotland Yard. Obviously that no longer holds true.' He looked witheringly at the Yard man as he continued, 'I shall remember this conversation when next you, or one of your colleagues, come cap in hand to Baker Street for my assistance.'

He turned on his heel and I was right behind him, when the inspector said, 'Mr Holmes.' We stopped and turned back. Lestrade asked, 'Do you have a client?'

Holmes nodded. 'Yes, I do as a matter of fact. A certain Miss Molly Wright, who was a friend to two of the victims.'

The inspector stood up and began pacing the floor. It was obvious to me that there was an inner conflict going on. Finally he stopped and said to Holmes, 'I cannot, with honour, let you leave in animosity. I recall the times when your help was invaluable to me. However, I can divulge nothing officially. If I tell you that my directive comes from the very highest level, I trust you will believe me. All I *can* say is that I firmly believe that the Strangler has killed his last victim.'

Holmes gave a nod of his head and responded, 'Well, thank you for that much at least, Lestrade. I will then endeavour to bring the fiend to justice on my own.'

Lestrade drew in a deep breath and said, 'Mr Holmes, I suppose it would be futile of me to ask that you drop this case?'

Holmes was aghast. 'I never thought I would see the day, Lestrade, that an officer of Scotland Yard would make such a suggestion.'

The inspector sat down on the corner of his desk and muttered, 'Neither would I,' then he continued, 'believe me, I have good reason.'

Holmes responded, 'Plainly you are under pressure from above to protect some privileged person; however, I am answerable only to my client, and am not so constrained. I'm sorry, Lestrade, but your assurance that the Strangler has killed his last victim is not good enough. Justice is not served unless he pays for the lives of the three women he has already murdered, and I will do my damnedest to see that he does. I shall not compromise you by asking for your help, except perhaps to allow Dr Watson and myself to see the body of the latest victim.'

Lestrade sighed and replied, 'Very well, Mr Holmes, but I shall deny having done so if asked. Come with me, and pray be discreet.' He led us down some stairs and, by a circuitous route, to the police mortuary.

As we entered, Holmes asked, 'Do you still have the medallion that was found at the scene of the crime?'

Lestrade replied, 'I know nothing of any medallion.'

'Come now, Inspector. It was torn from the jacket of the murderer. Surely Scotland Yard has not lost such a vital piece of evidence?'

'I tell you I have seen no such medal, Mr Holmes.'

My friend nodded. 'Very well, Inspector, no matter. Fortunately I have a good description of it.'

Lestrade uncovered the body of a young woman and said, 'These are the remains of Harriet Perkins.' She was small and slim with red hair and freckles, and was about the same age as Molly Wright. Around her neck was a thin line of purple bruising.

The British Museum

Holmes remarked, 'Plainly he used the cord he carried to strangle her.' I nodded in agreement. Holmes said, 'Help me turn her over, Doctor. I want to examine the back of her

230

neck.' I did as bidden, and Holmes pointed to a lesion where the skin was abraded. 'Just as I suspected,' he said.

'What caused it?' I asked, but he ignored the question. Turning to Lestrade, he said, 'Thank you, Inspector. We have seen enough, and it has been highly illuminating. Come, Watson.'

When we were outside once more, Holmes declared, 'I must visit the British Museum, old fellow.' Glancing at his half hunter, he continued, 'Though I should be back at Baker Street in time for lunch.'

I responded, 'Very well, Holmes. I have some patients to attend anyway, so I shall see you later.' In the event, however, he did not return until close to teatime.

I asked, 'So how goes the investigation?'

He replied, 'I think I know how to pinpoint the killer, though to do so I have been forced to enlist the aid of my brother.' I raised an eyebrow and he continued, 'There are times, Watson, when it is a distinct advantage having a sibling such as Mycroft.'

I said, 'But I thought you were going to the British Museum.'

He tutted and replied, 'Of course. Forgive me, I am leapfrogging again. The museum has, as I'm sure you would expect, a medal collection second to none, and I soon found an example to match the description given to us by Miss Wright. It is the 'Merito Militar' or 'Order of Military Merit'. Awarded for war services to all ranks, and the country of issue is Spain.'

'Ah! So the fellow is a Spaniard.'

He nodded. 'I knew that much anyway, but the medal confirmed it.'

'Oh! How did you know?'

Holmes answered, 'Two things pointed the way. You remember the cryptic utterance of 'ballet s.o.c.k.s.'? Well I finally worked out what it meant. One of the kings of Spain,

Phillip the second I think it was, spoke with a lisp and could not differentiate between the letters B and V. Both sounded like B when he spoke. The royal court, out of deference to the king, adopted the lisp, and as a consequence Castillian Spanish, or *Castellano,* retains the lisp in its pronunciation to this day. What the strangler said was not 'Ballet', but *'Vale'* which means "Right" or "OK". Once I had made that connection the rest was easy. S.O.C.K.S. was in reality, *"eso si que es,"* which means, "That's it". In essence what the fellow said was, "Right, that's it", once he knew that his victim was dead.'

I nodded in understanding. 'I should have realised that it was not English, for it made no sense at all.' After a moment I continued, 'You said two things pointed the way?'

Holmes nodded and replied, 'You saw the other clue yourself, Watson. The abrasion to the back of Harriet Perkins' neck. The poor girl wasn't just strangled, she was garrotted, which is the *official method of execution* in Spain!'

'I'm not sure I know the difference, Holmes.'

He explained, 'Garrotting is diabolically cruel, slow strangulation! In a Spanish judicial execution the seated criminal is secured to a post by a hinged metal collar around his neck and a slowly tightened screw dislocates his spinal column. Originally, however, the collar was a cord and slow strangulation was effected by twisting this cord. That was how the monster killed Harriet Perkins, and the lesion to the back of her neck was caused by this twisting action. Though we have not seen the other bodies, ten guineas says they all bore the same marks.'

I shook my head. 'I would not take that wager, Holmes.'

He went on, 'Garrotting also explains why the killer had Lizzy Banks prone on the bed and why he wore gloves. A thin cord can cut into unprotected hands.'

I nodded in agreement. 'I'm sure you are right, Holmes, it all fits. But even though you now know he is Spanish, there must be scores if not hundreds of Spaniards in London. It still seems like a needle in a haystack to me.'

He countered, 'Not quite, old fellow. I pondered about the medallion and wondered why he should have been wearing it. After all, it is not something one would normally wear when abroad hell-bent on murder. It occurred to me that perhaps he had been at some formal function and slipped away unnoticed, to carry out the dirty deed. Such a function would provide a perfect alibi, if he was to be questioned later by the authorities. Pursuing this line of reasoning, I remembered that all three murders had taken place in Mayfair, and Mayfair is the location of several foreign embassies, *including the Spanish Embassy!*'

I exclaimed, 'Of course! It all makes perfect sense to me. And,' I said, 'if the fellow is a diplomatist that would explain why Scotland Yard has been warned off. Obviously if he were to be charged with murder it would cause a diplomatic incident with far-reaching international repercussions.'

'My reasoning precisely, Watson, and if you recall, Miss Wright said she saw no carriage in the vicinity, which could indicate that the killer was on foot, therefore local.' Holmes was thoughtful for a few moments before continuing, 'However, if the fellow *is* a diplomatist, he cannot be arrested because he will have diplomatic immunity.'

I was aghast. 'Surely not, Holmes. Not for multiple murder?'

He nodded emphatically. 'Absolutely, Watson.'

'How can that be?'

Holmes explained, 'The principle of diplomatic immunity began in ancient times to protect messengers who carried news between warring armies. The Greeks and Romans granted immunity to foreign emissaries since they firmly believed them to be under the protection of the gods. The practice is vital even today because immunity allows diplomatists to work, in often-hostile countries, without fear of persecution. All this means that on the rare occasions when an ambassador transgresses, then hides behind the shield of diplomatic immunity, the only recourse for the host nation is expulsion.'

I shook my head and said, 'That seems grossly unfair to me, Holmes.'

'Nevertheless, that is the way of the world, old fellow.'

I was quiet for a few moments before asking, 'So just how does Mycroft figure in all this?'

Holmes replied, 'I have asked him to secure us invitations to an embassy soirée, and I've no doubt he will be successful, but that is not the full extent of his involvement.' Holmes pulled a sheet of paper from his pocket and spread it out on the table. 'This is a list of staff and servants currently occupying the Spanish Embassy, and few men in London could have procured it for me so quickly. Such is the measure of my brother and his connections along the corridors of power.'

He scanned down the list and remarked, 'Most of the people named can be discounted, for example the catering staff, maids, waitresses and so on, virtually all of whom are English. Even the chef is French. Of the Spanish contingent all but four can be eliminated on the grounds of age, gender and so forth.'

I looked at the list over his shoulder and saw that he had underlined four names: Ramon Margallo, José Phillipe Rodriguez, Miguel Frederico Lorca and Fernandez Angulo.

Holmes studied the notes beside each name and announced, 'We can eliminate Miguel Lorca because he does not have a military background. That leaves three possible candidates.' He sat back in his chair and put his hands behind his head. 'All in all we could hardly have asked for more, Watson, and when we visit the embassy we should be able to narrow it down even further.'

The elder Holmes was his usual efficient self, and the following morning a messenger arrived at Baker Street with invitations for the two of us to accompany Mycroft to a reception at the embassy that very weekend.

Saturday evening saw Holmes and myself resplendent in our evening suits, top hats and bow ties, and I wore my military medals. Mycroft collected us, as arranged, and the carriage drew up outside the embassy on time. A liveried commissionaire opened the door for us and escorted us up the steps, holding a large umbrella over our heads to protect us from the slight drizzle. Inside, another flunkey took our hats, capes and canes and we were shown into a large reception hall with a marble floor and crystal chandeliers. A wide sweeping staircase led to the upper floors, and paintings by the likes of Velasquez and El Greco adorned the walls. There must have been thirty or forty people already assembled, with others arriving, as we accepted champagne and canapés from the waiters. Mycroft pointed out various dignitaries to us and acknowledged many of them as old acquaintances.

Holmes asked, 'Can you identify any of the Spaniards on your list?'

Mycroft cast his eyes around and then singled out a young man with dark hair and olive skin. 'That is Fernandez Angulo, an attaché.'

Holmes nodded and said, 'Then plainly we can eliminate him as a suspect.' I asked why, and Holmes replied, 'Is it not obvious, Watson? The fellow is too short. Why, he is no more than five feet nine, yet we know from Miss Wright's description that the killer is my height at least.'

'Of course. I had forgotten that point.'

Mycroft said, 'The tall fellow over there by the window is, I believe, Ramon Margallo, another attaché.' He was at least as tall as Holmes and in every way matched the description given by Miss Wright. Holmes watched him intently for several minutes as the man sipped champagne and chatted amiably with a group of guests. As he moved off to circulate, however, Holmes declared, 'I believe we can also exclude Señor Margallo.'

'Why?' I asked, 'he seems a perfect choice to me.'

Holmes explained patiently, 'He has a stiff leg, Watson. In fact, since this fellow *does* have a military background, it may well be a false limb. That rules him out, because we know that the killer knelt over his victim on the bed.'

I nodded. 'As you say, Holmes.'

Presently we saw a tall distinguished looking gentleman carefully descending the stairs to be greeted with much deference by all and sundry.

Mycroft whispered, 'That is Don Pedro Garcia Manrique. The Spanish Ambassador to the Court of Saint James's. He is a highly respected and astute statesman.'

The fellow was lean and angular with chiselled features and an aquiline nose. His long grey hair was swept back from his high forehead, and he sported a goatee beard, which was as grey as his hair. I was strongly reminded of Don Quixote de la Mancha, by Cervantes.

Mycroft said, 'I will try to initiate an introduction.' Again he was successful, and presently he introduced Holmes and myself saying, 'Don Pedro, may I present my younger brother Sherlock and his friend and colleague, Dr Watson, late of the British Army.'

We shook hands and Holmes said, '*Encantado*, Don Pedro,'

The old man smiled and asked, 'You speak *Castellano*, Mr Holmes?'

Holmes shook his head and replied, '*Un poco, nada mas*,' (a little, no more.) 'Though I have promised myself I will learn your beautiful language one day when time permits.'

'What is it that takes up so much of your time then, Mr Holmes?'

Mycroft answered for him, saying, 'My brother is self-deprecating and would never reveal that he is one of the world's foremost criminologists.'

The old man raised his eyebrows. 'Of course! Sherlock Holmes. I had not made the connection. I have heard of some of your exploits and your powers of deductive reasoning. Commissioner Thompson of the Metropolitan Police holds you in high regard.'

Holmes made a little bow and responded, 'You are too kind.'

Mycroft excused himself and went to talk to a vice regent he knew, leaving Holmes and myself with the ambassador. At that moment a suave, urbane individual approached and spoke quietly, in rapid Spanish, to Don Pedro.

The old man said, 'Excuse me, gentlemen, but an urgent matter requires my attention. I will leave you in the hands of my deputy, Captain José Phillipe Rodriguez.' The introductions were made and Don Pedro left. Captain Rodriguez smiled at us with practised ease, revealing perfect white teeth. However, I noticed that the smile did not reach his eyes, which were dark and calculating. He was tall and athletic-looking, with a strong jaw line and black hair that glistened with scented pomade. I felt sure that rejection by the fairer sex would be an unknown experience for him.

He summoned one of the waiters imperiously, saying, 'Let me refresh your drinks, gentlemen.'

Holmes said, 'So, Captain, you have a military background, like Dr Watson here. Yours was an infantry regiment?'

'No, a cavalry regiment. Rather like your Royal Hussars.'

'Indeed, and from there you entered the diplomatic service?'

He nodded. 'It is not uncommon in Spain for diplomatists to be selected from distinguished army officers,' he replied, with no attempt at modesty.

Holmes said disarmingly, 'I am surprised you are not wearing your military medals. No doubt you have earned several?'

'But of course. However, they have somehow been misplaced.'

Holmes asked, 'Does your collection include the Merito Militar?'

The Spaniard looked keenly at Holmes and replied, 'Yes it does include the Merito Militar. Why do you ask?'

My friend shrugged and replied, 'Just one of my many interests, militaria.'

'You are not a military man yourself?'

Holmes shook his head. 'No, I am not.'

Rodriguez smiled a superior smile and remarked, 'I have met such armchair militiamen. Interested in militaria, but not men of action enough to risk personal involvement.'

Holmes did not rise to the bait, but responded, 'I am a pacifist myself, though I recognise the need for an army to safeguard that peace.'

'Then you must consider yourself fortunate indeed to have men such as myself to do your fighting for you.'

Holmes rejoined, 'I believe that the word is mightier than the sword, and that war is the madness that rages only when reason and tolerance fail.'

The Spaniard inclined his head and responded, 'Then we must agree to differ, Mr Holmes, for I am a soldier first and a diplomatist second.' The fellow drifted off to join a group of ladies, who greeted him enthusiastically.

I said to Holmes, 'There goes the archetypal ladies man.' He nodded thoughtfully, and watched the Spaniard discreetly for some time.

Presently we were rejoined by the ambassador. His face was grave and his brow furrowed. He regarded Holmes seriously for a moment before saying, 'It may well take you a long time to learn *Castellano*, Mr Holmes. Am I not right in thinking that you are, even now, pursuing your particular vocation?'

Holmes smiled and replied, 'Mycroft did not exaggerate when he described you as astute.'

Don Pedro asked, 'Will you both step this way please, gentlemen?' He led us into a ground floor room, which turned out to be his study. Bookcases lined the walls and a cheerful log fire burned in the marble fireplace. In front of the tall windows stood an antique writing desk and leather-bound chair, with two easy chairs facing it. Indicating the two chairs, the ambassador invited us to sit down. He then took a silver casket from his desk, opened it and offered us the long thin cheroots it contained. Holmes took one, but I declined. Don Pedro selected one also and lit them from the fire with a long wax taper. Sitting down at his desk he regarded us both for a few   moments as though weighing his words carefully. Finally he began, 'Gentlemen, what I am about to say must not go beyond these four walls. Do I have your assurance to that effect?'

Holmes nodded and answered for the two of us, 'Yes, Ambassador, you do.'

'I have just received word from your Secretary of State's personal representative that my appeal, on behalf of Captain Rodriguez, has been rejected. The Foreign Office have 'requested' that he be returned to Spain immediately.' He took a deep breath and continued, 'Though this may sound, in the diplomatic language used, to be of no great import, I assure you it is. This is tantamount to expulsion and is only warranted in the event of an extremely serious transgression, or suspected transgression. The Captain swears he is innocent of any such violation, and your Foreign Office refuses to reveal why they want him dismissed.' The ash grew on the end of his cigar, but he seemed not to notice. Still regarding Holmes, he continued, 'I am sure you could enlighten me as to what it is that you, and the F.O., suspect my deputy of, Mr Holmes.'

Sherlock drew on his cheroot before replying, 'Don Pedro, I am uncomfortable making unsubstantiated accusations against anyone, especially a foreign diplomatist, but at the moment my investigations seem to indicate that Captain Rodriguez is heavily implicated in the deaths of three young women, here in Mayfair, in recent weeks.'

The old man looked stunned. Making the sign of the cross, he whispered, '*Madre de Dios*' (Mother of God). His hand trembled so much that the ash dropped from the end of his cheroot onto the desktop. Placing the cigar in an ashtray, he said, 'Surely there must be some mistake. I have known the man for years and he is an officer and a gentleman from one of Madrid's leading families.'

Holmes replied, 'Do we ever really *know* anyone? We all have our dark side, but fortunately most of us manage to subjugate it in favour of the good side. Perhaps the Captain has lost that particular battle.'

Don Pedro rose and walked over to the fireplace. He leaned on the mantelpiece and stared into the flames. After a few moments he said, 'I had read the newspaper reports about those poor unfortunate women, but never in my worst nightmare would I have believed that a member of my embassy could be involved.' Turning to face us he asked, 'What was it that led you to suspect José?'

Holmes replied, 'There were several clues, but the most important was a medallion found at the scene of the second murder. It was the Merito Militar. Tell me, Ambassador, is it customary to inscribe the reverse of this medal?'

Don Pedro shook his head, 'Not normally, though some recipients choose to have it engraved themselves. The Merito Militar is awarded to all ranks and comes in four classes. The Captain's is a first-class award and I believe his *is* so inscribed.'

Holmes turned to me and whispered, 'Now we know how Lestrade picked up the scent so quickly.'

Don Pedro asked, 'Have you seen the medal?'

Holmes shook his head. 'It was handed to the police, who now disavow it.'

'Then it may not even belong to José.'

Holmes argued, 'If it does not, then why would the Foreign Office want him expelled?'

The old man slumped. 'Of course you are right. I am, as you say, clutching at straws.' He was quiet for a while before asking, 'What did you have in mind when you came here tonight, Mr Holmes?'

My friend replied, 'I wanted to size up the fellow first, and if I was satisfied, question him about the murders.'

'And do you still wish to question him?'

'Very much so.'

Don Pedro looked thoughtful for a moment, then asked, 'If, in the course of your questioning, you came to the conclusion that the Captain is not the guilty party, would you inform Scotland Yard and your Secretary of State to that effect?'

Holmes nodded. 'Of course, Ambassador.'

'Then I think you *should* question him. I shall suspend my own judgement until such time. However, if the fellow *is* guilty of such appalling acts then ...' The old man shook his head and clenched his fists.

I led him to his chair saying, 'Pray calm yourself, sir. Here, drink this,' and I poured him a glass of water from a carafe on the desk.

He sighed, 'Thank you, Doctor. You are right, I must watch my blood pressure.' Turning to Holmes he said, 'You may not be aware of this, Mr Holmes, but not all the staff live permanently here at the embassy. Rodriguez rents a house nearby. I will give you the address.' So saying, he quickly wrote it out on a piece of embassy notepaper and handed it to Holmes.

He glanced at it, put it in his pocket and said, 'Thank you, Ambassador.'

We stood up to leave and Don Pedro walked us to the door. He looked at his pocket watch and said, 'If you call after eleven he should be alone, for his manservant, Enrique, will have returned here to the embassy by then.'

We both shook hands with the old man, and Holmes said, 'I am indebted to you, sir; you are an honourable man. I sincerely hope that Captain Rodriguez proves to be one also.'

We rejoined Mycroft, who was just detaching himself from a group of dignitaries. The three of us chatted amiably and whiled away the time sipping champagne until eventually, looking at his watch, Holmes said, 'Thank you, Mycroft, for all your help. Watson and I will be leaving now. The evening has been a huge success.'

'Very well, Sherlock. I'm glad to have been of assistance. Let me know how your investigations conclude.'

Soon Holmes and I were settled in a hansom cab heading out of Mayfair. However, he did not immediately direct the cab towards the Captain's address, but instead told the driver to take us to 221b Baker Street. When I asked why, he whispered, 'I want you to collect your service revolver, Watson.' I was taken aback by this statement, but refrained from further discussion within earshot of the driver. After I had collected the weapon, Holmes directed the cab to an address on Elizabeth Street.

We found ourselves outside a large white residence with steps up to a portico. Holmes rang the bell and presently the door was opened by Rodriguez himself. His eyes narrowed when he recognised us, and he tried to slam the door shut in our faces. Holmes was too quick for him, however, and thrust his boot against the door to block it. He challenged, 'What are you afraid of, Captain?'

The fellow glared at Holmes and replied, 'I fear nothing, least of all you, Mr Holmes.'

'Then you will have no objection to answering a few questions.'

'How did you find this address?'

Holmes replied, 'Don Pedro gave it to me. He believes we *should* talk.'

Reluctantly Rodriguez opened the door and said, 'Very well, come in if you must.'

We went through into a large masculine study where a coal fire burned in a broad fireplace. The stuffed heads of boar and deer lined the walls along with sabres, foils and muskets. A bearskin rug occupied the floor space before the fire, and an imposing desk almost filled the window bay. Some of the drawers stood open and the contents were piled on the desktop. A leather valise had more papers stuffed in it, and there were several boxes with a miscellany of artifacts in them.

Holmes enquired innocently, 'Packing for a trip?'

Rodriguez answered, 'Not that it is any of your business, but yes. I am returning to Spain, for I weary of your grey London skies and foggy days.'

Holmes responded, 'I believe your reasons for leaving are far more serious than that.'

'What are you implying, Mr Holmes? If you have something to say, then say it.'

Holmes said, 'Indeed yes. By all means let us put our cards on the table. I believe, sir, that you are a multiple murderer, who has already killed three young women here in Mayfair.'

Rodriguez sat down at his desk and nonchalantly put his feet up on it. He picked up a letter opener, in the shape of a dagger, and began cleaning his fingernails with it. He sneered at Holmes, 'And what evidence do you have to support this incredible accusation?'

Holmes replied, 'I record the fact that you did not immediately deny the charge.'

The fellow shrugged. 'Very well, I deny it.'

Holmes said, 'You are probably unaware of it, but when you killed your last victim, Harriet Perkins, you also made an orphan of her baby daughter Emily.'

Unperturbed, he responded, 'I have killed no one, Mr Holmes, and you have still not revealed any evidence for these fantastic claims.'

Holmes rejoined, 'Why do you persist in denial, when Scotland Yard holds the Merito Militar inscribed with your name?'

The sneer vanished from his face and his dark eyes flashed. 'What are you talking about?'

Holmes replied, 'Give up this pretence. Your medallion was found in the woman's apartment.'

The Spaniard jumped to his feet and stared hard at Holmes. 'Have you seen the medal?' he demanded.

Holmes nodded emphatically. 'Of course,' he lied, 'Lizzy Banks tore it from your jacket and it was found by the man who disturbed you in the act.'

Rodriguez looked puzzled. 'The *man* ..?' he began, then immediately he realised that Holmes had tricked him. He smiled. 'Very clever, Mr Holmes, but it will avail you nothing. I enjoy diplomatic immunity and will not have to answer for my transgressions.'

'So you freely admit to these abominable crimes?'

The Captain shrugged. 'Why not? Though I prefer to think of them as *encuentras de apasionado*, passionate encounters.'

We were appalled at the ruthless arrogance of the man.

Holmes asked, 'Why, in God's name, did you have to *kill* them?'

Rodriguez strolled over to the fireplace and turned to face us. 'How can I expect a cold, unemotional Englishman like you to understand the passionate fire that burns inside a *madrileno*? How could you, with your reserved frigid morality, know what heights of rapture can be achieved when exercising man's dominance over woman?'

Holmes responded, 'And the ultimate domination is to take that woman's life?'

'Of course! Don't you see? When a woman has reached that pinnacle with me, no other man can emulate it, so she is better off expiring at the moment of supreme ecstasy.' He shrugged as he continued, 'In any case, these women were worthless.'

Holmes and I were temporarily speechless at this monstrous assertion. Finally I responded, 'No human life is worthless. Except perhaps your own, after what you have done.'

Seemingly indifferent to the suffering he had caused, Rodriguez countered, 'You probably don't even have a mistress of your own, do you, Mr Holmes?'

Sherlock nodded. 'Yes, I have a mistress, and I have been faithful to her all my adult life. Unfortunately, she is blind.'

The man sneered, 'With your looks it is perhaps as well.'

Holmes ignored the gibe and went on, 'She carries a sword in one hand and scales in the other. She is of course Justice, and you can be sure I shall continue striving to serve her to the best of my ability.'

He took off his cape and coat and placed them on a chair. Then taking one of his gloves, he walked over to the Spaniard and slapped him hard across the face with it.

The fellow's eyes flashed with anger, then he smiled. 'You are a fool, Holmes, and I feel honour-bound to give you the chance to retreat from the position in which you have placed yourself. I must warn you that I am a master swordsman with foil, epee *and* sabre and a deadly marksman to boot.'

Holmes responded, 'I do not retract. Choose your weapon.'

I was appalled and drew Holmes to one side. I whispered urgently to him, 'Have you taken leave of your senses? Duelling is outlawed. Even if you win, you will go to prison.'

He replied also in a whisper, 'This is the only way justice can be served. The fellow is above the law.'

I argued, 'But what if he *wins*? You heard him. He is a cavalry officer, a master swordsman and a crack shot.'

He replied, 'I have the angels on my side. However, if he *does* prevail against me, shoot him with your pistol. He must *not* escape justice.'

I blanched at the prospect. 'Holmes,' I whispered, 'I am sworn to uphold life, not take it. You are asking me to commit murder!'

He shook his head and countered, 'Not murder, Watson, judicial execution. The man is guilty by his own admission. Would you have the deaths of other innocent women on your conscience, if he should live? Tell Scotland Yard you were trying to save my life. They know he is a killer, so you will not be convicted.'

I could think of no other argument with which to dissuade him and so fell silent. I gripped the butt of the revolver in my pocket and trembled at the prospect of what was about to transpire.

Holmes rolled up his shirtsleeves and turned again to face Rodriguez. 'So, what is it to be, lady killer?' he taunted.

The Spaniard beamed. '*Estupendo*! You have nerve, Señor Holmes. I am almost sorry that I have to kill you.' He reached up for the crossed sabres by the fireplace and tossed one to his opponent. Holmes caught it by the hilt and hefted it in his hand, judging its weight and balance.

'A fine weapon,' he remarked.

'Finest Toledo steel, Mr Holmes,' Rodriguez replied. He kicked the bearskin rug out of the way and Holmes and I moved the furniture back to create an arena. Rodriguez slashed the air expertly with his blade and flexed his leg muscles in preparation.

I made one last attempt. 'For God's sake, Holmes,' I pleaded.

He smiled a tight-lipped smile and said, '*Jacta est alea*, Watson. The die is cast!'

Rodriguez cried, '*En Garde!*' and assumed the stance.

Holmes reciprocated, saluted his opponent and said, 'On your command, Watson.'

I was terrified. The conflict I was about to initiate had only two possible outcomes, and both were odious. On the one hand, my best friend would die and I would be forced to take a human life, or on the other, Holmes and I would be jointly guilty of murdering a high-ranking foreign diplomatist.

Taking out my handkerchief with a trembling hand, I said croakily, 'When this falls, gentlemen.' I took a deep breath, dropped the handkerchief and stepped back.

Immediately the two antagonists hurled themselves at each other with furious intent. I knew that Holmes had been a champion swordsman during his student days at university, but that was many years ago. Whereas Rodriguez had, until recently, been a cavalry officer highly trained with the sabre. He was also a younger man to boot. Holmes launched a blistering attack in an all-out attempt to gain a quick kill, and for a while he forced the Spaniard to retreat. However, the killer was indeed an expert and he parried every blow and riposted every thrust that Holmes delivered. Gradually he began to turn the tables, and before long Holmes was giving ground. Rodriguez began to smile. He was confident that he now had the measure of his man, and he hacked and slashed at his opponent with more and more vigour.

I could see that Holmes was tiring. The perspiration streamed from his face and his shirt was soon soaked through. Rodriguez leaped nimbly onto the desk, scattering the papers, and delivered a downward slash at Holmes, who only just managed to avoid the blow. Holmes' sabre swept in an arc aimed at the Spaniard's legs, but the captain skipped lightly over the blade as it passed by. Then leaping from the desk and dropping to one knee, the killer thrust his sabre upward at Holmes and managed to stab him in the thigh. I gasped in dismay as I saw the dark stain of blood spread over Holmes' trousers.

He hardly seemed to notice, and I knew this was because of the adrenaline that coursed through his body. His eyes shone with the intensity of battle that I had first seen amongst soldiers in Afghanistan.

He glanced down at the wound, exclaimed '*Touche!*' and resumed his attack.

The clash and ring of steel on steel filled the study as the two men cut and thrust backwards and forwards. Inevitably the younger man began to wear down his older opponent, and I feared the worst. Whatever ploy Holmes adopted, the Spaniard had an answer to it. In fact I began to suspect that he was deliberately prolonging the duel, like a cat with a mouse, because there were one or two openings which he could have exploited to finish off Holmes, but he spurned the opportunities.

My friend was now gasping for breath and was forced totally onto the defensive as Rodriguez mounted an exhibition of superb swordsmanship. He was laughing with delight as he hacked and slashed at his rapidly weakening adversary.

I made a decision. I would not let my best friend die at the hands of this arrogant murderer. I drew the pistol from my pocket and released the safety catch. As I raised the gun, however, Holmes did an amazing thing. He feinted to go left, then went LEFT! The captain's blade passed harmlessly over his right shoulder as Holmes thrust straight for the heart. His aim was true and the sabre plunged into the Spaniard's chest.

The smile on his face was replaced by a look of total surprise. He glanced down at the sword sticking out of his body, then looked questioningly at Holmes as if to say, 'However did you manage that?'

Holmes released his blade and stepped back. Rodriguez sank slowly to his knees, and his sabre slipped from his grasp and clattered on the floor. I rushed forward instinctively to try to aid the fellow, but Holmes commanded, 'LEAVE HIM BE, WATSON!'

I stopped in my tracks. The stricken man's eyes glazed over, then with a gurgle in his throat, he pitched forward onto the floor, driving the sabre right through his body and out the other side.

Holmes staggered to an armchair and collapsed into it, totally spent. I checked for a pulse in the Spaniard's neck, but the fellow was dead. Replacing the gun in my pocket, I went to aid my friend and found his injury was not serious. A puncture wound to the *vastus lateralis*, or outer thigh muscle, and I soon stemmed the bleeding. I dressed the wound, using an improvised bandage torn from Holmes' shirt, then poured him a glass of *Rioja* from a well-stocked wine cabinet.

Reaction had set in and Holmes was trembling so much he could not hold the wineglass. I held it for him whilst he drank, and gradually a little colour returned to his cheeks.

I said, 'I was sure you were going to die, old fellow. I fully intended to finish him off, but you beat me to it.

Holmes replied weakly, 'I did not want you to have to break your Hippocratic oath, old friend.'

'That double-bluff feint was remarkable. Wherever did you learn it?'

He smiled a tired smile and replied, 'I didn't, Watson. It was born out of desperation and was my last card. I knew that if it failed I would be dead.'

I responded, 'The angels really *were* on your side.'

He struggled to stand up, saying, 'We must vacate this place as quickly as possible before someone comes.'

I helped him to his feet and asked, 'What about Rodriguez?'

'We have to make it look like suicide. Pass me that onyx inkstand from the desk.' I did as bidden and Holmes said, 'Right, now help me raise the body and sit the sabre's hilt in the inkwell.'

I understood immediately what Holmes was planning. It would look as though Rodriguez had wedged his sabre upright, supported by the heavy inkstand, so that he could fall upon his own sword.

When we had done so, Holmes replaced the dead man's sabre on the wall, and the two of us tidied the room and rearranged the furniture to remove all signs of a struggle.

Holmes said, 'We really need a suicide note.' Casting around, he found a typewriter on a side table and put a clean sheet of paper in it. Sitting down to type, he muttered, 'I hope I can remember enough Spanish.' He typed: '*Yo tengo la culpa, lo siento. José.*'

I asked, 'What does it say?'

He translated, 'I am to blame. I am sorry, Josĕ.' Quickly donning his coat and cape he urged, 'Come, Watson. We must away!'

We hurried from the house, and I had to support Holmes as we descended the steps to the street. We turned left and almost immediately encountered a police constable walking towards us. Holmes, leaning heavily upon me, began to sing loudly, with slurred words, as though very drunk.

I was impressed with my friend's quick thinking and joined the role-play, saying, 'I told you not to drink so much.

Come on, let's get you home.' The constable shook his head and smiled at me sympathetically, before strolling on. Around the next corner I managed to hail a passing cab, and before long we were back at 221b Baker Street.

I cleaned and dressed Holmes' wound properly and gave him some laudanum for the pain. He looked totally exhausted as I helped him into his bed.

'Thank you, Watson,' he said weakly, 'I don't know what I would have done without you.'

'Don't mention it, Holmes. I prescribe complete rest for the next forty-eight hours. I'll check your wound again in the morning. Good night, old chap.'

He did not get his forty-eight hours rest, however, for the next morning we had a visit from Inspector Lestrade. I told him (in a voice loud enough for Holmes to hear) that my friend was in bed with a heavy cold, and was unable to receive visitors.

Lestrade said, 'This is official police business and I really *must* insist.'

Holmes came down in his pyjamas and dressing gown trying hard not to limp. He held a handkerchief to his nose and asked nasally, 'What is it, Lestrade?'

The inspector said, 'There has been another death in Mayfair.'

Holmes enquired, 'Another young woman?'

'No, not this time. A Spanish diplomatist by the name of José Phillipe Rodriguez.'

'Murdered?'

'Suicide, apparently.'

'Apparently?'

'I'm not convinced. Tell me, Mr Holmes, where were you last night between nine p.m. and midnight?'

'Why, Inspector? Am I a suspect?'

'Just answer the question.'

'Very well. I was at a reception held at the Spanish Embassy with Dr Watson here.'

'And did you meet the Deputy Ambassador?'

'Yes.'

'Did you visit his residence?'

'Yes.'

'For what reason?'

Holmes replied, 'Come along, Lestrade. We both know that Rodriguez was the Strangler.'

Lestrade insisted, 'Please answer the question.'

Holmes said, 'Very well. I wanted to be sure that he *was* the Strangler, so I questioned him to that end.'

'And?'

'He admitted it. In fact he gloried in it, *and* in his immunity from prosecution.'

'Then what?'

'I told him about baby Emily, orphaned by him when he killed her mother, Harriet Perkins. I believe that is what finally touched him. Indeed it must have been, since as you say, he later took his own life.'

'So he was alive when you left?'

'Of course.'

Turning to me he asked, 'You can confirm all this Dr Watson?'

I nodded. 'Absolutely, Inspector,' I lied.

Lestrade said, 'There are inconsistencies in the evidence.'

Holmes asked, 'Such as?'

'Well for one thing, there were drops of blood on an armchair some distance from the body. For another, all the swords on the walls showed dust on their hilts, except the second sabre.' He looked keenly at Holmes and asked, 'Did I detect a slight limp as you entered the room?'

Holmes shrugged. 'A mild ankle sprain, nothing more, Inspector.'

Lestrade tutted in mock sympathy. 'You really must be more careful, Mr Holmes. First a cold, now a sprain. Incidentally, your cold symptoms seem to have miraculously disappeared.'

Holmes sighed, 'Look, Inspector, if you have something to say, then for pity's sake say it. I wish to return to my sickbed.'

Lestrade stood up and replied, 'Rest easy, Mr Holmes. The coroner's verdict is bound to declare that Rodriguez took his own life, and the main evidence comes in the form of his suicide note, which only *he* could have written.' He put on his hat and continued, 'Take care of your wound ... I mean *sprain*, Mr Holmes. Good day, gentlemen.'

When he had gone, Holmes and I looked at each other. I said, 'He knows we were lying, Holmes.'

He smiled grimly. 'Of course he does, Watson, but what can he do? The scenario of a high-ranking diplomatist being murdered in his own home is almost as dire as of that same man being charged with murder. Suicide is the only option that will divert public scandal and international repercussions.'

I nodded in agreement. Shortly afterwards there came a ringing of the doorbell and Mrs Hudson ushered in a very distinguished visitor. None other than Don Pedro Garcia Manrique himself.

Holmes smiled, '*Bienvenido*, Don Pedro.'

'Good morning, gentlemen.' He sat down stiffly in the chair Holmes indicated and enquired, 'You know that Rodriguez is dead, Mr Holmes?' My friend nodded, but made no reply. Don Pedro asked, 'You questioned him at length?'

Holmes replied, 'I did.'

'Did he deny any involvement?'

'At first, yes. Though later he not only admitted his guilt, but also revelled in it. When I informed him that his evil had made an orphan of Harriet Perkins' daughter, Emily, he showed no remorse whatsoever.' The Ambassador watched Holmes intently as he spoke, and I got the distinct impression that he was gauging the verity of Holmes' statement.

'Did you question José about the Merito Militar?'

'Yes, but he claimed it had been lost or misplaced.'

'Did you believe him?'

'No I did not.'

Don Pedro sighed and said, 'He was telling you the truth.'

Holmes leapt to his feet, then winced with pain. '*What's that you say?*' he cried.

The old man sat back in his chair and responded, 'Pray calm yourself, Mr Holmes. *I* took his medal.'

Holmes' eyes narrowed and he resumed his seat, saying, 'Perhaps you should tell us the whole story.'

The ambassador replied, 'What you could not know, Mr Holmes, is that these murders were not the first. There was a spate of killings in Madrid last year, in which a number of prostitutes were garrotted. The killings stopped when the Captain came to England, but then they started here. I had to know for sure, so I followed him the night Miss Banks was killed. Unfortunately I was unable to prevent it, but I saw him leave the scene of the crime, to be followed soon after by Miss Wright. I slipped into the house and witnessed his handiwork. I was appalled, and for a while I pondered what to do.' The old man took a deep breath before continuing, 'I love my country, Mr Holmes, as you do yours, and the thought of her medals of honour being worn on the breast of a probable murderer was just too much to bear. I had earlier purloined his medallions until such time as I could determine the truth. José believed they had been misplaced by one of the servants. I decided to plant the Merito Militar in the room to assist the Metropolitan Police. I knew, however, that the authorities could only have him deported and such action would not secure justice, preserve the honour of the Rodriguez family in Madrid, or safeguard other women at risk. Finally I thought of you. Commissioner Thompson had spoken of your doggedness and total dedication to justice, so I followed Miss Wright to find out where she lived. Eventually, when I had formulated my plan, I suggested to her, by means of an anonymous note slipped under her door, that she contact you for help. Unfortunately this was too late to prevent the third murder, but I felt sure that you were the only person who would be able to resolve the situation, and you have succeeded beyond all expectations.'

Holmes asked, 'Why did you not reveal that you knew Rodriguez to be the killer?'

Don Pedro replied, 'I could not flout Spanish diplomatic protocol by overtly betraying a fellow diplomatist. It had to appear to be due solely to the efforts of the English law enforcement authorities.'

Holmes regarded the old man for a few moments before asking, 'My Spanish, in the suicide note, was flawed?'

Don Pedro nodded and replied, 'Only a little, but it needed a much more complete and personal message to convince the authorities of its authenticity, so I provided one.' Here he passed the flawed note to Holmes, who glanced at it, screwed it into a ball and threw it into the fire.

The ambassador continued, 'I confess that my forgery of José's signature was less than perfect, but I had anticipated that Inspector Lestrade would almost certainly ask *me* to verify if it was genuine. Which he did.'

Holmes shook his head and said, 'You really are a remarkable man, Don Pedro. I feel like a marionette whose strings have been manipulated by a master puppeteer.'

The old man replied, '*Lo siento*, I am sorry, but I really had no alternative.' He regarded Holmes for a moment before continuing, 'It is *you* who are remarkable, Mr Holmes, for apart from all your other talents, you must be a consummate swordsman to have defeated my deputy. Yet I notice that you did not emerge completely unscathed.'

Holmes gingerly touched his damaged thigh and replied, 'I'm fine now, thanks to Dr Watson's ministrations.'

Don Pedro stood up slowly and said, 'I am retiring from the Service, Mr Holmes. I have a yearning for some Spanish sunshine to warm these old bones of mine.' He handed Holmes his card, saying, 'I would be delighted to hear from you, in either English or *Castellano*, whenever you can find the time.'

Holmes smiled and shook the ambassador's hand warmly, saying, 'It has been an educational experience making your acquaintance, Don Pedro.'

The old man bowed his head slightly and said, '*Vaya con Dios*, gentlemen.' (Go with God).

When he had gone, I remarked, 'The man was a superb actor, Holmes. The way he reacted when you told him that Rodriguez was the likely killer was *so* convincing, yet he already knew the truth.'

Holmes nodded, 'As you say, Watson, but then what is diplomacy if not an act?'

The following day we had a visit from Molly Wright and Holmes said to her simply, 'The Strangler is dead. You may read in the newspapers of an apparent suicide by a Spanish diplomatist; however, it was *not* suicide.'

Her eyes shone. 'You have *killed* the beast?'

Holmes nodded and replied, 'I shall forever deny it, and you must never tell a living soul, but yes. I ran him through with his own blade.'

She clapped her hands in delight and cried, 'Bravo! Mr Holmes. Bravo!' She kissed him on the cheek and said, 'I thank you on behalf of my friends, both living and dead, and especially on behalf of baby Emily. You really *are* a man of honour.'

*One of the statues
outside Burslam Priory*

THE CHAMBER OF SORROW MYSTERY.

The following account has waited an inordinate time to be released to Sherlock Holmes' faithful public, even though I wrote it immediately upon our return to Baker Street from Epping Forest, all those years ago.

The memories of those few days are etched into my mind with a clarity that is undimmed by time, and I believe they will be with me to my dying day.

Of course the sole reason for the delay was that Mrs Hudson had asked me not to divulge her involvement, and I respected her wishes. Now however, since the dear lady has been in her grave these two years past, she can hardly object to the telling. Indeed, I believe that if the truth had been generally known at the time, she would have elicited more sympathy than condemnation for what she perceived to be her culpable gullibility.

As is often the case, it was the little things which alerted both Holmes and myself to the probability that things were not all they should be on the domestic front. Mrs Hudson had begun to let her usual high standards slide. The normally efficient and ordered regime she maintained and demanded of the maids and servant girls was conspicuously reduced. Our meals were late and often cold. The level of hygiene, normally clinical, was diluted, and she spent more and more evenings out, often not returning home until after midnight.

When Holmes broached the subject to me one evening I suggested, 'Perhaps she has formed a romantic attachment, old fellow. After all, she has been a widow for long enough and is still a handsome enough woman for her age.'

He replied, 'You don't detect any signs of illness in her then, Watson?'

I thought about it for a moment, then said, 'She looked fine to me, albeit a little tense and preoccupied. If I could examine her I would be able to tell you more, but as you well know I am not her physician.'

Holmes was thoughtful for a few moments before adding, 'In addition to all the other irregularities, did you know that she has increased the rent on these rooms twice in the last six months?'

I looked up in some surprise. 'No, I was not aware, Holmes. You never mentioned it, when I last presented my share.'

He waved a dismissive hand and said, 'I meant to tell you sooner. No matter, that is not the point. The point is that whatever is making demands on her time is also making demands on her purse.'

Now I was really intrigued. A genuine romantic involvement should not be costing her money. However, there are ever those tricksters and gigolos who prey on widowed and lonely women to separate them from whatever wealth they may possess. I said as much to Holmes, who nodded in agreement.

'Leave it to me, Watson; I shall get to the bottom of this before long and Mrs H shall be none the wiser.'

There matters rested for the next few days, until one night, after Holmes had retired to his bed and Mrs Hudson was out, I was getting ready for bed myself when I heard a key in the lock. I glanced down the stairs expecting to see Mrs Hudson returning, and was dismayed to observe a total stranger letting himself in with a key. The fellow was a hunchback and appeared to have a withered left arm.

I called down to him, 'You sir, who the devil are you, and how come you into this house?'

He looked up at me and his eyes narrowed. He had a shock of black hair to match his beard, and when he grinned he displayed yellow teeth. 'I'm here to see Sherlock Holmes.

Be ye him?' and he began to climb the stairs in an ungainly, lurching fashion.

I called down, 'No I am not, and stay where you are! I warn you I am armed and a deadly marksman.' The man just laughed and carried on climbing. I rushed into our room, seized my revolver from the drawer and, as I turned to confront the fellow, heard a familiar chuckle. 'Holmes!' I cried, 'you frightened the *life* out of me!'

He lurched into the room still laughing. 'Watson, you should have seen your face!'

I responded, indignantly, 'I should have thought you would have outgrown such schoolboy pranks by now.'

He apologised, saying, 'I'm sorry, Watson, but I had to be sure that the disguise was convincing, and I knew that if *you* failed to penetrate it then Mrs Hudson would surely be unable to.'

'But I saw you go into your room not an hour ago and you never emerged, I'll swear.'

He pulled off the black wig and began to carefully remove his stuck-on beard. 'Quite right, old fellow, but it is not the first time I have shinned down that drainpipe and gone out over the back wall. You must recall that occasion when the wife-killer Blake came to assassinate me and emptied all six bullets into the bolster. I had exited via the pipe and came in to nab him from behind. The poor fellow thought I was a ghost.'

'Yes, I remember, Holmes. I also remember that Mrs Hudson was not well pleased at the damage to both bolster and mattress. And speaking of Mrs Hudson, I take it that you have not yet actually followed her to find out where she goes?'

In between removing the yellow dye from his teeth he replied, 'Not yet, old fellow, but the next time she sallies forth you can be sure she will have company.'

He was as good as his word, for two nights later he returned in serious mood. As he removed his disguise he confided, 'She has fallen in league with a gaggle of spiritualists, Watson.'

I sighed with relief, saying, 'I'm fairly certain that the collective noun for a group of spiritualists is not a 'gaggle', but surely there can be no harm in that, Holmes.'

He shook his head. 'I'm not so sure. The leader of the group is a certain Madam La Conte, and if ever I saw a powerful and ruthless woman it is Madam La Conte. Oh, she is good. Very convincing, and her routine is impressive. She is operating from a small private chapel on the Edgware Road and is playing to full houses. They were queuing to get in, and I only just made it.'

'I take it then, that you are a sceptic so far as spiritualism is concerned?

'I do *not* believe in ghosts, Watson, and I think I am right in saying that virtually every medium ever investigated scientifically has failed to convince.'

I rejoined, 'There are many notable figures, including men of science, who believe in it.'

He smiled and countered, 'There are many people who still believe that the earth is flat, but it does not make it so.'

I said, 'So tell me, what was this Madam La Conte's routine that impressed you so?'

'Amongst other things, she exuded ectoplasm from her body whilst in a trance.'

'Ectoplasm? Isn't that the substance that ghosts are supposed to be made of?'

Holmes nodded. 'That's right, Watson.'

'I'm sure I have read somewhere that ectoplasm has been shown to have actual *weight.*'

'I too have heard such claims. I have also heard that it is "light fugitive", in other words it disappears in strong light. A trifle convenient, wouldn't you say?'

I argued, 'But what about all the photographs of ghosts there have been over the years?'

Holmes shrugged. 'I can't account for them all, but I'm sure that most of them will be fakes, accidents or double exposures. *I* believe in what I can see, touch, smell, hear or taste, and *none* of my senses has ever registered a ghost.'

'Some people are more receptive than others,' I countered.

'Have *you* ever seen one, Watson?'

'Well no. But I try to keep an open mind about such things.'

'In that case, old friend, you must accompany me the next time I follow Mrs Hudson. I will disguise you so that even your own mother wouldn't recognise you!' I was tempted by the proposition. I had never before in my life been to a seance, and I was intrigued to see how my friend would alter my appearance.

'By Jove! Holmes,' I said, 'I believe I will.' Then after a moment I asked, 'But why do you need to follow her again, now that you have established where she goes?'

'Because, Watson, I believe they have further plans for her. She is one of a small core of converts who are being groomed for something extra. There is talk of a special gathering to be held soon, and she will be one of those attending.'

I asked, 'When is the next seance of this Madam La Conte to be held?'

'Thursday at eight.'

I nodded. 'I shall look forward to it.'

Thursday evening saw me seated before Holmes' dressing table mirror undergoing a remarkable transformation. My friend's talent as a make-up artist is formidable. With padding in my cheeks, muttonchop whiskers and tortoiseshell spectacles, I was a different person. He brushed white powder into my already greying hair and I looked ten years older. Rouge red cheeks and nose completed the illusion, and I was amazed. I could not even recognise myself, so I was sure that Mrs Hudson would be unable to.

We left the house ten minutes after she did and hailed a cab to take us to the Edgware Road. As we approached the chapel, it became obvious that this was going to be another full house, for the queue was already extensive. Holmes dismissed the cab and we went to join the waiting throng. I had to suppress a chuckle as I glanced at my friend shuffling along beside me like the Hunchback of Notre Dame!

Near the front of the queue I could see Mrs Hudson in her feathered black hat and black coat with a fox fur around her shoulders.

Presently we entered the vestibule, where a thin, morose individual, in a long frock coat, held out a collection plate. Although the service was ostensibly free, everyone dropped silver coins onto the donation platter. We did likewise and passed through into the chapel. It was gloomy inside, being lit mainly by rows of candles. We took our places on the pews and waited for events to unfold.

An oval table, with a fluted central leg, stood with three chairs on a raised area before the altar, which was concealed by burgundy-coloured drapes. When the chapel was full, the curtains parted and Madam La Conte swept in. She was a tall, imposing figure who carried herself almost regally. Her chestnut hair was pinned back into a bun, and she wore a long black gown. Her only jewellery was a small gold crucifix on a chain. Her face was lean and angular and seemed unnaturally pale.

She took her place behind the table and smiled at the assembly. 'Welcome, my friends,' she said, with just a trace of an accent. 'May I present my two helpers, François and Henri.' On cue two swarthy individuals in black evening suits entered and sat down on either side of her. She remained standing and said, 'I feel the signs are auspicious for a positive session this evening. The ether is vibrant with energy and I'm sure we will not be disappointed.'

There followed a lengthy series of questions and answers along the lines of; 'Does the name Horace mean anything to anyone?' Whereupon a lady would reply; 'Yes, that's my husband who passed away last year.' Then Madam La Conte would relay a message of love and hope from beyond the grave. This sort of thing was repeated even to the extent that one message purported to come from Rover, a faithful spaniel, to his weeping mistress. I was beginning to fidget with boredom, when suddenly Madam La Conte exclaimed, 'I am detecting ripples in the ether! There is an unbeliever in our midst.' People began to look at each other and I glanced at Holmes, but he stared impassively ahead. She came to the edge of the dais and, raising her arms, she declared, 'Perhaps a little demonstration will convince the sceptic.'

She returned and sat down at the table, where she proceeded to go into a trance. Throwing back her head she began to shake and shiver as someone with the ague, and a piercing wail emanated from her mouth that raised the hairs on the back of my neck. It sounded like a soul in torment. Her eyes rolled upwards until only the whites were visible, and then she began to speak in a deep resonant voice.

She said, 'After his resurrection, Jesus spoke unto Thomas saying, Dost thou doubt that I am risen?' She stood up slowly and continued, 'Even as Christ arose, so shall ye,' and she pointed at Henri.

The man unbuttoned his coat and climbed onto the table. He laid himself down full length, with his head over one end and his feet over the other. Madam La Conte closed her eyes and waited. There was absolute silence in the chapel. Slowly she raised her arms like some fantastic puppeteer and Henri began to float up off the table! My eyes nearly popped out of my head. I could not believe what I was seeing. He was as straight and rigid as a ramrod, the only movement being the fall of his coat, as he continued to rise. Eventually he stopped a full eighteen inches or more above the table, and we could see the space beneath him quite clearly. While Madam La Conte seemed to hold him aloft on invisible strings, François passed his hands above and below Henri's head and feet to demonstrate the absence of wires. When he had rejoined Madam La Conte, she slowly lowered her hands and Henri settled gently back down onto the table. There was pandemonium in the hall. People were clapping and shouting, and at least two women fainted. There were cries of, 'It's a miracle! It's a miracle!' I had never seen anything like it before in my life. I turned to Holmes and he winked at me before standing up and shouting, '*I* was the unbeliever! My friend here, Major Thomas, tried to convince me, but I was sceptical. I am a sceptic no longer. The saints be praised. It *is* a miracle!'

Madam La Conte flopped back into her chair like a rag doll, and while Henri climbed down from the table, François chafed the lady's hands in an effort to revive her. Gradually she came out of her trance and passed a hand over her eyes. She looked around as though unsure of where she was, then smiled weakly at François.

Henri stepped forward and announced, 'Ladies and gentlemen, I am afraid that what you have just witnessed has taken a great deal out of Madam La Conte. This small miracle is extremely demanding of psychic energy, and the lady is spent. Please show your appreciation for our charitable causes on your way out, and may the spirits guide you.'

The congregation applauded then slowly began to file out. I started to rise, but Holmes gripped my sleeve and tugged me back into my seat. We sat on while the chapel largely emptied. It was then that I noticed that Mrs Hudson and a few others also remained. Presently Holmes rose and, motioning me to remain where I was, shuffled forward to speak with Madam La Conte. After a few minutes earnest conversation with her, he returned and indicated that we were leaving.

Outside, as Holmes hailed a cab to take us back to Baker Street, I said, 'That was the most incredible thing I have ever seen, Holmes. Of course I have *heard* of people being levitated, but I never thought I would live to see it with my own eyes.'

A cab pulled up, and we had settled ourselves inside before Holmes conceded, 'Indeed, Watson. Very impressive. Did I not say she was good?'

I asked, 'What was it that you discussed with her?'

He smiled archly and replied, 'I intimated that we are seekers of enlightenment and as such we have pursued our goal amongst the Mullahs of Persia, the Mahatmas and Fakirs of the Indian sub-continent and even amongst the Lamas of Tibet. The implication being that we are men of some financial standing and fruit ripe for the picking.'

'And as a consequence?'

'We are invited to attend a very special gathering this weekend, at an ancient priory in Epping Forest. She called it Burslam Priory, as I recall.'

'*What*!' I exclaimed. 'Are you sure?'

'I believe so, Watson. Why?'

'Good heavens, Holmes! You mean to say that you have never heard of Burslam Priory? Why, it is said to be the most haunted house in England and has been since the Middle Ages.'

Holmes shrugged. 'Unless it touches on crime or its perpetrators, Watson, it is doubtful I would have heard of it. I have enough to monitor as it is, with the criminals of this great metropolis, not to say these isles, without worrying about haunted houses.'

I argued, 'But this one is *renowned*. It is said to be stalked by several ghosts, the most famous of which is the

"Poor Postulant", one Jane Stiles. An unfortunate novice nun who was accused of witchcraft and tortured to death by the Witchfinder General. Her spectre is reputedly seen regularly to this day.'

Holmes commented, 'You seem to know a great deal about all this, Watson.'

'I read an article about the place and its history, just last month in the Empire magazine. Apparently the nun was killed by crushing. They placed a door on her front and piled stones upon it until she either confessed, or died. She would not confess to being a witch.'

Holmes shook his head and remarked, 'What a brutal race we were in those days, Watson.' The cab pulled up outside 221b Baker Street and we climbed out.

Later, as we sipped a glass of sherry each, I said, 'I should still have the magazine here somewhere... Ah here it is!' I opened it to the article and read: *There is a particular room in the priory tower which seems to be the main centre for manifestations. In the eighteenth century the then Mother Superior, Sister Benedict, saw the ghost of the Poor Postulant in that room and called it 'Cubiculum Dolor', The Chamber of Sorrow. She never again entered the room for the rest of her life. Over the decades the ghostly figure has been seen in or near that room on numerous occasions. When the Order of the Silent Sisters was dissolved by the Abbey early this century, Burslam Priory was locked and boarded up, its brooding air of mystery growing like the weeds of neglect around it. Then, some ten years ago, it was bought by a consortium of London business men and re-opened as a sort of guest house, trading on its reputation as the most haunted house in England. It has been maintained in its original state and is still lit by candles. Paying guests sleep in the cells, which were once occupied by the sisters, though they are not expected to cook their own meals or clean their own cells. Burslam has its own catering staff and chamber maids, none of whom, however, would dream of sleeping in the priory itself, preferring the unhaunted lodge house in the grounds. The atmospheric old place can be hired for ghostly parties, seances and the like, though anyone wishing to do so would be well advised to avoid such dates as October 31st, for it is in great demand during Halloween.*

Holmes nodded, 'Well well well. It seems we are in for an interesting weekend, Watson. Perhaps one of us will be lucky enough to be allocated The Chamber of Sorrow.'

'Or *unlucky* enough.' I countered.

'What's this, old fellow? Could that be a white feather I glimpse in your top pocket?'

I bristled, 'I'm not afraid, Holmes, and I'll prove it by sleeping in the accursed room if I have to.'

'Bravo, Watson! Stout fellow. You know I was only teasing you.'

I said, 'Nevertheless, you shall see.'

Saturday afternoon saw us well on our way to Epping Forest in a sturdy dogcart, ideally suited to the rough country roads. The track through the forest eventually opened onto a large clearing and we had our first view of Burslam Priory. It was a forbidding aspect. Its weathered sandstone looked as old as time itself, and the ancient ivy that covered two-thirds of the building marked the centuries it had stood there. In the dense shade of mature oak and ash trees the house seemed to brood in a timeless silence. Our carriage drew up at the huge iron gates and we climbed out. The path took us past the lodge and the gravestones of the Silent Sisters, until we came to a wooden bridge over a dry moat bed. Beyond, two weathered oaken doors with black iron studs and hinges barred the gothic arched portal. Standing like sentinels, on either side of the entrance, were life-sized statues of cowled women with heads bowed as if in penitence or mourning. At the eastern end of the building was a stout tower with castellations and stained-glass windows, and, as I looked, a large black raven took off from the battlements and flew silently away into the forest.

We were greeted by Frančois, who showed us into a spacious hall. This room at least was not too Spartan, for comfortable easy chairs and sofas surrounded a cheerful log fire. Religious paintings adorned the walls above dark oaken wainscoting, and hanging from the smoke-blackened, vaulted ceiling were two large unlit candle chandeliers.

There were several people already assembled, including Mrs Hudson and at least four others I recognised from the chapel. Mrs Hudson looked at Holmes and myself without a glimmer of recognition, and I found it strange that no introductions were made. Henri circulated with trays of drinks and refreshments and we sat around making idle conversation whilst waiting for Madam La Conte to put in an appearance.

Eventually she strode in, wearing a striking full-length crimson gown and matching headband. Again her only concession to adornment was the small gold crucifix.

She smiled at us and said, 'Welcome to Burslam Priory, ladies and gentlemen. I would like to start by assuring you all that I consider each of you to be particularly special. Very few people indeed are received into the Inner Circle of our movement. Gifted individuals with psychic auras, which are visible to me, stand out from the crowd as the chosen few, and all of you here fit that description. Over this weekend I hope to share with you the mysteries of the Cosmos and imbue each of you with powers beyond your wildest dreams.' Strolling amongst us, she looked each of us in the eyes with a confident candour that was impressive. She continued, 'Those with blue auras, such as yourselves, are almost always intelligent, artistic and sensitive and rarely materialistically minded. However, if wealth *is* what you seek, then the powers I am about to instil in you will make that achievement easily attainable.'

She sipped from a glass of red wine before continuing, 'You all saw me levitate Henri the other evening; well, the psychic energy that I tapped into to perform that feat is the life force that is in and around all of us. I've no doubt you have all heard of people called "diviners" who with the aid of a forked hazel twig can detect water, often hundreds of feet underground. Or people called "seers" who can foresee the future. There are even those who can read other people's minds. They all feed on this cosmological force for their power. If you trust me and place your faith in me, I can bestow those powers on each and every one of you. You will be able to perform minor miracles, bend people to your will, predict the future and even heal the sick.' She looked around to gauge the effect her words were having, and I too glanced about. Madam La Conte could hardly have been disappointed, for there was rapt attention and a gleam of desire in everyone's eyes. Evidently what she offered them was highly desirable.

She went on, 'Of course, as in everything, there is a price to pay. Most of the world's holiest men have forsaken all wealth and live an ascetic life on high mountains or in barren deserts. Indeed, it is written in the Holy Bible that 'It is easier for a camel to pass through the eye of a needle, than for a rich man to enter the kingdom of heaven.' She looked at us all in turn before saying, 'I have spoken with most of you already on this subject and will talk to the others later, but now I think we should have our first gathering.'

Outside the light was fading as evening approached, and a strengthening breeze blew falling leaves against the windows. Madam La Conte called Henri and asked him to light the candles in the chandeliers. We watched as he expertly lowered them on their ropes before lighting the candles with a long taper. After he had secured the lights,

Madam La Conte beckoned us all to join her around an oblong table by the window.

She sat down next to Henri, saying, 'François will join us later, but now I want you to hold hands with your neighbour and complete the circle.' When we had done so, she closed her eyes and breathed deeply and regularly for some time. The only sounds were the sighing of the wind outside and the crackle of the burning logs in the grate. Finally, after several minutes, our hostess threw back her head and said in that strangely resonant voice, 'Is there anybody there?' She repeated the question, adding, 'Give us a sign of your presence.'

For at least a minute nothing happened, then suddenly there was a loud rap on the table. I jumped with the shock of it and glanced at Holmes, but he was as impassive as ever.

Madam La Conte said, 'Do you have a message for anyone here? Knock once for yes or twice for no.' There was a single knock. She then said, 'Moving clockwise from me, indicate the recipient.' There were four further raps. She said, 'The message is for Mrs Hudson?' Another knock. Mrs H looked around nervously. Madam La Conte asked, 'Is it good news?' Again the single knock. Using a simple code of one knock for A, two for B and so on, it spelled out the message, 'This is your dear husband James. Trust the medium, my darling, and be guided by her. She is a good woman. I look forward to the time when we will be reunited. I love you.'

Mrs Hudson was overcome with emotion and her tears flowed freely. She went to reach for her handkerchief when Madam La Conte screamed, '*DON'T BREAK THE CIRCLE!*' Too late, I realised, as suddenly the table began to rise up off the floor! Madam La Conte urged, 'Hold hands again. Don't let go. An elemental spirit is trying to gain entrance to this world!' The table began to buck up and down like a wild thing. First one end would tip up, then the other. It was frightening to feel the power within it as it pulsed and trembled with a life force of its own.

Madam La Conte cried out in a loud voice, *'Allez-vous-en Diablo! Hypage Satana*!* For a moment the frantic activity seemed to abate, only for it to be renewed with even more energy. Now the table began to rise up and slam back down onto the wooden floorboards with loud crashes again and again. We had difficulty keeping our hands on its top and I half expected the thing to disintegrate. I was becoming more and more alarmed and started to stand up, but Madam La Conte shouted, *'REMAIN IN YOUR SEATS. DON'T BREAK THE CIRCLE.'* I hung on grimly to Holmes' and Mrs Hudson's hands, but now there rose up from beneath our feet an unholy wail which started as a low moan, then increased in pitch until it jarred every nerve in my body. It sounded like all the souls in purgatory baying for release, and it made my blood run cold.

Madam La Conte's body seemed to stiffen, and her eyes rolled upwards in her head until only the whites were visible. Then, as a series of shudders racked her body, a white mist began to issue from her torso just below the sternum. Almost immediately the banshee wail began to subside, and the table floated down to settle gently on the floor. As the last echoes of that hellish sound died away, the ectoplasm emanating from our hostess ebbed and Madam La Conte slumped forward onto the table in a dead faint.

I wanted to minister to her, but was afraid to break the circle. However, Henri seemed to consider it safe to do so and leaped to aid his mistress. I was just about to offer my services as a doctor, when Holmes squeezed my hand in warning. Of course! In all the excitement I had forgotten that I was masquerading as Major Thomas.

Henri's ministrations were hardly necessary, as Madam La Conte revived quickly and seemed none the worse for her ordeal. She smiled to reassure us and said, 'My apologies, ladies and gentlemen. I should have warned you not to break the circle. Demons are forever trying to gain access to our world, but as you saw, with the power, which soon each of you will possess, I was more than a match for him.'

There were murmurs of relief from the group, and Mrs Hudson apologised for her error. Madam La Conte said, 'Perhaps we have had enough excitement for the time being. I propose we adjourn for supper and re-convene later.' There was general agreement, and the group broke up.

When Holmes and I were out of earshot of the others, I asked, 'Well what do you make of that then, Holmes?'

He nodded. 'Fascinating, Watson. Absolutely fascinating.' He was thoughtful for a moment before saying, 'Look, old fellow, I wish to do a little ferreting. If anyone enquires, indicate that I am somewhat indisposed and will return presently.' Before I could protest at being left alone among strangers, he was gone.

I wandered aimlessly about before being buttonholed by one of the group, a Mr Sanderson, who enthused about what we had just witnessed. He confided to me that he was very interested in the occult and aspired to gain the 'power' that Madam La Conte had talked of. I feigned a desire to learn the secrets of re-incarnation and pretended to be interested in immortality.

Presently we were summoned to the refectory for supper, but there was still no sign of Holmes. When we sat down to eat, Madam La Conte enquired as to the whereabouts of my companion. I was just about to explain that he was feeling a little unwell, when Holmes shuffled in.

'My apologies, Madam, but a chronic condition of mine inconveniences me from time to time.' Without further elaboration he took his seat next to me at the table.

The meal was excellent and the wine plentiful. So much so that the whole group soon recovered from the earlier trauma of the seance, and when our hostess suggested another session, the proposal was greeted with enthusiasm. Once again we sat around the table, but this time Madam La Conte produced a ouija planchette, with a pencil attached and a large sheet of white paper. Written on the paper were the words YES and NO.

She arranged the objects in the centre of the table and said, 'For a little light relief, does anybody have a question to ask of the spirits?'

We looked at each other to see who would be the first to try. Mr Sanderson said, only half joking, 'Which horse will win the St. Leger next week?'

We all laughed, but Madam La Conte replied, 'With a little more preparation and the performance of a certain ritual, I could tell you.' She was deadly serious, and the smiles on our faces faded. She went on, 'You yourselves will be able to do such things. That is what having the power means.'

Holmes said, 'I have a question to ask of the spirits.'

Madam La Conte regarded him coolly and replied, 'Then do so by all means.'

Holmes asked, 'Which one of us should sleep in the Chamber of Sorrow tonight?' I glanced at him, but he held the Frenchwoman's gaze. A frown crossed her face for an instant, then it was gone. She nodded and closed her eyes. Again a silent expectancy descended, and as the seconds ticked by I began to feel uneasy. I remembered the wild bucking of the table and half expected it to start again. Outside, the breeze had strengthened to a gusting wind, which could be heard moaning intermittently in the chimney as it tugged at the flames and flickered the candles above us.

Madam La Conte suddenly gasped as though drenched with cold water and said, in that almost masculine voice, 'I feel a presence. Is there anybody there?' A log settled in the fireplace with a soft hiss, but nothing else moved. She repeated the question and waited, but again nothing happened.

I was about to ask, 'Should we not each have a finger on the planchette for this to work?' when, without warning, it suddenly shot across the paper of its own volition and pointed at the word YES. We were stunned. Even Holmes' sang-froid deserted him and he stared at the animated wooden pointer. At the collective gasp we all uttered, Madam La Conte opened her eyes and looked at the planchette, pointing rigidly at the YES. For the briefest moment I thought I saw a look of fear in her eyes, but it was so fleeting I could not be sure.

She asked, 'Who are you?'

The pointer started to move slowly and the pencil wrote the letter J, then the letter A, then N. As it did so it began to speed up, until soon it was flying over the sheet. It spelled out the name, JANE STILES.

I blurted out, *'The Poor Postulant!'* Everybody looked at me, and I wilted in my seat.

Madam La Conte asked, 'Who shall sleep in The Chamber of Sorrow tonight?'

With startling suddenness the planchette shot across the table and pointed directly at *me!* I almost fainted. My first impulse was to jump up and leave, but Holmes' earlier gibe about the white feather and my display of bravado came to mind. I nodded and said, albeit a little croakily, 'So be it.'

Madam La Conte asked, 'Do you have a message for anybody here?'

The planchette moved again to YES.

Madam La Conte asked, 'Who?'

The pointer wrote, *'Ye all.'*

'And what is your message?'

The planchette began to flow and its stylus scribbled the following appeal in a spidery hand;

'May ye never suffer the torment and despair that is my cup of bitterness. Was my sin so vile that the cleansing flame of Purgatory can ne'er be quenched? I pray there be one among ye of compassion and fortitude withal to hearken to the plea of this wretched supplicant. Deus det, Deus det, Deus det.'

The planchette stopped, and outside the wind moaned and sighed in counterpoint to this tragic invocation.

Holmes whispered to me, 'Deus det?'

I translated, 'God grant it be so.'

Madam La Conte asked, 'Are you still there?' But the planchette remained motionless. A minute passed by, then another, but still there was no movement.

Suddenly Holmes began to shudder and moan, and we all looked at him. I thought he might be having a heart attack, but he winked surreptitiously at me before standing up and crying, 'My arm! My arm!' His ostensibly withered left arm was uncurling and straightening with an accompanying creaking noise, which I realised he was making with his mouth. He shouted, 'IT'S A MIRACLE!' Then straightening his hunched back, he began to stand up to his full height. 'Look!' he cried, 'my crouchback is cured! Praise the Lord, ANOTHER MIRACLE!' The group around the table stared in wide-eyed wonder, and even Madam La Conte's self-assuredness was strained as she watched my friend in amazement. Finally Holmes pulled off his wig and beard, saying, 'Why, I feel like a different person altogether!'

Mrs Hudson cried, *'Mr Holmes*! Is it really you? What on earth is going on?'

He replied, 'Calm yourself, Mrs Hudson. It is indeed I, and I am here to expose these charlatans for what they are. You have fallen into the clutches of a gang of fraudsters bent on duping you into parting with property or wealth.'

She looked at him incredulously. 'Surely not, Mr Holmes.'

Madam La Conte cried, 'How dare you, sir? This is slander, gross slander.' Henri and Francois rose threateningly from their chairs, but Holmes suddenly produced my old service revolver from his pocket and pointed it in their direction.

'Remain in your seats, gentlemen,' he commanded in icy tones, and the two Frenchmen sat down again meekly. Holmes turned to me and said, 'You may as well divest yourself also, Watson. Those cheek pads can become uncomfortable after a while.'

I did as Holmes suggested and was indeed relieved to do so.

Mrs Hudson stared at me in disbelief. 'Dr Watson! I thought there was something familiar about your voice, but I would never have recognised you in a hundred years.'

Holmes, without taking his eyes off the Gallic trio, said, 'Tell me that the Madam has asked nothing of you, Mrs Hudson.'

Our landlady looked a little sheepish and conceded, 'Well, she did talk of signing over the deeds to the house on Baker Street, but she assured me that with the Power, I could afford ten such properties.'

Holmes nodded knowingly. 'I'm sure the rest of you can tell similar tales?'

Mr Sanderson said, 'She promised me I would be able to foretell the results of sporting events, if I would donate five hundred guineas to her charitable causes.'

Holmes nodded. 'Just as I suspected. The oldest confidence trick of all, the pot of gold at the end of the rainbow. Few indeed are immune to such temptation.'

Madam La Conte said defiantly, 'We are not charlatans. You saw the miracles I performed.'

Holmes laughed, 'Miracles? Why they were, without exception, nothing more than conjuring tricks. Albeit extremely sophisticated ones.'

I protested, 'Surely not, Holmes. What about the levitation? You saw Frančois prove there could be no wires suspending the fellow.'

'As you say, Watson, there *were* no wires, but as with any good conjuring trick, one has to watch the periphery of the action to detect what is real and what is illusion. You should watch the magician's left hand if he holds the cards in his right.'

I said, 'So you know how it was achieved?'

'Of course, old fellow. One of the reasons I went up to speak with the Madam at the chapel was so that I could get a glimpse at the table. That glimpse was enough to confirm my hypothesis.'

'Then pray satisfy our curiosity, Holmes.'

He asked, 'Do you recall, when the lady indicated she was going to levitate Henri, he unbuttoned his coat before climbing onto the table?'

'Yes that's right, he did.'

'Well that was *the* most important ploy and crucial to the success of the illusion.'

'How so?'

'Because when the central portion of the table rose up elevating him, his hanging coat hid the hydraulic piston which propelled him!'

I was stunned. 'The devil you say! A hydraulic piston?'

Holmes nodded. 'Concealed in the central leg of the table. When I looked at the tabletop I could see a slight circular gap around the floral marquetry inlay at the centre. This was the platform on which he rode! A man's centre of gravity in the supine position is in the small of his back, and Henri carefully positioned himself thus. Then, holding his body rigid, he appeared to float upwards.'

I nodded in understanding and added, 'And Frančois operated the hidden actuating lever?'

'Exactly! In hydraulics, Watson, there is a phenomenon called "mechanical advantage" which allows a large mass to be lifted by a relatively small force. It was this that enabled Frančois to elevate Henri with ease.'

I sighed, 'I feel cheated, Holmes. Here I was convinced I had finally witnessed something truly esoteric and you have shown it to be mundane.'

Holmes replied, 'Sorry, old chap, but you *did* ask.'

Mrs Hudson asked, 'But what about the table rapping?'

Holmes replied, 'Take a look at Henri's right hand. As you can see, he wears a rather ugly snake ring on his middle finger. When we all held hands at the start, I noticed that the ring was missing. Immediately realised that what Madam La Conte was holding in her left hand was, in fact, a fake hand inserted into the sleeve of Henri's coat. He, in the meantime, was using the ring on his finger to strike the underside of the table in response to the lady's questions.'

There were murmurings around the table at this revelation, and Madam La Conte blustered, 'This is absolute rubbish.'

Holmes responded, 'An inspection of the jacket should prove or disprove my assertion.' Pointing the pistol at Henri's head, Holmes commanded, 'Kindly remove the garment and pass it to Dr. Watson.'

The Frenchman looked to his mistress for guidance, but she was glaring at Holmes. Finally Henri sullenly acquiesced to the demand and handed me his jacket. I searched its pockets and almost immediately found what Holmes had predicted, a moulded rubber hand. It was extremely lifelike in appearance, but soft enough to be enfolded in my fist. 'Well done, Holmes,' I said, holding it up for the others to see.

Mr Sanderson muttered, 'Damned fraudsters!'

Another gentleman, whose name turned out to be Tavistock, asked, 'How on earth did they make the table leap about and hover in the air like that?'

Holmes smiled and replied, 'That was particularly clever. We all looked in vain for suspension wires, but the table was not lifted from above. It was supported from *below*. When my end of the table first raised up off the floor, I tried to pass my foot beneath the leg nearest to me. It encountered a thin metal rod. You will recall my indisposition before supper? Well in reality I was investigating the cellar beneath this room.' He looked at Madam La Conte with something akin to admiration as he went on, 'You have gone to a great deal of trouble to create these impressive illusions, but then of course the potential rewards were worth it.'

Turning back to us, he said, 'This table has thin steel rods screwed into the base of each leg. These rods pass through four holes drilled in the floorboards and hang down into the cellar. The table was raised and lowered on cue by Frančois and the other individual, the collection plate bearer from the chapel.' He looked at Madam La Conte, who now seemed to have accepted that the game was over.

She said, 'His name is Jacques.'

Holmes nodded and said to me, 'Don't let me forget Jacques, Watson. He is, as we speak, bound and gagged in the cellar with just the rats for company.'

I said, 'Good Lord, Holmes!'

He made a dismissive gesture and asserted, 'The fellow is fine. I know how to render a man unconscious without inflicting serious harm.' Turning again to the others, he said, 'There are some interesting devices below us, for example a hand-cranked wind fan that can emit anything from a low moan to a piercing screech, depending on how fast one turns the handle.'

Sanderson said, 'That accounts for the wailing we heard.'

Holmes continued, 'In addition there is a hollow metal tube and funnel inserted into a floorboard and a smoke-generating can of the type used by beekeepers. No doubt Madam La Conte was able to connect a thin rubber hose, concealed under her dress, to this tube which allowed her to exude her 'ectoplasm'.'

Mrs Hudson shook her head and said, 'I can't believe I have been so stupid as to be duped by these tricks, Mr Holmes.'

My friend replied, 'Don't be too hard on yourself, Mrs H. The illusions were cleverly done, and the setting of England's most haunted house contributed the perfect atmosphere.'

I asked, 'What about the last trick, the spirit writing produced by the planchette?'

Holmes, for the first time, displayed uncertainty. 'That trick was exceptional, Watson, and I have to confess that at present, I do not know quite how it was achieved. Perhaps Henri influenced the movement of the planchette with a strong magnet, from beneath the table.'

I picked up the planchette and examined its three feet. 'They look to be made of wood to me, old fellow,' I said.

Passing the revolver to me, he took the planchette and examined it carefully.

'And,' I added, 'I have searched the pockets of Henri's coat and I found no magnet.'

Holmes sighed and conceded, 'As I say, Watson, I can't yet explain it, but I am convinced it was a trick, nevertheless.'

Madam La Conte asked, 'What do you intend to do with us? Hand us over to the authorities?'

Holmes replied, 'That really depends on these good people here, whom you sought to defraud. If they so decide they can prefer charges on you through due process. However, since I have prevented any actual transaction of money or property being carried out, they may decide to be lenient. For my part I would not wish to reveal, to all the good people who have attended the chapel and received messages of love from beyond the grave, that you are a fake. If you each undertake to return to France and never come back, I would be in favour of releasing you now.' He looked around the table at the others, and there was general agreement and a nodding of heads.

Mr Sanderson sighed, 'It would have been so good to be able to always pick the winners.'

Holmes responded, 'Such stuff as dreams are made on, but of no substance.' Turning to Madam La Conte he presented his card and said, 'I shall expect a letter from you with a Paris postmark, within seven days, confirming that you are once again on French soil, or I shall inform Scotland Yard of your activities.'

She snatched the card from him with ill grace and rejoined, 'We will leave at first light, and you can be sure we shall not be coming back to your miserable little country.'

Holmes responded, 'Have a care, Madam, lest I contact my good friend Inspector Deschamps of the Sûreté to have him investigate your machinations in La Belle France.'

She sneered, 'You think yourself so clever, Mr high and mighty Holmes, but you won't fathom out the last trick. You won't work it out because it was *not* an illusion!' With that she swept from the room with her two cohorts in tow.

Holmes called after her, 'Don't forget Jacques in the cellar!'

Mrs Hudson, Sanderson, Tavistock and the others gathered round and sheepishly thanked Holmes for saving them from the tricksters. As they shook his hand, he said, 'All's well that ends well, but there is a lesson to be learned from this, and you don't need me to spell it out.' They all nodded and murmured in agreement.

Shortly afterward, the group dispersed to their rooms, and collecting my bag, I asked a maid to direct me to the Chamber of Sorrow.

Holmes asked, 'So you still intend to sleep there?'

'Of course, old fellow,' I said, displaying more confidence than I actually felt.

'Good night then, Watson, and I hope you have an undisturbed night.'

'Good night, Holmes.'

The maid handed me a candlestick with a new candle in it, and she led the way with one of her own. We went along a couple of gloomy corridors, lit by bracketed candles, and up a flight of creaky stairs. Then through a door, up a second, narrower staircase and into an octagonal room at the top of the tower. Tall windows on three sides reflected our lights back at us and by this feeble illumination, I discerned a large four-poster bed and an ancient dresser with a water jug and bowl on it. There was a fireplace in the room, but no fire in the grate. It felt cold and damp, and the moaning of the wind seemed louder up here than downstairs. The maid bade me good night and left, and I felt terribly alone.

Though I knew that Holmes and the others were not so far away, I felt totally isolated in that high, cold chamber. I went to one of the windows and peered out, but there was little to see. The dark forest seemed to press in on all sides, and overhead scudding clouds obscured the moon. I placed the candlestick on the bedside table and undressed for bed. Suddenly there came a scratching sound at the window which made me catch my breath, but it was only the branches of an old oak tree being blown by the wind. I jumped into bed and hugged the bedclothes up to my chin, peering into the flickering shadows of the room. I felt like a little boy again, gripped by nameless fears.

'Come along, old chap,' I chided myself aloud. 'You are a man of science! How would your fellow physicians react if they could see you now?' I lay down and closed my eyes, but I did not blow out the candle.

The wind grew stronger, and I could hear it sighing and moaning around the battlements. My eyes would not stay shut. At every new sound they popped open of their own volition. I was convinced that I would not sleep a wink all night, but I must have finally dozed off because something woke me with a start and I looked at the candle. It had burned down to less than half its original length. The wind had abated somewhat and I listened for whatever it was that had wakened me. There! A scuttling sound behind the wainscot. Just a mouse, old chap. Get back to sleep. But wait. What's that over near the fireplace? The shadows seemed blacker there. I blinked and rubbed my eyes. A draught flickered the candle flame and the other shadows danced on the walls, but this one did not move! My blood ran cold. As I watched, the shadow deepened and started to take form. I was immediately reminded of pictures I had seen of the grim reaper. A cowled figure in black, with no face!

I tried to pray. 'Our Father who art in heaven...' but the words would not form because my teeth were chattering with fear. The wraith floated towards me, and I felt the hairs on my head and arms literally stand on end. My heart seemed to be in my throat so that I could hardly breathe, and its pounding filled my ears. I was on the verge of fainting when the figure stopped, and by the candle's feeble light I saw that it was a young nun. She looked at me with such pleading that I knew immediately she meant me no harm. Her face was the most sorrowful countenance I had ever seen, and she spread her arms in silent appeal.

I tried to speak, but my voice was a croak. I tried again. 'Are you Jane Stiles?'

She nodded slowly.

'What do you want of me?'

She reached out her arm and with a long, slim finger beckoned me to follow her. Then she turned and glided towards the fireplace. I was in a quandary. I really did *not* want to go with her, and yet all my instincts and training as a doctor urged me on. Here was someone in dire need and, whether spirit or human, I could *not* refuse.

I scrambled out of bed, quickly donned my dressing gown and picked up the candlestick. I expected her to move towards the door, but instead she went to one of the oak panels beside the fireplace and pointed to a carved crucifix at its centre. Next moment she had disappeared into the wall.

I thought, 'Perhaps there is a secret door or compartment here,' and I pushed on the crucifix, but nothing happened. I was trying to slide it to one side when suddenly it rotated, and with a click the panel swung inwards a little. I pushed it open to reveal a narrow stone stairway curving upwards, built into the very wall of the tower itself. Steeling myself, I thrust the candle ahead of me and began to climb. Thick festoons of cobwebs brushed my face, and the air smelled of must and mildew. The stairway emerged into a small, windowless chamber above my own and barely five feet below the leaded roof of the tower itself. The place was sparsely furnished with a primitive narrow wooden bed, a small chest of drawers and a chair. Everywhere was thick with the dust of centuries, and the simple furniture was riddled with woodworm.

I had heard of such places, called Priests' Holes, in Abbeys and Priories, where clerics could hide in times of persecution, and was sure that this was just such a place.

The ghost of Jane Stiles knelt beside the chest of drawers and pointed at the bottom drawer, which was slightly open. Placing the candlestick on the chair, I bent and gripped the handles, bracing myself for what I might find. I tugged, and the rotten timber gave way, leaving me holding the drawer front in my hands. I finally managed to slide out the drawer, and immediately I understood. Lying in the drawer, wrapped in rags, was the skeleton of a very young baby. The anterior fontanelle, the gap in the bones of the skull, was still open to a degree that indicated the child had been only six or eight weeks old when it died.

I looked at Jane, and she was gazing down fondly at the pitiful remains. For a moment I saw the child as she did. Pink and warm and new, sleeping peacefully in its makeshift crib, and I seemed to know instinctively that it had been a little girl.

I asked, 'Why did you not tell them she was here, before they destroyed you?'

She looked at me and, covering her mouth with her hand, she shook her head, conveying to me graphically that she was a natural for the Order of the Silent Sisters. The poor girl was a mute!

The full horror of her ordeal hit me then, and I wept unashamedly. I could not even begin to imagine her torment as she was slowly crushed to death, knowing that with her demise her baby had no chance of life. Nobody would hear its cries of hunger as its young life slowly ebbed away.

She saw my tears and nodded, knowing that *at last* someone understood.

I said to her, 'I am a physician and a soldier, and I swear by all I hold sacred, my Hippocratic oath and my allegiance to Queen and Country, that I will have your baby's remains buried in consecrated ground and a requiem mass said for her soul.'

She smiled a ghost of a smile. Then with one last lingering look at her baby, she raised her face and her arms to heaven and disappeared.

I knelt there beside the tiny remains for some time trying to come to terms with what I had seen. I realised then that in all the years that had elapsed since the occurrence of those terrible events, nobody who had seen the Poor Postulant had ever tried to help her. Without exception they had all fled in terror. I sighed and retraced my steps back to the Chamber of Sorrow. The room held no terrors for me now, and I was undisturbed for the rest of the night.

The next morning I met Holmes heading towards the refectory. He announced, 'The French have retreated! Departed at cock crow and good riddance.' He peered at my drawn features and remarked, 'You look as though you have seen a ghost, Watson.'

I replied, 'How singularly perceptive of you, Holmes.'

His smile faded as he realised that I was serious. 'Good lord, Watson! Whatever has happened?'

As we sat down to breakfast, I said, 'This is perhaps best for your ears alone, so I will tell you later.'

For once in my life I had little appetite for what was in fact an excellent meal. Later, as the others prepared to depart, I said to Holmes and Mrs Hudson, 'I have some binding promises to keep and cannot return to London yet awhile.'

Holmes replied, 'If you've no objection, I would like to stay and keep you company.'

I shook my head. 'Not at all, old fellow, you are most welcome.'

Mrs Hudson said, 'Well, I shall see you both back at Baker Street presently.'

When we were alone again, I recounted to Holmes everything that had happened the previous night.

He replied, 'If I had heard this tale from any other living person but you, Watson, I would not have believed it.'

I took him up to the Chamber of Sorrow and opened the secret door. Then I led him up to the Priests' Hole and showed him the tragic remains of Jane Stiles' baby. Even the oft-times cold and cynical Sherlock Holmes was visibly moved by the sight.

When we were back downstairs once more, he said, 'Be assured, Watson, that I shall never again, even in jest, call into question your undoubted fortitude. It is an honour to call you friend.'

*   *   *

We extended our stay at Burslam Priory, and over the next three days I had crafted, by a carpenter in the village of Loughton, a beautiful little maple casket lined with white satin. I arranged for the local priest to come to the Priory chapel to perform the service, and paid a strapping farm labourer to act as gravedigger in the Priory cemetery.

Eventually, as the priest intoned the prayer for the dead, Holmes and I lowered the pathetic little coffin into the ground. The first leaves of autumn settled gently all around, as if the trees themselves were weeping, and I offered up the following earnest prayer; *'Fly away, little soul, to the waiting arms of your poor mother. You have been parted from each other for too long. Lord grant that thy servant, Jane Stiles, may comfort her baby with a mother's love forever and ever, Amen.'*

*   *   *

Later, after Holmes and I had collected our bags and were passing through the hall on our way out, I felt myself drawn to the Ouija planchette, which was still on the table. Its stylus had left a written message on the white paper, which read; *'Beatus Medicus, Tibi gratias ago. Hoc erat in votis. Deus vobiscum, Jane.'*

Holmes asked, 'What does it mean?'

I translated, *'Blessed Doctor, Thank you. This was the very thing I have prayed for. God be with you, Jane.'*

To this day, so far as I know, there have been no further sightings of the Poor Postulant at Burslam Priory.

* Begone Satan, in French and Greek.

Main Entrance to
Saint Bartholomew's Hospital

THE PEDDLER OF DEATH

One could say that it was I who, albeit indirectly, involved Sherlock Holmes in this case, which is arguably one of the most intriguing and baffling we were ever involved in. It came about because of my military background when a fellow officer, Anthony Purvis, from my old regiment, presented himself at 221b Baker Street with grave news. He knew that I shared accommodation with the great detective, and his visit was directed as much to Holmes as to myself. He was, of course, like me, retired from the military, but maintained contact at regimental reunions and the like. His hair was thinner and his moustache greyer, but he still carried himself with an upright military bearing and he had maintained a slimmer waist than I had. I invited him in and introduced him to Holmes. We drank a toast, to fallen comrades, with a glass of sherry each, and he updated me on current news of the regiment.

Eventually he said, 'I'm sure you gentlemen would appreciate it if I were to get to the point of my visit. I am the bearer of sad tidings, Watson. Your old Commanding Officer, Major General Wright Pullman, is dead.'

'Dear me, Purvis! I'm sorry to hear that. Whatever happened?'

'Heart attack, apparently. Nothing suspicious in that, of course, since he was advanced in years and a good deal overweight.'

Holmes observed, 'But *something* has aroused your suspicions?'

Purvis nodded and took an envelope from his pocket. 'Last Friday evening I was attending a regimental dinner at the Grand Hotel. We had finished the meal and the toasts and were passing the port when Wright Pullman showed me this note he had received saying he could make neither head nor tail of it.' Here he handed the note to me, and I held it so that Holmes and I could both study it. It read:

Wright Pullman.
I am nothing that breathes yet I'm dreaded by all.
And strange to declare owe my rise to a fall.
Mid the poor and the rich, before kings I've been rude.
At their gluttonous banquets I often intrude.
But say of intrusion, who justly complains?
The feasting enjoyed I but seize the remains.
The duty completed here ends my employ.
And I leave one and all's just desserts to enjoy.

THE PEDDLER

I was totally baffled by the rhyme, but Holmes drew in a deep breath. 'You were absolutely right to be concerned, Mr Purvis. Have you been to the police?'

Purvis shook his head, 'No, not yet. Should I?'

Holmes replied, 'Perhaps it would be a little premature, though it is an option we may act upon at a later date, if required.'

I asked, 'Why what does the rhyme mean, Holmes?'

'Isn't it obvious, Watson? I see it as neither more nor less than a death threat!'

'How so?'

He explained, 'Death does not breathe, but is feared by all. His rise depends on the fall of others. He is an uninvited guest at many a banquet and the dead can't complain. He seizes the remains, i.e. the body, and he leaves the just desserts. We all get our *'just deserts'* when we die, depending on how we have lived.'

'Good Lord, Holmes, how *macabre!*'

'Isn't it just?' Then turning to Purvis, he asked, 'Did anything untoward happen at the reunion?'

He shook his head, 'Nothing I can recall. It was like all the others, an excellent evening with good food and fine wines in stimulating company. Followed later by cigars and brandy.'

'Did Wright Pullman overindulge in any of those things?'

Purvis looked a little uncomfortable in replying, 'Well, as Watson will verify, the Major General was a food and wine connoisseur and enjoyed both to the full.' I nodded in agreement.

'Did he smoke a cigar?'

'No. His addiction is, or rather was, snuff, like several of the other officers, myself included.'

I asked, 'How did the end come?'

'Well, his face flushed even more florid than usual, and his breathing became laboured. I recall him clutching his chest and complaining of pains. We thought it a touch of indigestion, following the pheasant, but the next thing was he had collapsed on the floor.'

I asked, 'Was there an army doctor present?'

'Yes, old Smithers.' I recalled Smithers as being a year ahead of me at Netley. Purvis went on, 'Though he tried everything, nothing was effective. The Major General expired right there before our eyes.'

'Dear me. How dreadful!'

Holmes paced the floor deep in thought. Finally he asked, 'Do you wish me to investigate this death on behalf of the Regiment?'

Purvis nodded. 'I was hoping you would consider it, Mr Holmes. I am the treasurer of our group, and current funds will cover the expense. I already have the approval of the others to enlist your aid, if you were to suspect foul play.'

Holmes nodded in agreement, saying, 'So be it. Pray leave it with me along with the note and your card, so that I may contact you with any news.'

'Thank you, Mr Holmes, and you too, Watson. I feel a good deal more settled in my mind than before.' He handed Holmes his card, then took his leave.

'What do you make of it, Holmes?' I queried.

'It is very strange, Watson, and at this juncture one cannot rule out a bizarre coincidence; however, I am suspicious of coincidences. If this *is* murder then it is a singularly unusual method. In fact I can only recall one incident in my entire career where an *induced* heart attack was the modus operandi. I'm sure you will recall that was in the Golden Cockerel case, where a Durian fruit was used?'

I nodded, 'Indeed, Holmes, though in that case the murderer took his own life, so it cannot be *he*. However, the same method *could* have been used again by someone else.'

Holmes shook his head. 'It is highly unlikely that Durian was served at the meal, for if it had been, most of your fellow officers would also be dead now, considering how much alcohol is normally consumed at these functions.'

'A valid point, Holmes,' I agreed. 'So where do you go from here?'

Holmes picked up the note and its envelope and commented, 'Posted in Belgravia on the 16th. Common brown envelope and cheap white paper available from any of a hundred stationers. No watermark in the paper and written by hand in black ink. The fountain pen used has seen much service and is well worn on the edge indicating a right-handed person. From my limited knowledge of the analysis of handwriting I should say that the writer is male and strong-willed. He displays a singular obsessive personality with a marked indication towards egotism. There is no humour or sympathy in this hand, but there is a vengeful nature and the suggestion of a persecution complex.'

I was amazed. 'You can see all that in the writing?'

'Not so much the writing, Watson, as the slope of the characters, the shapes of the letters and the pressure of the strokes. All these signs are readable to the initiated.'

'I'm glad you are on the side of the angels, old fellow,' I remarked.

'Of course it tells us nothing about who did this or how it was achieved. However, I recall a similar rhyming message in the personal column of the *Evening Standard* of a week or so ago. At the time I did not attach any significance to it.' Here he began to rummage through the personal columns in the pile of newspapers in the hearth. He was always reluctant to throw away previous issues, for he was of the opinion that by backtracking on news and correspondence, the developing dramas could be seen to unfold. The ploy had served him well over the years and was about to do so again.

He exclaimed, 'Aha here it is!' He folded the paper at the spot and I peered over his shoulder. It read:

Havelock.
My first is in braid but not in twine.
My second is late but also on time.
My third you will find in many a tale.
Yet seek it in stories and you will fail.
My fourth is the very best drink of the day.
My fifth is essential when you're making hay.
Put them together, if ye be so brave.
For I am what carries you off to your grave.

THE PEDDLER

I exclaimed, 'By Jove, Holmes, you were right. It's The Peddler again!'

'Indeed, Watson, and the message is the same, *Death!*'

'You've already deciphered it then?'

'Of course! A child could do it. The letter D is in *braid*, but not in *twine*. E is in *late* and also in *time*. A is in *tale*, but not in *stories* and *tea* or T is, to many, the best drink of the day. So, Watson, what is the last letter?'

'Of course, the letter H. One can't make the word *hay* without it!'

'Exactly, and as it says, Death is what carries us off to our graves!'

'I wonder why the message wasn't sent directly to this Havelock, as was the one to Wright Pullman?'

Holmes answered, 'Perhaps The Peddler did not know Havelock's address.'

'So who *is* Havelock, and is *he* in danger?'

Holmes replied, 'I'm very much afraid that poor old Havelock may already have met his maker.' As he spoke he picked up that evening's paper and turned to the Births Deaths and Marriages section. Almost immediately he found the name Havelock, it read;

Sir Walter Frederick Havelock, Baronet, aged 63 years was suddenly struck down at his home, Grantmore Manor in St. John's Wood. Much beloved husband to Lady Mary Anne Havelock, Sir Walter will be sadly missed by his family, friends and fellow politicians on both sides of the House. Service and committal will be held at St. Marks church...

I read no further, but turned to Holmes saying, 'Just as you predicted, old fellow.'

Holmes nodded, 'I wonder if Lady Mary has seen this warning from The Peddler?'

'We could ride out there and enquire,' I suggested.

'Capital idea, Watson. Let us act upon it this instant,' and he jumped up to grab his hat and coat. Soon we were in a hansom speeding towards St John's Wood.

Holmes mused, 'We must establish the connections between Havelock and Wright Pullman, the former a politician, the latter a retired Army officer.'

I offered, 'They were both older men, both gentlemen and both professionals, i.e. financially secure.'

'As you say, Watson, but I was thinking more about what might mark them both out for murder.'

'You have me there, old fellow. I couldn't even speculate.'

'Nor should we at this stage, Watson. We have nowhere near enough data yet.' The cab pulled up outside Grantmore Manor and we stepped down. It was a sturdy Georgian edifice surrounded by high wrought-iron railings. The door was opened by a manservant, who ushered us into a waiting room.

Presently Lady Mary entered, and Holmes made the introductions.

He said softly, 'Our sincere condolences and apologies for intruding at such a time, madam, but I wondered whether you had seen this message in the *Evening Standard*?' She was a petite, mousy woman with grey hair and a careworn countenance. She was dressed in a long, black gown and wore a black lace shawl around her shoulders.

She read the message and looked at Holmes in confusion. 'What does it mean, sir?'

Holmes explained gently, 'It is a riddle that spells out the word *Death* and is, in effect, a death threat!'

Her hand flew to her throat and she gasped, *'Oh my dear God!'* She appeared on the verge of collapse and I rushed to her side and guided her into an armchair. She turned tear-filled eyes to Holmes, saying, 'Are you telling me that my husband was *murdered*?'

'It is a possibility that I can't ignore, madam, because your husband is not the only man to have received such a warning and then to die of an apparent heart attack.'

297

She dabbed her eyes with a handkerchief, saying, 'I can't believe it. There must be some ghastly mistake. The doctors assured me that Walter had died naturally from heart failure.'

Holmes replied, 'There are ways to *induce* a heart attack with certain poisons and the like.'

She shook her head and said, 'This has come as a very great shock, Mr Holmes. What should I do now, contact the police?'

'I shall do that for you, Lady Mary. You must believe me when I say how sorry I am to be the one to add to your suffering with all of this, but did your husband have any enemies? Anyone who may have wished him ill will?'

'Not a soul, sir,' she said emphatically with a shake of her head.

'Did your husband drink or smoke?'

She nodded. 'In moderation, Mr Holmes. He also enjoyed snuff on occasions.'

'Do you know if he was acquainted with Major General Wright Pullman, a retired Army officer?'

Again she shook her head. 'No, I'm sure he was not. I know all my husband's friends, and he was not one of them. Was he the other gentleman who died?'

'Yes, I'm afraid so. Well, thank you, Lady Mary. You have been most helpful. Here is my card; please inform me if you recall anything at all that you feel I should know.'

I was worried about leaving her alone after such a shock, but she assured me she would be fine and that she had a maid to look after her. We took our leave and re-boarded our cab. Holmes directed the cabby to take us to Scotland Yard, and presently we were seated opposite Inspector Lestrade in his office. Holmes informed him of the deaths and showed him the note from Purvis and the rhyme in the newspaper.

Lestrade's brow furrowed. 'This is the damnedest thing. *Two more of them!'*

Holmes exclaimed, 'What's that you say? Are you telling us that you know of *another* such death?'

The inspector nodded gravely. 'Indeed I am, Mr Holmes. We are currently investigating the suspicious death of The Reverend James Wentworth of St Stevens Church on Brompton Road.   He too received such a warning, before dying of an apparent heart attack. Here is the note,' and he handed it over to Holmes. This too had been posted in Belgravia, and the handwriting was the same. We read:

Wentworth
Man is afraid of the sound of my name.
But until he finds me, no rest can he claim.
They who have known me can't renounce me to brothers.
Those who don't know me introduce me to others.
There are many that call me when assailed by pain.
Yet when they're recovered won't mention my name.
I am the sure cure for every great ill.
Will we ever meet? We most certainly will.

THE PEDDLER

Holmes translated it as: 'Man is afraid of Death until he is finally at rest. If you are dead you can't renounce anyone, and people kill other people, thereby introducing them to Death. When in great pain people have been known to pray for Death, but not when they have recovered. All ills are wiped away by Death, and he waits to meet every last one of us!'

I nodded, and Lestrade said, 'Exactly, Mr Holmes.'

My friend asked, 'Could the reverend have been poisoned?'

Lestrade shook his head. 'The post mortem examination showed nothing. Certainly nothing that he had ingested.'

Holmes responded, 'There are ways to absorb poison other than by swallowing it. Wright Pullman and Havelock were both snuff takers. Perhaps *that* is how the agent entered their bodies. Do we know if Wentworth took snuff?'

Lestrade brightened considerably. 'Capital idea, Mr Holmes. I'm afraid I don't know, but I shall soon find out. This is the first possible lead we have had in this enquiry, and I've a feeling that you could be on to something. Pray leave it with me and I will have it checked out.'

'Thank you, Inspector. Until I hear from you then.' We left and headed back to Baker Street. As we rattled along, Holmes said, 'Whilst we wait for Lestrade I really must try to ascertain what else, if anything, the victims had in common.' He rapped on the ceiling of the cab with his cane and ordered the driver to stop and let him out. Turning to me he said, 'The search I'm about to conduct would bore you to death, old fellow, so I shall see you later, at Baker Street.'

'Very well, Holmes,' I replied. As it transpired, I did not see him until breakfast the next day. I asked, 'Any luck, old chap?'

'I'm afraid not, Watson. The three men were unknown to each other; they all went to different schools and they were not members of the same club. They are not related to each other by blood or marriage, neither did they share any sporting or recreational activities. In short they have *nothing* in common.' At that moment, Mrs Hudson knocked and entered with a message for Holmes.

'Thank you, Mrs Hudson,' Holmes said as he tore open the envelope. 'Ah the information from Lestrade. And I was wrong, Watson, they *do* now have *one* thing in common. *All three of them* took snuff.'

'I nodded and quoted a maxim favoured by Holmes himself, 'Once is happenstance, twice is coincidence, but three times...?'

'Quite so, old fellow, quite so.' He paced the floor in thought for a while before turning to me and asking, 'How much do you know about snuff?'

'Not much except that it is pulverised and ground tobacco.'

'It's much more than that. For one thing it is not just *any* old tobacco; it is made from carefully selected leaves, which are then aged for two or three years. After that it is fermented at least twice, ground, flavoured and scented, the preferred scents being attar of roses, jasmine, lavender and sometimes cloves.'

'For someone who does not use snuff you seem to know a great deal about it, Holmes.'

He replied, 'Though I'm not a user myself, I *have* tried it on occasion, and my brother Mycroft is somewhat of a connoisseur.'

'So where is this leading then?'

He replied, 'Because snuff is usually scented, it means that the smell of an added poison, unless very strong, could be masked by the snuff's aroma.'

'Ah yes, I see your point.'

He went on, 'We must find a poison which is strong enough to induce a heart attack when a very small amount is absorbed directly into the lungs. It also needs to be in powder form and preferably reddish in colour.'

'I understand the requirement for it's colour, but must it be a powder?'

He nodded. 'I think so, Doctor. Can you imagine what would happen if you tried to mix a liquid poison with snuff? It would clump together and probably dry into lumps. The fine dust-like consistency would be ruined. Even dampness is anathema to snuff.'

I nodded. 'Yes of course, you're right. I must say, though, that in searching for just such a poison, needles and haystacks come to mind.'

He nodded, 'You are not far wrong, Watson.' He stood and gazed reflectively out of the window for a while before announcing, 'I must visit The British Museum, old fellow, and again I hesitate to inflict hours of boredom on you.'

'No matter, Holmes. I have patients to attend anyway, so I shall see you presently.' It was nearly bedtime before Holmes finally returned and flopped down on the sofa with a great sigh.

He passed a hand wearily through his hair and said, 'I had no idea there were so many poisons out there, Watson. One book alone, *Lawson's Toxicology of Plants,* lists hundreds.'

'Do any of them fit the bill?'

'Surprisingly few, fortunately. Most of the toxins can be eliminated on the grounds that they need to be swallowed, or injected under the skin. I've excluded a great many more because they are in liquid form, and a significant number were ruled out because of their strong odours.'

'Must you *positively* identify exactly which poison it is, Holmes?'

I think so, Watson. If I can do that, it might lead us to where it was obtained, which in turn could help us to pinpoint who procured it.'

'Yes, I see.'

'Tomorrow I intend to find out which brand of snuff was used by each of the victims. With any luck they all used the same brand.' Here he took a small box of snuff from his pocket and sniffed at it. 'I bought this from the tobacconists on the corner,' he continued, and he offered it to me to smell. 'Jasmine, I think. What say you, old man?'

I sniffed at it and nodded. 'Yes I agree. Definitely jasmine.'

'There are a few tests I wish to subject it to,' he announced as he strode towards his array of test tubes, retorts and Bunsen burners.

'Then, I shall leave you to your experiments, old fellow. I'm off to bed now.'

'Good night, Watson.'

When I came down to breakfast the following morning, Holmes had already eaten and left.

He returned around mid-morning to announce, 'Good news, Watson! The three murdered men *did* use the same brand of snuff. It is called *Regency Gold* and is an exclusive and expensive mixture manufactured and distributed solely by Coombe Brothers of Mayfair.'

'That *is* good news, Holmes.'

'And that is not all. I have also managed to acquire the remainder of the snuff that was last used by two of the victims.' Here he showed me the two ornate red and gold boxes of *Regency Gold* that he had recovered. 'Now it should be possible to have it analysed and hopefully discover what toxin, if any, it contains.'

'Who will carry out the analysis?'

He replied, 'Professor Dunston-Jervis of Barts has been recommended to me as perhaps the most eminent toxicologist in England, so I have arranged to meet him this afternoon. Perhaps you might like to accompany me?'

'Very much so, Holmes. It promises to be very interesting and informative.' Holmes took one of the little boxes to his makeshift laboratory and began subjecting its contents to yet more tests. As I had already read the morning paper and was at a loose end, I stood behind him and watched. He took a beaker of clean water and sprinkled some of the snuff into it. Then taking a spoon, he stirred it in well and waited for it to settle. As we watched, about half of the snuff began to absorb the water, becoming saturated, and sank down to the bottom of the vessel. The remainder floated on the surface and did not sink.

Holmes cried out, *'Eureka!* I was *right!*

'What does it signify?'

'Well, Doctor, in my research into toxins I discovered that there are a few African hardwood trees whose wood is highly toxic. One in particular, Padauk or more correctly, *Pterocarpus Soyauxii,* is particularly noxious, causing heart failure if its sawdust is breathed into the lungs.'

'Well I'll be damned!'

He continued, 'I reasoned that if it *were* a type of sawdust that had been added to the snuff, it would float in water, whereas the tobacco-based snuff should sink once waterlogged.' He went on, 'Padauk is an interesting timber, Watson. Its outer sapwood is a creamy colour, but its heartwood, which carries the poison, is a rich mahogany red, just like *Regency Gold* snuff!'

'I'm amazed, Holmes. So is *this* Padauk?'

'We won't know for sure until the Professor subjects it to certain tests, but it is a distinct possibility.'

'I wonder how the Peddler managed to contaminate the snuff with his poison? And is *every* user of *Regency Gold* in danger?'

'Good questions, Watson. I very much doubt that he has poisoned an entire batch of the snuff, otherwise people would be dropping like flies. *Regency Gold*, though expensive, has quite a following. No, I'm sure he *targeted* his victims, and I suspect he must have had inside help. Someone who could supply him with a list of customers and who could also tamper with those orders. It is interesting to note that Wright Pullman, Havelock *and* Wentworth all obtained their supplies by post!'

'Ah. That *is* significant, Holmes.'

We had some lunch, then set off in a hansom to St Bartholomew's Hospital. As we alighted I was, as ever, struck by the impressive façade of the great medical school, which was founded in 1123. The building, with its complex of research laboratories, classrooms and libraries, has always been very special to me. After all, it was here that I studied medicine all those years ago and indeed where young Stamford introduced me to my good friend Sherlock Holmes at the beginning of our long association.

I followed Holmes inside and was immediately on familiar ground. Even the *smell* of the place was the same as I remembered. We found Professor Dunston-Jervis in the very same chemical laboratory where I myself had studied and where Holmes and I were introduced. The professor was tall and slim with grey hair and thick eyeglasses. We shook hands and Holmes made the introductions.

Dunston-Jervis smiled and said, 'Welcome to St. Bart's, gentlemen. Is this your first visit?'

I shook my head, replying, 'Hardly, Professor. I myself was a student here years ago and my friend Holmes has conducted many experiments in this very room.'

'Indeed, indeed. How very interesting.' Turning to Holmes he asked, 'So how can I help you then?'

Holmes outlined our problem and showed the professor the suspect sample of snuff he had brought along. He said, 'I believe it could be laced with sawdust from an African hardwood called Padauk. Are you familiar with it?'

The professor looked surprised as he answered, 'I have encountered it before, but it is *very* rare. Usually the victim is a wood turner or lathe operator making small wooden bowls or the like from the timber. If one breathes the dust into one's lungs it can induce a heart attack. Indeed most suppliers no longer use that particular wood because of the danger.'

Holmes asked, 'Can you test for the toxin?'

He nodded and replied, 'Yes, but it will take an hour or so. Could you leave it with me and call back later?'

'Of course, Professor; we are indebted to you.' We left him to it and strolled outside until we found a café where we whiled away the time over cups of coffee. Eventually we retraced our steps and Dunston-Jervis greeted us with a smile.

He said, 'You did all the hard work for me, Mr Holmes. It was *indeed* Padauk.'

'Excellent, excellent! Thank you very much, Professor. Now all I have to do is find out where the killer obtained his wood.'

'I'm afraid I can't help you there, except to suggest that you check on local manufacturers of hardwood items and furniture.'

Holmes smiled, 'No small task. Once again my grateful thanks, Professor.' We shook hands with the academic and left. Soon we were hailing a cab to take us back to Baker Street.

As we were about to climb the stairs at 221b, Mrs Hudson emerged from her rooms with a letter for Holmes, saying, 'This arrived for you this afternoon, sir.' He took it from her and froze into immobility. I looked at the handwriting on the brown envelope and immediately recognised it as being from The Peddler. It said simply, *Mr Holmes.*

'Did you see who dropped it through the letterbox, Mrs Hudson?'

She shook her head. 'I'm afraid not. I just found it lying on the mat. In fact I didn't even hear the sound of the letterbox flap when it was pushed through.'

'Thank you, Mrs Hudson.' We hurried up to our quarters and Holmes ripped open the envelope. As he read its contents his face paled.

He handed it to me saying, 'It seems that I am to be The Peddler's next victim, Watson.'

'Good Lord, Holmes!' I took the message and read,

Holmes
By hook or by crook the Crome moth flys.
And when it does somebody dies.

Death's Head Hawk moth? No, not quite.
It's only active during the night.
He needs not a mile, nor scarcely an inch.
He's often recruited with barely a pinch.
Say now, am I my brother's keeper?
I'm afraid you must ask that old grim reaper.

THE PEDDLER

I shook my head in puzzlement and said, 'This is even more incomprehensible than the others to me, Holmes.'

He took the message from me and read it through again. 'I have to agree with you, Watson. This *is* more difficult than the others. It is still a warning, but it does not spell out the word *death*. It refers to it indirectly by mentioning a Death's Head Hawk moth and the grim reaper. It also implies that Death is the one who '*needs not a mile, nor scarcely an inch.*' He began to pace up and down studying the message in his hand, then stopped and turned toward me. 'The implication is that I will be targeted during daylight hours, and the reference to '*barely a pinch*' agrees with what we have already discovered that the toxic agent is snuff. But I don't *use* snuff, so how am I at risk?'

I shook my head in bewilderment. 'I'm sorry, old chap, but I am completely out of my depth with this.'

He took down the dictionary, saying, 'I've never heard of a species called a *Crome moth*.' We looked up the word *crome* and it said, '*A hook or a crook, v.t. To draw with a crome.*'

I suggested, 'Could he mean the metal, Chrome? Perhaps it is a spelling mistake.'

He shook his head. 'I doubt it, old fellow. He already mentions *hook* and *crook* in the rhyme, also there is another deliberately misspelled word in the message, *Flys*. It should more correctly be *Flies*. Somehow I can't imagine The

307

Peddler being so clumsy. I'm convinced there is a reason for all this.' He looked at his watch, then said, 'I believe I shall enlist Mycroft's help with this one. He will be at the Diogenes club at this hour.' Grabbing his coat and hat, he added, 'I shan't be long, Watson.'

'Very well, Holmes, and good luck!'

It was barely two hours later that I was summoned by a very agitated young Wiggins, the leader of the Baker Street Irregulars, to go directly to the Diogenes club where a tragedy had occurred. My heart was in my mouth as I urged the cab driver to greater speed. I clutched my medical bag tightly and tried to imagine what could have happened to my friend. When we finally arrived I took the stairs two at a time and burst into the club to find Holmes slumped in an armchair, totally distraught. My relief at finding him still alive was short-lived. For lying on a stretcher, in the process of being covered with a white sheet, was the body of Mycroft Holmes! I was dumfounded. Behind Holmes' chair, with his hat in his hand, was a very subdued Inspector Lestrade, and beside the stretcher stood the eminent surgeon Sir Miles Holford, himself a member of the club. With a sigh, he replaced his stethoscope in his medical bag as two orderlies lifted the stretcher and carried it respectfully from the room.

Totally ignoring the club rule that bans speaking, I turned to Holmes and cried, 'What, in God's name, has happened?'

He looked at me through tear-filled eyes and replied, 'I was too late, Watson. My bumbling stupidity has cost the life of my brother. The Holmes targeted by the message was not *me* but *Mycroft!*'

'Oh my God! So *that* was what was meant by the reference, *'Am I my brother's keeper?'*

'Exactly. I finally deciphered that part of the riddle that says, 'The *Crome moth flys.*' There is no such species as a 'Crome' moth. The words are an anagram for *Mycroft*

Holmes! I *ought* to have realised, because the only one of us that used snuff was Mycroft.'

I said gently, 'You mustn't blame yourself, old fellow. I'm sure you did everything possible and I know that your brother would not want you to torture yourself so.'

He stood up and said softly, 'Thank you, Watson, for those sentiments. I feel the need to be on my own for a while to try to come to terms with what has happened. I shall go to an hotel for a few days.'

I nodded. 'Of course, old fellow. If there is *anything* I can do...'

'Good-bye, Watson.' He walked dejectedly from the building, and my heart ached for him.

Lestrade put his hand on my shoulder and said sympathetically, 'A terrible tragedy, Doctor. Rest assured that I shall throw the full weight of Scotland Yard's resources against this maniac.'

'Thank you Inspector.' I made my way back to Baker Street with a heavy heart, and our rooms seemed strangely empty without my friend's company. Holmes packed a suitcase with some of his clothes whilst I was visiting my patients, so we did not meet again that day.

Mycroft's obituary appeared in the following morning's newspapers, and there were glowing tributes from distinguished colleagues, though of course no mention of his governmental activities. At the inquest the coroner recorded an open verdict, pending the results of the police investigation. I had no contact with Holmes during the next week, apart from a card outlining the details of the funeral arrangements, which were to conclude with breakfast at the Excelsior Hotel.

It was a bright cold morning as I made my way to the cemetery for the service. The chapel was not as full as I would have expected, and Holmes sat somewhat apart from the other distinguished mourners, gathered to pay their last respects. He wore a long, black overcoat and carried a black bowler hat and his ebony cane in his gloved hands. The service was brief and the eulogy, given by Holmes himself, very moving. Presently we made our way behind the coffin for the committal and interment. As the priest intoned the prayer for the dead, three other mourners and I lowered the coffin into the ground. Holmes threw a handful of earth onto the casket, and I could not hold back the tears as my heart went out to him in his sorrow.

As the group began to disperse, two gravediggers, both of whom had kept discreetly in the background, came slowly forward, shovels in hand. I would not have noticed them if it had not been for Holmes, who was watching them intently. One was tall and thin whilst the other, a hunchback, was squat and thickset. Both wore coats, scarves and caps against the cold.

Holmes beckoned them forward and jingled some coins in his pocket, the implication being that he wanted to tip them for their task. The hunchback shuffled forward expectantly, but the other fellow lagged behind. Holmes dropped some coins into the hunchback's palm, and the man doffed his cap in gratitude, but still the tall one hung back.

Holmes strolled over to him, saying; 'Don't you want what's coming to you?' The man looked down at his feet and shook his head dumbly.

Holmes put on his bowler hat and gripped his cane with both hands before continuing, 'Nor would I, if what was coming to me was the *hangman's noose!*' The man's eyes flashed and he suddenly thrust at Holmes' midriff with the sharp edge of his spade. Holmes was ready for just such a move and parried the blow with his cane. Then as quick as a flash he whipped out the blade from his swordstick, for such it was, and held its point at the other's throat.

His voice was icy cold as he said, 'I sincerely hope that you give me reason to run you through where you stand.'

I was convinced that grief had unhinged my friend's mind, and I gently approached him saying, 'Holmes, for God's sake put away your blade. Have you lost your reason?'

Without taking his eyes off the fellow for an instant, he said, 'Aren't you going to greet an old acquaintance, Watson? I thought you would have recognised the despicable Jonas T. Rimmer, or should I say The Peddler? Surely you remember our last encounter? As I recall, you named your account of the case '*A Slaying in Suburbia*'.'

I was dumbstruck for a moment, but then something about the fellow's eyes *did* strike a chord. 'Is it *true*, Holmes?'

He nodded, saying; 'Absolutely, Watson.' Other mourners, who had been in the act of leaving, gathered around this developing drama, and from behind some trees and bushes in the distance Inspector Lestrade and two uniformed constables came forward. Holmes cried, 'Better get the derbies on him, Inspector, he's as slippery as an eel!' One of the constables took the spade from the man and the other forced his hands behind his back so that Lestrade could handcuff him.

He glared at Holmes with sheer malice and hissed, 'You've got nothing on me. I've done nothing wrong.'

Holmes responded, 'To a twisted mind like yours, killing three innocent men with poisoned snuff would not be considered wrong, but to the rest of society it is.'

I said, 'You mean *four* innocent men, Holmes.'

He smiled and replied, 'Three, old fellow. Mycroft is fine, in fact here he comes now,' and he indicated a bulky figure striding jauntily towards us, along the path, swinging his walking-stick. I was in a turmoil of emotions, relief being the strongest in that the elder Holmes was indeed still alive.

I pointed at the coffin and began, 'But who is…?'

Holmes answered, 'A couple of dozen house bricks have just been very reverentially disposed of, Watson.'

Mycroft was immediately surrounded by his friends and colleagues, who shook his hand and slapped him on the back as everyone started talking and asking questions at once.

He held up his hand and addressed them all, 'My sincere apologies to each and every one of you for this cruel deception, but it was necessary to trap the vicious murderer you see before you.' He strode over to the captive and looked him in the eye, saying, 'So this is the monster, eh Sherlock?' As he spoke he disdainfully knocked the man's cap off with the end of his walking-stick, saying, 'Not much of a specimen is he? I rather think it would take a better man than *this* to kill me!'

Rimmer began ranting at Mycroft, but the elder Holmes abruptly turned his back on the fellow and, dismissing him completely, addressed his friends. 'I've ordered a dozen bottles of vintage champagne to celebrate my return to the land of the living, and they await us at the Excelsior. It's not every day that one gets the chance to enjoy one's own wake, and I intend to do so to the full. Shall we?'

As he led the merry group out of the churchyard, Holmes called after him 'Save some champagne for Watson and me; we will join you there later.'

Rimmer taunted Holmes, saying, 'There's no evidence against me that would stand up in a court of law. You've got nothing to tie me to those murders.'

Holmes smiled and replied, 'You might well be right, but then I don't *need* anything. You seem to have forgotten that there is still a warrant out for your arrest for the murders of Thomas Pritchard and Cedric Tomkins and conspiracy to murder Arthur Dunn. Whether you hang for one murder or five, you still hang.'

Rimmer looked stunned at these words and swallowed hard, but then he snarled, 'This isn't over. You've not seen the last of me yet.'

Holmes replied, 'Once again you are right in what you say. I *will* see you again, in court. And after the verdict I shall be there to watch James Berry, the hangman, pinion your arms and legs, slip his noose around your neck and operate the drop that will send you plummeting straight down to Hell!'

Rimmer's face paled visibly at these words and, despite the cold, beads of sweat formed on his forehead and upper lip. He cast his eyes about desperately, and I could hear the chains on his handcuffs jingling as his hands trembled with fear.

Now he began to plead with Holmes, and his voice took on a plaintive tone, 'Go ahead, Holmes, do it. Run me through and put an end to it once and for all; you know you want to.'

Holmes shook his head and replied, 'I promised a long time ago that I would end your malignant existence and rid the world of your cankerous presence, and I have done my part. Now we must wait for Mr Berry to do his. Perhaps, in the time you have left, you might spare a thought for the poor unfortunates that you sent to their graves. In any case you will have plenty of time to reflect on and anticipate your own demise, the same death you were quite willing to inflict on the completely innocent Arthur Dunn. I am not usually a vengeful man, but in your case I make an exception. He's all yours, Inspector.'

Lestrade said, 'Jonas T. Rimmer, I arrest you for the wilful murders of Thomas Pritchard and Cedric Tomkins and for conspiring to murder Arthur Dunn...'

Holmes sheathed his blade and, turning to me, said, 'Come, Watson. Vintage champagne awaits us at the Excelsior!'

As we walked from the churchyard, he put his hand on my shoulder and continued, 'I know you have a hundred questions to ask me, old fellow, so perhaps we should walk to the Excelsior. It is but a few blocks from here.'

I responded, 'I barely know where to begin, but how did you know that The Peddler was in reality Jonas Rimmer?'

He replied, 'When I left you at Baker Street to find Mycroft, I studied the message again in the cab and finally spotted the anagram. I then recalled how the odious Rimmer had once tested me using an anagram of his name on his calling card when he posed as the solicitor Mister N. Major. Another tiny clue in the message was where it read, *'Say now am I my brother's keeper?'* "Say now" is more of an American expression than an English one.'

I commented, 'They seem to be very tenuous clues to me, Holmes.'

'Indeed they were, Watson, but then I thought about a pattern, or more precisely the lack of a pattern. None of the victims were connected with each other; they were totally random, which told me they weren't the crux of the mystery, just pawns in the game. When I remembered that the method of informing each victim wasn't only by posted messages, but also through a publicly announced warning in a national newspaper, I suspected that *I* was included in the killer's plans. Rimmer had been well briefed, by his mentor Moriarty, about my habits, including, presumably, my penchant for scanning the personal columns of the newspapers. I realised that my earlier notion that Rimmer might not have known Havelock's address was inconceivable; after all, the politician ordered his snuff through the post. So that raised the question, why warn him publicly? I became sure that the warning wasn't just for Havelock's benefit but also for *mine*.'

I said, 'But I still don't understand what Rimmer's motive was in killing those men in the *first* place.'

Holmes smiled at my naïveté. 'He was striking at *me* through *them* and challenging me to find him and stop him.'

'But why?'

'Because Rimmer is a psychopath. He has all those traits I pointed out to you, when analysing his handwriting, plus a few more. As far as I know, I am the only man who has ever bested him. I exposed him as the murderer of Cedric Tomkins and Thomas Pritchard, I exonerated Arthur Dunn and I had a warrant issued for his arrest. In his eyes, all of this would be enough to mark me out for destruction. First he must defeat me intellectually, hence the riddles. Next he must make me suffer, as he believes I made him suffer, by killing someone close to me, Mycroft. Lastly he would have killed me by some, as yet unknown, gruesome method.'

'But to take the lives of innocent people just for the sake of a battle of wills, Holmes?'

'That is the mark of a psychopath, Watson. They are without conscience or pity. I don't doubt for a moment that if *you* had been a snuff-taker, you too would have been targeted.'

I nodded in agreement, then asked, 'How do you suppose he knew about Padauk?'

Holmes replied, 'You have to remember the calibre of the man, Watson; he was very nearly the intellectual equal of Moriarty himself. When he set out to kill Mycroft, for that was to be his penultimate action in my destruction, he would have had him placed under close scrutiny. Once he had discovered that my brother used *Regency Gold*, he would then have set out to find the perfect toxin with which to contaminate it. His *modus operandi* in killing Cedric Tomkins was 1) Surveillance, to establish background information. 2) Plot to use that knowledge against the individual. 3) Execution, *literally* so. As for his finding the poison, he probably did what I did and searched the archives. The information is there for any diligent student to discover.'

I shook my head as I finally began to understand the nature of the beast we had been stalking. 'I can scarcely believe it all, Holmes, yet everything you say is so obviously true.' We walked on in silence for a while until I asked, 'So how did you know that he would be present at Mycroft's funeral?'

Holmes smiled as he replied, 'That *was* predictable. It would not have been sufficient for him just to make me suffer. He had to *see* me suffer, and what better place to do that than at the funeral of my only brother?'

I said, 'I'm a little disappointed that you did not confide in me about your plan, Holmes.'

He replied, 'I'm sorry, Watson, but I did not deliberately set out to exclude you. As I said, I only realised who The Peddler might be when I was on my way to see Mycroft. Incidentally, I was only just in time to prevent him from sampling his newly acquired supply of snuff. I do believe he considered me quite irrational when I dashed it from his hand. But to continue, when I explained the events to him and suggested my plan to trap Rimmer, it was Mycroft himself who insisted that as few people as possible be told. After all, we had no idea where Rimmer was or how many spies he might have watching us. With all due respect, old fellow, you are not the worlds greatest actor, and we needed you to be convincing in your reactions to the tragedy.' I smiled, for I had to agree with Holmes on that point.

I said, 'So presumably Sir Miles Holford was a party to the plan?'

'Yes, he was in the club at the time and agreed to help us once he knew that we were trying to trap a multiple murderer.'

'And Lestrade?'

Holmes shook his head, saying; 'Even Lestrade was unaware at that time, I only told *him* yesterday.'

'And the coroner?'

'Sir Miles arranged that side of things. Evidently the two men are old friends.'

I congratulated Holmes, saying; 'It really was a splendid strategy, old chap, and it worked to perfection.'

'Why, thank you, Watson, and here we are at the Excelsior already.'

The party inside was in full swing, and they had indeed saved more than enough champagne for us. I have to confess that I enjoyed it rather to excess, but then it really was an *excellent* vintage.

Also from MX Publishing

Close To Holmes

A Look at the Connections Between
Historical London, Sherlock Holmes and
Sir Arthur Conan Doyle.

Eliminate The Impossible

An Examination of the World of
Sherlock Holmes on Page and Screen.

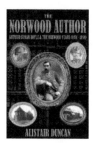

The Norwood Author

Arthur Conan Doyle and the Norwood Years
(1891 - 1894)

www.mxpublishing.com

Also From MX Publishing

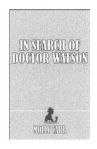

In Search of Dr Watson

Wonderful biography of Dr. Watson
from expert Molly Carr.

Arthur Conan Doyle, Sherlock Holmes and
Devon

A Complete Tour Guide and Companion.

The Lost Stories of Sherlock Holmes

Eight more stories from the pen of John H
Watson – compiled by Tony Reynolds.

www.mxpublishing.com

Also From MX Publishing

The Sign of Fear

The first adventure of the 'female Sherlock Holmes'. A delightful fun adventure with your favourite supporting Holmes characters.

A Study in Crimson

The second adventure of the 'female Sherlock Holmes' with a host of sub- plots and new characters joining Watson and Fanshaw

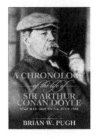

The Chronology of Arthur Conan Doyle

The definitive chronology used by historians and libraries worldwide.

www.mxpublishing.com

Also From MX Publishing

Aside Arthur Conan Doyle

A collection of twenty stories from ACD's close friend Bertram Fletcher Robinson.

Bertram Fletcher Robinson

The comprehensive biography of the assistant plot producer of The Hound of The Baskervilles

Wheels of Anarchy

Reprint and introduction to Max Pemberton's thriller from 100 years ago. One of the first spy thrillers of its kind.

www.mxpublishing.com

Also From MX Publishing

Murder in the Library

Chicago based thriller where one of the main characters is a Holmes fan. Murder, mystery and fun in the library.

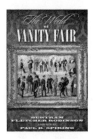

The World of Vanity Fair

A specialist full-colour reproduction of key articles from Bertram Fletcher Robinson containing of colour caricatures from the early 1900s.

Tras Las He huellas de Arthur Conan Doyle (in Spanish)

Un viaje ilustrado por Devon.

www.mxpublishing.com

CPSIA information can be obtained
at www.ICGtesting.com
Printed in the USA
LVHW01s1542111217
559406LV00012B/1477/P